To Patricia Langham, my sister, with much love

About the Author

Lynn Bryant was born and raised in London's East End. She studied History at University and had dreams of being a writer from a young age. Since this was clearly not something a working class girl made good could aspire to, she had a variety of careers including a librarian, NHS administrator, relationship counsellor and manager of an art gallery before realising that most of these were just as unlikely as being a writer and took the step of publishing her first book.

She now lives in the Isle of Man and is married to a man who understands technology, which saves her a job, and has two teenage children and two labradors. History is still a passion, with a particular enthusiasm for the Napoleonic era and the sixteenth century. When not writing she runs an Irish dance school, reads anything that's put in front of her and makes periodic and unsuccessful attempts to keep a tidy house.

Chapter One

It was cold. Along the lines, men were stirring, coming awake in the foggy morning with chilled reluctance. Autumn had brought mist to the heights above Bussaco and the camp nearby and although the days had been mild and pleasant, there was an almost wintery feel to the early morning.

Private Jamie Hammond shifted sleepily in his bedroll and cocked an ear for signs of life outside. It was still almost dark but almost four years of army life had given him a sixth sense for the state of the camp and he could tell that there was movement outside and was judging his moment. He was on mess duty at present and given yesterday's orders it was particularly important that hot food was provided this morning.

"You awake, Hammond?"

The voice was that of his Corporal, a Londoner like Hammond himself. During the few weeks that he had been with the 110th light company, Hammond had found himself forming a cautious bond with the other man. Carter was thirty, a tall loose limbed man with a long humorous face and a dry wit which appealed to Hammond. He had an instinctive distrust of officers and NCOs born of the brutal regime of his previous regiment, but even after a few weeks he was finding the 110th a very different experience.

"I'm up," Hammond said, uncurling himself from his bedroll. Outside the tent he sat on an upturned crate to pull on his boots and coat, shivering slightly. Carter appeared beside him and Hammond waited until he was ready and then accompanied him up the lines to collect water. It was not Carter's job, but in the 110th Hammond had realised that the workload was often shared unexpectedly. Around them the camp began to awaken with a variety of men shuffling about muffled in coats, struggling to light fires and wielding cooking pots and kettles.

On the way back, passing the larger tents of the officers, a voice hailed them and Carter paused. Sergeant Michael O'Reilly, wrapped in greatcoat and looking chilled, wandered over with a tin mug of tea in his hand.

"Morning Carter. Hammond. Bloody cold."

"It'll warm up, Sarge. Probably just about the time we're sweating our way up that bloody ridge with full packs."

O'Reilly grinned. "It won't be that bad, Carter. Wellington's had his engineers clearing access roads for us. The worst of it will be no fires or hot food. Hope the bloody French come quickly. He's not fed properly he'll be a pain in the arse in three days."

He jerked his head towards his commander's tent. Carter grinned. "Might not be this time, Sarge. Never seen him in such a good mood as this week. It could last through the battle although I'm hoping even she won't be up on the ridge with us. I wouldn't put it past her, mind."

"Neither would I. God help the French. No, she'll be down at the hospital with Norris."

"Just going to get the fires lit, Sarge," Hammond said. Carter nodded.

"I'll be there in a minute, Hammond," he said, and he and O'Reilly watched as the younger man moved along the lines.

"How's he doing?" O'Reilly asked.

"Good. Not seen him under fire yet, but he's a good lad, fits in well. Bit wary, mind, but given what he's been through I'm not surprised." Carter pulled a face. "I've seen some floggings, Sarge, but what some bastard did to his back beggars belief."

Michael nodded. "Bloody mess. Don't blame him for deserting. The surprising thing is that he was willing to give the army another go."

"Yes." Carter eyed his sergeant with a grin. "I'd love to know the rest of that story."

"You'll have to wait until he tells you, Danny. It's not mine to tell. To be fair, none of us know all of it yet, but I've got a feeling he's going to stay so we probably will. Morning, sir."

They were joined by two officers, both wrapped up in heavy greatcoats. Captain Johnny Wheeler was holding two mugs of tea. He passed one to Carter who took it with a smile of thanks and wrapped both hands around it.

Michael nodded towards the commander's tent. "He up yet?"

Captain Carl Swanson grinned. "He's awake," he said, and the four men laughed.

"Jesus, doesn't he get tired?" Michael said.

"Apparently not," Carl said. "We should move his tent further away, mind, the rest of us don't get much sleep and we're not enjoying it as much as he is."

Carter was laughing. "Leave him alone, you bastards," he said. "I bet you give him grief every time he steps outside that tent. He's been married less than a week and he's back on the bloody battlefield. Wellington could have let him miss this one, it's not like he's not done his bit. Has he even had leave since after Assaye?"

"Not really. Unless you count time in barracks, and it's not like he ever relaxes then." Wheeler laughed. "I'm making the most of this to be honest, we can say what we like to him at the moment, Carter, you can't wipe the smile off his face."

"Let's hope the French don't bloody manage it then," Carter said. "Wouldn't fancy their chances if they piss her off this week. I'm going to get some breakfast. If I'm living on cold food for the next few days I'm going to make the most of this."

The laughter had drifted down to the commander's tent, and Major Paul van Daan turned his head and smiled at his wife. "I think it's time I was up," he said regretfully.

"I know." She snuggled closer against him. "I need to go and roust out my orderlies and get down to the hospital. It's just so warm here."

Paul pulled her up closer and kissed her in a leisurely fashion. "On the other hand, I'm going to get roasted the minute I go out there," he said. "It's not much of an incentive compared to what I've got in here."

"They'll get over it eventually," Anne van Daan said, amused. "It's a novelty for them to see you in such a good mood. They think I'm the cause of it."

"You are the cause of it," Paul said, and slid his hand across her stomach and up to her breast. She gave a little gasp at his touch and he felt her heart quicken under his hand.

"Paul – we cannot!" she said huskily.

"I actually could, love. And I'm damned sure you'd like to. Although it would probably be dereliction of duty. What a pity. You are looking particularly beautiful just at this moment. On the other hand, I'm in charge of the regiment. Do I care?"

He bent his head to her breast and she made a little sound, hastily suppressed. "Stop it," she whispered. "I am quite certain that they are out there laughing about this."

"Well they'd have had a good chuckle about an hour ago then," her husband said, continuing to tease at her nipple with his tongue. "Don't worry, love, it's part of camp life. Privacy isn't possible here. Have I ever told you that when you begin to be aroused, your skin turns a particularly delicious shade of pink? And I love the sounds you make – the ones you're trying so hard not to make just now."

He slid his hand between her legs and Anne tried to bite back her response, and then he lifted himself onto her and she gave up the unequal struggle and made a little sound of enjoyment. Paul laughed and kissed her.

"You sure, bonny lass?"

"Get on with it, Major, before they come in to find out if I've murdered you," his wife whispered, laughing.

"They wouldn't bloody dare," Paul said softly, and shifted. "That feel good?"

"Very good. Don't stop now."

Anne seemed to have forgotten the need for quiet and his own consciousness of sounds outside the tent quickly disappeared as he lost himself in the girl in his arms. When they were done he rolled over onto his back, catching his breath. He was trying to remember the early days of his marriage to his first wife. He could recall being surprised at how much he enjoyed waking up with her beside him each morning but he was fairly sure he had not found it this difficult to get out of bed at all.

He lay still for a moment and Anne pushed herself up onto one elbow and leaned over him, the tousled curtain of black hair tickling his face as she kissed him.

"I am quite sure," she said mischievously, "that some of your men spend a considerable amount of their time wishing that they were where you are right now."

Paul grinned. He was sure she was right. Since Anne had joined them, he was enjoying watching the officers and men of the 110th trip over things because they were gazing at his wife. "As long as none of them is wishing that he is where you are just now, dearest Nan, I am well content," he said, and she began to laugh and could not stop. He was laughing too, and he pulled himself reluctantly out of the bed and reached for his clothes.

Stepping outside, he accepted a tin mug of tea from his orderly and moved along the lines towards his officers. A pretty brown haired girl came towards him and he smiled. "Morning Teresa. She's awake."

"Good morning, Major." Anne's maid went past him and ducked into the tent and Paul joined his officers.

"Anything from Hookey yet?" he asked.

Wheeler shook his head. "No. Half the lines are barely stirring. Can't blame them, it's bloody cold this morning."

"Although you're looking nice and warm, sir," Michael O'Reilly said pleasantly. His commander lifted a hand and smacked him across the back of his head. The others were laughing.

"You're an impudent bastard, Sergeant. Don't let my wife hear you, or she'll be out here with a bayonet."

"I doubt she's got the energy," O'Reilly commented, moving out of reach. Paul grinned and made his way up the lines towards the neat rows of smaller tents, which the men of the 110th shared, four to a tent. Cooking fires had been lit and the women and mess orderlies were busy with breakfast but few of the men had appeared.

"Get up you lazy bastards!" he yelled, thumping on the canvas of the nearest tent. "If the French decide to make an early move you're going to be caught with your trousers down, and that's not a sight that I need to see in the morning. If I don't see you out here feeding your faces and ready to march in half an hour I'm going to start throwing a few of you in the river!"

"That should get them moving," Captain Swanson said with a grin. "How the hell has he got the energy at this hour? I can barely speak."

"He's been awake longer than the rest of us," O'Reilly said, still laughing. "And let's face it, wouldn't we all be in a good mood if we were in his place?"

Their voices reached Paul, and he smiled, still rattling tents and watching his men drag themselves reluctantly out into the cold air. He had married less than two weeks ago and both he and his regiment were still adjusting to the arrival of his new bride in their midst.

It was a second marriage for both of them. His first wife had died giving birth to his daughter less than four months earlier, and like Anne she had often travelled on campaign with him. He could not imagine his officers making open references to his sex life with Rowena. They had liked and respected his fair-haired gentle wife, but if they had speculated on the state of his love life with her he was completely unaware of it, and he knew she would have been appalled at the idea. Her shyness had meant that he had found opportunities when they were living in tents, to make love to her away from the camp, and although he was sure that his friends must have known why their commander and his wife often took long walks or rides into the surrounding countryside in the evenings they would never have remarked on it. She was, and had remained, his lady in the eyes of both officers and men, treated as if she were a delicate creature in need of protection and shelter. He had been very fond of her, and still missed her at times with an ache of regret at her death.

The sound of a musical laugh made him turn and he surveyed his new wife from a distance. She had just emerged from their tent and was regarding Sergeant O'Reilly with an expression which told him that she was about to utter a crushing remark and was just deciding on the exact wording. She was dressed in her working clothes of a plain dark gown, and she wore no embellishments other than the long glory of her black hair, which fell loose to her waist. He felt the accustomed wave of sheer happiness at the sight of her, followed by a stab of desire, which he ought not, after the previous night and morning, have been capable of feeling at all.

She was unlike Rowena in every possible way, which was surprising given that they had been such close friends. Rowena had been a lovely woman, and from their early stolen trysts in the woods close to his family home in Leicestershire she had welcomed his lovemaking. But he was still adapting to his new bride's surprisingly uninhibited enjoyment of the sexual act. Her own first marriage had been unhappy and brutal, so she had come to his bed with no experience of a loving relationship, and he had expected that she would need some time and some coaxing before she was fully comfortable in his arms. He had been wrong. She had proved to be a passionate and imaginative lover, who made no attempt to hide her desire for him, and the combination of her almost delicate beauty with an earthy sensuality of which she was in no way ashamed or embarrassed, made her completely irresistible to him.

He had loved Rowena but he had never been faithful to her, and it had been a regret at her death that he must have hurt her so often. At his wedding to Anne in the crumbling church in Viseu he had made his vows with a very different determination to keep them. After less than two weeks he found it hard to imagine any circumstances, which would cause him to break them. Apart from anything else, he thought with some amusement as he went back up the lines towards her, she would probably stab him if she found him with another woman.

His mess sergeant, George Kelly, was handing out bowls of steaming porridge as he approached. Paul took one and passed it to his wife. "I think they're awake," he commented, glancing down the lines of tents, which were now bustling with activity.

"I should think Marshal Massena is awake as well, the racket you've been making," his wife commented. She seated herself neatly on the ground next to the fire and began to eat. His sergeant, with a commendable lack of formality, which made Paul want to laugh, sat beside her and passed her a tin mug of tea.

"Here you are, girl dear. You must be in need of sustenance, I should think."

Paul paused with his spoon halfway to his mouth and regarded Michael with disbelief. His wife blushed charmingly which was something he was beginning to think she could do to order, she used it so well.

"One more remark like that from you this morning, Sergeant O'Reilly and you're going into battle with a bone saw sticking out of your left eye!" she said succinctly, and took a mouthful of tea. "Thank you, George, this is good."

"You're welcome, ma'am. Plenty more if you're hungry. I think Sergeant O'Reilly might have just lost his appetite."

Paul finished his meal, his eyes on his wife. The enormity of her self-possession in this masculine environment was breathtaking. He watched as she finished eating and allowed Kelly to take her bowl and cup and Captain Swanson to pull her to her feet, and she distributed smiles as rewards and then looked around her. "Anybody seen my orderlies?"

"Not yet, ma'am," Corporal Carter said approaching. "Want me to go and kick them out of bed for you?"

"If they're not already up and loading my supplies they'll get more than a kicking," Anne said. "Morning Danny. Have you been fed yet?"

"Yes, ma'am. Hammond is on mess duty this week, which means it runs like clockwork. He's after my job, that lad, I've got my eye on him. But I won't say no to more tea."

Anne went to collect a tin mug and fill it, and Paul watched her hand it to his corporal with a smile. He was so accustomed to the ways of his regiment that he seldom thought about it, but since Anne had joined them he found he was seeing it anew through her eyes. She had fitted in seamlessly with the informality of the 110th and it felt as though she had always been part of it. Rowena had travelled with the regiment for many years but he reflected that he had never seen her taking tea to his corporal.

Anne came over and touched Paul's arm. "Looks like the General's orders are here, love."

Paul turned. Major Drydon, one of Wellington's ADCs was riding towards them. He looked tired and cold and Paul wondered how early he had been roused from his bed this morning. He looked as though he had been up half the night, and not as pleasantly occupied as Paul had been.

"Good morning, Chris. What news?" he asked.

Drydon dismounted. "Orders, Major," he said, handing Paul a folded note. Paul took it.

"Why in God's name doesn't he just tell you?" he asked. "Doesn't he trust you?"

"No, Paul, I don't think he trusts you," Drydon said with a grin. "Best to put it in writing so that there's no confusion when you decide to do something completely different to what he's told you to do."

"Good idea," Anne said, coming forward with a tin mug. "Although he can't think it will make any difference to the outcome, he's known Paul for years. Have some tea, Chris, you look as though you need it."

"Thank you, ma'am." Drydon took the mug. Paul observed his expression with some amusement. Anne was not new to Wellington's army, having been married for two years to an officer in the quartermaster's department. The death of her husband and her subsequent marriage to Paul had caused a scandal of impressive proportions, and Paul was well aware that Wellington had attended his hasty wedding purely to ensure that Anne's reputation survived enough to enable him to continue to receive her.

The entire army assumed that Paul had been sleeping with Captain Robert Carlyon's lovely wife long before the death of either Rowena or Carlyon, and although the ladies of headquarters would be obliged to follow the commander's lead in accepting the new Mrs van Daan, he knew that they resented having to associate with a woman they considered an adulteress. Their menfolk were less censorious although just as avidly curious. Paul suspected none of them blamed him for whatever he had been doing with Captain Carlyon's young wife for the past two years, but they were all slightly surprised that he had chosen to marry a girl whose virtue was so thoroughly suspect. At the same time not one of them was immune to her charm, and watching her laughing up at Drydon, Paul reflected that in six months she would have them as thoroughly under her spell as Lord Wellington and the rest of the 110th.

Drydon was looking around him. "You're about the only regiment looking anything like ready for action so far today, ma'am," he said, sipping his tea.

"Oh the Major has been up for hours, so he has," O'Reilly said, and then caught Anne's eye and grinned. "Sorry, ma'am. Forgot."

"At this point, Michael, if I were you I'd find somewhere else to be," Captain Clevedon said laughing.

"On my way, sir," the Irishman said. He saluted and took off in the direction of the lines shouting orders, which brought the light company from relaxed groupings into perfect lines within two minutes. Drydon watched admiringly.

"I'd love to know how you do that," he said.

"Sergeant O'Reilly is showing off," Paul said absently, reading Wellington's note. He grinned. "Apparently we are to get into place alongside General Craufurd's light division, gentlemen."

There was a shout of laughter. "Jesus, I'd like to have been there when Craufurd got his orders," Carl said. "Are we under his command, Paul?"

"It doesn't say so, but I think we may assume that we are. After the Coa he recommended to Wellington that I should be either cashiered or shot, and refused ever to command the 110th again, with particular reference to the light company, Carl. A bit harsh in my opinion because we undoubtedly saved his arse that day, even if one or two of us might have been a bit mouthy about it!"

Carl Swanson, who commanded the light company was laughing. "Mouthy? Paul, he actually could have had you up on a charge that day, even I was shocked when you let rip at him and I've known you all my life."

His commander gave a grin. "I did lose my temper a bit," he admitted. "But he was just as angry because he knew he'd been in the wrong, we should never have been on that side of the river, it was directly against Wellington's orders. He'll get over it. He's a bloody good general and he knows what we're worth. Wellington has put us next to him because he knows when the time comes

Craufurd will do the right thing. And I like serving under the grumpy old bugger. With that single exception at the Coa, he seldom puts a foot wrong. We've also got the two Portuguese battalions that Wellington mentioned, so I'd better get down there and introduce myself, tell them what I expect. Let's get them moving, gentlemen. Nan..."

"I'll take Bella down with the wagons to the hospital, love, and get out of your way. I expect to see you at the end of the battle and not before and if you get carried in to my surgery because you've done something daft you'll be sorry. And take care of this lot, I'm getting very attached to them."

She reached up to kiss him, and Paul drew her into his arms and kissed her with leisurely enjoyment. When he released her she smiled around at his officers and went off to find her horse and her supply wagons, her maid at her heels. Paul watched her go until she was out of sight then went back to his tent to finish getting ready, conscious of the amused sympathy of his officers and men watching him. Most of them felt that Lord Wellington could have granted him some leave with his new wife. Paul suspected that if he had asked for it, it might have been granted, not for his sake but for Anne's. Wellington was very fond of his wife. He had not asked and she had not mentioned it.

One of the many differences between Anne and Rowena was his new wife's alarming level of independence. She did not appear to require him to take care of her in the way that he was used to and it had not occurred to her to question his presence on the battlefield any more than she expected him to question her intention of working in the hospital alongside the surgeons. Paul knew that many of his officers were baffled by what they saw as his lack of control over his wife. Personally he found her competence immensely restful. He knew, without needing to ask, that he was free to do his job without further concern about her and that she would not require anything more from him until his work was done.

The ridge at Bussaco was one of the best defensible positions that Paul had ever seen. Starting at the Mondego River, a long, narrow, steep sided ridge ran to the north west, reaching its highest point at Bussaco where it turned north and lost some of its height, but not its steep sides, and continued on into the mountains. Wellington's engineers had been busy clearing an excellent access road, which would mean that his troops had good mobility up and down his somewhat thinly stretched line.

With his men in position, Paul wandered along the line, stopping occasionally to speak to one of the men. Private Hammond watched him curiously, hearing the laughter which followed his progress. Eventually he paused by Carter and Hammond.

"Settling in, Hammond? Try not to listen to anything Corporal Carter tells you, will you? He's a bloody liar for one thing, and he drinks too much." Paul reached into his coat, drew out his flask and passed it to Carter, who grinned, unstoppered it and drank. He passed it to Hammond who did the same after a slight hesitation, then handed it back to Paul.

"See, I told you," Paul said, shaking his head. "Drunkard."

"The thing is, Hammond," the Corporal said confidentially, "the Major likes to drink with the enlisted men. Not so keen on the officer's mess. He tends to get into fights there."

"There's a nice steep cliff just over that rise, Carter, and I doubt we'd find much of you left after you hit the bottom," his commander said cheerfully.

"I'll be extra careful, sir. Don't think your lady would like it, mind, do you?"

"Probably not, she's unaccountably fond of you." Paul studied Hammond for a moment. "I'm hearing very good things of you, Private Hammond."

"Thank you, sir." Hammond said. "I'll try not to let you down."

They watched as he moved away. Hammond shook his head. "I don't get him. He's a bloody strange officer," he said.

Carter laughed. "Isn't he? You'll get used to him, though. I remember him way back in India when he first joined. Arrogant little sod, he was. Followed the rules he felt like following and couldn't be arsed with sucking up to the senior officers. I didn't think he'd last a year, to be honest. Then we saw our first action under him, got attacked by Maratha cavalry while we were escorting a supply train. I swear to God you'd have thought he was a veteran, he didn't hesitate And he didn't hang back shouting orders either, he was in there fighting alongside us. Cool as you like, never seen anything like it from a lad of twenty-two. These days I can't really imagine serving under anybody else."

"No. He's certainly different. Very friendly with the men. How does he keep discipline? Don't they take advantage?"

Carter grinned. "Not twice. You wait until you hear him get pissed off, you'll wish you were the other side of the Coa. Still makes me flinch after all these years. He can afford to be friendly, the men would die for him."

"Yes, that's what I'd heard of the 110th. Always thought it was just army legend, most of them don't live up to it."

Carter grinned. "Wait and see," he said. He eyed the younger man and Hammond knew what was coming. He had been expecting it. A few weeks in Corporal Carter's company had been enough for him to recognise that his fellow Londoner was both intelligent and shrewd.

"Hammond – how the hell did you come to be here?" Carter said, lowering his voice. "I bloody know there's more to this story than anyone is telling me."

"Like I told you at the start, I deserted. Ran into Sergeant O'Reilly and he talked me into giving it another go."

"I believe some of that, I've seen what those bastards did to your back. I'd have deserted as well. But I'd swear there's more."

Hammond glanced at him, weighing him up. He liked Carter immensely, but that in itself would not have been enough to convince him to confide. But it was also very obvious that the Corporal enjoyed a close and easy relationship with his commander and the other officers of the 110th.

"Not sure what I'm supposed to tell you," he said. "If it was just about me..."

"It's going no further than you and me, lad," Carter said. "I normally know everything that's going on around here, but I've missed something. And I've got a feeling you know what it is."

Hammond jerked his head, making up his mind. "Come for a walk, I don't want the rest of the light company earwigging."

They walked up the lines towards a small copse of trees away from the bulk of the army. "You know what happened with Mrs van Daan and her first husband?"

"I know all about that bastard," Carter said grimly. "I was privileged to watch him smack her across the face in the middle of Viseu with half the officers in Wellington's army watching. If Captain Wheeler hadn't blown his bloody head off, he was in my sights, believe me."

Hammond smiled slightly. "Captain Wheeler didn't," he said quietly. "I did."

Carter stopped and stared at him. "Excuse me?" he said.

"I shot Captain Carlyon. Captain Wheeler took the blame. He said that he'd be believed. I'd have been hanged. Still can't believe he did that for a deserter he'd only just met." He met Carter's eyes and shrugged. "You know she was on her own up there, pretty much. I was trying to get to Oporto, hoped to stow away on a wine ship, trying to avoid Captain Vane or Sergeant Roberts catching up with me and finishing what they'd started."

Carter eyed him steadily. "It was a risk, lad. They shoot deserters."

"You know what, Corporal? I've been shot and I've been strapped to a post and flogged three times in six months and they'd just ordered another five hundred. My back hadn't healed properly. I think it was going to kill me. I think it was meant to kill me, and I'd rather take my chances of a firing squad. At least it's quicker."

Carter nodded soberly. "Fair point. I've been flogged a couple of times although not for years and nothing like that. Something wrong with those bastards if you ask me. So you ran into the Major's wife. Although she'd still have been Mrs Carlyon then."

"Came on the farm – it was obvious it had been used as barracks but seemed deserted now. I slept in the barn overnight. Following morning I was just about to leave and she wandered in. Must have heard me. I was trying to reassure her, but she wasn't scared. Asked if I was hungry and I was bloody starving. She invited me into the kitchen for food. Her maid was up at the hospital, nobody else about. To be honest, I was worried about her. Still can't understand him leaving her there on her own like that though I didn't know anything about her bloody husband. When I was ready to go she made up a bag with food for me. I was on my way when I saw him ride in."

"Carlyon?"

Hammond nodded. "Didn't know who he was, but she was on my mind. Kept thinking that a lovely looking woman like that should not be on her own up there. I thought I'd just double back and have a quick look. Make sure she was all right. If it all seemed fine I was just going to leave quietly again."

Carter was studying him with amused blue eyes. "And it wasn't fine."

"No. He'd got her pinned up against a wall, and he'd been hitting her, she was bleeding. He was pointing a pistol at her, threatening her. I didn't know who the bloody hell he was although I could see he'd an officer's uniform. But I wasn't going to walk away and let him do whatever the hell he was doing to her. I warned him. He didn't back down. So I shot him."

Carter gave a long low whistle, eyeing his new recruit with considerable respect. "You must have known you could end up on a rope for that, lad?"

"I thought I probably would," Hammond admitted. "I didn't know what the hell I'd walked into, but I couldn't leave her in that state, he'd beaten her bloody."

"He was a bastard. Hit her all their married life."

"What for, sleeping with a senior officer?" Hammond said unexpectedly.

Corporal Carter shook his head, pulling a face. "That been worrying you?"

"A bit. I'm not stupid, Corporal. They got married about two weeks after I shot Carlyon. Don't tell me they fell in love in two weeks."

Carter smiled slightly. "They didn't. But nor were they having an affair. Carlyon was a bloody lunatic. I'm friendly with Teresa,

Mrs van Daan's maid, and she tells me he hit her from the day they married, and the Major was nowhere near then. He mistreated her, lad. You shouldn't feel bad about killing him."

"I don't really. No excuse for what he was doing to her that day. I liked her, she's a lovely woman and if that's how her husband treated her you couldn't blame her if she did turn to Major van Daan since it's clear how he feels about her! She was in a bit of a state, shaking all over, so I got her up to her room and I sat with her for a bit. Couldn't walk off and leave her like that. I thought I'd wait until her maid got back and then run for it, but next I knew there was a noise outside and Captain Wheeler and Sergeant O'Reilly had arrived. I thought that was it for me, but turns out not. The Captain sent me off with the sergeant, and he went to the Provost Marshal and told him he'd walked in on Carlyon beating his wife and shot him. They don't seem to have doubted him."

"They wouldn't; he's got a good reputation, the Captain. Good think Major van Daan wasn't there. I'm not sure anybody would have believed he'd not done it. He beat the shit out of Carlyon in the middle of the officers' mess when he found out what he'd been doing to his wife. Couldn't have been more public."

"He's got a temper."

"He might have but he'd never hit a woman and he can't stand men who do," Carter said.

"I agree with him. Anyway, here I am. Pleased I did it. It's a funny regiment, this, nothing like my old one, but I like it." Hammond studied his corporal. "What made you think that story wasn't true?"

"Got a nose for a lie, lad. Honestly? Something about the way the Major is with you. He'd have given anybody a second chance, that bit wasn't odd. But he really likes you, and normally it takes him a while. I'm glad you told me. I'm guessing you didn't start out as Hammond?"

"No. But I'm getting used to it now."

Carter laughed. "I doubt you're the only one in this regiment under a name he didn't start out with. I'm glad you told me, lad. I'll keep it to myself. Although if the lads from the light company knew what you'd done for her, they'd make a hero out of you."

Hammond smiled slightly. "She's well liked for an officer's wife."

"It's more than that. I once stood in a barn and watched that woman step between me and a French dragoon who was about to cut my throat. She's not just another officer's wife." Carter smiled and shrugged. "You'll understand after another few months. Some of us were on the retreat from Talavera with her, she got left behind with the medical staff. What she did for our lads those weeks…well you know what it was like."

"I do," Hammond said feelingly. "I was wounded, probably should have stayed in the hospital but they said the French were on their way and I didn't fancy a prison camp so I got myself up and back on my feet for the march. Nearly bloody killed me."

"We got all our wounded out, the officers found a couple of wagons. But it was a miserable month." Carter glanced over at his commander who was further down the hill. "Although I don't recall either of them looking that miserable. He got shot in the chest, nearly died. She dug the shot out and nursed him. I'm not a sentimental man but watching them together that month…" He shook his head. "I liked his first wife, I was sad when she died. Childbirth. But I am not sad that you shot that bastard Carlyon, Hammond. It was a good days work."

Paul moved back to his command position where his officers, looking slightly gloomy in the thin fog, with no prospect of hot food, were huddled in great coats discussing Wellington's battle plans. He joined them. The Portuguese officers were looking slightly ill at ease. It was Paul's first time commanding Portuguese troops. In the early stages of his time in Portugal, they had the reputation of being ill-trained, ill-equipped and likely to run at the first sign of trouble. Since then, they had been under the rigid training of Marshal Beresford who had been placed in charge of the Portuguese army, and they had apparently improved in both training and morale. They were still mostly untried in the field, and Wellington had taken the precaution of dividing them up among his most experienced troops.

He had given Paul two battalions, both commanded by young and inexperienced officers. Their English was good, and they seemed keen to engage with his officers and to listen to their views on how and when the battle might commence. Paul had decided that he would send in his light company and first and second companies first and then allow the third, fourth, fifth and sixth to bring in the Portuguese. He was hoping that Beresford's training had paid off. The British were in a strong defensive position, but the line felt uncomfortably thin to him.

It was a miserable few days, enlivened only by daily visits from the local Portuguese population. Most of them were loading carts and wagons to move themselves and their families down behind the lines of Torres Vedras, and they had been instructed to leave nothing that the French could live off. Wellington was intending to scorch the earth as far as possible to make it impossible for Massena's army to survive the winter. To the delight of the soldiers, a constant stream of farmers toiled up to the ridge bearing gifts of fruit, wine, bread and meat which they gave freely to the men or sold at very reasonable prices to their officers.

On the fourth day news came that Massena's army had been sighted and Wellington was grimly pleased that the French marshal had taken the route he wanted him to. Paul sent his officers and NCOs through his regiment with ruthless thoroughness to confiscate any form of alcohol and to make sure that his men were armed, ready and capable of fighting. He observed that Black Bob Craufurd was doing the same with the rest of the light division. From a distance he caught the General's eye and saluted with a grin. After a moment, Craufurd returned the salute, and then made his way down from the disused windmill where he had set up his command post.

"Major van Daan. Men ready?"

"Yes, sir. Waiting for your orders."

Craufurd gave a grim smile. "Waiting to see if you'll obey them, sir."

"I almost always do, General."

"It is the insertion of the word almost that I take issue with, Major van Daan." Craufurd studied him. "How are your Portuguese?"

"They're keen enough. Won't know until they're under fire. What's the plan?"

"I want your light company out as advanced skirmishers alongside my rifles. They'll draw the French in, I'll keep in sight with the 43rd and keep the rest of your men and the 52nd out of sight."

Paul gave a grin. It was a familiar tactic of Wellington's who had more than once made excellent use of concealed troops. "Yes, sir. I'll put my experienced men at the front and then pull the Portuguese in behind them, when they see the French falter they'll gain confidence."

"You sound very confident yourself, Major."

"That's my job, sir."

"It is. I understand congratulations are in order."

Paul nodded. "Ten days ago. I'm sure you've heard about it in detail from the headquarters gossips, sir."

"Bunch of old women," Craufurd said contemptuously. I wasn't there the day Carlyon hit her in the middle of Viseu but if I had been I'd probably have shot him myself. They've been gossiping about you for years with that girl, no idea what the real story is and don't give a shit. Hope you'll be happy."

Paul was touched. "Thank you, sir. I'll pass it on to Nan, I know she'd value your support."

Craufurd laughed. "I like that girl, always have. Not one of these namby pamby females who faint at the sight of blood. Saw what she did on those wards after Talavera. Bloody amazing. You've done well for yourself."

"I think so, sir. Thank you. I'll await your orders."

"You better bloody had, Major, or your wife will be a widow before the end of the morning, because I am not taking any of your crap again!" the General said, and moved back up to the windmill, taking out his telescope. Paul went back to his officers, laughing. Craufurd had the reputation of being the harshest disciplinarian and the rudest man in the army but Paul was very fond of him although he knew that his own unconventional approach drove Craufurd mad. For all their differences he knew that Craufurd was one of the few officers who shared his own concern for the welfare of his men, and the light division would follow their irascible General into anything.

The French did not reach the foot of the ridge until night, and in the early hours of the morning, the Anglo-Portuguese army lay under arms and waiting. The valley was shrouded in thick fog, and apart from occasional shots exchanged between the rifles and tirailleurs there was little action. Gradually the mist began to clear as dawn came, and the sounds of battle commencing could be heard from the right as Reynier's Corps launched an attack on Picton's 3rd Division. Given that they were firing uphill, the French guns were ineffective, and Lightburne's brigade fired volley after volley. The combined effect of this along with the fire of two six pounders sent the French into chaos.

There was a second attack further to the south, which quickly degenerated into a long range fire fight which did little damage to either side. General Foy was bringing his force up to the centre of the battlefield against the forty fifth and three Portuguese battalions and had some success at forcing his way through. He was unaware that Wellington had already ordered Leith's division to move along the lateral road from the south-west. Paul, whose view was limited from his position concealed behind the ridge, paid silent tribute to the engineers who had cleared the road so effectively that it made it easy to move reinforcements from one part of the battlefield to the other. Paul glanced up as one of Wellington's orderlies reined in close by.

"Sir, Ney is moving his two brigades up against us in columns. Be ready."

Paul nodded. He glanced further along the line and saw the black browed figure of General Craufurd stomping along towards him.

"Your lads ready, Major?"

"Yes, sir."

"Hold them until you get my order."

"Yes, sir. On your word."

Craufurd glanced over at the watchful lines of the 110th. "Bunch of insubordinate bastards," he said dispassionately.

"They are, sir."

"Bloody brave, though. Proved that at the Coa. Let's see what they can do."

"Yes, sir." Paul repressed a smile as he moved back to his men. It was probably the closest his irascible commander could manage to an apology. Craufurd could never admit to a mistake and had justified his own near disastrous action even to Wellington. Paul had written to Craufurd with an apology of his own. He had been furious at Craufurd's risky decision and even more furious when the general had forbidden him to take the 110th back to cover the retreat. He had done so against orders, relying on his faith in their ability to hold discipline during a difficult retreat and it had worked spectacularly well.

Paul appreciated Craufurd's willingness to forgive. At the time Black Bob had been furious and had given Paul a dressing down in front of the entire light division which had made Paul feel like a junior lieutenant. He had responded with a few words of his own, and he was ruefully aware that he could have been in serious trouble both over his direct refusal to obey the order to retreat and his scathing criticism of a very senior officer. He had ridden back from the battle still seething and had arrived to the news that Robert Carlyon was dead, leaving Anne beaten and bloody. Managing that situation had driven Craufurd from his mind.

Since then he had married Anne, and in his own happiness it was impossible to hold on to a grudge. He had told his new wife what had happened and she had laughed and shaken her head.

"Paul, you don't want to be on bad terms with Bob Craufurd, you like him too much. He's senior to you, and from what I hear you were appallingly rude to him, very publicly. He can't make the first approach. Write to him."

He had done so and had received a stiffly worded acceptance of his apology. It had been enough. He was glad to be up here under Craufurd's command, and his commander's endorsement of his marriage warmed him. The General had met Anne many times at headquarters parties and on the wards of the military hospitals where she worked and they got on well.

Paul could hear them now, the steady drum beat of the approaching columns. He turned to O'Reilly.

"They're coming," he said, and raised his voice softly. "110th at the ready!"

"Ready, sir," Wheeler called back, and the order was passed along the lines. There was no bugle call on this occasion. Craufurd wanted the presence of such a large force to come as a shock to the French.

Michael checked his rifle and looked over his shoulder. "Nice and steady boys," he said. "No need to be heroic here, the bastards have no idea they're about to walk into us. Wait for my word, now."

"Light company ready, sergeant?"

"Ready as they'll ever be, sir."

Paul moved along the ranks his eyes checking for potential problems. They could hear the marching of the French coming closer through the mist and he saw the green jackets of the 95th further up beginning to move forward in skirmish formation. He nodded to Michael.

"Corporal Carter," Michael called.

"Yes, sergeant."

"Will your lads pay particular attention to not letting the Major get himself killed today? You know how clumsy he is, and if I have to take him down to the hospital with a hole in him, his wife is likely to be after us with a scalpel."

Paul looked back, startled, and then began to laugh. "Corporal Carter!"

"Sir."

"Let the lads know there'll be extra grog for the man who shoots Sergeant O'Reilly for me today. Make it look like an accident."

There was a muted rumble of laughter. "Do it now for you if you like, sir!" one of the sharpshooters called. "No need for extra grog, be my pleasure!"

"You'd better hope the French get you today, Scofield, you cheeky bastard!" the sergeant said, laughing. "Ready now boys."

"Get going," Paul said, and Captain Swanson called the order and led his men forward.

They watched as the skirmishers moved over the ridge, taking down individual Frenchmen with accurate rifle fire. It took some time. Paul grinned as he realised that his light company were getting carried away with their feinted attack and were actually pushing the French column back. He imagined that Craufurd was cursing them for delaying the French advance. He could not sound a retreat without alerting the French to his position so he settled down to wait for Carl and O'Reilly to pull them back. Eventually he saw them moving back up the ridge, saw Carter and young Hammond laughing, having just received an earful from their exasperated sergeant. The rifles of the light division were already back up the ridge and the French came on, causing the English gunners to limber up and pull back. Still they waited. The French came closer, pressing on, thinking that on this part of the ridge at least they had the English on the run. They could only see the thin line of the 43rd.

Craufurd held his nerve. The leading column was within twenty-five yards of the crest, and Paul could see the individual faces of each Frenchman when he heard Black Bob yell. "52nd and 110th – avenge Moore!"

It was an emotive cry. There were men of both regiments who had seen Sir John Moore fall at Corunna and he had been beloved of the men he commanded. Paul had done his early training under Moore and had always believed him to be one of the best commanders of light infantry in the army.

"Fire!" Paul roared, and along the line the 52nd and the 110th rose and fired a staggering volley of rifle and musket fire at point blank range into the enemy. No man at the front of the columns was left standing. Along the line his men were reloading, as the shocked Frenchmen reeled, and then steadied and clambered over the bodies of their comrades and ran into a second devastating volley. Some of his riflemen fell back to reload and manage a third, but the rest fixed bayonets and Paul drew his sword.

In the roar of the musket fire and the screams of wounded and dying men, Paul moved his lines steadily forward. He had deliberately allowed the experienced men of the 110th to bear the brunt of the first attack and seeing that they were holding their own without difficulty he ran back to his two Portuguese battalions leaving Johnny to lead the 110th on. These were raw inexperienced troops but he was hopeful that with him at their head they would stand.

He was not disappointed. As the musket fire tapered off, the men were fighting with bayonets and swords, and he led his Portuguese into the fray. With the example of the 110th already cutting their way through the French lines, they did not hesitate, and before long the French advance had halted and the whole line was wavering. Paul's marksmen found time to reload again, and as another barrage of fire crashed into them the French began to run. Some of the Portuguese chased after them, and Paul bellowed to stop them. Without being able to see what was happening all along the ridge he would not risk them charging through French lines and being cut off and hacked to pieces.

A small party of horsemen approached from the north. "Nice work, Major van Daan," Lord Wellington said. "Our allies are looking good today."

"Our allies are looking bloody brilliant, sir," Paul said. He was delighted with the performance of his Portuguese, and he could sense the high spirits of the troops. They had worked hard and trained well, but nothing improved morale as well as a successful action.

"Think you can make them even better, Major?" Wellington asked quietly, and Paul looked up sharply.

"Given some time, definitely, sir."

"I'll bear that in mind. They'll remain under your command for the time being until we have a chance to talk."

"Yes, sir."

Wellington looked along the line to where Craufurd was approaching. "General Craufurd. Superb work, sir. Couldn't have gone better. I think that will more or less do it for the day. They might rattle away at us a bit, but they've got the point. Well done, sir."

Craufurd's face lightened slightly. "Thank you, sir. Good tactics." He glanced at Paul, and his mouth twitched into what was almost a smile. "Well done, Major van Daan."

"Thank you, sir."

Wellington smiled as he watched Craufurd move back down the lines. "Nicely handled, Major. Your diplomatic skills have improved since India."

"I hope so, sir. I was an arrogant young bastard then."

"You still are, Major. You just hide it better. Hold the line and be ready in case I need you elsewhere, you're the fastest battalion I have. But I think we're mostly done."

"Yes, sir. We'll keep picking them off as we see them. Good shooting practice for the lads." Paul raised his voice. "Carter! O'Reilly still alive, is he? Why? Get on with it, lad, haven't got all day!"

"You're a murdering bastard, so you are, sir!" an Irish voice called, and Michael emerged through the smoke which hung like a pall over the battlefield and realised that Wellington was listening with great interest. "Oh sorry, sir, didn't know you were here. Major van Daan is just trying to talk the lads into shooting me, sir."

Wellington gave one of his alarming cracks of laughter. "Is he? Well I'd better get out of here then in case he decides to set them on me! Hope you survive the day, Sergeant."

"Thank you, sir, appreciate your support," Michael said. He watched as the general rode off up the line. "Peterson is down, sir, shot through the shoulder. I've sent him up to the back to get treated. Can't have him lying around to trip over if they come again. No other casualties."

"Good. Carl, do you know how the other brigades are doing?"

"All good I think. They'd no idea we had so many men. Brilliant tactics."

"Aye, Hookey knows his work. They don't know they're beaten yet, but they are. Let's keep it up, nice and steady. If it's French, shoot it." He looked at Michael and grinned. "Or Irish and wearing sergeant's stripes."

"Very funny. If I get caught in the crossfire you'll be laughing on the other side of your face, so you will."

"Stay alive, Michael. If I get you killed, she'll murder me. She likes you, you're always on her side if we fight."

"We're all on her side, sir, in case you'd not realised. She's prettier than you. And possibly a better soldier too, now that I've seen her in a fight."

Paul laughed. "She fights dirtier than you do, Sergeant."

"Good. I hope she shoots you on sight."

All across the ridge the French were being beaten back. Merle's division thrust up the ridge in columns and was met by Picton who had swiftly marshalled his defenders by making use of the road along the ridge. The French were met at the crest by the men of the 88th and the 45th along with two Portuguese battalions in a concave line. The French tried unsuccessfully to deploy into line but came under such heavy fire that they broke and fled down the slope. The final French charge was beaten back by Denis Pack's Portuguese brigade, and there were no further major attacks. By midday the battle was all but over although there were skirmishes up and down the lines throughout the rest of the day.

Chapter Two

Lord Wellington had established himself in the pretty convent at Bussaco for the night and summoned Paul to a meeting in the refectory. His officers sat around the long polished oak tables and ate lamb stew while Wellington outlined his plans.

"Massena is moving out," he said. "Major van Daan sent out scouts this afternoon. Report please, Major."

"Yes, sir. He's realised that he isn't getting past us over this ridge and so he's moving his troops out to the right to outflank us. I'd sent out one of my Portuguese battalions under Captains Swanson and Wheeler to try and cut them off, but the French reached the road ahead of them to the north."

"Our position is turned," Wellesley said. "No point in hanging around here. We'll march in the morning, back towards the lines. No hurry, no need to tire the men out. Once we're there we can hold out. Massena is going to get an unpleasant surprise when he sees what we've been up to." He nodded at Paul. "Good work today, Major. Your Portuguese did well."

"Thank you, sir."

Wellington picked up his wine glass and drank, signalling that the formal part of the meeting was over. "Manage to kill Sergeant O'Reilly?" he asked casually.

Paul grinned. "No, sir. But there'll be other battles."

"Surprised you could find the time or energy to join us, Major," General Picton said. The tone of his voice was offensive. "Given that you've finally married the Carlyon wench, I'd have thought..."

"What did you just say?" Paul demanded, turning towards Picton in furious indignation.

"Gentlemen..." Wellington said quietly.

"Come on, Major, we're all men here. Wouldn't say it in front of the ladies, but..."

"You'd better bloody not say it in front of me, General!" Paul said icily. "In the first place, I resent the implication that my marital status is likely to affect my ability to do my job. My first wife gave birth to my son on a ship in Naples and died giving birth to my daughter on her way back to Lisbon after being attacked by the French while I was elsewhere doing my bloody duty. And if you want to find out what my current wife is doing while I'm up here listening to your foul mouth, I suggest you take yourself down to the hospital where you'll find her on her feet, covered in blood, stitching up wounds and digging out shot! Give her my regards, would you, because I've not seen her for days, I've been on a battlefield. And feel free to call her a wench to her face, and then come back up here and tell me how that went. If you can still walk!"

There was a ripple of laughter around the table. Wellington smiled slightly. "I realise you must have been joking, General Picton, but I think an apology might be in order."

Picton was glowering but nodded. "Apologies. Didn't realise you were so sensitive, Van Daan."

"I don't need you to apologise for my sensitivity, General, I need you to apologise for insulting my wife," Paul said inexorably, and beside him Robert Craufurd, who loathed Picton, gave a snort of laughter.

"I apologise," Picton said again.

"Apology accepted," Paul said evenly.

"Excellent," Wellington said. "I think we're done here, gentlemen. A good day's work for all of us today. Once we're back behind the lines we can starve them out. Lisbon is secure and he can't maintain that army in this countryside for long."

The men around the table began to leave and Paul rose. Craufurd got up and went across to Picton. "Nasty, sir," he said shortly. "I realise he can't hit you, you're a senior officer. But you miscall his wife in front of me again, I won't hesitate. And I can."

He nodded at Paul who smiled slightly, watching him leave the room. Wellington had moved to stand beside him. "I find it singularly charming that General Craufurd actually believes that you wouldn't hit a senior officer, Major," he said quietly.

"Well I've never hit him, sir, so he has reason to," Paul said, equally softly.

"I can distinctly remember you threatening to punch me on one occasion," Wellington said, and Paul laughed.

"I caught you kissing my girl on the terrace, sir. You're lucky you're still here. Picton's an arse."

"Picton showed his worth today, Major."

"I didn't say he wasn't a good soldier, sir. And I know he's only repeating what half the army is saying about her. They're just not stupid enough to say it in front of me. But you might want to have a quiet word with him and let him know that he needs to keep his mouth shut. Because with his record with women in the Indies, I'd rather he didn't speak to my wife, let alone comment on her virtue!"

"Paul, nobody knows the truth of what happened there," Wellington said, watching Picton leave. "You more than anybody should know how stories spread."

"If there's a story out there about me torturing a sixteen year old lass to get a confession for theft, sir, I'd love to hear about it."

Wellington shook his head. "When I hear a story about you, Major, I tend to assume it's true, however bizarre. But you're right, it's unlikely to include abusing a woman. Calm down and go and find your wife. Does she know you're alive?"

"I hope so, sir, I told Carl to find her and let her know where I was. I've a feeling he did because I think if she'd not had a message by now she'd have been up here finding out why. And God help Picton then."

"Yes. You've got Robert's sympathy. He adores that wife of his."

"I know. He and I have more in common than you'd think. Perhaps that's why I like him so much." Paul glanced at his commander. "I'm sorry we missed Massena. I would have liked to cut him off."

"Paul, one of the things that always happens is that the French surprise us with their speed. It's unfortunate, but time is on our side now." Wellington smiled slightly. "Massena is going to get the shock of his life when he marches south to take Lisbon and sees what we've got waiting for him."

"One of the other things that always happens, sir, is that they recover quicker than we expect and they're a lot better than we are at living off the land."

"Not the state we've left the land in," Wellington said quietly. "Stop feeling responsible for everything and get yourself back to your wife or she'll be in that hospital all night."

"Yes, sir."

Collecting Rufus Paul rode back down to the lines. There was the smell of cooking as the army made up for several days of no hot food. By now his men would be settled around the fires drinking their grog ration and talking over the battle. He had lost none today and despite the disappointment of not managing to stop Massena, he was happy with how the day had gone. Picton's spite had not really upset him, although he had deliberately made a point of sounding furious. He had taken the opportunity to make it clear that he was prepared to defend his wife's good name against anybody. The gossip would die down soon enough, and the army would become used to their marriage, but he did not want to give the impression that he would tolerate snide remarks like Picton's.

Lamps were burning in the hallway of the seminary where the medical board had set up their hospital. Paul walked through, stepping over men who lay on the marble floor still waiting to be seen, and paused in the door of the ward.

"McGrigor, seen my wife?" he called.

The surgeon-general looked round. "In surgery with Norris," he said. "He's got a French colonel in there with an arm being amputated. Not sure if it's her needlework or her French he needed but she'll be done soon. You all right, Major?"

"Not a scratch, thank you. We'd hardly any wounded, do you know if they're here?"

"No, I think your wife sent them back up to the lines, they could all walk." McGrigor nodded. "Here's Norris now."

Paul turned to see Dr Adam Norris coming towards him. "Paul, how are you? Sorry I've kept her."

"I've only just come from Wellington's meeting anyway," Paul said. "Not a bad day."

"Worse for the French, to be honest. She's just getting Colonel de Galle settled and she'll be with you. If she doesn't come soon, go and find her, he might have just lost his right arm but he knows what he wants to do with his left, believe me and I don't think he gives a damn that she's married."

"I'll go now, I do not trust her with a Frenchman," Paul said with a laugh, and went through the ward and down into the long room at the back where he found his wife giving instructions to a ward orderly about the care of the colonel. Paul came forward. Colonel de Galle was lying back on his mattress, grey with pain and exhaustion, but his dark eyes were on Anne's face. Paul smiled slightly at his expression.

Anne finished and looked back at the French colonel. "I'll come and check on that tomorrow," she said in fluent French. "Try to get some sleep, the laudanum should help."

"Thank you, madame. You are as kind as you are beautiful," the colonel said.

"As long as you don't upset her, Colonel, and then believe me everything changes," Paul said, and came forward as she spun around, her face lighting up.

"Paul, I thought you'd gone back to Lisbon without me!" she said, laughing.

"No, that was your first husband," Paul said with a grin. He caught her to him and kissed her hard. She laughed and batted him away.

"Let me wash my hands and get rid of this revolting apron, you'll get covered in blood. Which for once after a battle, you're not! Weren't you there?"

"I was. It was surprisingly tidy. I don't always come off the field with a ball in my chest, you know. Besides which, I've been with Wellington so I had to clean myself up. Go on, go and get ready and we'll go back to the lines."

When she had gone he turned to the colonel who was watching him with a slight smile. "You are a lucky man, Major."

"I know," Paul said in French. "You haven't been so lucky, sir. Where were you?"

"I came up over the ridge expecting to find a small force," the colonel said wryly and Paul pulled a face.

"Ah. I'm sorry. I hope you make a good recovery."

"You were up there?"

Paul nodded. "Major Paul van Daan, 110th first battalion."

"Your men fought very well today, Major."

"Thank you. I'm proud of them."

"You should be. And of your wife. I was hoping to go back to see mine, but it may be a while now."

"You'll need time to recover," Paul said. "But I'll speak to Wellington, see if we can get you released quickly. He doesn't like keeping wounded men prisoner."

"Thank you, that is kind of you." De Galle closed his eyes. "Take your wife home, sir. And thank her for me."

"I will." Paul went in search of Anne and found her giving instructions to one of the young hospital mates. He grinned and approached.

"Nan, if you don't come with me of your own accord I'm going to pick you up. It is late and I'm tired and if you're not, you should be!"

"I'm coming." She smiled at the boy and turned, taking Paul's outstretched hand. They walked out to where an orderly held their horses and he lifted her up into the saddle and then swung himself up tiredly. They walked back along the ridge towards the lights and fires of the camp.

"All right?" he asked, sensing her mood. She looked over at him and nodded.

"Yes. Glad it's over. That's the first time I've watched you go into battle as your wife. It felt odd."

"Christ, I suppose it is. I hadn't thought of that. And you'd no experience of it with Robert."

"I wouldn't have cared anyway with him," Anne said candidly. "But I found myself riding up to the hospital the other day wondering if I'd said the right things."

"You always say the right things, Nan. And it wouldn't matter if you didn't. Just waking up with you beside me in the morning starts my day off well."

Anne laughed. "And gives your regiment a laugh," she said. They were approaching the lines of the 110th, easy to identify by the rows of small tents. In most other regiments only the officers had tents, with the enlisted men obliged to sleep in the open or fashion tents from their blankets. Anne was aware that other regiments looked askance at what they saw as the privileges granted to the 110th, but she knew that the tents had been purchased through money saved in other areas. She had spent hours with Paul and his quartermaster working out how it could be done. The 110th had the reputation of being one of the fittest and healthiest regiments in the army but she was aware that Paul's determination to ensure that his men were dry and warm and properly fed had a good deal to do with that.

Paul dismounted at the tents and Private Jenson, his orderly, came to take the horses away. Anne's maid got up and came forward.

"You eaten, ma'am?" Corporal Carter asked. "I'm guessing the Major ate with Lord Wellington."

"I did, but he's stingy with it so if there's any left..."

"I'm hungry, Danny," Anne admitted. "I just want to get changed."

"I'll heat it up," Carter said, getting up. Anne smiled and ducked into the tent. Teresa appeared with a jug of hot water and Anne stripped off the dark gown and washed, then dressed in a loose dark green velvet morning robe. She possessed several of them and found them warm and comfortable, but until recently she would not have worn them in camp. Her first husband would have disapproved of her appearing in dishabille in front of other men. Paul did not appear to care, and she suspected that privately he enjoyed her unconventionality. Slipping her tired feet into soft shoes she allowed Teresa to brush out her long hair. Leaving it loose she went outside and joined the group around the fire. Paul was already there, eating paella from a tin mess bowl. Anne sat down in the folding chair and accepted a bowl and spoon from Carter with a smile of thanks. Michael O'Reilly came forward with a drink and Anne sipped and lifted her brows at the quality of the wine.

"Very nice. Did we have a good battle?"

Paul laughed. "The local farmers have been plying us with drink. Nobody wants to transport it back to the lines and most of them are moving out, so we thought we'd make the most of it. We're educating Carter's palate, he'll be ruined for army grog by the end of the week."

"I'll still manage to force it down, mind, sir," Carter said placidly.

Paul glanced around. "Where's Hammond? I don't often see you without him these days, Carter."

"In the tent. He's not feeling so clever, sir. Got a crack across the head with a French musket."

"I didn't know he was hurt," Paul said.

"Not really much you can do about a lump on the head, sir, but he's got a headache, didn't feel like eating."

"Hopefully he'll sleep it off and be fine later," Anne said. "But if he needs me to look at him, Danny..."

"I know."

"How did he do today?" Paul asked. Carter grinned.

"Bloody good," he said. "I'd a feeling he would be, mind, but you never know until you're out there. He's very cool under fire, and smart. Took that whack on the head from behind while he was bayoneting one of the bastards. Kept on going, didn't realise it was hurting so much until later. He's a good lad, worth holding on to, sir." He glanced across at Anne.

Paul smiled slightly. He was beginning to suspect that Carter knew the full story of how Hammond had joined the light company. "I rather thought he would be," he said. "You can have his share, Carter, you've earned it today. Although I'm surprised Craufurd didn't shoot you lot when you forgot you were supposed to be drawing them back up."

"Don't even talk to me about it!" O'Reilly said gloomily. "Stupid bastards nearly pushed the French back off the ridge. Which would have been fine if the light division rifles had been doing the same, but they were following orders and retreating. If the French had been quick enough they could have cut us off and taken us to pieces!"

"Sorry, sir. Not used to that strategy. Our lads start killing Frenchmen, it's hard to stop them. But we got it back, although Captain Swanson came surprisingly close to losing his temper out there."

"I want a transfer," Carl said, reaching for the wine bottle. "Clevedon, want to take over the light company?"

"No, thank you, Captain. I don't like that bit where they run off down the ridge after the French when they're not supposed to."

Paul was laughing. "I expect we'd have come to your rescue, but I just know Craufurd would have blamed that on me! And he's in a good mood with me today."

"Yes, I gather he stood up for me with General Picton in the meeting," Anne said mildly, setting down her empty bowl and sipping her wine. Paul gave her a startled look.

"How the hell did you know about that?"

Anne laughed. "Colonel Grant came down to the hospital to check on some of his men, just before you did. Actually he didn't tell me, he was telling Adam Norris the story, but I was operating in the next room and he has a nice clear voice."

"Jesus, you'd think with Bonaparte's bloody army to kill they'd have better things to do than gossip," Paul said, irritated. "Don't let it bother you, lass. Picton is an arsehole, and if he starts again I'll deal with him. But I think Wellington intends to speak to him anyway."

His wife sipped her wine. "I'll try not to lie awake worrying about it," she said sweetly. "To tell you the truth, Paul, I'm not sure it has much to do with me. He sees you as an ally of General Craufurd and he hates him. Can't do much about Craufurd, he's of equal rank. But he can amuse himself winding you up at headquarters and see if he can get you to blow. As Craufurd demonstrated today, you might drive him crazy but he'll stand up for you if he needs to."

Paul looked at her with an arrested expression. "That's an interesting thought," he said. "I'll bear that in mind. Have you finished? It's been a long day and personally I'm shattered."

Anne nodded and got up. Around them the other officers were getting to their feet. Carl watched as his commander said goodnight and ducked into his tent with his wife.

"I wonder if she's right about Picton," he said to Wheeler as they made their way back to their tents.

"It wouldn't surprise me. Not just because of Craufurd. Paul has never liked Picton and doesn't always bother to hide it. But one thing is for sure, now she's put that in Paul's head he's going to keep his temper better around him. He won't want Craufurd baited."

"No. I wonder if she knows that?"

Johnny laughed. "I try never to underestimate our commander's wife, Carl."

In the tent Paul lay in the bed watching his wife undress. She slid in beside him and curled up against him. "I'm tired," she said, and he gave a soft laugh.

"Which is your way of saying you know that I'm tired."

Anne laughed. "We're both tired," she said, and reached up to kiss him. They lay still and quiet, his arms about her and he thought about the day, about the battle and the bloodshed and about the miracle of coming back to camp to lie like this beside her.

"Nan."

"Mm?" She had not been feigning her tiredness he realised, smiling. She was almost asleep, her body warm and relaxed against his. He kissed the top of her head gently.

"I love you, bonny lass."

"I love you too, Major. Let me go to sleep or I'll slap you."

He lay there in the darkness smiling to himself, thinking that the strangest things about her made him happy.

The retreat back to the lines was an orderly affair, unlike Anne's previous experience of the retreat from Talavera. Wellington was well prepared and Paul marched his 110th and Portuguese companies down towards Pere Negro with a sense of confidence. Bussaco had been a neat and useful victory. Like Wellington he believed that the important work would be done this winter, with the completion of the lines and the systematic starvation of the French army. As they marched, the 110th saw long straggling columns of local villagers, carrying as much as they could, walking to take refuge under Wellington's protection. He pitied those who stayed behind. The French were brutal in the towns and villages when provisions were short and he had seen rows of hanged and tortured bodies during their march. Better to enter the lines as refugees than to endure what a starving French army might do to the countryside.

One village had been completely destroyed; the entire population massacred other than a local priest who had hidden in the burnt out ruins of his church. He informed Paul with tears in his eyes that before the massacre the French had rounded up every woman between twelve and thirty and marched them away for the use of the soldiers. Paul glanced at his wife and saw her blinking away tears as she led the priest to find him a horse to accompany them back to the lines.

"You shouldn't have let her hear that," Johnny Wheeler said quietly.

Paul glanced at him, startled. He realised with rueful amusement that it had not occurred to him to send Anne away during the conversation. "She's all right, Johnny."

"She's crying, Paul."

"That doesn't mean she's not all right."

"You wouldn't have had that conversation with Rowena there, Paul. I know Nan is an unusual woman, but she's still a woman. In fact she's still little more than a girl. How old is she now?"

Paul was watching his wife talking quietly to the priest. "She'll be twenty one in December," he said.

"She's twenty, and she wasn't raised to this any more than Rowena was." Wheeler glanced at his commander and smiled slightly. "You treat her like she's one of us, you know that, don't you? And I can't for the life of me understand it, because you were so bloody protective of Rowena. I've never forgotten that day in Dublin when that arsehole Tyler grabbed hold of her and tried to kiss her at Wellesley's reception. I thought you were going to kill him."

"It was tempting," Paul admitted with a grin. "But out of curiosity, Johnny, what do you think Nan would do if Tyler grabbed hold of her and tried to kiss her against her will?"

Wheeler thought about it then grinned. "I don't know. Does she still carry that knife up her sleeve?"

"Yes."

"I know she's tough, Paul. I just think sometimes you might forget how young she still is."

They completed the march through two days of torrential rain, with baggage carts sticking in the thick mud, and officers and men soaked through to the skin and shivering in their tents at night unable to get dry or warm by lighting fires. Anne slept wrapped in the warmth of Paul's arms and looked forward to reaching the lines where at least there was a good chance of a dry billet.

They were well into the morning's march the following day when Paul observed that his wife was no longer among the officers where she had been riding. He glanced back down the lines and saw her slight figure through the rain, well at the back of the long column, and he turned and rode back. She was close to the baggage wagons where the women and children who accompanied their men on campaign trudged through the mud in sodden misery, their skirts heavy with red mud, weighed down by bundles and packs and heavy children. Paul reined in. She had not seen him, was swinging down lightly from Bella, talking to some of the women. One of them was heavily pregnant, holding the hand of a small boy. Anne talked for a few moments and then called one of her medical orderlies over. The young man hoisted the pregnant woman up onto Bella's back and under his wife's instructions passed up the boy, and a small girl who was stumbling behind with her mother. Anne smiled her thanks to the lad, took Bella's reins and fell into step beside the women. One of them was talking to her and he saw Anne laugh, indicating her soaked riding dress with resigned amusement.

He smiled and shook his head, rode forward. Anne looked up. She was so wet that there were droplets on her eyelashes. "You look freezing," he said.

"I am. Dreaming of a hot fire and a cup of wine at the end of it."

"We'll be there before dark and they're good billets, plenty of outbuildings for everybody to keep dry."

He could sense the uncertainty of the women at his reaction to his wife walking with the men's wives. Glancing over he spotted another woman, struggling with an infant in her arms and two children clinging to her soaked skirts, a boy and a girl of around four or five. He grinned and moved his horse round. "It's Mrs Clifton, isn't it? Pass them up, it'll give you a break for a bit."

She looked up, startled. "Sir, it wouldn't be right."

"Nonsense, Rufus is strong enough and there's nothing of these two." He grinned at the boy. "Although there will be, he's tall for his age. Up you come, lad, come and see how it feels to lead the regiment."

He trotted the horse gently back up to the front, talking quietly to the two children. After ten minutes, he was aware of Captain Wheeler moving past him. "Your wife looks like something a corporal picked up at the roadside," he said with a grin.

"I wouldn't blame him, Johnny, if I came across something looking as good as she does at the roadside I'd pick her up myself," Paul said laughing.

"She's a bloody menace! Every single one of these brats is going to be crawling with lice and I'm going to itch for days."

Paul watched as he rode back down the lines, rain streaming off the back of his hat. He saw him bend down and lift up two children onto his horse. Paul was laughing. He glanced across at Carl who was shaking his head. "I bloody hate her!" he said. "If Wellington comes past he's going to go up the wall!"

"Not when he knows who started it. She can get away with pretty much anything with him," Paul said, still laughing. "Go and collect your share of muddy brats, Carl, and I'll pay for your laundry."

"Your wife should do my bloody laundry!"

"My wife should do my laundry, but I don't recommend you tell her that!" Paul said. "Cheer up. At least we're on horseback. She's got so much mud on her skirts she won't be able to walk by the time we get to Pere Negro!"

Carl glanced across at his commander's soaked, muddy wife. "Much she bloody cares," he said. "I think I love your wife, Paul."

"Thank you. I do myself." Paul smiled, watching his friend ride back to join Anne and scoop up two wet, shivering toddlers. Carl drew the older girl back against him and settled her sister in the crook of his arm letting his coat shelter them from the driving rain.

On reaching Pere Negro the 110th had been allocated billets in a large unoccupied convent on the edge of the village not far from Wellington's headquarters which was situated in a big graceful house loaned by a local dignitary. Paul's companies occupied outbuildings and barns and the officers took over the main convent building, while Anne set up her hospital and surgery in the church.

The quartermasters and orderlies had moved ahead of the main force and as they rode into the main yard there was the smell of smoke which told them that fires had already been lit and George Kelly had been busy in the kitchen. Paul rode over to the barn and delivered his charges back to their mother. He dismounted and gave Rufus to his orderly to stable, then turned to find his wife. She was standing in the shelter of the barn door as the men streamed past her out of the rain, holding a swaddled baby in her arms, talking to three of the women. One of the men stopped and spoke. Anne handed back the baby, and the private took her hand and kissed it. Paul smiled slightly and went forward.

"You flirting with my wife, Private Murphy?"

The man looked around startled. "Sir? No, sir. Just wanted to say thank you. My wife, sir – the children..."

"I know." Paul surveyed Anne. "You look like a mermaid," he said quietly. "Come inside and get dry before you catch your death."

"He's right, ma'am, you need a bath!" the woman said. "Let me get the bairns settled and I'll start heating some water."

"Thank you, Josie, but don't hurry you've enough to do."

"It's no trouble, ma'am. Sir."

She bustled away and Paul put his arm around Anne and led her firmly over to the main convent building. Teresa was already at the top of the stairs unloading boxes with the help of Corporal Carter. She studied Anne and rolled her eyes.

"I know," Paul said. "You try telling her, Teresa, she takes no notice of me."

"You don't bloody try, sir," Carter said, laughing.

Paul led Anne into the bedroom allocated to them and went for towels, stripping off his soaked clothing. He wrapped a towel around him and went to help her out of her drenched riding clothes, and into a dry shift then seated her on a wooden stool and stood rubbing her soaked hair. She sat in tired silence letting him tease out the tangles with her brush and comb.

"You all right? You were freezing."

"Probably warmer walking than riding," she said. "I need to find a bootmaker, those shoes are hopeless for this."

"We'll ask around. You must be exhausted."

"I'm tired, but so is everybody else."

She looked up over her shoulder and smiled at him and he set down the brush and drew her up into his arms. "Christ, I love you, lass."

"I love you too, Major."

"Supper will be ready soon. I'm starving."

"How long?" she asked softly, and Paul took her hand and raised it to his lips.

"Long enough to test that bed out," he said with a grin and led her across the room.

Anne had been aware of the lines of defence that Wellington had been working on since the retreat from Talavera. Both Paul and her first husband Robert Carlyon had been involved in the project in different ways, Robert in helping to organise labour and supplies, and Paul in working with Fletcher and the engineers on the design and defensibility of the lines. But she had not realised until now the sheer scale of the project. With his men settled, Paul took her on horseback to tour several sections of the lines and she was astonished at how much had been achieved with very few people knowing about it. Standing in one of the hilltop forts looking down on the country through which the French would come, Anne glanced round at her husband.

"This is what Robert was working so hard on," she said.

Paul nodded. Anne very seldom spoke of her dead husband. They were able to talk freely of his wife, who had been Anne's friend, but the horror of Carlyon's treatment of Anne and his final attack, which had led to his death, was too recent. But there had been another side to Carlyon, and Paul had always known that although Wellington was glad that he was no longer alive to hurt his wife, he missed the man's undoubted talent as an administrator.

"Yes. It's why Hookey promoted him. He was virtually in charge of supplies and labour."

"No wonder he was so often away. He never spoke of it, and I assumed that it was because we just did not talk. But of course he could not."

"No."

"Are the French on their way, Paul?"

He nodded. "Yes. Massena will probably be here in a week or so. It's going to be a nasty surprise for him. We're ready."

The lines had been created from two ridges of hills by local labour working under the supervision of Fletcher and his engineers. Closed earthworks with a series of small redoubts holding 3-6 guns and 200-300 men, were sited along the high ground of each ridge. Buildings, olive groves and vineyards had been destroyed, denying any cover to an attacking force. Rivers and streams had been dammed to flood the ground below the hills and sections of hillside had been cut or blasted away to leave small but sheer precipices. Ravines and gullies were blocked by entanglements. As she rode beside Paul, listening to him explaining the work that had been done, Anne was amazed at Wellington's achievement.

"We'll wait behind the lines," Paul said. "The fortifications are manned by the Portuguese militia, some Spanish and a few British gunners and marines. He's set up a communication system using semaphore, which is the best I've seen since my navy days. He can mobilise his troops faster than Massena will believe, and the roads he's created mean we can move up and down the lines to where we're needed very fast. And he's scorched the terrain for miles outside. The French are very good at living off the land, but I think he's got them beaten this time. It just depends on how long it takes them to realise it." He smiled at her. "And then we wait, and collect reinforcements and supplies and train our army. Next year we'll be ready for another advance."

Anne nodded. She was watching him. "What is it, Paul?"

He glanced at her and smiled. "How do you always know?"

"Your voice. Your face. Something has been bothering you for a few days."

"Nan – do I expect too much of you?"

Anne stared at him for a long time. Eventually she said:

"Carl or Johnny? Actually it could be any of them, but they're the two most likely to say it to you. The rest just think it."

He burst out laughing. "Johnny," he said. "He noticed you were upset that day in the village. Hearing what they'd done with the girls. And at the murder of the villagers. He pointed out that I'd never have let Rowena hear that story. And he was right, I wouldn't."

"Paul, I can't comment on your marriage to Rowena. I only know what I want. Right from the start you have refused to treat me like an idiot or a child, which is how most men treat most women. It is probably a big part of why I love you so much. But that must be difficult because sometimes it means I will get upset, or frightened. And you can't protect me from that."

"Johnny reminded me how young you were," Paul said quietly, reaching for her hand. "And as I heard myself say it, I realised that he might have a point. That at twenty you should be thinking about parties and fashion and jewellery and all the things that I should be able to give you. I'm taking you on a tour of redoubts and blockhouses instead of riding in the row and introducing you to George Brummell and the Prince of Wales."

Anne began to laugh. "Should I like either of them?"

"I think you'd like George, I do myself. Not so sure about Prinny. Although he'd definitely like you! Now that I think about it, you're probably safer out here with Wellington, who actually does know how to behave although he wishes he didn't. But seriously..."

"Paul, seriously, what is this about?"

"I never asked you," he said suddenly. "About any of this. I walked into the villa and I carried you to bed and five days later you're my wife and in an army camp up to your ankles in mud with no prospect of a normal life, and I never once asked you if that was all right."

"Did you ever ask Rowena?"

"No. She was pregnant and completely desperate. I took her to Naples deliberately so that she could have Francis away from home. By the time we came back the gossips had forgotten to add up dates and there was no scandal. I never asked her because she had no bloody choice, I'd already had what I wanted out of her, she could hardly say no! And that was unbelievably selfish of me. I meant to do things so differently with you. But I didn't, did I? By the time we got married I'd already created such a bloody scandal with you that you didn't have much more choice than Rowena did."

"And that has been bothering you for days hasn't it?" She was smiling.

"Yes. We laughed about it at the time, but I don't think I even asked you to marry me properly. I just took what I wanted. Again."

"Oh love, stop it!" Anne realised suddenly that he was genuinely upset. "I am going to kick Captain Wheeler for this!"

"It's not his fault, Nan. It just made me look at this differently. I've been so happy. And so completely wrapped up in myself. And that's what I do. I met you in Yorkshire, and..."

"Paul, stop! What is it you think you should have said to me back in Lisbon?"

"I should have asked you to marry me. I should have told you that I know I am not offering you even a part of what you should have, and that the life is hard and painful and often very sad. There are risks and dangers and you'll see and hear things that will stay with you all your life. I should have told you how much I love you and that if you wanted you could stay in Lisbon or even go back to England, and I'd still marry you. I should have told you that if I have to choose between this life and you, I choose you. And I should have left you time to make up your mind." The blue eyes were steady on hers.

Anne put her arms about him. "Yes, Major," she said quietly. "My answer is still yes. And I'm not going either to Lisbon or to

England unless that is where you are going too. I love you, and I love this life. I love your regiment no matter how foul mouthed and filthy they are, and I even love Captain Wheeler although I feel sorely tempted to throw him off Bussaco Ridge the next time he does this to you! I am exactly where I want to be. With you. If you show any signs of trying to shelter me in the way you did with Rowena, you are going to find yourself in serious trouble. And how can I doubt what you'd give up for me when you'd have given up your career if you'd fought that duel with Robert?"

"Nan..."

"I love you, Paul. The way you are. I am not going back to England to sew cushion covers and dance at the hunt ball. Since I've been out here I've discovered there is a lot more to me than that. I'd like to find out what else I'm capable of. And I want to be with you. So please, stop listening to your officers trying to tell you that you're doing this wrong, because you're not. Being married to any one of them would drive me mad! And drive them even madder."

He nodded, his eyes on her face. "What did I take on when I married you?" he said softly.

"Just me. I'm not easy, Paul."

"I know. But somehow I don't seem to find you difficult at all."

"Prove it," she said quietly, and he laughed suddenly and reached for her, scooping her up into his arms.

"You don't have to tell me twice, lass," he said, laughing. "Good thing they've not manned this fort yet, it's nice and sheltered in there."

Anne was laughing too. "Serve you right if a company of Portuguese militia marches in while you're busy," she said. Paul bent his head to kiss her.

"I'll take the chance," he said.

Chapter Three

On 11th October the first of the French reached the lines of Torres Vedras. Wellington's intelligence agents had been frantically trying to establish the most likely place for the French to attack. Montbrun's cavalry reached the lines close to the village of Sobral, which was actually outside the lines and held by the picket line of Sir Brent Spencer's 1st division.

Montbrun's supporting infantry brigade clearly outnumbered the defenders of the village but the French commander could see that the hills to the south were lined by fortifications, and was aware that if he attacked Sobral there was real danger that his force would be overwhelmed by superior numbers. Spencer's men abandoned the village overnight but by the next morning they had been ordered back into place.

As Montbrun moved east, towards the Tagus, he was replaced by the first part of Junot's 8th Corps, Clausel's division. This time the French decided to push the British outposts back. At least six battalions of Clausel's division moved into Sobral, and forced the pickets from Erskine's and Löwe's brigades to retreat 300 yards, crossing a ravine that separated Sobral from the lower slopes of Monte Agraça, the highest point on this part of the line. There the British formed a new picket line and built a barricade to block the high road and then waited while Wellington's semaphore sent out messages across the lines, testing the system which Wellington hoped would stop the French advance permanently.

On the morning of 14 October Junot decided to push the British outposts further away from his lines around Sobral. After a short bombardment, Junot sent the 19th to attack the British outposts, that day manned by the 71st Foot. The French attack forced the British pickets to abandon their advanced line, but the rest of the 71st then launched a counterattack, which forced the French to retreat back into Sobral. The British pursued as far as the village, before being themselves forced to retreat by the presence of Ménard's brigade. Junot paused at this point to assess the situation, and the British were able to reoccupy their original picket line. This skirmish cost the

British 67 casualties and the French at least 120 but the arrival from further west of the 110th and two Portuguese battalions under Major van Daan caused the French to pull back quickly.

While this skirmish was taking place, Masséna finally made his first visit to the front to view the Lines of Torres Vedras. He arrived at Sobral in time to see the failure of the French attack, and to decide not to press the attack . Seeing Wellington's army in a strong position, and remembering the losses he had suffered at Bussaco, Masséna decided not to risk attacking the Lines, and instead on 15 October the French settled down outside the lines, remaining there for the next month. During this period no more serious attacks were made on the Allied outposts, and on 14 November Masséna pulled back as far as Santerem in search of supplies.

Paul was resigned. He had hoped, as Wellington had, that the French could be lured into another Bussaco, but Massena had begun to realise, with considerable surprise, the extent and strength of the English defences, and the waiting game had begun. With the outposts secured, the 110th returned to their billets and Paul set to work to plan drilling and training which would keep his men busy and ready for action. He was still in command of his two Portuguese battalions, and he placed them under the command of Carl Swanson and Johnny Wheeler, to work with their companies on drilling, musket and bayonet training. He was also keen to begin working with the rest of his companies on skirmish drill. While officially it was the role of the light company to act as skirmishers, he was aware that the skills they had learned could be applied throughout his regiment to improve their fighting skills overall.

When Anne was not busy at the hospital or working with Paul's quartermaster she rode up to watch training. Her husband and his officers became accustomed to her presence, and took turns to spend time with her explaining what was being done and why, and she was fascinated to watch the process which had made a legend of the 110th. She suspected that very few of the other regiments were working quite so hard with no immediate prospect of a battle and she began to realise with some amusement where Paul's reputation for perfectionism had come from.

In the relative comfort of their billet she had time to settle in to the life of the regiment and to get used to being married to Paul. Up and down the lines, Wellington's officers hunted and gambled and attended parties, and she watched her husband rise each day to join his officers and men on the training field, observed his watchful eyes scanning the lines for mistakes and inefficiencies, and laughed at their grumbles as they left the field, knowing that what had already been good was expected to be perfect.

"Every other bloody officer in this army is applying for leave!" she heard Carter commenting, after a particularly gruelling afternoon of skirmish drill. "What the hell is wrong with him? Can't he take furlough and give us a break? Or even a day off!" He caught sight of Anne's laughing face and grinned. "Sorry, ma'am. Didn't see you there. You sure you aren't due a honeymoon?"

Anne laughed. "Not sure what my chances are, although I hear that even General Craufurd is going home to see his wife for a while. You're just unlucky that I'm out here, Danny. But it's looking good."

"It is bloody good, ma'am. But according to him, it needs to be bloody perfect!"

"It does," Paul's voice said, coming up behind Carter. "Stop complaining to my wife, Carter, she doesn't care."

In the relative isolation of the convent, the 110th maintained it's usual level of informality. The officers ate together in the main convent building but from the start, Paul insisted that Anne join them for dinner. She was surprised, knowing that married officers usually dined separately with their wives, but she was the only lady attached to the 110th and it was clear that her husband intended to start a new custom. When the meal was over Anne removed herself tactfully to allow the other officers to relax, but she enjoyed the sense of belonging that eating in the mess gave her and within a few weeks the officers of the 110th had settled to the custom and vied for the privilege of sitting beside her.

After dinner most of the officers drifted down to the field behind one of the barns where the men tended to congregate on fine evenings. Two of the women had set up informal grog tents there, and Private Flanagan of the light company was often to be found playing his fiddle, sometimes accompanied by one or two of the drummer boys. Anne would perch on a hay bale at the edge of the barn sipping wine and laughing and talking with Paul and his officers and men. It was a very different experience to life in the army with her first husband. She was busy and challenged and realised, when she gave herself time to think about it, that she had never been so happy in her life.

They were sitting one evening in camp chairs, sharing wine and watching with amusement an impromptu wrestling tournament, taking place on the field. The noise filtered through to Anne gradually, and she turned, noticing that each one of Paul's officers was suddenly alert, setting down drinks and getting up. Anne looked over to the source of the noise, which seemed to be coming from the stable blocks, which housed the third and fourth companies. Johnny Wheeler who led the fourth glanced across at his lieutenant and moved forward, but before he had taken more than a few steps he heard the voice of Captain Edmonds.

"Carter, what the bloody hell are you doing? Get off him and get out into the yard! Are you drunk? Because if you are, I swear to God you'll get the same treatment as everybody else would!"

Paul glanced at Wheeler, smiling slightly. "And that was definitely an accusation of favouritism," he said softly.

"You do favour him, Paul," Wheeler said equally quietly. "But only as much as you do any of your friends."

Corporal Carter appeared on the field with another man, a private from the third company. Captain Edmonds had a hand on each man's shoulder, pushing them forward, and Paul could sense Carter's solid resistance to being pushed. He suppressed a grin and glanced at Carl who nodded and stepped forward.

"What's going on, Captain?" he said pleasantly.

"Two men brawling over by the chapel," Edmonds said. "Carter was kicking the hell out of him. I suspect he's drunk."

Carl surveyed his corporal. "Are you, Carter?"

"No, sir. Although it's possible that Simpson might be."

Carl glanced at the other man. He was holding his sleeve to stem the blood flowing from his nose and one eye was swelling. "Hard to tell," he commented.

Captain Edmonds was looking furious. Paul was trying not to smile. "Do you two want to sort this out or would you rather I did?" he said quietly.

"It'll be the same verdict either way, won't it sir?" Edmonds said shortly. Paul sighed and jerked his head. "Come into my office," he said. "So much for a night off." He glanced at Carter and Simpson. "Wait outside," he said quietly. "Carter if you hit him again, I will hit you."

"Yes, sir. Mind if I have a brief word with your wife while I'm waiting? Might need her help."

"You don't look injured, Carter."

"Mrs Simpson, sir."

"Ah." Paul nodded, enlightened. "Sort it out then come back and see me."

He led the way into the convent, unhooking a lantern on the way and into the small room where he had set up a regimental office followed by Carl and Edmonds. Paul went to light the oil lamps and two candles. "It's too late to deal with this, and I'm irritated," he said shortly. "What the bloody hell is going on?"

Carl smiled sweetly. "Captain Edmonds feels that I favour my men in matters of discipline, sir."

"That is not, however, what you just implied Gerry. What you just implied was that I did," Paul said, looking at Edmonds. "And you said it in front of the men."

"I didn't say it, sir."

"Bollocks, Gerry, you implied it. Don't equate uneducated with stupid. My guess is that Carter just came across Simpson battering his wife and has given him a kicking. I don't propose to discipline him for that because in my opinion, it's his job. I might give the bastard another kicking depending on what I find out."

"How did you work all that out...?"

"Because I'm not stupid either. And because you're absolutely right, I started from the assumption that Danny Carter isn't drunk on duty and doesn't beat the men for no good reason. I make that assumption not because he's my friend – although he is – but because he's served under me for eight years and I know what he'll do and what he won't do. If he's given you lip, you deal with him and you won't see me complain because I bloody well know he probably has it coming. But you imply I let him off of serious disciplinary issues because I like him, and you're going to piss me off." He looked at Carl. "And you just stood out there and let this happen because you thought it was funny."

His friend grinned. "I did. And I'm sorry, Gerry, I shouldn't have laughed. Been practicing a straight face with Carter for years, still can't always manage it."

Edmonds nodded grudgingly. "Does Simpson hit his wife?" Paul asked.

"I've no idea, sir. He's not really supposed to have a wife, she's not officially on strength."

Paul bit back his instinctive response. He knew that some of his officers found the informality of the regiment difficult but he expected them to know the basics about the men of their companies. He glanced at Carl, who knew the family circumstances of each one of the light company and probably a lot of the other men as well. Carl shook his head. "I don't really know him," he said. "I've an idea the lassie came out here with somebody else and took up with Simpson recently, but I don't know for sure, I just noticed her in the lines." Carl met his commanders gaze and grinned. "Surprised you didn't. She's very pretty."

"I am a reformed man. I expect Nan will get the information out of her. Gerry, do you want to deal with this or would you rather I did?"

"I'll talk to Simpson, find out his side of the story. Carl can do the same with Carter. I'm sorry, sir." Edmonds gave an apologetic smile. "Sometimes I do find it hard."

"Everybody does. I'm bloody awkward, Gerry, I know it. But it works for me, and I don't want you to get pissed off and leave because you're a good officer and the men like you."

Edmonds smiled and saluted. "I'll let you know about Simpson."

When he had gone Paul looked at his friend who grinned. He opened the door. "In you come, Carter, I know you're lurking there."

"Not so much lurking, sir. Being tactful."

"Which you weren't earlier."

"Sorry, sir. Just the sight of me annoys Captain Edmonds, but he's very good about it."

"I know, it's not your fault. What happened?"

"You'd got it right. Found him at it round the back of the small chapel. There's four or five storage sheds round there, sir, we've let the women and children camp out in them."

"Yes, Nan told me."

"It was her idea, sir. Bit run down but some of the men have been repairing them in their off hours to make them watertight and they've made quite a nice little family camp down there. Keeps the women out of barracks and the men go down to spend time with them when they're free."

Paul smiled slightly. "Very domesticated. What's the story with Simpson?"

"Simpson's a drunken bastard. Picked up this lassie about six months ago in Viseu. She came out here with her childhood sweetheart, he got fever a month later and died within a week. She wasn't on strength, didn't know what to do and Simpson got hold of her. I've not seen it before, don't spend a lot of time around the third, but I'd heard rumours he's rough with her." Carter eyed his Colonel thoughtfully. "I don't like men who hit women, sir, at all. But it's not unheard of for a couple to get into a fight when they're both in drink, and I've known some of these women to be as bad as the men for throwing a punch. They don't complain and the following day they're back to normal. I don't like it, but that's life."

"I know, Danny."

"I might intervene to break up a fight if I thought it was getting out of hand but what goes on with a man and his wife isn't my business if nobody is getting hurt. But what he was doing to that lassie in the field at the back of the chapel wasn't a fight, it was a rape and a beating and I wasn't going to let him do it. Sorry if I dropped you in it, but it's a good thing Captain Edmonds came round when he did because I was going to fucking kill the bastard!"

"Jesus, is she all right, Danny?"

"Don't know, sir, your wife took off to find out. Thought I'd better come and see you. You want me to apologise to Captain Edmonds?"

"Will you? Although I'm not sure what you did wrong."

"Not sure I did much wrong, sir, but my first sergeant used to tell me I'd a face to be flogged for. Might be that."

Carl laughed. "I know what he means," he said. "Thanks, Danny. I'll talk to Edmonds."

"No, let me," Paul said. "Now that Nan is involved, I'd like to follow it up. Do you know where she is, Carter?"

"Up at the hospital, I think. She's in one of the small rooms."

Paul stood up. "I need a night out where nobody can find me," he said wearily. Carter laughed.

"We'll go down to the Grapes, sir, on the other side of the village. Good food, good wine and I don't think even Lord Wellington's heard of it."

"Doesn't matter if he has, Carter. He can track me down anywhere, don't know how he does it. Other officers in this army get leave and days off and free time. I only have to move outside his range and he's onto me like a bloody hawk!" Paul smiled. "You did the right thing, Danny. I'd have kicked him a lot harder."

"Christ, sir, you'd have killed him."

Paul walked up to the church where Anne had set up the regimental hospital and found her in a small chapel at the back. There was a single mattress on the floor and he paused in the doorway.

"Nan."

Anne looked up. "It's all right, Paul, come in, she's asleep."

He stepped into the room and looked down on the girl on the bed. "Christ, she's so young," he breathed.

"She's eighteen. Stowed away with her sweetheart when he joined the 95th. He never saw a battle, died of fever in Viseu. She was alone and desperate and Private Simpson offered to take her on. They're not formally married, she never has been."

Paul studied the girl. She was very attractive with a mass of dark curly hair and a sprinkling of freckles across an adorable tip tilted nose. He was faintly surprised he had not noticed her in the lines before, and presumed his complete absorption with his wife had distracted him. She was definitely a girl he would have looked twice at in the past.

"What happened?"

"He beats her. Fairly badly and very regularly. She puts up with it. Sees it as the price of his protection. When he's been drinking she tries to keep out of his way if she can. This evening he found her hiding. Wanted his marital rights and she wasn't keen, given the state of him. If he can't manage it it's her fault and he hits her instead. He took her out into the field at the back and took what he wanted, giving her a few good punches along with it to remind her not to refuse him again. Nothing new for her, but this time Danny Carter stopped off on the way back to barracks to relieve himself and heard her crying."

Paul nodded, his eyes on the girl's bruised face. "Well he can bloody well stay away from her," he said quietly. "I'll see him in the morning, he's in lock up when he's not training, and he can forget his grog rations for a while, nice fresh well water will do. But if she goes back to him he'll do it all over again." He looked at Anne steadily. "At her age, you were in a similar position."

"Similar, not the same. Robert didn't often get drunk, and I did get better at managing him. Except when he was jealous."

"At which point he held you down and thrashed you with a riding crop," her husband said caustically. "Perhaps she has it slightly worse, Nan, but not by much I'd say. God knows what we're going to do with her. I could probably get her back to England, but..."

"She'd never get there in one piece, Paul, you and I both know that. She comes from Cornwall, a miner's daughter, worked in the sheds before she came out here. She lands up on a transport back to England without a man, she'll be picked up by somebody. It might be a decent lad or it might be another Simpson. I thought she could bunk in with Teresa for now, help out with laundry and mending. We could do with another pair of hands to be honest, given how extremely undomesticated your wife is. She can earn her keep for a while and he won't come looking for her if she's under my protection. Or not twice, anyway. Maybe she'll take up with somebody better. I'm hoping she doesn't feel she has to go back to him."

Paul nodded. "I'll leave it to you, Nan. The best I can do is make sure the lads know she's to be accorded the same respect as Teresa. She's not had any trouble, I assume."

Anne grinned. "No. Apart from the way Danny Carter is looking at her, but I'm not so sure she minds that."

He shot her a startled glance. "Carter? Are you sure?"

"He's just flirting. Michael does it sometimes as well. She enjoys it. I just have a very slight suspicion that she enjoys it from Danny more." Anne glanced at the sleeping girl. "I'm going to ask Teresa to come and sit with her for a bit. I don't want her waking up alone, she'll be scared. Tomorrow she can get her things and move into Teresa's room."

"Yes. I'm going to speak to Gerry Edmonds, let him know I'm dealing with bloody Simpson. He got arsey with me earlier over Carter, implied that I'd take his side in a dispute because I like him."

"He doesn't know you that well yet, love. You'd be harder on Carter than one of his men if you thought he'd stepped out of line."

He slipped his arm about her as they left the church. "I would. Ah look, Michael O'Reilly, my so-called Regimental Sergeant Major, in charge of what laughably passes for discipline in my regiment. Good evening, Michael."

O'Reilly studied him. "What did I miss?"

"Simpson from the third half killing his girlfriend, and Corporal Carter then half killing him, while Captain Edmonds gets into a spat with Captain Swanson about discipline and being over friendly with the enlisted men – that will be a reference to me and Carter by the way – and Nan now having to find a place for a beaten and terrified eighteen year old lassie. Had a good evening yourself, Sergeant?"

"It was until now," O'Reilly said. "Bugger Carter why didn't he just kill him, we could have hidden the body and called it a desertion."

"If bloody Edmonds hadn't intervened that's exactly what would have happened," Paul said, feeling his wife's shoulders shaking with laughter. "I'm going to find Edmonds now."

"No, sir, I'll deal with it, I'm back now. Go to bed, if you go back out there it'll all start up again and you look in the mood to punch somebody. Edmonds won't give me any trouble, I saved his neck at Talavera, and he's never forgotten it."

"This evening I can't help wondering if you were wise, Michael, but it's possible that I'm just in a bad mood."

Michael grinned. "Take him to bed, ma'am, and see if you can cheer him up," he said.

"I'd slap you, Michael, if I weren't grateful that you're back," Anne said with a laugh. "Goodnight."

"Night, ma'am."

He turned to go.

"Sergeant?"

"Sir?"

"What's her name?"

The Irishman grinned. "Madalena, sir."

"Is she pretty?"

"Very. Come down to the Grapes one night and I'll introduce you."

"Does that invitation include me?" Anne asked sweetly, and Michael chuckled.

"No, because I know you'd come! Night, sir. Ma'am."

Paul was supervising rifle drill with the first to fourth companies the following morning when he saw his wife's maid on her way up to the main house with the girl. She held a very small bundle of possessions. He glanced across. Private Simpson was in line, his face battered and bruised.

"Captain Swanson, take over, will you?"

"Yes, sir."

Paul walked over and Teresa stopped, her hand on the girl's arm. Paul looked down at her. "How are you feeling?" he asked gently.

The girl looked up at him. She had melting brown eyes and her body under the shabby cotton dress was pleasantly curved. He reflected that it was unlikely that she would remain unmarried for long and hoped his wife would persuade her to choose better this time.

"I'm better, sir, thank you."

"Has my wife spoken to you about her plan for you?"

"Yes, sir. She's been very kind. I'm willing to work, I don't need charity."

"I know."

She glanced across at the lines of the third company and he saw her go pale. He did not look around. "Simpson, get over here!" he bellowed.

He heard running footsteps. When they stopped he turned and surveyed the man. "Are you listening to me?" he said, very quietly.

"Sir."

"I didn't hear you, Simpson."

"Sir. Yes, sir."

"Good, because I won't be repeating myself. Your relationship with this lass is over. You don't look at her or speak to her or go anywhere near her again. Is that clear?"

"Yes, sir."

"Louder, Simpson, I must be going deaf."

"Yes, sir!"

"She's a very pretty lass and I doubt she'll remain on her own for long, but what she does next is entirely her choice and you don't get involved in it. I don't like men who beat women, Simpson, it's a bit of a thing of mine. Ask any of my men, it makes me grumpier than General Craufurd. So if I find out you've touched her or even looked at her wrong I am going to shoot you in the head, bury your body and cross you off my list as a deserter and nobody will even bother to look for you! And if you don't think I mean that, you go

An Irregular Regiment

and have a chat with my light company and they'll set you straight. Now piss off back into line and keep your eyes down! Move!"

"Yes, sir!"

Paul watched him go, then nodded to Teresa who looked as though she was concealing a grin, and looked at the girl. She was looking at him in complete astonishment.

"I'm sorry, I didn't ask your name."

"It's Keren, sir. Keren Trenlow."

"Try not to worry about him, Keren, he won't give you any more trouble. If he does, go to Nan or come to me." He gave her a friendly nod.

He encountered his Corporal on his way back from training that afternoon. "Did Sergeant O'Reilly speak to you Carter?"

"He did, sir. Did a fine job with Captain Edmonds too. Was going to ask if you mind a few of us going out tonight. Seeing as we've worked so hard, and all?"

"Where to, the Grapes?"

"Yes, sir. You could join us."

Paul glanced at Anne who had walked to meet him and she laughed. "Go. Gives me a chance to catch up on some letter writing. My parents will think you've murdered me, apart from that five line scrawl I wrote them from Viseu after the wedding, they've heard nothing from me."

He laughed and put an arm about her, scooping her against him for a kiss. "Thank you, girl of my heart. Shall I take you to Stuart's reception tomorrow evening so that you get an outing too?"

"That is noble of you!" Anne said admiringly. "Yes, you may, because it will be my last chance to see General Craufurd before he leaves for England."

"Are you setting up a flirtation with Robert Craufurd now as well as Wellington?" Paul demanded indignantly. His men were laughing openly. "He'd better bloody go back to England in that case, we can do without him. Perhaps he can take the commander-in-chief with him and I can get you to myself for a while." He glanced across at Carter. "I'll see you down there later, Carter, I'm going to eat first." Paul caught sight of Private Hammond approaching, with what appeared to be a letter in his hand. "Oh bloody hell, you don't even have to tell me who that is from! How does he know when I've decided to take a night off?"

Anne began to laugh as Paul opened the letter and read it. "Is it?"

"It is. He wants to see me, and that is never a good sign." Paul glanced at Carter. "I'm going to ride up there now, Carter, I'll catch him at this hour, I know his habits. Tell Mr Swanson and the others. Nan, why don't you eat without me and I'll get something down at the Grapes later."

Anne kissed him, still laughing. "Give Lord Wellington my best wishes," she said.

"Much more of that," her husband said succinctly, going to change his coat, "and I'll give you a box on the ear, lass."

As Paul had hoped he found Lord Wellington in his office reading through some letters from London. He looked up as his aide showed Paul in.

"Major – come in. Sit down." Wellington smiled. "You're very prompt."

"I was on my way out, sir."

"With your wife?"

"Not tonight. I imagine we will see you tomorrow."

"I wondered if you would."

"We need to get it over with some time, sir."

"Is she worried?"

Paul smiled slightly. "Nan would rather be down in the hospital dealing with a difficult amputation than going to that reception, sir. But you won't see that tomorrow evening. She isn't like Rowena."

"No. I don't have to tell you that you both have my full support, do I, Major?"

"No, sir. And we both appreciate it. In fact she asked me to give you her good wishes."

Wellington grinned. "Did she? I like your wife, Paul."

"I am well aware of that, sir."

Wellington seated himself. "Massena has dug himself in. I'm surprised. He isn't going to be able to last for long without supplies, and he will run that army into the ground if he tries. But he knows he isn't getting past our defences. So for a few months at least we have reached a stalemate."

"Yes, sir."

"It gives us a chance to recuperate. I'm concerned about the men. We've lost too many to sickness and wounds. Fever is laying some regiments so low they wouldn't be able to march if we needed them to, and the hospitals are full to bursting."

"I know, sir, Nan tells me."

"I've received news that supplies and men are coming in from England. Transports should be arriving during the next week, to Lisbon. Some of them are for the 110th from the second battalion. You'll decide where you want them."

"We could do with them, sir, although they'll need training."

"They certainly will to get them up to your standards. There are also guns, ammunition, food supplies and medical supplies, along with some extra personnel – surgeons and whatnot. In addition I need grain for the horses and rations for the men. Now that we're back close to Lisbon we need to look to supplying our army for the campaign next year. We need to investigate better means of transport and we need to get the supplies we have to where they're needed."

"Yes, sir."

"Major, I want you to go back to Lisbon to work on this. The quartermasters department is understaffed and the commissariat is hopeless, they need somebody to put a rocket up their backside to get them moving! Take a sizeable escort of your ruffians – the route to Lisbon should be secure, but I'm not taking any chances especially on the return. And take your wife. Spend some time in Lisbon with her while you're working on this. I'm aware that you got married and were back on the battlefield forty-eight hours later. Most of my officers would have been petitioning me for leave to take a honeymoon. You're out chasing the French and she's stitching up sabre cuts by lamplight."

Paul gave a grin. "She's an unusual woman, sir."

"Don't I know it, by God! Most competent female I ever met in my life. And probably the loveliest. But she's earned a few months of comfort, so take her home and make a fuss of her."

"I will, sir. Thank you."

"That's not the only reason I'm sending you to do this, Major. Most of my other officers would welcome a trip to Lisbon, but would kick up a fuss about being used to fetch and carry. Not you. You're one of the few men here, beside myself, who really understands the logistics of war. You know how important this is to our success. So you'll make sure it's done right."

"Yes, sir." Paul smiled slightly. "I'm flattered of course, but I'm also well aware how much of this you're expecting that competent female to do."

Wellington returned the smile. "We all take shameless advantage of your wife, Paul, don't think I don't know it. But at least it will make a change from being up to her elbows in blood in my field hospitals."

"Yes, sir."

"Also the new recruits. In addition to those of the second battalion, we are bringing out the seventh and eighth companies of the first battalion of the 110th. They've been in Sicily as you know, and they're much depleted. Sickness as well as injury. There are also a couple of companies of artillery men, I understand, and a contingent of engineers for Fletcher."

"We're in sore need of those, sir."

"We are. Then there is a battalion of the 112th infantry. Eight companies. They're in barracks and their last outing in the Indies was not a success. Their colonel was cashiered and most of their officers sold out or were transferred elsewhere in the hope they could do less damage. Morale is not good, and the men need training. I have all this from my brother in London. They are travelling under two very young lieutenants with little experience, and they have no commanding officer – as yet."

"Sir."

"Paul - the timing of this is no accident. I've had word from Horse Guards. Colonel Johnstone is retiring. His health has not been good since Alexandria and Corunna, and he almost died in Walcheren. He's done enough."

Paul sat very still, looking at Wellington. He was trying hard not to hope and he wondered if Wellington was deliberately prolonging the suspense. A new colonel might not be as tolerant as Johnstone had been of Paul's flexible approach to army regulations and Wellington knew it. After a moment, his chief said:

"Think you can raise the funds for a colonelcy, Major van Daan?"

Paul felt his heart leap. "A full colonel?"

"Yes. Unorthodox I know. But the 110th is too valuable now to risk anybody else taking over from Johnstone and interfering with what you've done." Wellington studied him and laughed. "Don't look so shocked, Paul. Who else am I going to offer it to? Johnstone has already made the recommendation to Horse Guards and for once they did not argue. I am promoting you to Colonel, effective immediately, in full command of the 110th along with the 112th first battalion. I want you to get these men out onto the training ground in Lisbon and whip them into shape. You'll command them along with your two Portuguese battalions."

"Yes, sir." Paul was conscious that he was trying to conceal his joy. It was what he had wanted from the start, but he admitted to himself that he had not expected it to happen so early. He felt sorry for Johnstone, the loud, bewhiskered borderer who had given him his support from the start in the 110th.

"Will Colonel Johnstone be all right? I've written to him but not heard for a while."

"He's gone home to Melrose, to his wife," Wellington said. "He needs rest and careful nursing and time away from this war I'm told. It's been hard on him these past few years. But he's happier now that he knows his regiment is in good hands. As am I. Any questions, Colonel?"

Paul smiled. "Yes, sir. Had you thought about throwing in a few companies of the German legion while you're about it, because I don't want to find myself without enough to do."

Wellington gave a crack of laughter. "I'll take it under consideration, Colonel. There will be a lot to discuss but we'll come to that later. I imagine you'll need to recommend some other men for promotion to handle this and I know better than to try to inflict new officers onto you. They'd never survive it. Let's have it."

Paul thought for a moment. "Johnny Wheeler to Major," he said. "He can act as second in command. Carl can stay with the light company, although I'll leave him here to manage the Portuguese for now, he and Johnny are working well with them. I've already men in mind for sergeant and corporals; I'll let you have a list before I leave. Nick Barry to Captain, serving in the fourth and he'll have Lieutenant Denny who is invaluable. Nick and Peter can afford the purchase. Johnny can't, but there's nobody else I'm willing to promote. Do I need to have this fight or will you do it?"

Wellington gave a wry smile. "I'll award a field commission, Paul, and I'll write to them. I can't promise they won't try to send somebody in from another regiment, though, if they can afford it."

"Tell them I won't accept them."

"You'll do that for yourself, Paul. And they can't force you to take anybody else. Most regimental commanders will, partly for political reasons and partly for the money but if you want Wheeler all you have to do is refuse anybody else."

"Good. I am not having some over bred, inexperienced twat with money to pay promoted over Johnny Wheeler. I'll make sure they know it at Horse Guards. Although I won't phrase it quite like that."

Wellington smiled slightly. "You've always managed to get your way so far, Paul. Any others?"

"The Portuguese have their own officers; I'll let them stand. The rest of the companies are settled enough."

"And for the 112th?"

"I don't know what they need yet, but if they've only got two junior officers in charge of eight companies I'm going to need some new officers. Let's wait until I've seen them and then I'll talk to you about it. I'll promote Danny Carter to sergeant, and young Hammond to Corporal. I know he's young and he's new but he's good and the men will follow him. We can see what NCOs they've already got with the 112th and Carter and Hammond can bring them up to scratch." Paul eyed his commander warily. "And I'd like to take Michael O'Reilly with me as newly promoted lieutenant."

He saw Wellington blink. "Raised from the ranks, eh? I don't often do that, Colonel."

"I know that, sir."

"Is he up to it?"

"Sir, you've met Michael O'Reilly many times over the years, you must know he's as responsible for my light company as I have been. I know you don't like doing it, but it's different with Michael. If he'd had the money when he joined he'd have come in as an officer."

"I've often wondered why he didn't join as a gentleman volunteer and get made up that way."

Paul gave a slight smile. "He's Irish, sir, I've always thought it best not to ask why he was in such a damned hurry to join and why he was so keen to be anonymous in the ranks. It hardly matters now, he's got ten years of service behind him and an excellent record. But my point is that he isn't going to struggle as some men do if they come up from the ranks, he was at Trinity before he joined and he'll fit in at the mess without difficulty."

Wellington snorted. "As if any of you ever go there!"

"You wrong me, sir, I make a point of it every now and again, just to remind them I'm still here. If you're giving me a battalion of flogged men with low morale and no training, to whip into shape for you in a couple of months, you're giving me Michael O'Reilly's promotion; I bloody need him. Your choice."

Wellington gave a short laugh. "You haven't changed since the day I first told you you'd been reported for drinking with the men, Colonel van Daan," he said. "Very well. Anything else?"

"Yes. There's an officer of the Irish brigade, Captain Corrigan. Knew him back in Dublin."

"I remember him well, Colonel."

"He's in Lisbon currently, wounded at Bussaco and what was left of his regiment has been shipped back to England to recover. I'd like him to join us when he can, he can take over a company of the 112th."

"You can have him."

"What about the second battalion?"

"They're under the command of Major Flanagan and will return to Melton for a while, they'll need to recruit."

"I know Sean Flanagan, he's a good officer. I'll write to him myself and find out all the details."

"Are you proposing to try to manage the second battalion from this distance, Colonel?"

"I don't need to, sir, I just need to manage Major Flanagan. And that is my job, isn't it?"

Wellington gave a small grim smile. "Officially yes, although I doubt many regimental colonels out here give much thought to what is going on in their other battalions."

"Well if I can get it right, we'll have better trained recruits when they get here, sir. But don't worry, I know where to concentrate my efforts. Is that all?"

"It is. Let me have the list before you leave." The General gave a small wintery smile. "Good luck."

"You may say so. What Nan is going to say about this, I shudder to think."

"If I were you I would be more worried about what the rest of the army is going to say about it, but I am well aware that you don't give a damn."

"Nor do you, sir."

"No, I don't. I shall see you tomorrow evening."

Paul smiled. "Thank you, sir. I'll try not to let you down."

He arrived at the tavern to find most of his officers and almost all of his light company there, eating and drinking. Paul sat down opposite Carl who pushed a platter of bread, cheese and cold meat towards him.

"Help yourself. The olives are good. What did Hookey want?"

Paul smiled. "It's a long story. Let me eat and then I'll tell you all together."

Carl nodded, and watched his friend for a while. "Is Nan all right?" he asked.

Paul looked up. "Why?"

"I was talking to Johnny."

"Ah. Did you get the lecture about how I need to shelter her more from the realities of warfare?"

"Along those lines."

"Well before you join in, you should know that her response was to threaten to kick him off a cliff. She's not so keen on being sheltered, she sees it as insulting."

"You told her?"

"Actually I needed to make sure. It did occur to me that I might have ridden roughshod over her on the subject of marrying me."

"I am assuming that she has not decided to return to England and be a lady."

"She didn't seem keen on the idea. But I'm actually grateful to Johnny, I realise it's a conversation I should have had before. I feel better."

"Paul, this may be the most eccentric marriage I've ever seen but I've known you all my life and she's bloody good for you. I've never seen you as happy as you are now," Carl said quietly.

"That's what Wellington thought, so he's come up with a plan to put a stop to that!" Paul said, laughing. "Come and join the others, I'm fed now and feel human again." He rose and moved to the centre of the room, gathering his officers with his eyes. As they crowded around him he pulled up a chair. "Gentleman, give me a brandy. Make it a large one and refill your glasses and then I'll tell you what the good general has in store for us all."

Carl poured a generous measure and pushed it toward his commander. "Not sure I like the sound of this," he said.

"It comes with a promotion or two, which is seldom a good sign," Paul said with a grin.

When they were settled, he outlined briefly the mission that Wellington had given them. Some of the enlisted men had begun to gather around to listen as well, and Paul made no complaint. Soon the whole room was quiet.

When he had done he hesitated, unsure of how to tell them the rest. Johnny Wheeler said:

"I'm guessing there's more."

Paul looked at him and Wheeler smiled and lifted his glass. "That's an awful lot of responsibility for a Major, Paul. But I'm guessing I'm no longer addressing Major van Daan?"

Paul met his eyes. "No," he admitted. "But I am addressing Major Wheeler."

"Oh Jesus Christ, Paul! Did you have to do that in the middle of a tap room?"

"Couldn't resist it." Paul laughed at his friend's expression. "How do you feel about taking command of my first battalion, Johnny? Colonel Johnstone has retired due to ill health. Sorry lads, you got stuck with me."

There was a brief silence and then a cheer, followed by another and then they were yelling. Paul laughed, watching them and Wheeler moved to join him.

"Is this definite?"

"Yes."

"Full colonel?"

"And full Major."

"Paul, when you were an arrogant young bastard on that first voyage to India you told me to stick with you if I wanted promotion."

"Don't even talk about it, Johnny, it makes me cringe. I still can't believe I said that to you. But I was joking."

"No you bloody weren't." Johnny put his hand briefly on Paul's shoulder. "Congratulations, Colonel. And thank you."

"You're welcome." Paul raised his voice. "All right, you noisy bastards, that's enough!"

He waited until the impromptu cheering died down. "I'm leaving the Portuguese here for the duration under Captain Swanson. Paul looked across at Johnny Wheeler. "And the rest of the 110th will be under the command of Major Wheeler. Congratulations, Johnny."

Wheeler lifted his glass amidst the cheering. He said nothing, but his eyes met Paul's and Paul smiled and raised his glass in silent salute. He looked across at Nicholas Barry. "Captain Barry will take over with the fourth company. Peter, you'll serve under him as Lieutenant. Carl, are you happy with the Portuguese officers?"

"Aye, they're coming on well, I've no need to change them. What about you, though? Did you say they've officers with them?"

"Two brand spanking new lieutenants, poor bastards. Wellington has agreed I can have Corrigan when he's fit for duty again. The rest of his regiment sailed without him, and he's worked with us before, knows how we do things. He can work with the 112th and in the meantime I've asked Wellington for some new officers. Preferably ones with brains." Paul glanced across at Corporal Carter. "Corporal Carter, feel like taking over as sergeant of the light company?"

Danny Carter's eyes lit up. "Gladly, sir. Are we going with you or staying with Captain Swanson?"

"I'll want you with me. I'm taking the light company as escort. They can help with training. Johnny can have Rory, who is promoted to Sergeant-Major and they can select their own NCOs." Paul looked across at Michael O'Reilly who was regarding him with a puzzled frown. "I'll be taking Lieutenant O'Reilly with me."

There was a slightly stunned silence, and then another cheer, which looked set to bring down the crumbling tavern walls. Two chickens, which had wandered in through the open door gave a squawk and rushed back outside. Men clapped O'Reilly on the shoulder, and Carl got up to shake his hand. O'Reilly sat still, looking at Paul. He looked genuinely shocked.

"We'll make preparations to march out as soon as possible," Paul said. "It should be an easy run, but we'll keep alert. We all know how easy it is for a small party to get behind the lines, even lines as formidable as ours, and it would be embarrassing to get into trouble on a journey like this. We'll use the barracks on the east of town; it'll be empty now and it's big enough. At some point we'll be joined by the seventh and eighth companies of the 110th. Any questions?"

"Just one, sir," O'Reilly said. "Would you tell me, for the love of God, what made you think it was a good idea to make me into an officer?"

Paul got up, reached for the brandy and refilled Michael's empty cup. "Because you already are one and have been for years. The rest is just paperwork. Although we'll have to do something about that uniform, mind."

Johnny held out his cup for a refill. "Paul, if they're shipping out the seventh..."

"I know what you're going to ask. Captain Longford. And I don't know. Forgot to ask Wellington. I'll ask him tomorrow at the reception."

"Jesus, I can't imagine Longford serving under you."

"Nor can I, but we'll see. I'm hoping to see all of you at this bloody party tomorrow if you can bear it. It'll be the first headquarters party Nan has attended as my wife, and it may not be easy."

"We'll be there," Carl said quickly. "Do you happen to know if the Cartwright woman will be around?"

"I've no idea. She had gone back to Lisbon last I heard. Nan will be fine, but she'll feel better if you're there." He glanced at Michael. "You're let off this time, but once I've got you a dress uniform there are no more excuses, Michael."

"Isn't it my job to provide my own uniform and horses, sir?"

Paul grinned. "You can choose the horses," he said. "As to the rest, piss off." He stood up and drained his glass. "I'm heading back to tell Nan the news. Enjoy yourselves."

Michael got up and walked with Paul to the door. "It sounds like an interesting assignment – the 112th. Know anything about what happened?"

"No. I'm going to write to my brother and get him to ask around. There's bound to have been talk at Horse Guards. I owe him a letter anyway. I scribbled off a few lines to tell him I was getting married, but other than that I've been too busy."

"Did you write to your father?"

"Only the barest details. He'll disapprove, of course, but then he's not met Nan. I hope I'm there when he does."

"Where is she tonight?"

"Writing to her family. They got the same as mine did, so I imagine it will be a long letter. I've no idea what she is going to tell them about Carlyon. They know his family, of course, and I don't know what the army told them. Interesting challenge."

Michael snorted. "You raise a son like that bastard, you've got it coming."

"No, they didn't. I stayed with them for a while, and they were good people. I've wanted to write to them but I've no idea what to say. Wherever Robert got his nasty streak from it wasn't from his parents. I'll see you tomorrow, Michael. Oh and I wanted to see Jamie Hammond. If he turns up can you tell him to come and see me tomorrow?"

"I will." Michael put his hand onto Paul's shoulder. "Thank you," he said quietly. "I know this was your idea. I'll do my best to make sure you don't regret it."

"I won't regret it, Michael," Paul said. "Goodnight. Get drunk. It might be your last chance for a while."

"I will. Goodnight, sir."

Paul found Anne just sealing her letter. She regarded him with some surprise. "You're early. I thought you'd be out until the small hours."

"Wellington's news. I wanted to come back and tell you. And I've a job for Teresa since I know better than to ask you to sew anything other than battle wounds."

She looked in silence at the insignia, and then up into his face. "Dear Lord, however am I going to remember to call you Colonel?" she said. "Congratulations, love, I'm very proud of you. Should I have a drink before you tell me the rest?"

He gave a choke of laughter. "Yes, let's take it to bed. It's a long story."

Paul was in his office the following morning when there was a tap on the door. "Hammond. Come in. I thought Michael had got drunk and forgotten to tell you I wanted you."

"No, sir. I was up at the hospital last night seeing how young Browning was doing."

"How is he?" Paul asked. Browning was from the third company, slowly recovering from an amputation of his lower arm after an injury at the battle at the Coa.

"All right. Mr Guthrie did a good neat job on him and it's healing. He's worried, mind, about what he'll do next. Pension's not much and his wife's expecting their first."

"I'll go up and see him tomorrow, see what he wants to do. If he wants to go home I'll find something for him. He's a bright lad, and my brother can always find space for a clerk. If he'd rather stay I'm damned sure my wife can find a use for him. Or he can work with Jenson. We'll work something out."

Hammond was smiling slightly. "Yes, sir."

"Did Michael tell you why I wanted to see you?"

"Only that we'd new orders, sir."

"Yes. I'm taking the light company back to Lisbon, Hammond. Wellington wants me to take charge of his supplies while training up my new recruits and a battalion of the 112th who sound as though they're going to be hard work. There are one or two promotions."

He outlined briefly what Wellington had said, noting with amusement the young man's pleasure at Wheeler's promotion. Wheeler had effectively saved Hammond from being hanged for killing an officer, and the boy was passionately grateful to him.

When he had finished, Hammond regarded him enquiringly. Paul reached into his chest and drew out a bottle and two cups, which he placed on the table. "Sit down, Jamie," he said quietly, and poured. Hammond lowered himself into the second chair and accepted the cup. Paul smiled.

"A few months ago when you first joined, you'd have found it hard to do that," he said. Hammond laughed.

"Yes, sir. Hadn't much experience of drinking with an officer. Got more used to it now."

"You've got used to us very quickly. I'm taking Michael with me, and Sergeant Carter. I don't know what the situation is with the

NCOs for the 112th but I'll need a couple of experienced men. I'd like to promote you to Corporal, Jamie."

"Sir?" Hammond looked startled. "There are a lot of men ahead of me..."

"That's not how I work. I've been watching you for months and you've not put a foot wrong. And it doesn't escape me that you're up at the hospital keeping an eye on young Browning when you could have been getting drunk with your mates. But it's more than that."

"Sir, you can't do this as a reward for saving your wife," Hammond said quietly.

"I'm not. But it is because of that. I'm choosy when I promote, Jamie. Some regiments promote and demote all the time. I've never yet had to demote one of my NCOs but that's because I pick the right ones. In my regiment it's not a reward for sucking up to the officers, it's a reward for being bloody good. And you are. I knew that from the first, because you were a man who risked his own life to save a helpless girl from that maniac, and you didn't know who the hell she was. You just did it. You'd do it again. That's why I want you. But if you want this, there is one thing that I do need."

"Sir?"

"I need to know the story you've never told me. I need to know why you were flogged so badly in your previous regiment that it nearly killed you and drove you to desert. Because I can't promote a man with a gap that big in his recent history. It's up to you. I know you didn't want to talk about it at the time because I know you didn't trust me."

"Not you, sir. Didn't trust any officer."

"Why would you? This is between you and me, Jamie. No need for it to go further. But if there is something that's likely to come back and bite me in the arse I'd like to know what it is."

He waited as the younger man thought about it, giving him time. Hammond was frowning slightly. He looked up. "All seems like a very long time ago to be honest, sir, although it wasn't. I was with the 80th, served three years. Wounded at Talavera."

"You joined young."

"Aye, sir. Eighteen."

"Your choice?"

"Not entirely, sir." Hammond smiled slightly. "I was apprenticed to a printer. Was doing well, had ideas above my station."

"Not a bad thing. Why did you leave?"

"I had a falling out with the master, sir."

Paul looked at him steadily and suddenly began to laugh. "Wife or daughter, Hammond?" he asked.

"Wife, sir. Very young, very pretty. He was a lot older than she was."

"Did he catch you in the act?"

"Pretty much. Got into a bit of a fight with him when he started hitting her. He came off worst and called the constables. I decided to be somewhere else." Hammond smiled wryly. "It was a bit of a problem for me, sir, back then, the lassies."

"Would it surprise you to hear that you have all my sympathy, Jamie?"

"Not that much, no, sir. I've heard the stories."

"I just bet you have. It's Michael's favourite party piece after the second bottle. One of these days he'll say the wrong thing in front of my wife and she'll castrate him. So you joined up and came to Portugal. And you did well. I've seen you fight, lad. What went wrong?"

"Lieutenant Vane, sir. Second company. We'd a captain who was never there. He was a drinker, so Mr Vane pretty much commanded the company. He picked his NCOs for different reasons to yours, sir. And I'm not the only man in the 80th with scars like mine. Not all of them survived. I've seen two men flogged to death. And I knew he'd do it to me."

"Why, for Christ's sake? I know some officers believe it improves discipline, but this was murder!"

"Only if he didn't get what he wanted, sir."

"And what did he want from you, Jamie?"

"My girl, sir. It's what he did. Any of the men with a young, pretty wife or girl. He'd go after the men, flog them, punish them for things they didn't do, withhold pay and rations. Make a man's life a living hell until she agreed she'd go to him. He'd use them for a few months and then move on to the next one. Most of them gave in after a while. It's hard to see your man flogged to death."

"Bloody hell. Did none of the other officers do anything about him? Surely they must have known?"

"Some of them must have done. Don't suppose they cared. It wasn't rape, the lassies went to him of their own accord. One or two might have complained, but I don't suppose anybody listened. These girls are just army wives or local lassies from the villages. Most of the officers think they're whores anyway." Hammond regarded his colonel with what looked like amusement. "Sir – other regiments aren't like this one. As long as discipline is good and the men can fight, the officers don't care."

"What happened to you?"

"She was Portuguese – her name was Lucia. Lovely girl. Met her just after Talavera. Should have known better really, but you know how it is, sir. He was onto her real quick. Three floggings in a few months, and I wasn't getting rations at all although the other lads kept me fed. He'd got me up on another charge and my back still hadn't healed. I told her to run, go back to her village, but she was worried he'd kill me. And I think he would have. So I ran, took her with me as far as her family then tried to get to Oporto. I wasn't letting him get his hands on her. That's when I met your wife, sir."

Paul reached for the bottle and refilled both cups. "I wonder where the 80th are now? They weren't at Bussaco."

"I think Cadiz, sir."

"Pity. I'd have liked to meet Lieutenant Vane. Although his absence has made it easier for you. Do you think he'd remember you?"

"I doubt it, sir. He didn't administer the floggings. His sergeant probably would. Mean bastard called Roberts."

"Well God help either of them if they show up anywhere near the light company, they're going to be found dead in a ditch with a bayonet up their arse! Corporal Hammond, you're coming to Lisbon with me."

"Thank you, sir. You won't regret it."

"Christ, Hammond, it didn't occur to me that I would. I needed to know for your benefit, not mine. And don't worry about Browning I'll go up first thing and set his mind at rest. Dismissed."

"Thank you, sir." Hammond got up. "I wouldn't want everybody to know, sir, but I don't mind if you tell Major Wheeler. He should probably know. And it's all right to tell your lady."

"Thank you. I probably will but only because Mr Vane is nowhere she can get to him."

"Bloody hell, sir, wouldn't want her to run into him."

"Neither would he. Off you go, Corporal."

Hammond saluted. "Thank you, sir. And good luck tonight."

Paul gave a wry smile. "How the hell does everybody in this regiment know everything so quickly, Corporal?"

"Mr O'Reilly, sir. He was trying to decide if he's glad he doesn't have to go so that he doesn't have to remember his company manners, or whether he'd like to be there if somebody says the wrong thing to your lady and you punch them."

Paul laughed aloud. "Impudent bastard," he said. "Remind me to kick him, will you?"

"Yes, sir. Although I can see his point, you just might."

"I might be tempted. I shall restrain myself, however. I'm not worried, give them six months and every one of them will be falling over their own feet when she smiles at them, I've seen it before. Get going, Hammond, I've work to do."

Chapter Four

There was no opportunity to speak to Anne privately during the remainder of the day. Paul went into their room that evening to find Teresa putting the finishing touches to her hair. Teresa smiled and nodded, moving silently out of the room. Anne turned and smiled at him then stood up and he studied her. She was wearing a gown of dark crimson, with her hair arranged in smooth braids high on her head, a style that highlighted the shape of her cheekbones and the smooth planes of shoulders and neck. She was breathtakingly beautiful. Paul smiled slightly and held out the package he had brought with him. She took it, looking puzzled.

"It's not my birthday yet, Paul."

"Call it a belated wedding present."

Anne unwrapped the paper and opened the velvet box then looked up. "Paul, they're beautiful."

He stepped forward and took the ruby necklace from the case. Anne sat down and allowed him to fasten it around her neck, then took the matching earrings and put them on. She stood up and he studied her and then smiled. "You don't need them, lass, but they look good."

"Thank you."

"I'm well aware that on campaign they'll look somewhat out of place. And you're probably laughing at me..."

"Love, I'm not." She reached up to kiss him. "I understand. And although I might be unusual, I'm still enough of a girl to enjoy the man I love buying me expensive jewellery. Especially tonight."

"Nan – are you sure you want to do this? Because you know very well..."

"Hush. I'll be fine. Especially now. Trust me, every woman at this party is going to be too busy trying to work out the cost of this necklace to worry about my virtue. Come on, let's get this over with and then we can go to Lisbon."

They were among the later arrivals at the reception and were met by Lord Wellington. Paul was conscious of the expression in the hooded blue eyes as they rested on Anne. "Mrs van Daan, you look beautiful."

"Thank you, my lord. And for inviting me."

"I'd rather have you here than half this room, ma'am." Wellington bowed over her hand. "Welcome."

They moved into the room, and Paul glanced at his wife. She looked relaxed and at ease and nobody would have guessed at any discomfort.

"Colonel van Daan. Congratulations on your promotion, sir."

"General Craufurd. Thank you. You know my wife."

"I do." Craufurd kissed Anne's hand. "I understand you are off to Lisbon, ma'am. I hope you enjoy it."

"I hope you enjoy your time in England, sir. Your wife will be happy to see you."

"I'll be happy to see her, ma'am." Robert Craufurd's dark eyes gleamed. "Now. Will you take a turn about the room with me and let's see if anybody is prepared to cut you dead when you're on my arm?"

Anne broke into laughter. "Oh sir, you are such a troublemaker! Truly, this delights you, doesn't it?"

"It does, ma'am." Craufurd looked at Paul. "Go and talk to your officers, sir, and leave your wife to me."

Paul grinned and moved away to join his friends. Carl was laughing. "Has she run off with Craufurd already?"

"It was inevitable," Paul said, accepting a glass of champagne. "I'm waiting to see if any of them dares to cut her. I doubt it, myself."

"She'll be fine, Paul. Better that he does it than you."

At the end of the evening Anne was quiet on the way back to the convent, and he waited until they were alone in their room. He came to help her with her gown, and watched as she removed the pins from her hair. Picking up the brush he ran it through the long dark tresses.

"Glad it's over?"

"It was fine. One or two of them were frosty, but they were all civil and that's all I require. Now that it's done, it will get easier.

Gossip like this is a five minute wonder. General Craufurd was lovely. And so was Lord Wellington..."

"You're never going to have any trouble with the staff officers, Nan. They all adore you."

"And I adore you." Anne stood up and drew him to the bed.

"I had a chat with Jamie Hammond today," Paul said, lowering himself tiredly onto the mattress.

"Did you tell him about the promotion?" Anne asked. She could sense his weariness, and reached up to kiss him very gently on the lips. "Lie still. You're shattered tonight, and so am I."

He laughed and gathered her to him. "I could probably be persuaded, but you're right," he said. "I love this. Just lying here in the dark next to you. It's strange. Rowena was a very peaceful woman. Very serene. It's one of the things that attracted me to her in the first place. And yet I'm more at peace with you. Why is that?"

"God knows. Nobody has ever called me restful. Your officers think I must drive you mad."

"That's because they spend all their time worrying about the things you say and do that an officer's wife isn't supposed to. Whereas I..."

"You just don't care."

"I actually don't. I think I find you restful because I don't have to worry about you all the time. You're so competent, I know that if I'm busy or distracted or even if I'm just to tired to be bothered, you'll still be all right. You're like the other half of me, and yet you're completely independent. You don't need me at all."

"Yes, I do."

"No, you don't. You want me, which is not the same thing. With Rowena I always needed to take care of her. To make sure she was all right. I didn't mind, it's what men do. But it is enormously restful to have a lass who takes care of me from time to time." He kissed her gently. "I got distracted, I was going to tell you about Hammond. I finally got the story of his desertion out of him."

"Can you tell me?"

"Yes, he's happy for you to know. And Johnny, but nobody else. And believe me when you've heard you'll be a lot less relaxed."

He told her quietly and she lay listening in silence. He reflected that her ability to listen without comment or interruption was another attribute that he found restful. When he had done he waited in the darkness for her response.

"I do hope I get to meet Lieutenant Vane at some point," Anne said. Her clipped tone told him how angry she was and he laughed.

"Yes. Bad enough when I thought somebody had done that to him from ignorance. But this is worse. And what pisses me off the most is that a lot of other officers must know what he's doing and are too lazy or too cowardly to step in and put a stop to it. And he's probably still doing it."

"Paul, a lot of them just assume that it doesn't matter to a woman of that class who she has sex with," Anne said quietly.

"No. I on the other hand call it rape, and believe me, at some point I'm going to catch up with that bastard. Nothing I can do about it now. But he'll keep."

There was something about his tone that caused her to tilt her head back to study his profile in the dark. "You have always hated men who rape," she said quietly. "More so than any other man I know. Paul – you don't have to answer this. Was there somebody you knew…somebody close to you?"

"Apart from you?"

"You didn't know what Robert had done to me until fairly recently. It's not that."

He was silent for a long time, and she sensed him turning over in his mind what to tell her and how to tell it. She remained quiet, cuddled up to him. He would tell her or he would not. They had known each other for three years but only been married for a few months and there would be many things still to discover about each other. They had time.

He took so long she was ready for a refusal. Then he said, his voice quiet but very steady. "It was me."

For a long moment she absorbed the sense of his words. Time froze in the horror of what he had said. Keeping her voice as neutral as she could, Anne said:

"Can you talk about it?"

He let out his breath in one long whoosh and laughed softly. "Apparently yes," he said, sounding more like himself. "Christ, Nan, you've no idea how difficult that was to say."

He readjusted his head so that he could reach her and kissed her properly for a long time. Outside it had begun to rain, and the sound was soothing against the window. She held him, wishing there were some way she could convey to him how she felt about him. Words never seemed enough.

Eventually he lay looking at her, and she could see the lines of his beloved face through the darkness. "As you can probably guess I was not quite fifteen and had just been pressed into the navy. Which is completely illegal given my age but happens all the time. We were only a couple of nights out of port and he was a big Scot, mean bastard. The boys were all in terror of him. I found out why the hard way. It was quick and unpleasant and it changed me. After it happened I lay in my hammock and thought about what I could do."

"I rather think I know what you did, Paul," Anne said calmly. "How long did he last?"

He gave a soft laugh. "Do you? Yes, you know me better than anybody, don't you? It took a couple of days for me to find the opportunity. He was a drinker so it wasn't hard. I killed him in his hammock, and I did it in a way that made it obvious why he was dead. He was the first man I ever killed. What a bloody way to start!"

"And nobody else had thought to stop him?"

She saw his lips curve into a smile. "That's an interesting way to look at it. No, they'd all known what he was like. But he was a good seaman, been in the navy for years, and everybody looked the other way. He wasn't going to stop. And I wasn't going to live like that until he got bored or found a new victim. Afterwards I found out that at least two lads over the years had killed themselves because of him. Oddly enough that didn't even occur to me as a solution."

"Did they realise it was you?"

"They'd no proof, I was very careful. When I look back now I am horrified at how ruthless – how calculating I was. My father's blood in me, I fear. They questioned me, threw me in the brig for a few days, even tried flogging me. I simply said nothing. In the end they couldn't hang me without some proof and they were short handed with a battle coming up. So they let me go. I got together with the other lads and they agreed to tell me if anybody else gave them any trouble, but nobody did."

"Why does that not surprise me? It clears up the mystery of why you were flogged, I'd always wondered."

"The bosun was a good man. He knew what I'd done and why. And I think he was interested in the way I seemed to have got the other lads organised. Suddenly nobody was stealing their rations or pushing them around. He used to come and find me in our off hours, taught me how to use a sword, how to fight. I'd learned to shoot as a boy at home. I suppose he is one of the reasons I'm here now. I settled, I learned, and I healed. To some degree."

"But you didn't forgive your father," Anne said quietly.

He gave a soft laugh. "You're right," he admitted. "Of course I was resentful. He sent me off to sea because he didn't like the way I was. To change me into the kind of son he thought he needed. He succeeded beyond his wildest dreams, but for years I think I was determined not to give him the satisfaction of knowing that. I was furious with him, but he never actually knew why."

"Do you think you'll ever tell him?"

"No. God no. It would hurt him beyond belief, knowing what happened to me. When I was younger I didn't tell him because I couldn't tell anybody. Except Carl. Now? Now I simply wouldn't do that to him. I have everything I've ever wanted, right here. I'm exactly where I want to be, exactly where I'm meant to be. And I have you. I'd rather him think I was a resentful brat who got over it than know what he inadvertently sent me to."

"I'm glad you told me," Anne said, snuggling close into him.

"You're only the second person I've told. I was drunk one night at Oxford when I told Carl. He was more or less as you would expect – horrified, and accepting. I'm fairly sure Michael knows, since Carl seems to have told him everything else about my history over the years."

"Not Joshua?"

"No. Like my father he would have felt personally responsible, even though he begged my father not to send me to sea. It would weigh on Joshua. And I've no need to unburden myself. I've lived with it and I've recovered from it in my own way. Although it has left me with an awfully poor view of rapists, which is why my lads spend far too much of their pay on brothels. They know what would happen to them if I caught them." He leaned forward and kissed her gently. "You survived," he said quietly. "Not just once, but two years of it happening repeatedly."

"They don't call it rape in marriage, Paul."

"I do."

"Then you'd be fairly unusual. When Robert thrashed me with a riding crop, I think most men would agree that was wrong. But those nights when he held me down and forced me…I think you'd find even some of the best of men would see that simply as my duty."

"Yes. If I'd have known about it, lass, he'd have been dead in a ditch within the day, and I would definitely have considered that my duty."

Anne laughed. "Why do you think I didn't tell you?" she said.

He kissed her again, very gently and they lay still together, letting the pattering rain on the windows soothe them. She lay awake longer than him, feeling his breathing deepen as he relaxed finally into sleep. It was hard for her to shut off the images conjured up by their conversation. She imagined him as a fair, slender boy, already terrified of the unexpected change in his circumstances, the wreck of his ship and the time in the lifeboat, struggling ashore, cold tired and hungry. The press gang, hauling him off before he could reach safety, and his attempts to convince them who he was, which they would have laughed off, having heard every excuse before. The shock of the new ship, the new life, the harsh discipline and poor rations. And then the attack, before he had even had time to acclimatise to his new world.

At fifteen, it should have killed him. It had not. He had adjusted, and fought back, had found his feet quickly in the new circumstances. He had adapted. He had killed. All of which, she thought wryly, shifting his weight gently off her arm, was evident in the man he was today. Colonel Paul van Daan of the 110th had been born during those dark hours below decks, when at the worst time in his young life, he had not faltered or broken, he had simply calculated how to survive. And he had managed, somehow, to retain his humanity throughout it all.

The rain died away gradually and the wind dropped, and Anne drifted into sleep warm in his arms.

Accompanied by the 110th light company, Paul and Anne arrived back in Lisbon after an easy march and went directly to the villa, which Paul rented from a wealthy Portuguese family who had fled to Brazil at the start of the war. Anne was amused at the consternation caused in the elegant neighbourhood at the presence of over a hundred men of the light company. She sent them into the stable yard and arranged for Mario, who ran the household, to take cold drinks to them.

"I'm just going to see Captain Corrigan, and I'll find out if the transport is in yet and if so, where they've put them. I'm assuming that the quartermaster got my letter and has sent them to the Sir John Moore barracks as I asked."

"If he didn't I'm sure he'll soon hear about it," Anne said in amusement. "Are we going straight out there?"

"I am, but I'd rather you stayed here tonight." Paul caught her eye and laughed. "Only for one night, Nan. Those barracks have been unoccupied for at least half a year, I don't know what condition they'll be in. I know you can rough it as well as my men, but for one night why on earth would you want to? Besides, Mario will want to fuss over you, he's not seen you since we married, and I can tell he's beside himself."

Anne laughed and nodded. "One night," she agreed. "What about Captain Corrigan?"

"I'll see how he is. He might not be ready to come back yet. Have you met him?"

"Actually I stitched him up after the battle, but I don't think we had much of a conversation."

"You'll like him. I'll be back soon and take this lot off your hands."

Paul found Captain Corrigan alone in his billet, a pleasant room in the home of a grain merchant. He appeared delighted to see Paul. He was a round faced Irishman in his thirties with a mass of curly dark hair and gentle brown eyes.

"How are you, Pat? Did you get my letter?"

"I did. Congratulations, sir. Not that it's a surprise to me, I knew you'd command that regiment from the day you stood on that parade ground in Dublin yelling at everybody because the accommodation wasn't up to your standards."

"Not changed much, I'm afraid. I'm going in search of my new troops after this. Not sure if they're here yet."

Corrigan smiled. "I can give you news of them, Paul. They've already arrived, about three days ago. The quarter-master has allocated them to the Moore barracks on the eastern side."

"Excellent, that's where I was going to put them. I'll take my lads over and get them introduced. How are you, Patrick?"

"Much better," Corrigan said. "I'm going for short walks every day, and eating much better now. Bizarre, how you lose your appetite after an illness. The surgeon here has kept an eye on me, but he's happy with the healing. He also said the stitching was the best he'd ever seen, asked me for the name of the surgeon. I take it you know who did it?"

Paul gave a shout of laughter. "I hope you told him!"

"I did. He went puce and asked no more." Corrigan eased himself out of the chair and went to pour wine for them both. "I hope I'll have a chance to see her while you're here, Paul. I want to thank her. If it were not for her I would most assuredly be dead by now. She must be an extraordinary woman, I'd like to meet her properly."

"She is. I wouldn't be here myself if it weren't for her, she saved my life at Talavera."

"So I heard. Paul, I was sorry to hear about Rowena."

"Thank you. It's been the strangest year of my life. Losing her and marrying Nan...and I've a daughter I barely saw shipped off back to my family." Paul studied his friend. "You'll have heard..."

"I've heard nonsense. It's already dying down in favour of the latest gossip about the Prince Regent from London. I know what Rowena meant to you Paul, I remember from Dublin. And if anybody has anything to say about it to me, I'll happily put them straight."

Paul smiled. "I know you will. As to meeting Nan, I hope we'll see a lot of you, Pat. With your agreement, I'd like you to come back when you're ready to serve with the battalion. Your regiment will be spending a while in England, I imagine, with the losses you suffered. Recruiting takes time and is expensive. Unless you especially want to join them?"

"No – God no! Can't think of anything worse. I'd love to serve under you, sir. I'll not be much use for a while yet, but I can help with the administration. Sounds like you've got a job on your hands."

"Then you'll be a Godsend, because getting together the supplies Wellington wants plus the means to transport them, is going to be hell," Paul said frankly. "Nan will do a lot of the letter writing, and haggling with suppliers. The local merchants are already so terrified of her they wouldn't dare try to cheat her. If you can work with her, it will cut down on my headache considerably. Thank you, Pat."

"Good luck with the new regiment," Corrigan said with a grin.

"Any idea what went wrong?" Paul asked, sipping his wine.

"I know what gossip said," Corrigan replied. "Apparently there was a big scandal, quickly hushed up, over the Colonel selling recruits to other regiments with money to pay, while his own lads were struggling to keep going overseas. I think most of the officers were in on it or turned a blind eye. The man who commanded them in the Indies – a Major called Andrews – was a nasty bastard, who ruled by fear. My cousin tells me he sold out quietly over a story that he beat a local servant to death in front of the whole battalion. They've shipped out what remains of them to Wellington, although I believe he didn't really want them. Too much troubled history. They've not had long in barracks to recover from the long voyage and the sickness they picked up from the Indies."

"This gets better and better," Paul said. "Wellington managed to make this sound like a honeymoon granted as a reward for good behaviour."

Corrigan laughed. Paul drained his glass. "I'd best get over there and see my lads settled, introduce myself," he said. "Don't get up, Pat. It's good to see you on the mend. I'll send Nan over to visit you."

"I look forward to it," his friend said. "Good luck, Paul. Let me know as soon as there's space for me and I'll come out to stay in barracks. I'm bored senseless here."

The barracks named after the late Sir John Moore who had fallen gallantly at Corunna, were long low buildings constructed several years earlier in local stone to house the growing numbers of Wellington's army. The buildings were set around a large central square which was used for parades and training. They had been empty for some time since Wellington moved his headquarters further north. After the sea voyage, Paul suspected that he would find little activity from his new troops. He did not begrudge them a rest. He would see the new officers and get his own men settled, and then they could go through a plan for starting training on the following day. He must see the Lisbon quarter-master to discuss rations and supplies, and would need to make sure all the men were properly equipped. If he were lucky the new uniforms he had ordered through Anne's father for his men would have arrived. Some of his men's garments were practically threadbare, although he thought it unlikely he would prise many of them out of their beloved coats. Each stain and mend was a badge of honour to them.

Leaving O'Reilly and Carter to line up the men and march them to the barracks, Paul rode on ahead. He was surprised to hear signs of activity on his approach. Perhaps after all their new lieutenants were managing drills already. If that were true, it was a good sign. Touching his heel to Rufus' flank he cantered further ahead of his company and rode in through the arched gate of the barracks, noticing that the painted sign was hanging down. He would set somebody to righting it tomorrow.

Abruptly Paul reined in, staring at the open square. The battalion was lined up around three sides, around three or four hundred men, he would guess. In the centre was a triangular wooden frame, and a man was tied to it. A corporal, sweating in the heat of the late morning sun, was wielding a lash and as it fell, the victim gave a scream of pain. His back was a bloody mess. Around a hundred, Paul estimated, as he swung down from the saddle.

The back rank of men noticed his arrival, and Paul motioned to the nearest man to take his horse. The infantryman did so with hesitation. Paul still wore the coat he had ridden in, with no insignia and there was no sign that he was anything other than a civilian. He walked forward. The two officers of the battalion were standing at the front of their men. They were young, probably no more than twenty-one or two, and both wore sparkling new uniforms, their hats cocked at exactly the right angle. There the resemblance ended. One was watching the flogging with an expression of apparent approval. He was tall and dark with a thin handsome face and hazel coloured eyes. The other lieutenant was shorter and slighter with soft brown hair and a pair of fine grey eyes, which watched in apparent horror. His face was white and he did not look well.

It was the dark man who saw him first. Paul walked past him towards the whipping post. The corporal paused in his work, looking uncertainly at Paul and then over at the two officers.

"I think that's probably enough for today, Corporal," Paul said quietly. "Take him down. Carefully, now."

"Who the devil are you, sir?" the dark lieutenant demanded. He had a clear baritone. "This man's punishment is not yet finished!"

"I was going to ask you the same question," Paul said turning to him. "Who is in command here?"

"I am. Lieutenant Lionel Manson, 112th foot. Don't know who the devil you are, but you've no place coming in here interfering with discipline, sir! If you've a message, it can wait until we're done!"

"You are done, Mr Manson. Cut him down, Corporal – don't make me ask again, I've had a long ride." Paul unbuttoned his great coat. He beckoned to a thin, white-faced private in the front row, who ran forward looking terrified. "What's your name, lad?"

"T…T…Terry, sir."

"Well, Private Terry, will you take this to the officers quarters for me, please?" Paul said, taking off his coat and handing it to the boy with a pleasant smile. He turned to find that both officers had sprung to attention and were saluting. "Ah, that's better."

The corporal called out two names, and the men ran to help lift their comrade down, just as the rest of the light company marched through the gate. Paul walked over to the man and inspected his damaged back. "How many, Corporal?"

"A hundred ordered, sir. Ninety given."

"What offence?"

"Don't know, sir."

Paul nodded. "Take him to the infirmary if you've one set up yet. If not, lay him on his bunk, face down, and give him some rum. I'll get somebody to look at him presently."

"Yes, sir."

Paul turned to the two officers. Michael O'Reilly had dismounted and was coming forward. "Have you introduced yourself, sir?"

"I've not had time," Paul said. "It's busy in the 112th I can tell you, Mr O'Reilly."

The Irishman surveyed the two lieutenants genially. "Lieutenant O'Reilly, 110th light company. You'll be under the command of this officer for the foreseeable future, gentlemen – Colonel Paul van Daan who commands the 110th, and now your battalion. We've a bit of work to do, I can see, but for the time being lets get our men settled and see what arrangements you've already made and then we can have a bit of a chat. I didn't catch your names."

"I've met Lieutenant Manson here," Paul said, indicating the dark lieutenant. "And this gentleman...?"

"Lieutenant William Grey, sir."

"Welcome to Portugal, Lieutenant Grey. I'll see my quarters and get settled in but you can both meet me in my office in – shall we say half an hour?"

"Yes, sir," Manson said. "But...will you not want time to wash and change and..."

"Yes," Paul said gently. "Which will take me approximately half an hour. Carry on."

He was talking to Private Jenson in his bedroom when there was a tap on the door of the outer chamber and O'Reilly entered. "All settled, sir?"

"Yes, thanks, Michael. How's the flogging victim?"

"Carter is seeing to him." Michael cocked an ear. "That sounds like the noisy bastard approaching now. Carter, you've the subtlety of an elephant so you have!"

"I didn't know I needed much subtlety to come up a flight of stairs, sir," Carter said straight faced.

His lieutenant clipped him smartly over the ear. "You're as cheeky a bastard as you were the day you joined," he said. "How's the lad?"

"Not so clever, sir. I've cleaned it up and got him lying on his bunk. They've no infirmary set up but then they've only been here a few days and the barracks have been empty. It's bloody filthy mind, they could have cleaned it."

"Well get them started on cleaning and repairs straight after drill in the morning. I feel like setting Lieutenant Manson to shovel out the latrines, but I'm aware that would be seen as undue provocation."

"Your wife turns up here and sees what he's done to that lad's back and she'll shove him head first into the latrines, sir," Carter said caustically.

Paul laughed. "How well you know her, Carter." He glanced across at the doorway where Corporal Hammond had appeared.

"What is this, my quarters or the meeting place of the tribes? What do you want, Hammond?"

"Begging your pardon, sir, but the two officers are waiting for you in your office. It's a bit dusty in there, sir, but…"

"Well it will do for today, but tomorrow perhaps we can stick a broomstick up Mr Manson's arse and see if he can do two things at once."

O'Reilly grinned. "This takes me back to our arrival at Melton with that bastard Longford. Whatever happened to him?"

"Still in command of the seventh company, I believe," Paul said ruefully. "I asked Wellington. Although once he realises he's about to be sent here to serve under me I rather imagine he'll be looking to transfer to pretty much anywhere. It's impressive that Colonel Johnstone managed to keep us apart all these years but Longford's luck has just run out."

"God help the poor sods serving under him all these years," Carter said. "He was a spiteful bastard."

Paul went to the basin to wash his hands. "You think Melton was bad, you should have seen the 115th in Yorkshire when I got there," he said. "I've never seen such a mess! I should have taken you with me, Michael, you'd have had a fit!"

"Aye, sir, although I'm surprised you had enough time in Yorkshire to be messing about with regimental duties and all," the Irishman said blandly. "Being so busy with your social life."

Paul turned to look at him, the towel in his hands. He had first met Anne in Yorkshire. "You two have been with me too long and have far too much information that you shouldn't!" he said severely. "I'm having the pair of you transferred to the West Indies and promoting Hammond in your place, Michael. He knows nothing about me."

"Apart from what Carter has told him," Michael said. "Pretty much everything, I imagine. Ready to go down now?"

Paul nodded and went to the door. They paraded down the stairs and met Lieutenant Manson in the hallway. At the sight of Hammond he stopped and glared.

"What the devil are you doing in here?" he demanded. "Didn't I tell you...oh – Colonel..."

"Just so, Mr Manson." Paul turned to Hammond and Carter. "Get the duties assigned, Sergeant, and organise a meeting with any existing NCOs for tomorrow. You can make your own arrangements but I'd like to speak to them briefly myself so let me know when it's happening."

"Yes, sir." Corporal Hammond saluted. "Just one thing, sir. There's no food in the mess."

Paul stopped and stared at him. "I beg your pardon?"

"Food, sir. The men have had a long march and..."

"Yes, I'm aware of that, Corporal. It wasn't the need for food I was questioning it was the lack of it."

Manson cleared his throat. "No time to sort out supplies yet, sir. We've no quartermaster..."

"Well I don't carry one tucked under my arm, Lieutenant, but I am still able to arrange food for my men! What have they been eating for the past three days?"

"Apparently they were told to forage for themselves, sir. Local farms and villages." Hammond was keeping his face perfectly blank. He was going to make a fine successor to Carter, Paul thought. He turned his eyes to Manson in amazement. By now Lieutenant Grey had appeared in the doorway.

"Forage?" Paul said. His voice had risen to a pitch, which could have been easily heard through the noise of a battlefield. "You mean loot? Christ almighty, these people are our allies!"

He turned to Carter and took a deep breath. "Carter, get a party together and go and buy food for the men, please," he said in tones of extreme patience. "See Jenson about the money, he's in charge of it until we get arrangements in place. I'm leaving Captain Breakspear and Mr Fallon where they are so we've no quartermaster and assistant, but for the time being Captain Corrigan will be joining us tomorrow and he'll act as temporary quartermaster until we rejoin the regiment. Any applications for money will go to him. I rather imagine my wife will organise supplies when she gets here." He looked at Manson. "I presume you've up to date records of the men, their pay owing and similar?"

"Yes, sir. They're in a box in my quarters."

"Go and get them, please," Paul said.

Manson turned to Hammond. "Get the chest from the corner of my quarters!" he said. "And hurry up about it!"

Paul's voice raised another notch. "Just because I use the word 'please' doesn't mean it's not an order!" he said. "Get the bloody box, Mr Manson, and do it now!"

He looked at Michael who was keeping a perfectly straight face. "Will you check on the injured man, Mr O'Reilly? Let me know if you think he needs my wife to come and have a look at him. She'll be here tomorrow. Carry on Sergeant Carter, Corporal Hammond." As they moved away he looked at Manson. "Don't make me tell you again," he said, and his voice had dropped to a dangerous quiet. Finally Manson moved.

When they had all left, Paul looked across at Lieutenant Grey who was still standing in the doorway. "At ease, Lieutenant," he said pleasantly. "Come and sit down."

He seated himself behind the desk and ran a finger across it, looking down distastefully at his finger. "It's odd how I can spend months on campaign living in the filthiest conditions and then feel irritated by a layer of dust on a desk," he said, and looked up at the boy opposite him. "Sit down, if you're not too fussy about your uniform. Ah, Jenson. I was wondering when you'd turn up, you're practically the only member of the light company who has not invaded my quarters in the pa\st twenty minutes!"

"Sorry, sir. Just unpacking and cleaning your rooms, sir."

"You'd better! My wife is expected here tomorrow and if she sees the state of this place we'll all be allocated cleaning duties which will take us until sunset!"

"That's what I thought, sir. I thought you might have a use for these." He set a brandy bottle on the desk and four pewter cups. Paul gave a broad grin.

"I take it back, Jenson, you are a prince among orderlies and I'm thinking of promoting you to Colonel!"

"Don't want it sir. Too much aggravation, and I bet you've not been paid for six months any more than we have!"

"You never spoke a truer word!" Paul said. "Jenson, let me introduce you to Lieutenant Grey. Mr Grey, this is my orderly, valet and chief intelligence officer for my wife, Private Freddie Jenson. He has a wooden leg as the Marathas blew the other one off for him at Assaye, but please don't bet against him in a race for the grog at the end of the day. Have you opened this, Jenson?"

"No, sir, don't like brandy that much." Jenson grinned. "Don't check the rum, mind."

"You can have the rum, I had a surfeit of it during my navy days. Thank you, Jenson. While you're down here, will you go and find Mr Manson who has apparently lost his way to his own quarters and tell him to wait please until I have had a chance to talk alone with Mr Grey. I'll send a message when I want him."

"Yes, sir. Be upstairs if you need me."

"Thank you. I'd suggest you get yourself something to eat but it appears that in the 112th they are tougher than us and don't require food. A good thing I left Nan at the villa tonight. If she'd been with me and there was no dinner, Wellington would have heard her yell from Torres Vedras."

"If Mrs van Daan had been here when we arrived, sir, he'd have heard her yell a lot sooner than that," Jenson said sagely.

When the orderly had left, closing the door, Paul looked across at his new officer. "When did you join?"

"Four months ago, sir. My uncle bought me a commission."

"Going cheap, was it? I'll just bet there wasn't a rush on to serve in the 112th."

"No, sir."

"Any training?"

"Not much, sir. When I arrived a few days before Mr Manson there was only one officer left in barracks and he showed us around, gave us a few pointers and explained about drill and sentries and so on. Other than that we were left to get on with it. Mr Manson knew more than I, he did some basic training with another regiment before coming to us, so I've been following his lead, sir."

"Yes. With regard to that, Mr Grey, may I suggest that from now on you stop following Mr Manson's lead, it is likely to get you into all kinds of trouble. Have a drink."

He poured for both of them and pushed a cup towards Grey who took it nervously and sipped. Paul laughed. "Don't look so worried, Grey, I'm not that bad."

"You actually are, sir," Grey said, and than coloured as he realised what he had said. Paul gave a choke of amusement and put his cup down.

"Don't do that while I'm drinking!" he said. "I shall endeavour to improve your opinion of me in time."

"I'm sorry, sir, I didn't mean to be rude," Grey said.

"Actually it was very funny. I probably am that bad when you're not used to me."

Grey was regarding him. Some of his nervousness was receding. "May I ask a question, sir?"

"Of course."

"I don't have much experience, sir, but I've spent time around other regiments, other officers, on the transport, and since we arrived. You don't seem much like them, sir."

"Ah. Was that a question?"

"Not really, sir." Grey admitted.

"Are you asking if it's me who is strange or them?"

"Trying not to put it like that, sir."

Paul gave a broad grin. "There's a novelty having an officer who at least makes an attempt not to insult me," he said. "When I was young and raw and almost as inexperienced as you are, Grey, I met a general by the name of Wellesley in India whose first remarks to me were that other officers had complained that I drink with my men."

"Lord Wellington, sir?"

"The very same, although he was not even a knight back then. He sent me out in charge of the light company and almost got me killed but we achieved what he wanted and when I came back he presented me with a couple of bottles to share with my men." Paul refilled both cups. "My point is that you are completely right – I am somewhat eccentric for an officer. Nobody cares because I can lead and I can fight and when I say jump, my regiment jumps. Unless, obviously, my wife has issued a counter order."

Grey smiled for the first time. "I've also never heard any officer talk about their wife the way you do, sir."

"My wife is a somewhat unusual female, Grey. You will meet her in the morning. She wanted to come with me but I am very glad I persuaded her to remain in Lisbon overnight."

"I know, sir. We're not prepared to receive a lady."

"You're certainly not prepared to receive this lady. The reason I'm glad she wasn't here is because if she'd ridden in to that scene on the parade ground earlier she'd have taken that whip and obliged Mr Manson to eat it. And I am not speaking metaphorically here. What had the man done?"

"Late for drill, sir."

Paul's brows furrowed. "A hundred lashes for being late for drill?"

"Mr Manson thinks it sets an example to the men."

"What do you think, Mr Grey?"

Grey hesitated. "Perhaps it was a bit extreme, sir."

"I didn't ask you to try to guess what I wanted to hear, Mr Grey, I asked what you thought."

"I hate it, sir."

The reply was so quietly definite that Paul smiled. "Welcome to the 110th Mr Grey," he said. "I think you'll fit right in." A sudden thought occurred to him. "By the way, where have you put my new recruits?"

"Sir?"

"For the 110th. There were supposed to be a contingent of new recruits for the 110th on the transports."

"Oh – yes, sir."

"And?"

"When we landed…there was nobody there, and there was a Major Armstrong from the…"

"I know who he is," Paul said grimly. "Go on."

"He took them, sir. Said his battalion was short and…"

Paul sighed, got up and went to the door. "Jenson!" he bellowed. "Go and get Lieutenant O'Reilly. And Mr Manson as well."

"Yes sir."

Paul listened to his orderly clumping down the stairs. "And don't break your bloody neck hurrying," he said.

"Not a chance of it, sir," Jenson said.

Paul returned to his desk and sat down. O'Reilly appeared almost immediately and Manson a moment later.

"Sit down, Mr Manson. Mr O'Reilly, are you particularly busy just now?"

"No, sir. Just chatting with the lads, sir."

"Excellent. Will you take Mr Grey and two of the light company and ride over to the southern barracks. Ask to see Major Simon Armstrong and tell him that he has stolen my new recruits and I'd like them back immediately please. March them back here and get them settled with the light company."

"Yes, sir."

"And Michael – if he attempts to argue with you, tell him he is a reiving Scottish bastard and that I'm going to check the records and if even one of my men is missing I'm going to ride over there in person, kick his arse and take whichever of his battalion I like the look of to make up for it."

"Happily, sir."

"Carry on, Mr O'Reilly. Off you go, Mr Grey. Who knows, by the time you get back there may even be dinner."

When the two men had gone, Paul sat back and regarded Lionel Manson. He was aware that he needed to set aside his initial prejudices and discover if he could work with this man.

"Not a good start, Mr Manson. Are those the records?"

"Yes, sir."

"Thank you." Paul hesitated. "I'm aware that neither you or Mr Grey had the training or the guidance you deserved at the start of your careers in the army. I am prepared to set all this aside and start again. While you are serving under me, you will answer not only to me, but also to Mr O'Reilly. He has seniority…"

"How long has he been an officer, sir?" Manson said.

"Excuse me?"

"You spoke about seniority, sir? How long has he…"

"His seniority, Mr Manson, comes from the fact that he was fighting for three years before I joined. That he fought beside me through numerous skirmishes in India and then at Assaye, Rolica, Vimeiro, Talavera, Bussaco and many other battles. And most importantly, because I have given him seniority. Feel free to take this issue up with him at any time. When he kicks you down the stairs for impertinence, I shall support him wholeheartedly. Shall we move on?"

Manson nodded sullenly. Paul took a deep breath. "I am aware that each regiment has its customs and traditions. In the 110th we do not use flogging as a punishment."

"It's in the army regulations, sir."

"I could give you a list of the army regulations which I choose to ignore, Mr Manson, but it would take a great deal of time that I do not have. When I have you and Mr Grey together I will go over how I want discipline to be handled. It will be strict and it will be enforced but it will not involve strapping a man to a post and thrashing him half to death. Tomorrow there will be a general meeting for all officers and NCOs and we will go over my plan for training and drills to bring the men up to scratch so that when we march to join Lord Wellington they will be ready – and so will you." Paul studied the younger man. "You have a choice, Lieutenant Manson. You can work with me and learn how to be a very good officer. It will get you promotion and it will keep you alive. Or you can work against me in which case you will have a very miserable time and if you apply for a transfer better make it a long way away from me. Go away and think about it. Good day, sir."

Chapter Five

Anne van Daan rode through the gates of the Sir John Moore barracks at noon the following day. She was followed by her two maids and a carriage bearing Captain Patrick Corrigan, and she reined in her horse for a moment to watch her husband attempting to teach a simple turning manoeuvre to the men of the 112th, a sight which brought a smile to her face.

Paul was conscious of the stir her arrival was causing, and when the drill was complete, he nodded to his sergeant. "Line them up, Sergeant Carter."

"Sir!" Carter turned, bellowing orders and the regiment fell into line by fits and starts as Anne walked her cavalcade over to the main barracks entrance and allowed her husband to lift her from the saddle.

"Paul. I see that you are going to be busy for a while then."

He bent to kiss her, laughing. "Where is your respect for the colonel in charge of the regiment?"

"I have no idea. You know how I misplace things…." Anne laughed up at him. "And you cannot kiss me like that on the parade ground. You are causing a scandal in the lines, Colonel."

"And not for the last time, I imagine."

"Not for the first time either." Anne saw Sergeant Carter approaching and held out her hand. "Danny, how are you?"

"Very well, ma'am. Better for seeing you. A right mess we walked into yesterday."

"I want you to be there when I hear the full story. You'll tell me the bits that he misses out."

"That's a promise, ma'am."

"Paul, I don't want to interrupt training. Can you…"

"No need, love, they can take a break. It's only half of them, I have the rest scrubbing the place. It's been unoccupied for a while and it was a mess." He turned. "Pat, thank God you are here. I have a tale of horror to unfold. Sergeant Carter, can you stand them down and get the other half up for drill. O'Reilly will take over from me with Grey."

"Yes, sir," Carter said. "Glad you're here ma'am. Captain Corrigan, good to see you again, sir." He glanced at Paul. "Sir – do you think we should get Mr Manson out here as well? He's been supervising the cleaning crew all day now."

Paul grimaced. "If you must. Don't let him make an ass of himself, Sergeant."

"Can't promise that, sir, but I'll try."

Paul turned to Anne's maid but she had made her own way out of the saddle and he regarded her seriously. "Teresa – is there any way you are ever going to learn to wait for a man to help you?" he asked.

The girl laughed. "Me, I take care of myself, Colonel."

"Welcome anyway." Paul went to lift the other girl from the saddle. "You look slightly stunned, Keren. Don't worry, you'll settle down. Jenson, there you are. Fall down the stairs?"

"Not yet, sir. You'll probably be the first to do that, the way you drink with the men."

"Jenson, you are dismissed. I can do without an orderly with a mouth like yours."

"Do I get my back pay then, sir? This way, ma'am. I'll show you to your quarters."

Several hours later, in the Van Daans' sitting room, Paul and Anne were joined by O'Reilly and Corrigan. Anne had unpacked and already the room had the subtle air of homeliness that she brought even to a tent. There was a scarf thrown across the arm of the sofa and Paul picked it up idly and ran his fingers over the soft texture. It smelled of Anne.

"So I am your new quartermaster, Paul?" Corrigan said. He was still smiling at the lengthy tale that Paul had told.

"If you will. I'm going to ride over to talk to Colonel Simpson as soon as I can. I don't think there will be a problem. I got the money out of Wellington before I left. But it's a mess, Pat. I've made no attempt yet to find out whom they robbed during those three days…"

"Sir." Jenson arrived in the doorway.

"Oh for God's sake, Freddie…"

"It's important, sir, or I wouldn't have called you."

"I'm coming. Do we need Michael?"

"I think so, sir."

They arrived in the hall before Paul's office to find Lieutenant Grey trying to deal with what appeared to be a domestic dispute. A middle-aged Portuguese who looked as if he might be a prosperous farmer, was talking at Grey in a stream of completely incomprehensible language. Behind him, were a young man and a girl. The youth was probably about nineteen or twenty, the girl probably slightly the younger. Both were silent, he looked angry and she had been crying. She was slim and dark and very attractive and there was a massive bruise coming up under her right eye.

Grey looked at Paul with relief. "I'm sorry, sir. I know your wife has arrived. I…"

"At ease, Lieutenant." Paul walked forward, ignoring everything else. He took the girl's face in his hand and turned it to the light. Then he looked at her father. "What happened?"

There was a flood of rapid Portuguese which was too fast and too complex for Paul to follow. Paul held up his hand. "Enough. Lieutenant Grey…"

"Shall I try to find an interpreter, sir?"

"No need. Will you go upstairs and get my wife please?"

Grey obeyed, puzzled. The colonel's wife was seated with her two female companions and Captain Corrigan but at his request she rose and accompanied him to the door.

"Lieutenant? I'm sorry, I don't know your name?"

"Grey, ma'am."

Anne preceded him down the stairs and into Paul's office. Her husband smiled. "We are in need of your language skills, love. My Portuguese isn't bad, but I'm not getting this."

Anne was looking at the pretty dark girl. "Of course." She looked at the farmer. "My name is Mrs van Daan and I am the Colonel's wife," she said in fluent Portuguese. "Will you tell me why you are here?"

The farmer regarded her. "I come to complain of a theft and a rape, Señora," he said, calmer now that he was being addressed in his own language. "Three nights ago they came to my farm. They stole food and wine and killed a pig. And then one of them took my daughter from her husband's side, and into the barn and they took turns with her."

Anne's eyes widened and she turned to the girl. "Are you hurt?" she asked gently.

"Some bruises. And I am sore…and shamed."

"There is no shame to you, Señora." Anne looked at the boy, who had put his arm about his wife. "I am sorry. They will be punished for this. And we can recompense you for what was stolen. But not for what was done. How many of them were there?"

"Three, Señora."

Anne looked at Paul who was regarding her steadily. She could see by the look in his eyes that he had understood enough and there was no laughter there now. "Will they be able to identify the men?" he asked.

Anne turned to the farmer. "Can you show us these men if we line up the battalion?"

"I can," the boy said. "I will never forget them."

Paul nodded. "Mr O'Reilly, I want every man in the barracks on the parade ground in ten minutes."

"Yes, sir."

"Why did you not report this before?" Anne asked the farmer curiously.

"I came the morning after it happened," the farmer said. "The officer did not understand me and told me to leave. I heard today from my neighbour that men came to him yesterday to buy food, which they paid for. They told him that there was a new commander so I came back."

Anne looked at Paul. "Did you get that?"

He nodded. "Grey, were you here when this gentleman came to complain?"

"I didn't see him, sir." Will Grey looked white and slightly sick, Anne observed. A nice lad who would probably do well with his new commander once he had learned not to be afraid of him.

"I honestly didn't think you had been," Paul said. He looked at Anne. "Nan, will you take care of the girl? She shouldn't have to see them again, although she'll probably have to give evidence at the court martial."

Anne nodded. "I'll take her up to our sitting room," she said.

When they had gone, Paul put his hand on the boy's shoulder. "I am so sorry," he said simply in Portuguese. "They will be punished, but it does not take away what they did."

"Will they die?" the boy said in heavily accented English.

"The court will decide, but almost certainly, yes," Paul said. "Ah, Mr O'Reilly."

"Carter's just lining them up, sir. They're that slow at the moment that if the French slipped past the lines and came calling they could have dinner cooked in the mess before this lot could find their boots and their muskets."

"The state of the mess arrangements so far, that might not be a bad idea." Paul looked at the two Portuguese. "This way."

There was silence out on the parade ground. Paul looked for Manson. As he had expected the lieutenant showed every sign of recognising the farmer. He said nothing, and went to the front of the square to address the men in a voice trained to carry across the sound of cannon fire on a battlefield.

"You've been in barracks here for a week. Crimes were committed during that time. Looting and theft is not permitted in the 110th, or anywhere else in Lord Wellington's army, and you'd best remember that, because if he catches you he'll hang you on the spot. But I'm aware that you're new and you were hungry and you knew no better. The people you stole from will be paid and the matter put to rest.

"Three men did more than steal. They took a woman into a barn and they raped her, each one of them. For that there is no amnesty – ever! I want those men to step forward now."

There was a murmur of shock through the ranks of the light company. Each one of them knew, Paul was aware, how serious this was. Nobody else moved. Paul looked at the Portuguese boy.

"Cowards as well as rapists," he said clearly. "Will you point them out to me?"

There was a movement, and a man stepped forward. After a few seconds two others followed suit. Sergeant Carter walked over to the rank and motioned to them to follow him and they lined up before Paul. Two of them looked terrified and did not look up. The third, a burly man of forty or so looked defiant. Paul glanced at the girl's husband.

"Are these the men?"

The boy nodded. Paul looked at Carter. "Lock them up, Sergeant. I'll send a message to the provost-marshal."

"Yes, sir."

"Carter. I don't know if the gaol has been cleaned yet, but if not, don't bother," Paul said.

"Yes, sir." Carter jerked his head to the men. Two of them fell into line, the third did not move.

"She was willing enough," he said. "Didn't want her man to know that though! I served three years in the Indies, sir, and what you call rape my old officer called sport."

A collective gasp went through the ranks of the light company. Paul raised his hand and hit the man backhanded across the face, a tremendous blow, which knocked him off his feet. Before he could get up, he was on his back with Paul's boot on his genitals. Paul applied pressure and the man screamed, a high-pitched sound, which echoed around the parade ground. Paul took the pressure off and the man curled up, clutching his privates.

"If we were in the field," Paul said in measured tones, his voice carrying clearly through the ranks, "you'd by over by that wall lying dead with a bullet in your head by now. As we're in barracks we'll go through the proper channels and I'll leave it to the provost marshal to deal with you. And you'd better pray that he does his job right and hangs you nice and quickly, because if he sends you back to me you're going to wake up one dark night screaming with your balls hanging from a hook by your bunk! And if your former fucking officer were here, his would be nailed right next to yours!

That's what I call sport!" He looked at Carter. "Get them out of my sight, Sergeant."

"Yes, sir," Carter said. He motioned to the light company. "Taylor, Berry, get him up. Try not to be too gentle with him."

Paul turned to the two Portuguese men. Both were watching him with steady eyes. "I am sorry," Paul said quietly. "Will you come into my office and tell me what you are owed for the thefts. And then I think you should take your wife home."

The boy's English was clearly much better than his father in law. He nodded. "Thank you," he said.

"You've nothing to thank me for. It should never have happened."

O'Reilly watched as his commander led the two men back into his office. "Sergeant Williams, Corporal Hammond. Stand the men down and assign them to cleaning duties until dinner time. Let's get this pigsty fit for a man to live in. Williams, were those bastards from your company?"

Sergeant Williams, a skinny Yorkshireman with yellow complexion nodded. "Yes, sir."

"Well put them on latrine duties for the rest of the week. Some of them must have known about this, and if they knew, I should have known!" O'Reilly surveyed the second company with a disgusted expression. "Perhaps shovelling shit for a week will teach you when to keep your mouth shut and when to open it. And in case any of you are in any doubt, right now is the time to keep it shut, especially when the Colonel walks by. He's forgotten about the rest of you. You'd better pray he doesn't remember until he's in a better mood. Battalion dismissed!"

He turned back to Grey and Manson. "I need to talk to you to about the NCOs," he said. "We need more of them, and I need to know whom to recommend to the Colonel. Come into the mess and get a drink, I need one after that."

He led the way into the two-storied building, which housed the officers' quarters and the newly cleaned and equipped mess. O'Reilly collected a bottle of wine and three glasses and seated himself at the long table. Grey sat down, looking around him. "How have they managed this in one morning?" he said.

"Elbow grease, organisation, and a fellow by the name of George Kelly on their arses. He's our cook and runs the officer's mess. The colonel pinched him from the Dublin barracks a few years back and he can make a meal out of anything so you'll not starve here. Have a drink, Manson, you look like you need it."

Manson took the glass with a grunt of thanks. "Christ," he said. "Is he always like this?"

"Like what?" the Irishman asked mildly.

"Bloody crazy! I know we were told that Wellington likes to keep the locals happy. But those boys had just come off a transport, for God's sake, they've had a foul few years in the Indies…"

"I'm going to stop you there, Mr Manson," Michael said gently, sipping his wine. "Because if I let you say what I think you were going to say, I'd have to punch you in the face and then George would be in my ear about making a mess in his nice clean dining room." He regarded the other officer's startled expression and laughed. "I don't know what you expected when you joined up, laddie, but clearly it wasn't this! The colonel was a little cross earlier, not because he's following Wellington's directives but because he doesn't like rapists. I admit I'm with him on that one, but we all know it happens. It just doesn't happen in the 110th. Ever. When the colonel joined us many years ago with Captain Swanson, whom you've not met yet, he was a lad of twenty-one who looked like butter wouldn't melt in his mouth and I remember Mr Swanson helpfully telling me that the lieutenant didn't like rapists. I bore it in mind and I told the lads as a good sergeant should, and then I forgot all about it until six months later when a man of our company had a few drinks and decided to get himself a woman. And when he realised he couldn't afford one he went and found the fifteen year old daughter of one of our sepoys and he used her instead."

"What happened?" Grey asked.

"She went crying to her father, who went to his commanding officer. His company just happened to be serving with the light company, which was under the temporary command of Lieutenant van Daan. We were in the field and a little short on provost marshals and the like, and I stood and watched that twenty one year old fair haired laddie, who still, by the way, looked like butter wouldn't melt in his mouth, put a bullet through a man's brain at six inches, and then go and have his dinner." O'Reilly took a long drink. "Like I said, the colonel doesn't like rapists. And that little gem about cutting off the man's balls? Well I didn't know him then but rumour has it that he's done it. And when I hear a tale about the colonel, I'm usually inclined to believe it's true. Now then, about these NCOs."

He reached for his notebook. Grey picked up his glass. Michael looked up, sensing Manson's eyes on him. "Is there a problem, Mr Manson?"

"I don't like rapists either and I'm not keen on the implication that I do."

"Oh bejesus, don't be challenging me, I'm not impugning your honour, I'm trying to teach you the rules. Learn them, for God's sake, or you'll have a miserable time. Let's start with the first company – you've no light company have you?"

When the discussion was over, Manson excused himself and left the mess. Grey hesitated and began to rise, and Michael motioned him to sit down again, and poured a second glass of wine. "I think Mr Manson needs some time alone to re-evaluate his views on army life," he said. "It's almost dinner time, and the job I should be doing involves going through supply lists with Captain Corrigan and Mrs van Daan, so I'm happy to delay that until the morning. It's been a long day."

"The colonel's wife helps the quarter-master?" Grey said, bewildered.

"The colonel's wife is the quarter-master. Whoever else gets the job is just for show. She's also the company doctor, by the way, if the men need anything. Which reminds me I must get her to look at that poor bastard's back."

"Is that usual?"

"No. On campaign the wives and women of the enlisted men usually help out with cooking, washing, nursing – that kind of thing.

One or two of the officers' wives sometimes help in the surgeon's tents but only nursing officers and light duties. Mrs van Daan can amputate a man's leg faster than most surgeons. And they often live through it."

"How long have they been married? She doesn't look very old."

"They've been wed less than a year but he's known her for longer. They were both married to other people. His wife died in childbirth, her husband was killed. She's not that old, but don't let that fool you, she's a lass who had to grow up fast."

"He's a strange man," Grey said. "I can't decide if I like him or not." He reached for his glass. "I know I'm terrified of him. Would he really have shot those men?"

"Yes."

Grey drank deeply. "Does he get many desertions?"

"Very few."

"And you. You came up from the ranks?"

"Very recently. I've been Sergeant of the light company for many years. He joined us in Melton as a very new lieutenant when I'd served for about three years. Like you, my first reaction was that this was a very strange officer. I was right, too. I've been with him pretty much ever since." Michael lifted a hand to a brawny Irishman who had entered from the kitchen. "Evening George, how's dinner going? My stomach is cleaving to my backbone!"

"Won't be long, Mr O'Reilly, sir. Evening Mr Grey." Kelly looked at Michael. "Heard the Colonel had a bit of a chat with some of the men in the yard earlier."

"He did so," Michael said. "Somebody tell you about it?"

"No, no, heard it for myself, nice and clear. He's in fine voice."

Michael grinned. "Hope it's a good meal tonight, George. He could do with something to put him in a better mood." He looked up as a soldier from the 112th appeared in the doorway. "What is it, lad?"

"Begging your pardon, sir, but I've come about Barker, sir. The man who was flogged."

"What of him?"

"He's awful bad, sir. Burning up and trying to turn over. Couldn't find Sergeant Carter, sir or Corporal Hammond, and I didn't know who else to talk to. Sergeant Williams said I should leave it and not bother anybody but I couldn't do that."

"Of course you couldn't. What's your name, lad?"

"Burns, sir. Second company."

"Well done, Burns. You've just saved your company a days worth of latrine duty. Take yourself off to the Colonel's quarters. Give them my compliments and ask if the colonel's lady will come and have a look at him."

Burns looked shocked. "His wife, sir?"

"Unless he's got another lady stashed away up there, and if he has he'd better start running now. I'll explain later lad. You should find Carter and possibly Hammond up there, by the way, making eyes at the colonel's wife. If you do would you tell them to get their lazy arses down here." He saw the boy's face, grinned, and amended. "Just tell them I'm looking for them, will you?"

"Yes, sir." Still the boy hesitated. "But he's in the barracks, sir. She can't come in there."

"I wouldn't advise you to try and stop her," O'Reilly said. "Excuse me, Mr Grey, I must see to this."

Grey got up. "I'll get a couple of the men to make up a bed in the infirmary. It's cleaned although we've not stocked it yet, but he'll be quieter in there."

"Good man. Mrs van Daan will be in charge of the infirmary, she'll organise her own supplies."

He found Barker moving restlessly on his bunk. Somebody had laid a cloth across his back and Michael grimaced. It had stuck to the wounds. He knelt beside the man and felt his forehead. Burns had been right. There were three or four men in the room, all from the second company, come to change their shirts after the unpleasant duty of emptying the latrines. They had jumped to attention as he entered. Michael waved them to carry on.

The door opened and Anne van Daan came into the room carrying a black bag. Michael stood up and then grinned as the men once again jumped to attention, one of them without a shirt on. "He's over here," he said.

Anne ignored the men and knelt down by Barker. O'Reilly looked across at the flustered men. "Carry on, lads," he said. "Get yourselves decent and go and get your dinner cooked and eaten."

There was a cry from Barker as Anne began to gently peel the cloth away from his back. Michael stood back and mentally counted. He had not reached ten before a furious expletive worthy of a guttersnipe emerged from her lips. The four men jumped, and then turned to stare.

"Who the hell authorised this butchery?" she demanded.

"Now ma'am…"

"Don't 'ma'am' me, Michael O'Reilly! Who was it?"

"It was Mr Manson, ma'am. But he's a very new officer and…"

"He's unlikely to make an old officer the way he's going!" Anne said ominously. She glanced at the avidly listening men and clamped her lips together with an effort. "He can't stay here."

"No, there's an infirmary block over the back and Mr Grey is getting it organised."

"Good. I can clean it and dress it, and I've some salve that will help. I'll give him some laudanum for the pain and to help him sleep. But I don't like this fever. Has he been ill before?"

"I don't know. I'll find Sergeant Williams and ask him."

"Thank you. Paul has organised a formal dinner in the mess tomorrow, did he tell you?"

"Yes. My uniform has arrived, so I've lost my excuse."

"You'd better bloody be there, O'Reilly! If I have to, you have to!"

Michael laughed down at her. "Girl dear, it's worth it to see what you'll make of Mr Manson. He's not going to last three weeks with your man, trust me."

"If he flogs another man in these barracks he isn't going to last three weeks with me."

Anne was curious to see the new officer who seemed to have thoroughly set up the backs of both officers and men of the 110th. Paul was currently the only officer with a wife in barracks with him, which meant she was the only lady at the table. Paul handed her to her place with teasing ceremony, his eyes moving over her appreciatively. She had dressed for the occasion in an ivory satin gown with a jonquil evening robe, and she wore the pearls her father had given her on the occasion of her first marriage. From the satin evening slippers to the top of her shining dark hair, secured with pearl-headed pins, she was every inch the colonel's lady and she could sense Paul's pride as he took his place at the opposite end of the table. The officers arranged themselves about the table. In addition to his own few officers, Paul had invited several other officers currently in Lisbon and Anne could sense their curiosity to see how she would handle her first formal mess dinner. Michael O'Reilly, resplendent in his new uniform, looked at her as they seated themselves and she saw the gleam in his eye.

"Girl dear, you're looking very lovely," he said. "I don't remember that gown from the retreat from Talavera, did you have it then?"

Anne gave a peal of laughter. She had travelled back from Talavera with the 110th wearing the same shabby gown for over a month. "Mr O'Reilly, you're only safe because I am not going to get blood on this," she said. "Mind you, you're looking very pretty yourself, almost like an officer and a gentleman."

Paul grinned, sensing the surprise of the visiting officers. He was accustomed to the relationship between Anne and his former sergeant and their banter had dissipated any sense of formality which he knew had been her intention. Conversation became general and easy. Anne had seated the two newest officers of the 112th on either side of her. She had already met and approved Will Grey. Lionel Manson was another matter. Anne regarded him thoughtfully. He was a tall young man, dark haired and good looking with a thin face and a pair of unusual coloured eyes, hazel but with golden flecks in them.

"Welcome to the 110th, Mr Manson," she said.

Manson seemed to sense the irony in her words. "Thank you, ma'am," he said stiffly.

"Are you settling in well enough?"

"I'm trying, ma'am."

Anne glanced at Will Grey. "Mr Grey, how about you?"

"Same, ma'am. It's very different to my previous experience, but that's been very limited."

"Don't worry about it, you aren't the first to say that and you won't be the last," Anne said with a laugh. "Did you get any training at all before they put you on that transport?"

"No, ma'am. Mr Manson had a little."

Anne looked at him. "Where was that, Mr Manson?"

"Norfolk, ma'am. Only a few weeks."

Paul watched his wife with amusement. He could see that she was trying hard to draw out the young lieutenant, and unusually for her, she was struggling. Will Grey was already a lost man, his eyes seldom leaving her face. Manson was looking rigidly uncomfortable, speaking civilly when he needed to but volunteering no information.

Anne excused herself when dinner was over, knowing that her presence would constrain the visiting officers from getting as drunk or speaking as freely as they wanted to. Paul took her hand to escort her back to their quarters, and to his surprise found Lionel Manson beside him.

"I'll escort your wife, sir."

Paul lifted surprised brows at Anne and she nodded. "Thank you, Mr Manson. Stay and behave like a Colonel, Paul, I'll see you later."

He laughed and lifted her hand to his lips. "I'll try. Thank you, Mr Manson."

Manson took her arm and escorted her in silence out of the mess and across the dark, deserted parade ground. Halfway across, Anne said:

"Normally I'd walk this by myself, but we don't know your men that well yet, Mr Manson."

"Judging by their record so far I'd say you've reason to doubt their behaviour around women, ma'am," Manson said, and it was so unexpectedly natural that Anne burst into laughter.

"You have a very good point," she said, laughing up at him. The thin lips quirked into the first hint of a smile she had seen. Anne studied him openly. "I was beginning to think you couldn't smile," she said quietly.

"Not finding it easy, ma'am."

"No, I can see that. But I'm not sure anybody does at the start. And if you've spent even a few weeks with another regiment, it won't have prepared you for this one, trust me."

"I'm surprised you'd care, ma'am."

Anne picked up the edge to his tone. They had reached the door to the officers' block. Anne stopped and looked up at him. "I see. Who told you I blew up over the flogging?"

"Several people, ma'am."

"Well I am sorry about that. I was completely furious, but I should have told you about it, not sounded off where other people could hear. Very poor form for the Colonel's wife. I do apologise, Mr Manson. But I find it hard to believe that Paul, Michael or Pat Corrigan passed what I said onto you. Are you having trouble with the enlisted men? NCOs?"

"Not your problem, ma'am."

"No. And I understand you cannot possibly want to discuss this with a girl who is probably not much older than you. But Mr Manson, you can't let them get away with it, you know. I rather imagine that you're not sure how to handle it given that the 110th doesn't use the traditional methods of discipline. But it's disciplined, believe me. You won't want to talk to Paul, but you could talk to Michael."

"I'm all right, ma'am. But thank you."

"Thank you, Mr Manson. Now turn around and go back to the mess. You're not going to help yourself by separating yourself from the others. I know perfectly well that's why you offered to escort me, but you're not getting away with it. If you disappear into your room, I'm going to stand outside kicking your door until you come out."

"Ma'am, nobody particularly wants me to be there and I don't want to."

"That sounds exactly like me with most headquarters parties. You need to trust me when I say that listening to them whispering behind my back is not enjoyable. But I still go."

Manson stood looking at her for a long time then nodded, turned, and walked back towards the mess. Anne watched him until he entered, then turned and went upstairs.

Having appeared to improve, Private Barker took an abrupt turn for the worse the following day. The wounds on his back were not infected but his fever was getting progressively worse. Going in search of information, Anne found his company practicing dry firing with Michael and Manson.

"Michael, I'm trying to find out what's happening with Private Barker. This fever is getting worse. Is there anybody who has served with him for a while?"

"I'll ask, ma'am," Michael said. Manson came forward.

"Burns and Campbell," he said briefly. "Would you like to speak to them, ma'am?"

"Yes, please, Mr Manson."

He nodded and moved away. Anne watched him. "How is he doing, Michael?"

"He's a miserable bastard with a poker up his arse," Michael said shortly. "He's not right for us, that's for sure."

Anne did not reply. Manson returned leading the two men, and she questioned them about Barker. As she had suspected, the episodes of recurring fever had begun in the Indies and returned regularly ever since. He had survived them all, but she suspected that the shock of the flogging had weakened him.

He lingered on for some days, but Anne sensed that he was fading and by the end of the first week she found herself surprised that he had lasted so long. Paul came to visit the infirmary during the evening and found her sitting beside him. He studied the man.

"He's not going to make it, is he?"

"No, he'll be gone by morning. I'm going to stay with him, Paul."

"Want me to?"

She looked up and smiled. "No, love, not the hours you're working at the moment. I can sleep in tomorrow if I'm up all night."

"We ought to put Lieutenant bloody Manson in here for the night, but that would be unfair on Barker!" Paul glanced at her. "This is a first for me, Nan, and I am seriously pissed off about it."

"I know you are, love. I am myself, but to be fair it's the fever that's killing him rather than the flogging."

"And he's survived it so far."

"I know. The flogging will have weakened him. I'm not excusing it, Paul."

He bent to kiss her. "I'd tell you to leave him, but I know you won't. Come and eat, Teresa can watch him for a while, and then I'll leave you to it."

"I'll be over soon."

"Make sure you are or I'll come and get you."

Returning after the meal, Anne sat quietly into the night, listening to the laboured breathing of the dying man. It was not the first time she had sat beside a man as he breathed his last, and she had learned the rhythms. Lighting a lamp she sat beneath it and read a scholarly paper, which Dr Norris had sent her on amputation techniques. Engrossed in the subject, she was surprised when the door opened and Lieutenant Manson was standing in the doorway.

"I came to see how he was," he said. Anne thought that he sounded suddenly younger and less sure of himself.

"Come in and close the door," she said.

Manson did so hesitantly. Anne indicated a wooden stool. "Sit down, Mr Manson. There's no need to hush. He can't hear you."

Manson sat down. "Is he going to die?"

Anne nodded. "Listen to his breathing. He's shutting down. I think he'll be gone by morning."

"Why are you here?" Manson asked.

"If it can be helped I don't think a man should die alone."

"I'm surprised the colonel would let you."

"He offered to do it himself, but he's working fourteen hours a day. He needs to sleep. I can catch up later."

Manson nodded. Then he said:

"Do you mind if I stay?"

"Not at all, it will be company for me," Anne said, setting aside the booklet she was reading.

Manson picked it up and looked at the cover. "A medical book?"

"It's a paper about surgical techniques. My friend Dr Norris sent it to me." Anne smiled at him. "This is all very new and very strange to you, isn't it, Mr Manson? What made you join the army?"

"I was always going to join the army. My father was a colonel – retired now. He married late. Since I could walk I was intended for a regiment. He wanted me to go into his own old regiment, but there were no vacant commissions, so he said I should start where I could and transfer over. There's not much money and the 112th was cheap."

Things were becoming much clearer to Anne. "And you no doubt received a lot of advice and information from him. What were his views on flogging?"

"He always said it was the only way to keep control. That an officer who couldn't control the common soldiers was lost. Hit them hard over the smallest thing, he'd say, and they'll learn to fear you more than they fear the enemy. So they'll fight better."

"Or desert," Anne said mildly. "Do you mind me asking how old you are, Mr Manson?"

"I'm nineteen," Manson said. Anne made a mental note to make sure that her husband knew this piece of information.

"You look older," she said.

"I didn't expect that the first man I killed would be one of ours," Manson said suddenly.

"No, I don't imagine you did." Anne hesitated, then decided to take a chance. "This fever wasn't caused by your flogging, Mr Manson. I questioned those men and he's had it before. Malaria, possibly, or some other recurring fever he picked up in the Indies. But if he was already ill when he was flogged he'd have been too weak to resist it."

"He said he'd been ill – that's why he was late that day. I didn't believe him. They all lie all the time. And I knew that none of them respected me, or Grey. I could hear them laughing at us behind their hands. They thought we were incompetent greenhorns. And they were right. But I thought…"

He stopped. When he did not continue, Anne said gently:

"You thought a show of strength would get them into line."

"Yes, ma'am." Manson looked up suddenly. "How do you know all this?" he said. "You can't be that much older than I am and you're a woman. But I swear the men of the light company would obey you faster than they would me or Grey."

"They'd better," Anne said succinctly. She laughed. "Don't take the 110th as your model as an average regiment, Mr Manson. Paul's leadership style is acknowledged to be a little eccentric. But he does get things done."

"I thought he was soft," Manson admitted. "I saw him laughing and joking with the enlisted men and the NCOs, and refusing to flog the men. And all I could think about was getting a transfer to a better regiment, with a real officer in charge. The kind of man my father would have respected."

"And what changed your mind?" Anne asked.

"On the parade ground, when he called those men out for rape. You didn't see it, ma'am."

"I heard a fair bit of it. The colonel's voice tends to carry when he is irritated."

"He would have shot them down on the spot," Manson said. "I could see it in his face. And I was watching the men – his men as well as the 112th. They all knew he meant every word he said. None of them dared move a muscle. That isn't an officer who is considered soft."

"No, I imagine the light company marched out on tiptoe just in case he noticed them," Anne said with a grin. "They know what he's like."

"He thinks me a fool and he's right," Manson said bitterly. "So I think I had better apply for that transfer."

"Mr Manson, I'm not in any position to give you advice. I hardly know you. But when you're on a battlefield and the French are advancing, there will come a moment when you realise you've got it wrong. You went the wrong way, you misunderstood your orders, you underestimated the enemy. I can think of at least one occasion in Viseu when Paul came back having lost half a dozen men because he'd underestimated the strength of the enemy and nearly got his battalion slaughtered."

"What happened?"

"He lost men. They fought, and they were good enough to get themselves out of it. But he's made mistakes. We all do, but when you do it, people will die. And you don't have the option in the middle of a battle to transfer out and start again somewhere else. You need to learn how to stand."

Manson nodded silently. Anne had the impression that he was genuinely listening. "No. I see that. You won't tell anybody that I spoke to you?" he asked, and he sounded very young.

"No, I give you my word." Anne smiled. "Word of a light company man. Or woman. May I ask your name – your Christian name?"

"It's Lionel, ma'am."

"Is that what your mother calls you?"

Manson laughed unexpectedly and it changed him beyond all recognition. "My mother calls me Leo."

"Now that, I like." Anne leaned over and checked on the dying man. "Go to bed, Mr Manson. He doesn't need two of us here and however long it takes him to die, the colonel will expect you on that training ground at six o'clock with your wits about you."

"Yes, ma'am." Manson got up and went to the door. "And ma'am."

"Yes?"

"Thank you."

Chapter Six

With what seemed like painful slowness, the new recruits to the 110th and the first battalion of the 112th began to adjust to the routine of drilling and training which their exacting Colonel had put in place.

Of the two groups the new recruits were doing better. It was often easier, Paul had noticed, to train men who had never worked the drills before than to retrain those who had learned sloppiness. Because of this, he had deliberately kept the two groups separate, forming a company of reserves from the new recruits. They were beginning to pick up skills quickly under the leadership of Michael O'Reilly, and gradually Paul began to work them together with his light company more. He intended them to learn not only the physical skills required to fight in the 110th, but also the discipline and work ethic. The light company was legendary not only for their formidable fighting skills, but for their unconventional attitude, and Paul was aware that some of this would also be passed on to the new recruits, but Sergeant Carter and Corporal Hammond would deal with any tendency to step out of line very quickly.

In between the mountain of work involved in working with the commissariat and quartermasters departments in sourcing transport and supplies for Wellington, Paul supervised the training of the 112th. Lieutenant Grey was settling well to the work and although the men did not leap to obey him they afforded him a level of respect. Lieutenant Manson was clearly finding it more difficult. Paul regretted that his light company had been witnesses to the flogging, which had killed Private Barker. Seven years of serving under Paul with his unusual attitude to discipline had fostered a healthy contempt for an officer who relied on flogging to earn the respect of his men, and Paul was very sure that their scorn had filtered through to the new recruits and the 112th. It was going to be difficult for Manson to come back from that, and Paul wondered if a transfer to a different regiment for a fresh start might be the only answer. He knew that Manson had considered it and wondered if he had written to Horse Guards to make the request. He did not ask. Manson was under enough pressure and although Paul had his doubts about the man he did not want to imply that he expected him to leave. Despite his disastrous start Manson seemed to be keeping his head down and trying to learn.

Curiously, the only person who had no criticism to make of Manson was his wife. After her first fury about the flogging and the failure to follow up the complaints of the farmer about his abused daughter, she seemed to have fallen silent on the subject. At dinner in the mess she had developed a habit of seating herself beside Manson. He was not talkative with her, but he would listen to her chatter, and make the occasional remark, even laughing occasionally. Paul watched thoughtfully. He had begun to realise that his wife's instincts about his men were often correct, and he wondered if she saw something in the young officer that he had missed.

As training began to improve, Paul chose a warm afternoon to lighten the mood by introducing lessons in swordplay. Enlisted men were not issued with swords, and fencing was the prerogative of officers and gentlemen, but most of Paul's light company and many of his other men had acquired weapons looted from the enemy over the years and many of them had developed some skill with them. He had begun to teach them for fun some years ago, and although it was not a main part of training, his men enjoyed the lessons, and he knew they felt privileged to receive them.

He fought, as he had since India, with an elaborately worked tulwar, which had been given to him as a prize by his men after his first action in command of the light company. It had taken some time to adapt his style to the different shape of the sword but he was as adept with it now as with a traditional blade, and he would not have swapped it, any more than he would go into battle wearing a coat without the white armband he had been given on the same day. It had been a light-hearted joke, giving the symbol of a chosen man to an officer who could not be expected to wear it. He had worn it and valued it, and he was aware that the story had become part of the folklore of the regiment, which was passed on to new recruits as they joined.

Having issued swords to the new recruits and the 112th he taught them the grip and stance of a swordsman and got them to practice for a while. Michael O'Reilly was working with the light company on slightly more advanced techniques. After watching them for a while Paul called them round and drew his sword.

"Mr Grey, let's see how you get on."

The young lieutenant stepped forward, looking nervous. The light company were grinning having seen their commander fight before. Paul tried a few simple passes to test his skill. Grey had been well taught, but he was hesitant and his nerves were obvious. Paul did not press him too hard, but he could sense that the boy was struggling with the strength and speed of his attacks. Within five minutes Grey was breathless, and his guard was beginning to drop. Paul allowed him two mistakes and then pressed forward, broke through his guard, and touched the point of his sword to the younger man's chest. Grey acknowledged the hit with a gesture and stepped back.

Paul lowered the sword with a grin. "Not bad, Mr Grey. You need to strengthen that wrist. But you'll get there." He glanced across at Michael. "Mr O'Reilly?"

"You've had years of opportunity to kick my arse in public, sir. Why not give Mr Manson a try?"

"Coward," Paul said with a laugh.

"Not frightened of the French, sir, just of you. When I fence with you I'm always distracted trying to remember how many times in the past week I've pissed you off."

Paul turned to Manson. "Mr Manson. Up you come."

Manson stepped forward with obvious reluctance and drew his sword. There was a rustle of anticipation around the square. Paul was wryly aware that the men would love to see Manson humiliated. The light company in particular would take a long time to forget the flogging and death of Private Barker, and Manson's distant manner did not endear him to any of the men. Paul was not sure that anything could retrieve Manson's position in the regiment after such a disastrous beginning. He lifted his blade in salute and Manson did the same. He looked as though he would prefer to be somewhere else.

The two men circled each other, each making exploratory passes. Paul made the first attack, moving forward quickly with a series of thrusts and parries, testing his opponent. Manson gave way steadily, his blade meeting Paul's in a quick defensive sequence and then he counter attacked with astonishing speed and strength and Paul was on the back foot, both blades flashing until Paul turned and parried and Manson shifted back out of reach. Paul looked at his face and the golden eyes were steady and watchful and Paul gave a slight smile.

"Well, well," he said softly, and for the first time ever he saw an answering gleam in the boy's eye. They circled each other slowly, watching for an opportunity. Around them there was complete silence on the parade ground. Nothing could be heard except the clash of metal on metal as the combatants met again, Manson taking the lead and almost managing to get through Paul's guard. Paul's defence held solid but he felt the boy's strength jar through his wrist and arm. He met Manson's eyes again and gave a nod of acknowledgement, then lunged forward at speed and almost had Manson over backwards with the speed and force of his attack. Manson took a leap back and landed with cat like grace in time to parry again. Both men were breathing harder now.

The attacks moved back and forth and the combatants flew across the parade ground, sunlight bouncing off the flashing blades. A pattern was emerging from Manson's combinations. He had no obvious weakness, he was strong and fast and very skilled, but he was younger and less experienced than Paul, and it was possible to draw him into a repeating cycle of moves. Paul did so, watching as the younger man allowed himself to be pulled in. On the fourth cycle, Paul suddenly changed his stance and twisted his wrist and his sword curled around Manson's, and the boy gave a sharp exclamation of pain as the blade flew from his hand and clattered to the ground two feet away. He stood breathing hard, holding his wrist as the tip of Paul's blade touched his chest very gently. Then

Paul sheathed his blade and came forward, breathless and laughing and clapped the boy on the shoulder.

"Are you all right? I'm sorry, I was a bastard there, that can really sting."

"Yes. What was that?"

"I learned it years ago from a Spanish naval officer. Not often had to use it, mind. When we've time I'll teach it to you. Where did you learn swordplay, Mr Manson?"

"I had lessons as a boy. Just took to it, I suppose. You're very good, sir." Manson rubbed his wrist with a rueful grin. He looked to Paul's appreciative eyes, much younger and more relaxed. He appeared to suddenly notice that around him the men were applauding.

"I'm almost ten years older than you and I've been fighting for most of that time. That was impressive." Paul bent and picked up Manson's sword, handing it to him with a smile. "Are you all right to carry on with training or do you need to rest that?"

Manson took the sword and tested his wrist with it. "No, I'm fine."

"Good. Take over from Mr O'Reilly with the light company, they've done more of this than the others and you've more to teach them. Mr O'Reilly, take Mr Grey over to the 112th and get them started on the basics."

He watched Manson move towards his men and saw Sergeant Carter step forward with a grin, and offer what sounded like congratulations. Paul smiled, and went to join the new recruits for the 110th.

He was vaguely conscious of a new atmosphere as he worked. Across at the light company he could hear the clash of blades and the voice of Manson, correcting and instructing. For the first time his young lieutenant seemed to have forgotten his dignity, and he was surprised to hear him laughing at something Sergeant Carter had said to him. At the end of the afternoon Paul dismissed the men and watched as Manson and Grey walked off to their quarters to wash and change.

"Interesting afternoon, sir," Michael O'Reilly said, coming to join him.

"Yes. I didn't expect that."

"Neither did I. He's very good."

"Yes. But I didn't really mean the swordplay."

"Neither did I," Michael said quietly.

Paul had wondered if Manson would allow his unexpected success to go to his head, but at dinner there was very little change in his manner. He sat quietly as usual, although Paul had a sense that he was listening more to the conversation around the table than usual. As the meal ended, Anne rose to leave the officers to their drinks. She caught Paul's eye and he came to join her.

"Don't disappear, Mr Manson, I wanted a word. Get another drink, I'll be back."

He slipped his arm about Anne and walked across the dark parade ground. "How was he this evening?" he asked.

"Happier."

Paul laughed. "How the hell could you tell, Nan? He gives nothing away, I've never seen a boy of his age so contained."

"Well he's not going to sit in that mess and laugh his head off, Paul. He knows very well that nobody wants him there. But he's definitely more relaxed this evening."

Her husband regarded her thoughtfully. "You've been quietly working at this haven't you? What is it you see that I've missed, bonny lass?"

"Determination," Anne said. "And courage."

"Meaning?"

"Paul, he's still out there, every day, facing those men, knowing how much they despise him. He hasn't sold out and he hasn't transferred, and don't tell me he couldn't have, there are officers out there who would pay to get in with the 110th. In all these weeks he's not missed a day, he's not been late one morning, and he's not complaining. At all. That's what I see."

They arrived at the officers' block, and Paul stopped and looked down at her. "All right, girl of my heart. You're not often wrong.

But he has to find a way to get them back. I can't tell him how to do that."

"I know." She reached up to kiss him, and Paul pulled her closer, kissing her harder. He was tempted to forego the rest of the evening in the mess in favour of picking her up and carrying her to bed, but he knew that Manson would be waiting for him. Reluctantly he released her.

"Don't go to sleep," he said softly. "I'll be as quick as I can."

"You can always think of a way to wake me up, Colonel," Anne said mischievously, and he laughed and kissed her again then walked back to the mess. He could hear the voice of Captain Corrigan, and the laughter of Michael O'Reilly as he entered and he stood listening.

"Corrigan, are you telling my new officers stories about me that they should not hear?" he demanded.

"Sorry, sir, I didn't think you were coming back," the Irishman said, grinning. "I was just about to explain your method of waking up an officer who had offended your wife."

Paul reached for the wine bottle and refilled both his and Manson's glasses. "I am never going to live that down am I?" he said.

"What did you do, sir?" Grey asked. He was losing a lot of his awe of his Colonel, Paul had noticed.

Paul shook his head, and Michael laughed and reached for the wine. "He arrived on the parade ground for early drill that morning, collected a waste bucket from the barracks, kicked down poor Tyler's door and poured a bucketful of piss and shit over his head, followed by a bucket of freezing cold water from the pump! Poor Tyler nearly exploded. Threatened to call the Major out, but he decided against it."

"I bet you didn't point out that this whole thing started with you showing off on the parade ground, O'Reilly," Paul said, laughing. He glanced across and suddenly noticed that Manson was laughing. Paul caught his eye.

"I also didn't mention that it ended with me getting flogged and demoted," Michael said pointedly.

"It's a miracle that didn't happen more often to you, it probably should have."

"What did Mrs van Daan say when she heard?" Manson asked.

"I don't think I told her," Paul said. "It wasn't Nan, it was my first wife. Rowena died in childbirth. She was a very gentle soul and she would have been horrified. If I'd been married to Nan at the time, the whole thing would never have got further than the cry of pain from Tyler as she smacked his face for him at the reception."

"If he was lucky," Michael said. He looked at Manson. "That was a very impressive display out there today, Mr Manson. What made your father give you fencing lessons?"

"He was a soldier," Manson said. "A colonel in the cavalry, married late, after he left the service. I'm his only child, I was always intended for the army and my education was aimed at that."

Paul studied him. "Did you want the cavalry as well?"

The boy shrugged. "I'm not really sure I ever thought that much about it. He wanted me to follow him into his regiment, but there were no vacancies, and it would have been too expensive anyway, there's not much money. As you once said, sir, the 112th was cheap."

"Do you know what happened in the Indies?" Paul asked.

"I know there was a scandal over fraud in the barracks," Grey said. "They were still talking about it when we arrived."

"The Major who commanded in the Indies was cashiered," Manson said. "I don't know all the details, but I was told he beat a servant to death in front of the whole battalion."

"Sounds like a mess," Paul commented. "No wonder it's taking them a while to settle down." He glanced across at his two newest officers. "They'll get there. Believe me, I've seen worse. The 115th Yorkshire would have made this lot look good when I first got there." He laughed. "I decided to take a very direct approach with them and after a few weeks of me, one of them had got so tired of it that he hid behind a tree and threw a rock at my head as I was riding to barracks one morning."

"We've all thought about doing that, sir," Michael said. "Mind you, you're not mentioning that the lass who found you and cleaned you up is the one you're married to. I reckon he did you a favour."

"Cheeky bastard," Paul said, laughing. "I've had enough of your mouth for one evening, O'Reilly, I'm going to bed." He looked across at Manson. "Look on the bright side, Mr Manson, you've been here longer than I had then, and none of them has thrown anything at you yet."

Manson drained his glass. "Doesn't mean they won't, sir," he said, and Paul laughed aloud.

"After that display out there today, Lieutenant, I can assure you my light company will think twice about it, they're not going to piss you off with a sword in your hand. Good night."

He found little time in the following two weeks to spend with his new officers. Even with the help of Corrigan and his wife, the sheer scale of the task Wellington had set him absorbed most of his time. He was aware that O'Reilly was keeping up a gruelling training schedule, and he joined them as often as possible, observing a marked improvement of his new recruits. The 112th were coming on slowly, and he could sense it was a matter of attitude rather than ability. He was tempted to spend time with them himself, but he knew it would not help Manson.

He could sense his officers beginning to feel the strain, and there were one or two incidents on the parade ground, which suggested that tempers were becoming frayed.

"What's the matter with them, Michael?" he enquired, after the Irishman had delivered a report of the penalties given after a drunken fight between two members of the light company and half a dozen of the 112th. "Do I need to get involved here?"

"They're tired, Paul," Michael said quietly. "You've been pushing them hard for weeks."

"I know," Paul said. He sounded tired himself. "Time for some light relief, you think?"

"I think so."

"We'll do it on Friday. Talk to Kelly and tell him what we need. Danny, does Flanagan have his fiddle with him?"

"What do you think, sir?"

"See if you can round up a few girls who are happy to come and share the party."

"Wives invited, then, sir?"

"Well mine is," Paul said. "Do we have any wives with us here?"

"No, sir, but a few of the lads have set up shop with local girls."

"Jesus, it doesn't take them long, does it?"

"And that from the man who managed to acquire a woman on the voyage to India back in '02 when as far as we knew there weren't any!" Michael said.

"Did he really, Michael?" Corrigan said with interest. "I didn't know that."

"Whose wife was it, sir?" Carter said with what appeared to be genuine curiosity.

"Whose wife was what?" Anne said, coming into the room with a pile of paperwork.

"On the first voyage to India in '02," Carter said. "The colonel was commenting that some of the lads have been quick workers with the local girls, and Mr O'Reilly said…"

"I'm sitting right here, you know?" Paul said in some exasperation. "And that is my wife you're talking to about my past indiscretions, Sergeant."

"Is that what we're calling them now?" O'Reilly said genially. He caught Paul's eye and laughed. "I'll be off then."

"You can all be off!" Paul said. "I've got work to do. Go and pretend you know something about running a regiment."

"It would have been Nell Kemp, Danny, Grace's mother," Anne said unconcernedly, and the men dissolved into laughter. "Am I kicked out as well, love?"

"No. You can stay and go over these transport arrangements with me to see if I've missed anything." Paul said. He pressed his fingers to the sides of his head. His wife studied him for a moment, then set the papers down on his desk.

"I've a better idea," she said. "I'm going to get changed and then we can go for a ride. Poor Bella has barely been out this week. And more to the point neither have you."

Paul smiled ruefully. "I'd love to, Nan, but I need to finish these. Wellington wants us back in the field."

"Do you need me to describe in detail how much I care about Lord Wellington's requirements right now?" his wife asked. "And if he starts moaning given the amount of work he's expecting you to do, I'll have a chat with him myself! Danny, on your way past will you get somebody to saddle up Rufus and Bella, please?"

Sergeant Carter gave a smile. "Yes, ma'am."

Paul closed his eyes tiredly. Then he opened them. "I suppose there is literally no point in me countermanding that order, is there?" he said resignedly.

"Don't be daft, sir. Go and get your riding clothes on. Mr Corrigan can go over these with you later."

Lieutenant Will Grey was somewhat bewildered at being informed that he was required to attend a regimental party. He was fascinated by the concept of the officers and men mingling freely together at a social event, and he was very sure that almost every other regiment would have frowned on the idea. Casually he mentioned it to Manson who gave him a wry smile.

"Don't ask me, Grey, it's beyond me. There are so many things I don't understand about this regiment that being told I have to turn up to watch my men dancing jigs is the least of my worries."

"You still looking to transfer?" Grey said quietly. He was very aware of his fellow officer's struggles, and was beginning to feel a good deal of sympathy for him. He had not liked Lionel Manson to begin with, but during the past weeks he had warmed to him. There was a reserve about the other man which made him appear completely inflexible but he had begun to let down his guard a little around Grey and had displayed a dry humour which Grey liked.

To his surprise, Manson shook his dark head. "No. If I transfer out, I might as well sell out and give up. Word will get round that I couldn't cut it with the 110th, it always does. And besides, I'd always know that I gave up." He glanced at Grey. "You're doing well. Get on all right with O'Reilly."

"I like him," Grey admitted. "I know he came up from the ranks, but..."

"He's not a ranker," Manson said positively. "Might have come through that way, but he's an educated man. Irish rebel, I suspect, although I don't think I'll ask him. We're not on those terms." He looked up. "What is it Sergeant Carter?"

"Sorry to disturb you, sir. Lieutenant Chapman from the quartermasters department is here with supplies and he isn't prepared to let either myself or Corporal Hammond take delivery of them. The other officers..."

"Yes, I know. I'll go." Manson got up. He walked with Carter across the parade ground to where a cart waited. The Lieutenant saluted.

"Wasn't going to leave this lot in the hands of an enlisted man," he said, nodding at the wagon, which was loaded with crates and barrels. "I gather there's some kind of celebration planned, your colonel has paid for this himself. Madness if you ask me, they'll be rioting before sunset." He handed a sheet to Manson. "It's all there."

"Good." Manson glanced at Carter. "Sergeant, can you get Hammond and Jenson to come and help go through this lot with me."

"No need for that," Chapman said briskly. "It's all there."

Manson glanced down at the list. "This is your order sheet," he said. "Where's the original order Mrs van Daan sent?"

"I don't know, how the hell would I? I've just given you my word that it's all there."

Lionel Manson felt a flicker of suspicion. He glanced at the Sergeant whose face was professionally blank. "Sergeant, is Mrs van Daan around?"

Carter shook his head. "Out riding with the Colonel."

"Who else would know where she keeps copies of her orders? I'm rather guessing she does."

"Hammond would know," Carter said. His eyes met Manson's in sudden enlightenment. "There's a few of us help her out from time to time, but she uses him a lot."

"Get him to look for it would you, and join us here." Manson was studying the Lieutenant's face. He was almost sure now.

"Yes, sir." Carter saluted, more smartly than Manson was used to, and left. He was back in minutes with Corporal Hammond who bore several sheets of paper covered in Anne van Daan's elegant copperplate. Manson took them.

"Won't take long," he said pleasantly to Chapman. "Tell you what, Hammond, why don't we unload as we go, and we can check them off and put them straight into the stores. Start with these barrels."

He hoisted one of the wine barrels onto his shoulder and his suspicions were immediately confirmed. The barrel was far too light. Carefully he lowered it to the ground and moved to unstopper it.

"Well I've heard a lot about this bloody regiment," Chapman said contemptuously, "but officers acting as porters alongside scum like these two seems a bit much even for the 110th. To say nothing of letting a female get involved in ordering!"

Leo Manson looked at him for a long moment. Without warning he kicked the barrel, which tipped up, splashing red wine all over Chapman's trousers and shoes. The lieutenant jumped back with an oath. Manson looked down at the wine pooling about the other man's feet. "Hard to get the smell of wine out of leather shoes, I'd have thought," he said. "Mind, I thought it would have been a lot worse than that, especially if the barrel were full." He looked up at Chapman. "I've got an idea, Mr Chapman. Why don't you try your hand at portering for a bit, pick up that barrel and put it back on that cart, piss off and bring us what the colonel paid for before I lose my temper with you and send you back with a broken nose as well? Puts my back up when a man caught trying to steal from another regiment calls my men scum. You've got a count of ten."

Chapman did not move. Manson looked at him steadily. "One," he said. "Two."

Chapman yelled an order and the private who had been standing by the box goggling ran forward and lifted the barrel back onto the cart. Manson gave a short laugh.

"Christ, you could do with joining us for training, Mr Chapman if you're too feeble to pick up a half empty barrel. I'll expect you back up here with what we ordered by the end of the day and if I don't see you, I'm coming over there to find you myself. Get lost!"

He stood watching as the cart left. "Better keep that list handy, Hammond. Let me know when he gets back here, will you? Or if he doesn't."

"Oh I think he'll come, sir," Carter said. "Probably fairly quickly too."

Manson glanced around in surprise at his tone and found that the light company sergeant was grinning. Hammond looked equally amused. Carter saluted, nodded and moved away.

He came back three hours later as Manson was finishing a musket session with the 112th at the range. "Thought you might like to know Mr Chapman is back. Hammond and Jenson are unloading and checking off. He doesn't seem to mind so much this time, but I thought you might like to come and see him."

"Be my pleasure, Sergeant," Manson said. He glanced across at his Sergeant. "Williams, finish up here will you and stand them down?"

"Yes, sir."

Manson walked in silence up to where Hammond and Jenson had almost finished unloading the wagon, helped by the same private. Chapman remained on the box seat. Manson watched as Hammond ran through the list, looked up and nodded. "All there, sir."

"Excellent." Manson looked at Chapman. "Thank you," he said briefly.

"It was a mistake, that's all," Chapman said stiffly.

"I'll bet they happen all the time, don't they Mr Chapman?" Manson said pleasantly. "But not in the 110th, just for future reference. Best let the rest of your staff know that. Next time you might not be so lucky, you might get my colonel's wife, and you need to trust me, there's a reason we leave the ordering to a female."

He nodded and watched the wagon leave. Beside him, Sergeant Carter said quietly:

"Somehow, I don't think he's going to offer to buy you a drink if he runs into you in the mess next week, sir."

"If he was buying, Sergeant, it would be watered down anyway," Manson said without thinking.

Carter began to laugh. Manson looked at him and smiled. "Thank you, sergeant. Let Mrs van Daan know when you get a chance will you? She'll want to keep an eye on him."

"I will, sir. Wouldn't want her to miss this story. Thank you." Carter saluted and left.

Manson watched him go, still smiling. He was beginning to realise why Colonel van Daan seemed to have such a good relationship with his light company NCOs.

On the evening of the party, Will Grey found himself standing on the steps to the officers' block watching the men of the 110th and 112th dance to the fiddle of Private Flanagan on the parade ground. They had eaten roast meat with bread and fruit and rice, and grog and wine were flowing readily, although Grey was fascinated to watch the level of control exerted by Carter and the other NCOs who took turns to man the drinks tables.

Colonel van Daan was dancing with his wife. Grey watched them moving down the line, both laughing. She was wearing a rose coloured silk gown, which displayed the curves of her shoulders and breasts, her hair caught up in two combs but loose down her back. Grey could not take his eyes from her. There were a number of other women present, mostly local Portuguese girls who had taken up with some of the men in recent weeks, and he saw Anne's pretty Spanish maid Teresa dancing with Private Dawson of the light company while Keren Trenlow was dancing with Corporal Hammond. But his eyes, along with most of the men present he imagined, kept returning to Anne van Daan's laughing, vivid countenance.

Paul and Anne returned to the group. He was flushed and laughing, and Will Grey thought that he looked suddenly much younger. He realised that had no idea how old his colonel was. He was standing in shirt-sleeves with his arm around his wife drinking from a pewter cup, watching the dancers with amusement.

"It occurs to me, Nan, that you can no longer shock the enlisted men by dancing with Michael," he said. "It is now perfectly acceptable to do so, he's an officer. What are you going to do to get a reaction tonight?"

"Well Danny Carter has promised me a dance, but I don't know that is going to get much of a rise out of them," Anne said. "They all know he practically lives in the infirmary when he's off duty."

"They probably don't realise that he practically lives in my sitting room," her husband said with some asperity. "I'm beginning not even to notice he's there, he's such a familiar sight. Like the coat stand or the armchair. I'm going to sit on him one day." He looked at his wife and narrowed his eyes. "What are you thinking, Nan? You are having an expression."

"Am I?" Anne said innocently. She reached up, wound her arm around his neck and pulled him down to kiss her. He did so, hard on the mouth. After a moment she squirmed away from him and stepped backwards, laughing back at him, the dress sliding low down her shoulders. Grey watched her fascinated. He had never seen such blatant sexual flirting in a woman of his own class. He glanced at his commanding officer and there was an expression on his face, which Grey had never seen before.

Grey had wondered idly, as he supposed they all had, about their relationship. At times Anne seemed almost like another member of the regiment, she was so involved with every aspect of regimental life and he was used to the easy day to day banter between the Colonel and his wife. Suddenly he found himself wondering how it must feel to have a woman like Anne van Daan look at him that way. For a moment the couple looked at each other, and the group around them were silent, the atmosphere suddenly heavy and strange. Anne leaned forward, and the rose silk of her gown strained across her breasts, and she kissed her husband again. Grey saw Paul's hand tighten on the cup he was holding and Grey could sense the self control needed not to pull the woman into his arms. And then she stepped back and laughed at him. Her own colour was heightened; she was as affected as he was. Grey was suddenly horrified to realise that he was visualising her with that hair falling around bare shoulders, and he was immediately aroused, thankful of the dark. And then she turned in a swirl of black hair and was running across the parade ground.

"Breathe, Grey," an amused voice said softly in his ear, and Grey glanced up to see Captain Corrigan standing behind him. Corrigan handed him a drink and Grey gulped it gratefully. "Don't feel bad. I've only been here for a couple of months, but I heard all the rumours before that, and I can see where they came from. You would need to be a bloody eunuch not to react when she turns it on like that. Look around you. We're all drooling like idiots. You'll be all right in a minute."

"How does she get away with it in a place like this?" Grey whispered.

"She's Paul van Daan's wife. Who would touch her? Although to be fair, if she was mine, I'd lock her up."

"She'd pick the lock," Paul said without turning around. "And then she'd come after you. With a blade. Trust me, I've considered the options."

Grey blushed a fiery red, but Pat Corrigan just laughed. "I'd forgotten you'd bats' ears," he said. "She's a menace to the peace of mind of your regiment, Paul."

"No she isn't," Paul said, still watching her as she caught the hand of Danny Carter and pulled him laughingly onto the dance floor. "She's the best asset I've got. Because they see her like this but they also see her trudging through thick mud when her horse can't carry her any more, or picking up some flea ridden camp brat whose mother is too tired to carry him, or up to her elbows in blood and gore trying to save their friend's life. You think any one of them would touch her? They'd die for her quicker than they would for me." He laughed suddenly. "Although I would guess there are going to be some awfully unsuitable dreams tonight. Look at poor Carter's face."

The dance ended. They were all still watching the dark girl. She swept a laughing curtsey to her partner, and then glanced across at Paul, her face brimful of mischief. Grey saw his mouth curve in an answering smile. "What the devil is she up to now….oh no!"

Anne was walking across to where Lieutenant Manson sat, solitary on one of the benches. He looked startled at her approach, looking around as if he were expecting there to be somebody else there. Anne was speaking to him, and holding out her hand.

"He'll never do it," Grey said positively. "He'll never get up and dance to an Irish jig in front of the enlisted men. He just won't."

"Offering odds, Mr Grey?" O'Reilly said.

"Don't take them, Will, he's trying to fleece you," Paul said without turning round, and then Anne bent and took Manson's hand and tugged it and he was getting up, setting his drink down on the bench. They watched as she drew him into the circle that had been formed, and another woman caught his other hand and he was dancing around with the men. Initially he did not seem to know how he had got there, but then the girl said something and he laughed, and watching him Grey thought he looked as though a weight had been lifted from his shoulders.

Danny Carter stood watching his colonel's wife with a slight smile on his face. Beside him, a voice said:

"Tired already, Sergeant? Or do you only dance with the colonel's wife?"

Carter glanced around and saw Teresa watching him. She looked amused.

"She's a good dancer," he said.

"She is. And very beautiful tonight."

Carter studied the Spanish girl. She was wearing a gown of primrose yellow that he had not seen before. It highlighted the bright brown of her hair and the pretty flush of her cheeks. "She's not the only one," he said quietly. "Is that new?"

She laughed. "It was a gift from Nan."

He was amused at her casual use of Anne's name. They had grown close over the past two years and he had often thought that she was more like a friend to his colonel's wife than a maid.

"It suits you, lass. I'm surprised you've time to hang around a mere sergeant with the officers queuing up to dance with you, but I'd be honoured...."

She took his hand. "Sergeant Carter, you talk a good deal of nonsense," she said, looking up at him. Carter felt a familiar stab of desire.

"I do, lass. Are you by any chance choosing this evening to start talking nonsense back to me?"

She allowed him to lead her into the dance. "Would you object?"

"No, Teresa. Just been waiting for you to make up your mind."

The girl studied him from thoughtful brown eyes. She reached up and smoothed the cloth of his red coat over his shoulder. "Very nice, Sergeant. This is new. What happened to the green one with the holes in it and the bloodstains."

Carter laughed although he felt himself flush slightly. "I gave in," he admitted. "Been hanging on to that damned thing for years. I found this on my bunk. I used to be in the 95th. Half a dozen of us were seconded to the 110th years ago in India. We never went back. Been on the 110th's payroll for years, but I've been stubborn about that bloody coat. When I got this promotion the Colonel must have ordered me this. And honestly I've thought of myself as a member of the 110th for years."

"I like this better," Teresa said. She moved her hands to the buttons and straightened the coat slightly with a familiarity which caused Carter's pulse to beat faster. He held out his hand and she took it.

"Dance with me, Teresa," he said and swung her into his arms. She looked up at him, the brown eyes laughing at him.

"You've been very patient, Sergeant," she said, surprising him.

"I like a girl who's picky, lass. Makes it feel worth my while." Carter watched her as the set drew her away from him, and then caught her hand again as it swung her back and held her slightly closer than the dance really required. Her eyes widened slightly. "Not prepared to get into a pissing contest with Mr O'Reilly over it and that's what he was looking to do. You're a lass with a choice, not the subject for a bet."

Teresa met his eyes and smiled. "You're an interesting man, Sergeant."

"You should spend some time getting to know me, Teresa."

"I think I might," she said. She glanced across to see Michael O'Reilly dancing with Keren Trenlow. Carter followed her gaze and sighed.

"He'll need to watch himself there as well," he said. "That lass is not available for a tumble in the straw at the moment, and..."

"Neither was I!" his companion said sharply and he stopped suddenly and drew her out of the dance, still holding her hand and drew her over to the shadows beside the first hut.

"Teresa, that was not what I meant. I've been watching him turning it on with you since the retreat from Talavera, but I know very well it's not gone beyond flirting."

"What makes you so sure?" Teresa said, looking up at him. Carter looked down into her eyes.

"Because you're picky," he said. "And you're bright. And Michael O'Reilly – who by the way is a friend of mine – has eyes for only one lassie, although he's very willing to make use of a whole host of others since he can't have her. I think you've more value for yourself than that. Am I right?"

The Spanish girl studied him for a long time. Then she said:

"Yes. So what are you looking for, Sergeant?"

Carter did not look away. "You," he said evenly. "Surprised you've not noticed before."

"I've noticed. But I wasn't sure that it was any more than..."

"It is."

Suddenly, unexpectedly, she stepped forward and reached up to kiss him. Carter took her into his arms and drew her closer. He had thought about this for so long but he had not realised that she was ready for him. Gently he parted her lips under his and felt her shiver in his arms.

"Danny," she whispered, and he moved his mouth to the soft skin of her neck, his hands sliding down her body. "Oh God..."

"I'm very tempted, Teresa," he said, laughing softly against her skin. "But do you know what, lass? I'm not going to tonight. You've had more wine that you're used to and so have I. I'm not having you waking up next to me wondering what you just did. We'll wait until you're stone cold sober and I'll make very sure you know why you did what you did. Although I'm not saying no to this in the meantime. Kiss me again."

She pressed herself against him, laughing softly. "Danny Carter, you're more of a gentleman than most of the officers who claim to be so," she whispered. "I'll wait, if that's what you want. Just don't make me wait too long."

"I won't," he said huskily, and kissed her again.

They stood, finally, in the shadows watching the dancers. Her back was against him, her head reaching just to his chin, and in the cover of darkness he slid his hand to her breast, stroking her through the muslin of her gown. She leaned back against him with a little murmur of pleasure. "That feels so good."

"It does, lass." Carter laughed suddenly. "Looks like the colonel has noticed what Mr O'Reilly is up to."

She laughed with him, watching as Colonel van Daan cut in on his lieutenant's dance with Keren Trenlow, and sweep the embarrassed girl into the dance. O'Reilly was laughing, and went to take the hand of his colonel's wife. They watched in silence as the couple danced.

"Does she know?" Carter asked suddenly.

Teresa nodded. "She knows. She is very different with him to the way she is with you. Or some of the others. You all look at her with desire sometimes and she is used to that. But she is more careful with Michael. Him, she could hurt."

He nodded. "Poor bastard. Of all the lassies in the world to fall in love with, he had to choose her. I wonder if the colonel realises it."

"He doesn't miss very much. Danny..."

"Yes, lass?"

"This is not fair," Teresa said quietly. "You need to either stop what you are doing or take me somewhere we are not going to be disturbed. Because I cannot..."

He laughed softly. "Have you made up your mind, then, lass?"

She turned into his arms, her mouth on his. "Yes," she whispered. "I'm not going to regret this."

"Let's get out of here then," he said.

The evening went on and turned into night and gradually the cooking fires died down and the men began to straggle in ones and twos towards their bunks. Paul set his cup down. His wife was still dancing. Michael touched him on the shoulder. "Go on," he said gently. "You've waited long enough, so you have. I'll see all safe here and I've got the watch."

Paul turned to smile at him, and Grey saw, like a tangible thing, the bonds of friendship and understanding between the two men. And then Paul turned and walked down onto the parade ground, and Michael O'Reilly was laughing. "She really asked for this," he said.

Colonel van Daan approached his wife and in front of his regiment he picked her up into his arms. She gave a startled gasp and then looked up at him and began to laugh. Paul bent to kiss her and walked with her across the parade ground. Somebody began to cheer and then they were all cheering, drunk and raucous, and the girl was blushing, but with no shame, Grey realised, as the colonel carried her through the door to his quarters, kicking it shut with a bang. He had never seen anything like it before and despite Corrigan's assurances he could not avoid feeling guilty at the fierce stab of envy he felt towards the man he had come to admire so much.

"And you know, I've known the two of them almost from the first," the Irishman said. "And I still don't know how much of that was pure theatre and how much of it was that he just couldn't keep his hands off her a moment longer." He sighed. "Let's get them settled down, then, Mr Grey, and then off to your bed. No early morning call for them tomorrow, although I might call you when I need a nap."

"You're staying up?"

"God love you, somebody has to do guard duty and make sure no fool burns the place down, and I doubt any of these are up to the job."

"I'll stay up with you."

Grey and O'Reilly turned. Manson shrugged. "I've not drunk that much. I'll be fine."

"I'd appreciate it," Michael said. "Come on then, let's get the last of these drunken bastards to their bunks."

In the commander's bedroom, Paul van Daan lay with his wife in a tangle of bedsheets, trying to catch his breath. Beside him she was quiet and still after the storm of passion, and he pushed himself up onto one elbow and looked down at her. She was naked with her black hair tumbled about her shoulders and her eyes still dreamy with pleasure and he felt an ache of awareness of how much he loved her.

"I wonder if I am ever going to learn to take you for granted?" he said softly.

Anne smiled. "You're showing no sign of losing interest, Colonel, so I'm hopeful."

He bent to kiss her. "Hush. I love you more than I can possibly tell you, even if I am painfully aware that most of the men in barracks are going to spend this night dreaming about you! On the day I met you I told you that you were a flirt and you haven't changed at all. Except that now you have a few hundred men to flirt with."

She reached up to touch his face. "I only want you," she said.

"I know it, love. And I you."

She gave a slight smile. "You're not looking so tired, Colonel."

"I'm not even close to being tired, lass, and after this evening's performance you'd better damned well not be," Paul said with a grim smile. "They've all enjoyed you very much out there. Now it's my turn."

Anne laughed and pulled him down to her.

It was cold and clear, and the smell of wood smoke and roasted meat hung in the air as Lionel Manson paced the perimeter of the barracks. He saw Lieutenant O'Reilly coming towards him and raised a weary grin.

"Give it another hour and I'll rouse Grey and Carter and we'll go to our beds," O'Reilly said.

"I'm fine."

The Irishman eyed him. "Aye, you look it," he said. "It was a good night."

Manson laughed. "I can't imagine my father dancing a jig with the men from his regiment. Or even speaking to them that much."

O'Reilly did not speak for a moment. Then he said:

"Would you take a piece of advice from a man who came up from the ranks, Mr Manson?"

"I'll listen to it."

"Good man. Don't try to be like anyone. There will come moments, somewhere along the way, when you'll know who you are. Just listen to them." Michael studied him. "Danny Carter told me about the incident with Mr Chapman."

"Did he?" Manson said, startled. "I wondered if Chapman would complain to be honest. One more screw up and I suspect the Colonel is going to tell me to sell out or be kicked out."

Michael shook his head slightly. "Mr Manson, if that had been Paul he'd probably have tipped that barrel over the little shit's head. Carter was still laughing when he told me. What he said was that it was a pity you didn't deal with the 112th the same way you dealt with Lieutenant Chapman. I wish I'd heard it, it takes an impressive mouth to rouse Danny Carter to enthusiasm." He looked beyond Manson and grinned suddenly. "Officer approaching," he said, and to his astonishment Manson saw Colonel Paul van Daan, fully dressed, approaching them. He sprang to attention.

"At ease, gentlemen."

"You're up early, sir," O'Reilly said. "Good sleep?"

Paul shot him a grin and shook his head. "Go to bed and don't piss me off, O'Reilly."

"Yes, sir."

Into the silence after his departure Paul said:

"You volunteered to stay up with Michael?"

"Yes, sir."

"Tired?"

Manson laughed. "Not sure, sir."

"Me either. I'm either going to be fine or I'm going to have a really bad day."

"Be grateful if you'd let me know which when you work it out, sir," Manson said and his commander gave a choke of laughter. He studied Manson for a long time. Finally he said:

"I was absolutely convinced at the beginning that I was never going to be able to work with you."

"Me too, sir." Manson said.

"I have reconsidered," Paul said quietly. "Go to bed, Mr Manson. Goodnight."

Chapter Seven

Over the following weeks as Paul finally began to send supply trains up to Wellington's lines, he watched Lieutenant Manson with growing appreciation. His wife had been right and in his anger at the stupid waste of Private Barker's life he had failed to notice that despite the enormity of Manson's mistake, there was a lot about the boy that he respected.

Surprisingly Manson seemed to have developed a rapport with Paul's two senior NCOs from the light company. He had heard Carter laughingly telling the story of the hapless Mr Chapman, but something about the occasion had caused the prickly Carter to let down his guard, and the light company gave Manson no further trouble as a result. The same was not true of the 112th and Paul watched in frustrated sympathy as Manson tried to find a way to get the best out of his recalcitrant men.

He had received word that transports with the rest of his reinforcements and the final two companies of the 110th first battalion were due any day and he had hoped that by then he could leave the 112th to Corrigan and the two lieutenants and deal with whatever officers arrived with the new men. He was aware that he was desperately short of officers, and while it was manageable in barracks, it was going to expose him when back in the field. Reluctantly he admitted that he might need to speak to Wellington about finding him some new juniors, although he hated taking on officers he did not know at any level above ensign or possibly lieutenant. In a month or so he would have finished his work on the supplies and would be ready to march his men north to join Wellington for the new campaigning season and he needed to be able to concentrate for the last month on the new recruits.

After a full afternoon of training, Paul was hot and tired and thinking with some longing of a drink and a meal. Michael was working with him and the light company, and Corrigan and Grey were busy with the company of 110th recruits. Manson was working with his NCOs and the 112th on close order drills and it was not going well.

Paul looked up, aware of a disturbance in the lines of the 112th and glanced across. Manson was trying to run the drill again. The men were moving in square, but slowly and raggedly, moving reluctantly. Michael O'Reilly glanced across at him.

"Idle bastards, sir. Want me to go over there?"

"No."

O'Reilly smiled slightly. "You're bloody hard on him, sir."

"I'm not. Believe it or not, I'm trying to help."

"Bollocks, sir. If that was Grey you'd help him out."

"I would. But he's not Grey."

"Give him a break. He's trying really hard."

"I know he is, Michael. Will you just trust me?"

"I always do, sir. But it's painful to watch this."

"Only another half an hour," Paul said with a grin.

He was aware of the steady tones of Manson's voice in the background as he finished his own drill and lined up his men. He said a few words and dismissed them. It was growing cooler. Manson had got his eight companies into line. Paul glanced across. "Done, Mr Manson?" he asked quietly.

Manson turned to look at him. His hazel eyes were stony and his face was expressionless.

"Not yet, sir."

Paul studied him for a long moment. Then he nodded. "Carry on then," he said neutrally.

He jerked his head to Michael and they walked over to the officers' quarters. Inside Michael glanced at his commander. "Sir?"

"Leave him alone, Mr O'Reilly. Get changed, I'll see you in the mess."

Michael nodded. Paul went up to his room and found his wife sitting before her mirror brushing her hair. She smiled at him, and then lifted her eyebrows. "What is it?"

He beckoned and she got up and walked to the window. They stood together watching the 112th on the parade ground. After a few moments, Anne said:

"What do you think?"

"I think Mr Manson has just lost his temper," Paul said quietly.

She glanced at him. "Really? I can just see him running drill."

Paul took out his watch and looked at it. "Yes. I'm going to get changed. Let's get dinner."

"You're not waiting for him?"

"I'm not expecting to see him for dinner," Paul said.

The atmosphere in the mess was slightly strained. Conversation flowed, but Paul was conscious that all of them were listening to the sounds coming from the parade ground. Manson's voice was clear and steady, repeating his instructions over and over again. Darkness fell and Sergeant Kelly lit lamps and candles. Across the table Paul watched his wife, beautiful in a gown of midnight blue silk. She was talking to Will Grey, telling him some story, which was making him laugh. The other officers were listening, drawn into the enchanted atmosphere she created. He thought how quickly the 110th had become accustomed to Anne being part of their mealtimes and he knew it would never have occurred to any of them to want her excluded. They had created their own rules and she was a part of them.

Gradually the other officers drifted away, leaving only Paul and Anne. Paul got up, finally, glancing at his watch. It was almost midnight. He walked over to the window and stood watching. It was completely dark on the parade ground, but there was a faint light from the partial moon, which glinted off belt and buckle. Across the ground he heard Manson's voice.

"One more time, sergeant."

Anne came to stand beside him. The companies moved into line and then back into square as one man. Their footsteps echoed into the darkness, as one. Not a man moved out of place. Paul glanced at his watch again.

"How long?" Anne asked.

"Seven hours."

"They seem to have improved. How on earth can they see what they're doing in the dark."

"They can't. But they're still doing it."

Anne glanced sideways at her husband. "Is this what you've been waiting for, Paul?"

He nodded, his eyes still straining through the dark, watching the drill. "He had to do this himself, Nan. Partly because of what happened at the beginning. Grey is different. He's young and unsure but they expect that in an officer, they'll cut him some slack and let him grow into the role. Manson doesn't have that luxury; they know bloody well he's capable of throwing his weight around. Now they need to see what he will and won't put up with and they need to know he's not going to take the easy way out again."

"This doesn't seem like the easy way out," Anne said.

"No. He's a worker. But it's more than that. He's got something…I can't describe it."

Anne regarded him in amusement. "You don't need to, love."

"No. You saw it before I did. Michael thinks I'm too hard on him, but he needed to do this. Not for my sake, I'm already convinced. But for his sake. And he needed to come to it on his own."

"Sergeant," Manson called. "Into line, please."

The 112th moved smoothly into position and Manson surveyed them through the darkness. His voice echoed eerily across the parade ground. "Better," he said. "You're working together now but I've still seen garden slugs move faster than you. We'll try it again in the morning. Let's see if we can finish before dark tomorrow, shall we? Because if you don't start working your lazy arses, I'm warning you I'm prepared to do this every bloody night until we march to join Wellington. Your choice. Dismiss!"

He walked across to the mess building, which was lit only by lamps. "Sir. Thought you'd be asleep."

"Would have been, Lieutenant, but some noisy bastard kept me awake drilling half the night," Paul said mildly. "Drink?"

Manson nodded. He looked exhausted. Anne went to kiss her husband, smiled at Manson and left. Paul watched her go, thinking appreciatively that her sense of timing was impeccable. He sat down and poured two glasses of wine, pushing one towards Manson. The door to the kitchen opened and George Kelly emerged with a tray, which he set down before Manson. "Eat it while it's hot, sir," he said.

Manson grinned tiredly and reached for the bowl. "Thanks, George. Hardly worth going to sleep," he said, beginning to eat.

"I'll take the early drill with them," Paul said quietly.

"Thank you, sir. But no. I need to be standing out there waiting for them looking at my watch. Even though I'll probably be too tired to read it."

Paul felt a little rush of pleasure at the response. He smiled. "You're right, Mr Manson. In fact I'm staying out of it. They're yours. You know them, you know what they need. Work out your own training plan with Grey. Ask me if you need anything."

"Lieutenant O'Reilly..."

"He's got enough on his hands with the new recruits for the 110th, and we've got our two extra companies coming in next week. I'm leaving the 112th to you."

"Thank you, sir. I'll try not to let you down."

"I'm not worried about that, Leo. Finish that wine, it'll help you get off to sleep quickly."

"Don't think I'll struggle with that, sir. Thanks for waiting up."

"It was a privilege to watch, Mr Manson. What's your feeling about your sergeants?"

"Williams is a good man, lazy but he knows what he's doing. Bryan is a troublemaker. If it were up to me I'd demote him and bring up young Cranston. Talbot and Devlin aren't bad, I think they might improve without Bryan there to stir them up."

"Do it in the morning."

"Thank you, sir." Manson finished his meal and drained the glass. "Permission to..."

"Go to bed, Leo. I'll see you in the morning. Don't worry, I'll make sure you don't oversleep."

"Thank you, sir."

Paul walked out onto the dark parade ground with him and over towards the officers block. "Leo?"

"Sir?"

"I don't know if you ever put in that request for a transfer, but if you did, you need to know I'm refusing it when it comes through. You want to leave, you'll need to sell out."

Manson laughed. "Or get myself killed in my first battle, sir."

"Don't you bloody dare, Mr Manson, it will piss me off!" Paul said. "Good night."

During the following week Paul worked frantically to complete the supply requisitions before the arrival of his remaining troops. He had not hated his time in Lisbon, and he was aware of the amount that he had learned about the complex business of supplying an army in the field, but he was tired of the long hours of paperwork and he was missing being in the field with the rest of the regiment. He was ruefully aware that both the quartermasters and the commissariat in Lisbon were longing to see the back of him with his incessant demands and meticulous insistence on accuracy and perfection and would be even happier to see the back of Anne who was just as bad. Both Carl and Johnny were good correspondents and had kept him up to date with the news but he was ready to return. There were rumours that Massena was finally on the move and Wellington was keen to try to cut him off from his retreat back into Spain.

He was in his office when a knock on the door announced the arrival of Michael.

"Transports just landed, sir. The rest of our reinforcements plus the seventh and eighth companies."

"Ah. They off yet?"

"No, it'll take them a while. You want me to go down there?"

"Please. Take Corrigan, Grey and Manson with you. What's that?"

"Letters, sir, off the packet. The messenger brought them." Michael handed them to his commander. "You worried?"

"Not exactly. A few weeks ago I might have been more concerned, but it's going well. I'm especially pleased with the new lads."

"You're especially pleased with Leo bloody Manson, sir," Michael said with a grin. "I look at him and I see a very strong resemblance to an arrogant little shit who walked in to my barracks in Melton eight years ago and took over."

Paul laughed. "I never flogged anybody, Michael."

"Only because you happen to know what it feels like. But you nearly killed Rory Stewart on that parade ground at the end of week two."

"I nearly killed you that day, Michael, although you might not realise it!"

His friend laughed. "I do now. Didn't know at the time how close I came, I didn't know your temper back then. Anything interesting?"

Paul was reading the letter. "It's from Johnstone," he said.

"Really? How is he?"

"He says the fever seems to have gone finally but he's still very invalidish. Sounds happier than the last few letters I've had from him, though, I think it's a relief to have handed over the responsibility. He's become a grandfather again. And…oh."

"What is it?" Michael asked curiously.

"Captain Longford. It appears he's bringing a wife with him."

"I didn't know Longford was married."

"It's very recent," Paul said, still reading. Johnstone apologises for giving him permission to marry without checking with me first, but it seems that there was reason for haste."

"Bloody hell. So is she bringing the brat?"

"No, she miscarried soon after the wedding. Poor lass. I feel sorry for anybody married to Longford, let alone in those circumstances."

"Irresponsible bastard," Michael said, and then stopped. Paul laughed aloud.

"That's all right, Michael. You will notice I did not call him names over that one, I was just as irresponsible with Rowena. And at least he's married her."

"Yes. Somehow I never got the impression Longford was much of a ladies man."

"He wasn't when I knew him, but that was a long time ago. And I'm aware I'm judging him unfairly, he might be genuinely attached to the woman. Will you let Browning know to make sure that Captain Longford is allocated extra space, Michael?"

An Irregular Regiment

"I will, sir. Be strange to have another officer's wife around. I wonder how she'll cope with Nan?"

"I'm more interested to see how Longford will. I wish he'd managed to transfer out. I wonder why he didn't."

"Probably because word has got round that he's bloody useless, sir. Who is in charge of the eighth?"

"Man called Kerr, transferred in from one of the border regiments about three months ago for promotion. I know nothing about him, but at least he won't have been around Longford for too long which is good. We've got about a month to get this lot up to scratch so it's going to be hard work."

"I'll be off then, sir. See you later."

Michael found that the troops had disembarked as he arrived at the dock. Their officers had lined them up beside the gangplank. Even at a distance he recognised Longford. He was standing in a small group with five other officers, a Captain and four lieutenants. Michael glanced around at his companions.

"Best come and be introduced, gentlemen."

He led to way to the group, and saluted. "Gentlemen, welcome to Lisbon. Hope you've not been waiting long."

Captain Longford stared. "Christ, I remember you!" he said. "That bloody insolent Irish sergeant from the light company! What the hell are you doing in an officer's uniform?"

"Captain Longford, I remember you too," Michael said keeping his voice pleasant. "Field promotion, sir, to lieutenant in the light company. Recently approved by Horse Guards. And Mr Zouch, good to see you again too. Let me introduce you. This is Captain Corrigan, and Lieutenants Grey and Manson. They're with the 112th, serving with us now. This is Captain Longford who commands the seventh company of the 110th and Lieutenant Zouch, gentlemen."

Longford snorted. "This is Kerr, in charge of the eighth. Lieutenants Lloyd and Heron serve under him and Lieutenant Fenwick serves with me." He looked back at Michael. "Gentlemen, I'd heard Wellington was desperate for officers but it's worse than I thought if he's promoting scum like O'Reilly from the ranks.

Although I suppose you're still sucking up to Paul van Daan which will have helped."

Michael gave a small grim smile. Before he had time to speak, he heard Lieutenant Manson's clear tones.

"Sorry, sir, would that be Colonel van Daan you meant? I'm new as well, might be confused."

Michael glanced around at him with a grin. "All right, Mr Manson. Go and get the spare horses will you? These officers mounts won't be fit to carry them for a day or two and we can't have them getting sore feet on the journey up to barracks." He became aware of the woman suddenly, standing to one side. "Captain Longford, would this be your wife?"

Longford glanced across indifferently. "Yes. Been ill on the voyage. Don't know if she's up to riding, but she'll have to be if there's no carriage..."

"I can ride," the woman said quietly. Michael moved forward.

"Mrs van Daan sent her spare horse down for you, ma'am, she's a gentle thing. But if you need a carriage, we can arrange one..."

"No, really. The fresh air will do me good."

"Have you no maid with you?" Michael said.

"No."

"No matter, it's a short journey and then the colonel's wife will take care of you."

"I'd forgotten he married that blonde filly, didn't he – Carleton's niece," Longford said. "And in a big hurry too, from what I remember. She out here, then?"

Michael was watching Manson and Grey supervising the leading of the spare horses. "I'm afraid the first Mrs van Daan died, sir, bearing her second child. A little girl, she's at Southwinds now with the family. The Colonel remarried fairly recently, a young widow. You'll meet his lady soon enough."

"I'll try not to be a trouble," Mrs Longford said quietly. Michael looked at her and saw that she had coloured deeply at her husband's tactless reference to the circumstances of Paul's first marriage. Longford did not appear to notice but one of his Lieutenants came forward.

"Are you all right, ma'am? We'll be there soon and you can rest."

Mrs Longford smiled at him. "I'm fine, Mr Fenwick. But thank you."

She moved to join her husband and Michael glanced at Fenwick. He was older than the other juniors, tall and fair with bright blue eyes and a humorous mouth. "She had a bad voyage?" he asked.

Fenwick's eyes were on the woman. "She just married my captain. So far she's had a bad year," he said and Michael gave a choke of laughter.

"Mr Fenwick, you should probably try for a little discretion when you speak to an officer you don't know," he said.

Fenwick glanced at him. "Mr O'Reilly, given the way he just spoke to you, I'm not sure you're likely to care. Anyway, it's not like I need to worry about him blocking my promotion, is it?"

Michael put a hand on his shoulder. He felt an immediate and instinctive liking for Fenwick. "I'm guessing that's why you're still where you are, lad," he said. "I wouldn't worry. Doesn't matter how broke you are out here, if you're any good you will get what you deserve eventually."

Fenwick shot him a sharp glance and then smiled. "I was hoping that," he admitted. "I've been stuck under that bastard for years because I don't choose to kiss his backside every time he wants."

As the officers mounted, Manson moved to speak to the NCOs in charge of the troops. Michael watched him with some amusement. The boy seemed to have acquired the habit of taking control of any situation, which Michael remembered in his commander from the first. It looked like arrogance, but it was not intended that way he knew. Part way through issuing instructions Manson remembered and turned to look at Michael. Michael grinned and nodded, and relieved, the boy carried on.

On their way to the barracks, Michael took the opportunity to observe the other new officers. Captain Kerr was fairly young and probably newly promoted, a wiry red haired borderer with amused green eyes. He said little but gave the impression of taking things in. His lieutenant, Heron, was slight, probably close to Manson's age.

Lloyd was a stocky dark Welshman who looked as though he would be good in a fight. George Zouch he remembered well from Melton many years ago. He was surprised to see that he was still a lieutenant and was fairly sure that a promotion was on the cards once he was back in Paul's orbit. He had always liked Zouch. None of them had much to say during the ride. Corrigan took the lead in explaining about the barracks, and listing the troops there. Michael dropped back beside Mrs Longford.

"How are you doing, ma'am? Rough crossing?"

"Yes. I've not been well anyway."

Michael studied her. She was fair-haired and blue eyed, a slender woman whom he would guess to be in her early to mid twenties. She looked as though she had been unwell, but she was still a very pretty woman. She also looked desperately unhappy and he could imagine why. If Longford had been pressured into marrying her because she was pregnant only to have her miscarry he was unlikely to be a gentleman about it.

He glanced at her again and remembered his commander's first wife, another blonde, when she had joined the light company on the transport to Naples many years ago, sick and frightened and bitterly ashamed that every man there knew she had married because she was with child. Michael was aware that Paul's fellow officers, especially Johnny, had been deeply concerned for Rowena Summers.

He had seen a new side to his arrogant young commander during those early weeks of marriage. Paul had treated his shy wife with a gentle affectionate respect, which had set the tone for both officers and men around him. No matter how busy he was or how difficult his situation, he had never become impatient or irritable with her. Never once had he referred to the circumstances of their hasty marriage, and he had given the impression that marrying her had been a privilege and a joy. Michael had watched her thaw and then melt under the onslaught of his commander's steady charm. Within two weeks she was smiling and within a month he heard her laughing with Paul. A year later he was aware that very few people even remembered that Rowena had been pregnant when she married Paul, and despite his infidelities, they were considered by other officers to be an unusually affectionate couple, who managed the difficulties of army life better than most.

Captain Longford had barely looked at his young wife. Michael looked ahead at Longford's indifferent back and thought how much he would like to punch him.

"Not far now," he said quietly to the girl, and she gave a wan smile.

"I am not usually this feeble, Mr O'Reilly."

"It's not feeble, ma'am. Half our lads get sea sick, and I'll bet they make more fuss about it than you do."

As they rode through the barrack gates, Michael observed Sergeant Carter and Corporal Hammond putting the 112th through bayonet training. Carter's voice bellowed across the parade ground and the new officers heads turned. Standing on the far side, Colonel van Daan was watching the exercise intently. He looked up at the sound of arrival.

"All right, Sergeant, thank you. That will do for now. Stand them down and we'll have a look at our new recruits."

Carter gave the order, and Michael reined in and dismounted. Paul walked forward. "Mr O'Reilly. Will you get the new men lined up on the parade ground, please, and I'll let you know where to allocate them."

The officers were dismounting. At the back, Mrs Longford hung back uncertainly, and Michael shot a look at her husband who continued to ignore her, and began to move forward but his colonel was quicker. He reached up and lifted her down, and stood looking down at her with some surprise.

"But I know you, don't I? Were you not Miss Mason?"

Mrs Longford smiled for the first time, confirming Michael's suspicion that under normal circumstances she would be a very pretty woman. "Yes, but I cannot believe you remember that, Colonel. It was so long ago and for about fifteen minutes."

"You've a memorable face, ma'am." Paul raised her hand to his lips. "Welcome to Portugal – and to your father's regiment. I had hoped that my wife would be here to welcome you but she's out chasing up a consignment of missing boots and has obviously been delayed." He glanced across at Lieutenant Zouch. "George, I am delighted to see you again."

"You too, sir." Zouch was grinning. "You've come a long way since Melton. Congratulations."

Paul turned to the other officers, who saluted. "Welcome to Lisbon, gentlemen. I'll have my officers get the men settled and you can go to your quarters. The baggage wagon will be here at any moment. I don't know if any of you have brought your own orderlies, but if not I'll get a couple of my lads to help you unpack and get settled in. Nothing formal today, we'll have a chance to talk over dinner and in the morning I've called a meeting with all my officers after early drill and we'll go over my requirements then. After that, Sergeant Carter will hold a meeting with all the NCOs to make sure they are up to scratch. Most of the new recruits will be for my first and third companies, which are up at the lines, but we'll start training them all together as a reserve company for now, as we've done with the previous lot and I'll appoint NCOs from my existing men."

He looked across at Carter who had cleared the parade ground. "Line them up, Sergeant, and get them allocated. Corporal, you have my lists?"

"Yes, sir."

"Carry on then. Oh and Carter."

"Sir."

"Keep an eye out for anyone likely, will you. The light company is pretty much up to strength, but if you see anybody you like the look of we could do with another half a dozen."

"Yes, sir."

Paul grinned across at Lieutenant Manson. "I've got my eye on one or two from Mr Manson's companies, but he's making an awful fuss about it..."

"If you pinch my best men after the work I've put in to them, sir, you'll hear me make a fuss!" Manson said.

"Wellington would probably hear it, Leo, with the mouth on you," Paul said with a laugh. "Carry on. Ah, Jenson. Wondered when you'd turn up. Where's Browning?"

"Just finishing up, sir."

"Good. Would you show the new officers to their quarters, please? Make sure they have everything they need."

"Yes, sir."

"One more thing, by the way." Paul glanced at Caroline Longford. "Traditionally I am aware that ladies do not dine in the officers mess. In the 110th we work slightly differently and my wife joins us for meals – she has been the only lady in barracks so far. She doesn't outstay her welcome, there will be plenty of opportunity to be as rowdy as you like. Mrs Longford, we would be delighted if you would join us too. If you prefer not to, you can have meals in your sitting room of course, with your husband. Decide it between you and let Sergeant Kelly know."

"Bloody stupid idea!" Longford scoffed. "Whoever heard of women in the mess? Can't believe Wellington allows that!"

"Perhaps not in his own mess, Captain, but I can assure you he would be very disappointed to come to mine and find my wife absent, he's very attached to her. You can ask him when you meet him. Remind me to be present." Paul's voice was chilled. "Jenson, would you escort Mrs Longford to her quarters for me, she looks tired. Ma'am, I'll send up my wife's maid and she'll get you unpacked. Jenson, will you see to it? And ask George to send up some tea, will you? Captain, will you join me in my office for a drink please? I'll speak to all of you individually at some point today."

He led the way through into his office. Longford followed him. Paul closed the door and retrieved a brandy bottle and two cups from the cupboard. When he turned, Longford was sitting down leaning back on the chair with his foot on the edge of the desk. Paul placed the bottle and two cups on the table, moved forward, lifted his foot and placed in on the back of Longford's chair. He pushed hard and the chair fell with a crash tipping the man onto the floor with a yell.

"Get to your feet, pick up the chair, and let's try this again," he said quietly.

Longford obeyed, his dark eyes furious. Paul sat down behind his desk and watched as the man stood to attention and saluted. He nodded.

"Sit down," he said. Longford sat, and Paul reached for the bottle and poured two drinks. He pushed one towards the Captain.

"That's better. Have a drink. Welcome to the regiment. At least the part of it that does any work. I am very surprised to see you here, Longford, I thought you'd have been out of here by now! Couldn't you get a transfer?"

"No – sir."

"I wonder why? I suppose it's been a few years, word must have got around. Still, in your position, I think I'd have sold out before turning up here with me in command. I've got a long memory."

"Yes, sir."

"Are you planning on it?"

"No, sir. Not all of us can afford what you can – sir."

"Longford, if you don't change your tone I'm going to kick you off that chair again. Well if you're staying we need to discuss a few rules. You're an officer of the 110th, God help us, and you need to keep your head down, learn your trade and try not to be an arsehole. And I know that is going to be difficult for you. I know all about you, you were a bully and a brute and I'll just bet that I find that morale is low and training appalling in the seventh company. We can fix that, but you're serving under me now which means you don't get to sit on your arse and do nothing. You don't bully the men and you don't flog anybody. I'll go over my views on discipline in the general meeting tomorrow, but I just wanted to make it clear that you will not get away with any of your crap in my regiment. You lay a hand on one of my lads without good reason, and I will beat the living shit out of you in front of the entire regiment. And if you can't accept that, make other plans."

"Sir."

"That's better. And while we're on the subject, you should know that I received a letter from Colonel Johnstone on the subject of your marriage. He thought I should know."

"Sir – my marriage is my own affair."

"It actually is. And given the circumstances in which I married my first wife, which you know very well, I am in no position to lecture you. I'm sorry you lost the child. It must be hard for both of you."

"If I'd known I wouldn't have married her."

"I'm assuming this wasn't a love match, then. But please be clear that I will be keeping an eye on you with her, and I'll expect to see you treating her with respect. Every other man in this regiment will." Paul picked up his cup and drank. "I don't like you, Longford, and I don't want you here. But I've thought that before, quite recently, and been proved wrong. If I see you working and trying to fit in, I'll give you the benefit of the doubt. But if I see you causing problems, I'll remember that you sent a man from your company to try to slit my throat all those years ago, and I will bury you, I promise. Now piss off and give it some thought. I'll see you at dinner."

Longford stood up and went to the door. As he opened it, he stood back, an expression of surprise crossing his face.

"Ma'am."

Paul rose. "Ah. Come in, Nan, and be introduced. Captain Longford has just arrived. He commands the seventh company. Captain, this is my wife Anne."

Anne held out her hand. "Captain, welcome to Lisbon. I understand your wife is with you."

"Yes, ma'am."

"I look forward to meeting her." Anne glanced across at her husband. "Paul, the boots will be on the next transport. I'm going to speak to George about dinner tonight. I'm assuming your wife will be joining us, Captain."

"Yes. Yes, ma'am. She'd be delighted."

"Excellent. I won't stay, but if I may I'll come up and introduce myself in half an hour."

"I'll tell her, ma'am."

Anne smiled and left. Longford stood staring after her. "By God, Van Daan!"

"It's Colonel, Longford. Or Sir. I don't mind which. But I take your point."

"Where did you find her?"

Paul smiled slightly. "Nan was married to an officer from the quartermasters department. He was killed. We married fairly soon afterwards."

"I don't blame you! You couldn't let her get away!" Longford said frankly. "Christ, your first wife was a pretty little thing, but this one..."

"Don't get carried away, Captain, you might piss me off again. But she is very lovely, I agree. She's also slightly unusual, but you'll learn that as we go along. And just in case you find yourself expressing your appreciation in somewhat broader terms at any point, I suggest you don't do it anywhere near any of my other officers. Or indeed my light company. They're very protective of her and you'll get hurt."

Longford looked at him. "It's a death sentence to strike an officer, Colonel."

"It is. But they probably wouldn't do it in front of witnesses. I'm just trying to keep you safe, Captain. Best go and see how your wife is doing. I'll see you both at dinner."

In honour of the new arrivals Anne had arranged a more formal meal that evening. Having confirmed arrangements with Sergeant Kelly she took herself off to the apartments allocated to Captain Longford and found Mrs Longford drinking tea while Teresa completed her unpacking.

"Welcome to Lisbon, Mrs Longford."

Caroline Longford came forward. "Thank you. And thank you for so much help." She indicated the tea and Teresa with a sweep of her hand.

"Think nothing of it, I remember when I first arrived feeling completely bewildered for a week or two. How are you, Michael said you've not been well?"

"I was ill aboard ship. And shortly before that I...I lost a child."

"I'm sorry, that must be very hard," Anne said quietly.

"Do you have children, ma'am?"

"No, although Paul has three from his first marriage. They are in England with his family. I travel with him out here, which makes it impractical to have them with us. In fact I've not even met the older two, we've been married less than six months. But I was married to another officer before, so the life isn't new to me."

Caroline studied her. "You don't look old enough," she said.

"I was not quite eighteen when I married for the first time. It wasn't a big success. Paul tells me your father was his first Captain."

Caroline smiled. "Yes. He came to visit me in Melton after Assaye to bring me my father's personal effects. He was so kind."

"And you married into the regiment. A daughter of the 110th and no mistake."

The other woman indicated that Anne should sit down. "I suppose so. I travelled with my father when I was young, but I was eleven when my mother died and he did not want me growing up in camp without her so I went to live with my aunt. I seldom saw him but he was a good correspondent."

"I remember Paul telling me that he hoped to do the same with his children. I rather suspect that if he is killed he wants them to have something of him to remember him by. You haven't been married long, there is plenty of time for other children."

"Yes. I...it is all so new."

Anne nodded. "Give it time," she said quietly. "I've been married twice. Paul and I...I'm not sure that many people have what we do. But my first marriage took work."

The door opened and Captain Longford entered. He saw Anne and bowed immediately. "Ma'am. Good of you to call." Anne saw his eyes flicker towards his wife.

"I came to see if your wife needed anything, sir. Will you be joining us for dinner, or would you rather be quiet this evening?"

"We'll be there, ma'am," Longford said.

Anne looked at his wife. "Caroline?" she asked quietly.

"Oh – yes. Thank you."

"Good. I'll see you then. We dress, but not too formally unless it's a special occasion. And please call me Nan, you'll feel out of place if you don't."

"Thank you."

Anne smiled impartially and left.

Letters from Wellington had given Paul instructions to re-join his regiment after Christmas in preparation for the new campaigning season, and with that in mind, and with most of the administrative work completed, Paul passed responsibility for the remainder over to his wife and Captain Corrigan, and set about bringing the seventh and eighth companies of the 110th and his second reserve company up to scratch. Over the years he had never had either of these two companies under his direct command. Colonel Johnstone, his predecessor, had chosen to keep the final two companies of the first battalion separate, and Paul knew that the main reason for this was his own antagonistic relationship with Captain Longford.

Longford had already been a Captain when Paul had joined the light company at the age of twenty one and been sent, almost immediately, to India. He had returned almost two years later, wounded and exhausted after the horrors of Assaye with a Captain's commission earned in the field from General Wellesley and a reputation for being an expert in training. Colonel Dixon, who had commanded the regiment had placed him in charge of training for the second battalion and the final two companies of the first battalion which had put Paul in the slightly difficult position of giving orders and instruction to a dozen men of his own rank who were older and longer serving than him. There had been a lot of resentment but over the months he had managed to win over all the other officers with the exception of Captain Vincent Longford, who on one occasion had sent a man from his company to attack Paul. Paul had never known if his instructions had been to kill or injure and had never really thought that it mattered. His own early promotion to Major had infuriated Longford and the new commander, Colonel Johnstone, had sent the seventh company to Ireland to keep Paul and Longford apart.

The relationship had not improved, although now that there was such a clear separation of rank it required less effort on Paul's part to manage it. He was aware very quickly, however, that among his fellow officers there was an immediate dislike of Longford. Michael and the other members of his light company were well aware of his history with the man, as was Anne, but he had said nothing to any of the others. He observed with weary irritation that within two weeks, Longford had managed to set up the backs of most of the other officers.

He was consistently rude to Michael O'Reilly, who treated him with a gentle courtesy, which made Paul want to laugh out loud. His remarks about the inferiority of the Irish were getting under the skin of Pat Corrigan, and he was scathing about all the new officers who were learning their trade. He seemed to have a difficult relationship with both of his Lieutenants, particularly Giles Fenwick and in the mess he was openly scornful about the unusual ethos of the 110th, comparing Paul's style of leadership unfavourably to that of Colonel Dixon and Colonel Johnstone in terms clearly designed to infuriate the other officers. And he had discovered with unerring accuracy that Lieutenant Manson was the must susceptible of the new officers to his persistent baiting.

As far as he could Paul kept the two of them apart. He was ruefully aware of how much of a headache it must have been for Colonel Johnstone over the years to find ways of keeping two of his officers at loggerheads from having to work together. He had not looked forward to Longford joining him, and he had every intention of getting rid of the man as soon as he was able, but he had not expected to feel so furiously protective of Leo Manson, who had just found his feet after several months of misery, and was now having to deal with persistent bullying from Captain Longford.

He was handling it well for such a young officer, better, Paul suspected, than he would have done himself at the same age. But it was taking its toll. For a short time Paul had a glimpse of Leo Manson coming out of his shell and he had liked what he saw. He had retreated back into silence again, and Paul was furious about it. None of it happened when he was within earshot and all he could do was watch and listen and work his companies as hard as he could. He gave Longford no opportunity to slack and he hoped that the relentless pace of life with the 110th would push the man into sending in his papers.

"I'm not optimistic," Anne said, getting ready for dinner in their room one evening. "I've been spending a lot of time with Caroline – who is lovely by the way - and I think money is a big problem. He lives on his pay, she's fairly sure he has debts and he has no other profession, he has always been in the army. She had a small amount of money put aside when they married and he's gone through that. I think this is literally all he has."

"Then it makes no sense why he doesn't just bloody well knuckle down and get better at it!" her husband said. "His company is clueless, and what they have learned over the years they've had from George Zouch. When I get back up to Wellington, I'm getting a promotion for him, it should have happened years ago. And Fenwick should be a Captain as well, he's very good, it's ridiculous he's still a lieutenant at his age! Johnstone was bloody lazy about that, he hated fighting with Horse Guards over promotions on merit, but I'm very willing to take them on!"

"You'll wear them down, Paul, you always do. And Wellington will support you."

"He'd better, the mess he dropped me into here. But with Zouch gone, we'll get a couple of new young ensigns for Longford to bully. And in the meantime he's clever enough to keep out of my sights and wind up Leo Manson until he blows and gets himself into trouble. It's how Longford has survived all these years. I'm watching that boy out there and he's practically running training for that battalion and he's getting better every day. And if I can't find a way to get bloody Longford off his back legitimately I'm going to shoot him and bury the body!"

Anne was laughing. "It's driving you mad, Paul. Calm down. It's Christmas next week, everybody will get a few days break and perhaps the seasonal cheer will improve Longford."

"Girl of my heart, a fucking bayonet up his arse is the only solution for Longford," Paul said feelingly, taking her into his arms.

"Come to dinner. In three weeks time I will be back with my regiment and hopefully if I have the opportunity to kill the French it will prevent me from murdering one of my officers."

Chapter Eight

The first battalion of the 110th was reunited at the end of January in their billet at the edge of Pere Negro. Paul had set Johnny Wheeler to finding accommodation for his extra men, and Wheeler had managed to obtain the use of an empty farm two miles further across. The barns and buildings were in poor repair having been badly damaged during the first French invasion several years ago, but he had set his companies to repairing them to give dry billets to his Portuguese battalions and the men of the 112th when they arrived. There was space for the officers at the convent, but Paul was only faintly surprised when Lieutenant Manson, during the last stage of their march, suggested that he and Grey find space in the deserted farmhouse.

"You can if you like, Mr Manson, but I don't know what condition it's in," Paul said.

"That's all right, sir. I got pretty good at cleaning duty during my early days with your regiment," Manson said straight-faced and Paul began to laugh.

"You're a cheeky bastard, Mr Manson. I'm not sure I noticed that to start with although I'm damned sure my wife did."

Manson smiled, something Paul wished he would do more. "Your wife is the reason I'm still here, sir," he said.

"I knew she was up to something. Good thing I've got her, I'd have made a thoroughgoing balls up and got rid of you."

Manson gave him a sideways glance. "I rather thought the balls up was mine, sir."

Paul studied the younger man. He was aware that he had a different relationship with his officers of long standing, to the one he maintained with younger and less experienced officers, but there was something about Leo Manson that blurred the boundaries. Impulsively, he said:

"Not wholly. I'm a bit odd about flogging, to be honest; it will have clouded my judgement. I should have asked you a lot more questions in those first weeks, found out why you did what you did.

I'm guessing my wife did that for me. I'm surprised she didn't tell me."

"I asked her not to. I wanted to work it out for myself. Probably stupid of me. But I'm impressed that she said nothing to you. She's a woman of her word."

Paul smiled. "She is. But honestly, Leo, the mistakes you made could have been made by any new officer with no guidance and no training and no experience of service overseas. I could kick Sym Armstrong's arse for him, he could have found something better to do than steal my recruits, and helped you to get your supply situation sorted out. And you couldn't possibly have known what those men would do."

"No. And you never said a word to me about that. But I thought it was my job not to show any weakness or admit to any mistakes. I was a bit of a twat, sir."

Paul laughed aloud. "You were in places. But you should see some of the cock-ups I've made over the years. I was luckier than you, had really good training at the start, and I already had two and a half years of experience in the navy, so I wasn't green at all."

"Navy?" Manson said, startled. "I didn't know that."

"I don't advertise it. It wasn't intentional; I got picked up by a press gang when I was fourteen. My father thought I'd gone down with his ship and I couldn't get anybody to believe who I was. No opportunity to write to him; you don't get shore leave as a pressed man. I was sixteen when I fought under Nelson at the Nile. And I was flogged. Fairly badly."

Manson said nothing for a while. Then he said:

"Jesus, sir, you must have wanted to punch me that day."

"I want to punch anybody who orders a flogging, Leo, including Lord Wellington. The army thinks I'm mad. But I seem to manage all right without it."

Manson glanced over at him. "Some nights I dream about him," he said abruptly. "Barker. The man I killed."

Paul did not speak for a moment. Then he said:

"Good. That means I'm not wrong about you."

Manson laughed. "You are nothing like my father," he said. "Thank you for telling me that, sir. And it won't go any further."

"You're welcome, Leo. And since I am not currently speaking to you as your commanding officer should, let me complete my indiscretions by telling you that I know exactly what bloody Longford is doing and I know that is why you don't want to join us at the convent. I'd prefer to stick him in that farmhouse especially if it's cold, damp and filthy. But I don't want him out of sight with your men."

"Neither do I, sir." Manson glanced at him. "I wish I knew what I'd done to piss him off."

"I never worked it out either all those years ago. I came back from Assaye into barracks. We were the same rank, but I was the youngest and newest of all the captains in barracks. I'd done well in India, caught Wellesley's attention, made Captain on merit very young. And I'd had some success with training the light company. Major Johnstone wrote to Colonel Dixon suggesting he put me in charge of training for all the companies in barracks at the time. I was twenty-three, and I was bloody good at managing my enlisted men – could get them to do anything for me. But exercising tact and diplomacy with my fellow officers was something I struggled with for years. And still do, to be honest. They all resented me, I was a young upstart with new fangled ideas and I was bloody arrogant. But gradually they all came round. All except Longford."

Manson looked at him steadily. "What did you do?"

"I made one of my fabled cock-ups. I lost my temper with him in the mess one day, very publicly. He was trying to wind me up, just as he is with you. I'm not sure what made me blow that day. Probably his reference to my daughter, Grace. I'd recently brought her back from India with me, it was a sensitive subject, I called her my ward but one glance at my girl tells anybody who her father is, she's the image of me. These days I don't even bother, just admit she's my daughter. Whatever caused it, I made a short and pointed speech about Longford and his shortcomings as a soldier in front of the whole mess. They all laughed a good deal. Later that evening I was on my way out and a man from his company jumped me and tried to cut my throat."

"Bloody hell, sir."

"You might say so. I was furious. But it wasn't his fault, Longford had threatened him and he was scared shitless. I had him transferred into the light company to get him out of Longford's way."

"You did what?"

Paul laughed. "I told you at the beginning I was eccentric. Danny Carter knew what he'd done and I think he had a hard time for a while. But he stayed. Back there in line now."

Manson laughed. "How did you solve it?"

"I didn't. Dixon and Johnstone worked hard at keeping us apart for years, which is why the seventh and eighth companies weren't with us in Portugal before as they should have been. I'd got a bit of a reputation for losing my temper and I think Johnstone thought if he put Longford and I in barracks together I'd end up killing him. I kept hoping he'd sell out. I was promoted over him which he bloody hated. But unless he does something concrete so that I can get him court martialled, or he transfers out, I'm stuck with him. I'll find a way or he'll slip up, no doubt about it. In the meantime he's got you in his sights. And I don't know why, unless he's worked out that it is getting to me. Or perhaps it is just that he can't stand to see somebody who is a lot better than he is ever going to be. But none of this helps you right now."

"Sir, all of this helps more than you can imagine," Manson said quietly. "I'm really grateful. I thought..."

"Well don't. If I've not said anything it's because I've not known what to say. I've thought about hauling him in and threatening him, but short of murder, which believe me I'm considering, I have to stick within army regulations and they allow officers like Longford to get away with being bullying bastards in the name of good discipline. When we're settled I'm going to talk to Wellington. Perhaps he knows of another regiment that really needs a captain and can be induced to take him. Eventually he'll be gone,

Leo, I promise you. In the meantime, try not to punch him and if you need to talk, both Nan and I are here."

Manson glanced over at Anne who was riding beside Caroline Longford. "Thank you, sir. One thing..."

"Yes."

"It's about Mrs van Daan. And Captain Longford."

"He isn't her type, Leo. If she leaves me it will be for General Craufurd or Lord Wellington, that is well established."

Manson laughed. "She isn't going to leave you, sir. She doesn't trust you to manage on your own."

"She's bloody right as well, isn't she?"

"Yes, sir. But I don't like the way he looks at her."

Paul stared at his junior. "Mr Manson, being married to Nan is a challenge, believe me. My entire regiment looks at her in a way that makes me want to punch them all the time. I am gradually learning to adjust."

"I know, sir. It's hard not to sometimes. But she's...she's so friendly, so comfortable with all the officers. And she's the same with him. She is literally the only person in barracks he is pleasant to, and that includes his own wife. But I'm not sure he gets the point with your wife. It's hard to explain – I've not that much experience, and - it's just that the way he looks at her is different to all the others."

Paul was silent, looking at the younger man with troubled eyes. Eventually he said:

"Thank you, Leo. I can hardly tell Nan to change who she is because there is an arsehole in camp. But I'll keep an eye on her."

They rode into camp in the late afternoon as the men were making their way back from training and other duties. Carl Swanson emerged from the convent and came forward, and Manson watched as Anne van Daan slid down into his arms and hugged him. Behind him other officers emerged, and as Carter and Lieutenant O'Reilly began to organise the men to their respective billets, Manson watched his commander's wife being greeted by her husband's officers. He had long since ceased to wonder at her unique position in the regiment.

"Mr Manson. Get your eyes off the Colonel's wife and attend to your men, sir. Christ, if I saw you look at my wife that way I'd be tempted to thrash you for it!"

Manson took a deep breath. "Yes, sir," he said evenly and turned away. Longford reached out his riding crop and held it across Manson's chest to stop him.

"Having a nice cosy chat with Colonel van Daan on the way here," he said. "What about?"

"Training, sir."

"Liar."

"No, sir. Permission to see to my men, sir? Can't leave it all to Mr Grey."

"Carry on, then. And watch your attitude, Manson. It'll get you into trouble."

"Captain Longford," a voice said quietly behind Manson and both men turned. A brown haired, grey-eyed man, wearing the insignia of a Major was watching them both.

"Wheeler. Didn't realise you were still here."

"Major Wheeler, Captain. I command the first battalion." The man looked at Manson. "And you must be Mr Manson."

"Sir."

"Welcome to the 110th. I've been hearing a fair bit about you in correspondence." The grey eyes were amused.

"Really hoping the last letter was fairly recent then, sir," Manson said feelingly, and Johnny Wheeler laughed aloud.

"It was," he said. "Go and get settled, lad, and I'll see you in the mess. I hope you're well rested because we've orders coming through I'm told. Unload your kit and get your men sorted and come up for a drink and dinner." He gave a friendly nod and moved over to greet some of the other new officers. Manson moved away, smiling slightly. He instinctively liked Major Wheeler.

It was strange to sit at table in the mess at dinner with the full complement of officers of the 110th around him. There were more than thirty of them, the captains of the ten companies and their assorted lieutenants arranged around two long refectory tables in what had once been the convent dining room along with the officers of the two Portuguese battalions under Paul van Daan's command. Leo was seated between Captain Swanson of the light company and Captain Clevedon of the second company. He was content to listen to the general conversation, much of which revolved around speculation about the orders they were expecting from Lord Wellington although he could hear Michael O'Reilly regaling his neighbours with the story of Paul's tussles with the commissariat in Lisbon to considerable hilarity. Occasionally one of Manson's neighbours addressed a question and he answered readily but otherwise he sat quietly. At the far end of the table he could hear Anne van Daan's musical laughter, as she talked to two of the Portuguese officers in an easy mixture of English and Portuguese. Both were gazing at her, fascinated. Looking past them down the table Anne caught Manson's eye and smiled at him. He smiled back at her, feeling immediately better.

"Mr Manson, I hope I don't have to speak to you again about your behaviour towards the Colonel's wife." Longford's voice cut across the table, and Manson felt himself flush much to his irritation. He was considering whether or not he needed to reply when Captain Swanson gave a laugh.

"If you're going to start complaining every time one of us smiles at Nan, Longford, you've taken on a full time job. I'd concentrate on improving your company's drill performance if I were you. Nan chooses her own friends."

Longford scowled. "You know nothing about my company's drill performance, Swanson, and you don't give me orders, you're still only a Captain!"

"It's true. Although I am Captain of the Light Company, Vincent, and you know how fond they are of you. But if your company knows it's right from it's left that'll be a big improvement since I last saw them in action." Captain Swanson turned to Manson. "I'm sorry, so busy proving to Johnny that he's wrong about our orders I've forgotten my manners. It's probably a bit overwhelming at the moment."

"That's all right, sir, I've been listening. If there's one thing I've learned so far it's to keep my mouth shut until I've some idea what I'm talking about."

Carl Swanson's lips quirked into a smile. "Congratulations," he said quietly. "You've only been here a few months and you've already learned considerably more than Captain Longford has in ten years."

Manson gave a surprised choke of laughter and looked up startled into Swanson's amused green eyes. "Didn't start so well, sir," he said.

"Doesn't matter how you start, Mr Manson, what matters is where you end up," Swanson said. "I've been having a chat with Sergeant Carter about your companies. We're very short of officers out here. Some of that is due to sickness and wounds and some of it is due to the fact that the Colonel is so bloody difficult about whom he'll take on, and Hookey indulges him beyond permission. He's going to talk to Wellington about getting George Zouch a captaincy but he'll want him to take over the third company while Edmonds is on sick leave, he's got camp fever rather badly. We have several very young and very new ensigns on their way up from Oporto and I think Paul intends to place them with the 112th. Carter's idea is that we combine your eight companies with the light company for training purposes while you're here. He tells me it will work. What's your view?"

Manson thought about it. "It might. We've kept the new recruits for the 110th separate and I know the Colonel wants to integrate them into the companies that are short. Our eight are all under strength, we've left too many of them in the fever ward after their time in the Indies, and most of our NCOs are fairly new although two of them, Quirk and Grisham came from the light company. I'm not convinced my lot have your level of discipline yet but they're a lot better than they were, and I think they'll learn by example. It's up to you, sir, but if Carter thinks it's worth trying it would be less of a headache than trying to work them all between Captain Corrigan, Grey and I. It's good of him to think of it."

"I was amazed, Carter's very fussy. Not sure what you've been up to, but you've done something right. We'll talk to the Colonel about it tomorrow. I'm going to try to talk him into asking for more junior officers."

Manson laughed. "Why is he so against it?"

"He's not too bad with new ensigns, but by the time they get to us a lot of them have purchased on to lieutenant. Christ knows why he's such an arse about that, it's what he and I both did when we joined, but I suppose he struggles with men who have worked in other regiments for a while."

"Perhaps I can see why. It's a shock to the system. But I don't believe there aren't plenty of men out there who can adapt. If I managed it, anybody can."

The light company captain grinned. "Perhaps you can talk some sense into him."

"Me?"

"Why not, you're closer in experience to what we're talking about than any of the rest of us. Tell him he's getting old and stuck in his ways...."

"I heard that, Swanson," the Colonel's voice came down the table. "Stop trying to suborn my junior officers!"

"Sir," Swanson said with a grin. "What makes you think I can?"

"Long experience. You leave Mr Manson alone, he's doing fine without your influence, and currently he's still relatively respectful towards me."

"Give him three weeks and that'll change," Captain Clevedon said.

"Mr Manson, you are forbidden to sit anywhere near those two again," Paul said with a grin. "You can sit beside my wife tomorrow."

"And what makes you think she'll be any better, sir?" Major Wheeler said.

Manson was laughing. His colonel raised his glass, smiling slightly, and Manson felt a rush of pleasure and was amused at his own reaction.

"He likes you," Captain Swanson said quietly.

"I don't know, sir. He's very good at making people feel good about themselves, certainly," Manson said without thinking, and then coloured slightly. Swanson laughed.

"Isn't he? We all fall for it, even when we know what he's doing. But the compliment is genuine. He only does it with people he values. But it's interesting that you can see it. I begin to see what he means about you. I gather it's been tough, but the Colonel tells me you've done well."

"I've had a lot of help," Manson said, glancing down the table. His colonel was talking to Caroline Longford, and she was smiling back at him, looking far happier than he had seen her.

"That's rather the idea," Carl said. "If you don't feel you can go to Paul, come to me, Mr Manson. I know Longford of old."

Manson looked at him sharply. "Does everybody know?"

"No, just Johnny and I. We needed to, Paul can't always be there. He's a bastard, it's not you."

"I was beginning to think it was. Does everybody have this much trouble at the start?"

"No, mine was remarkably smooth. But I joined with Paul, I was so busy covering his arse I didn't have much time for trouble of my own."

"Was he really that bad?" Manson said with a slight smile. "I can't imagine him anywhere other than in command."

"That was rather the problem. Neither could he."

Manson laughed aloud. Obscurely he felt better. There was something very steadying about both Carl Swanson and Johnny Wheeler, and he was beginning to understand more about how the regiment worked so spectacularly well with their understated support for their unorthodox colonel.

Paul was standing up and the room fell quickly silent around them. Amused blue eyes surveyed the room. "It's good to be back," he said, and there was a barrage of cheering. He laughed and shook his head. "Missed your noise, the lot of you. Welcome to all our new officers. It isn't always going to be this bad, believe it or not.

"Some of you already know that Lord Wellington has orders for us which I'll find out in the morning. Frankly I'm surprised he let me get dinner first, he doesn't usually, but I'm grateful for it. I rather suspect there's not much to eat where we're going, and you know how I get if I'm not fed."

There was more laughter. Paul smiled and picked up his glass. "In addition to the new officers, we have Captain Longford's wife with us, and I'd like to welcome her back to the 110th. A few of you will remember Captain Mason who commanded the light company when I first joined back in '02. He was a brave man and a good officer and I always wished I'd had time to know him better. He died during a skirmish on the day before Assaye, and General Wellesley gave his command to me. I only met Miss Mason once and didn't know she'd married into the regiment that she'd grown up in. It's good to have you with us, ma'am. I'd like to propose a toast to Captain Mason of the 110th and his very lovely daughter."

Manson raised his glass, glancing at Longford. His wife was visibly moved by the speech but he was not looking at her. He was looking down the table at Anne van Daan.

"That's all for now. I'll let Johnny say a few words, and propose the loyal toast since he does it better than I do, but there's one salutation I always make when I get the chance." He looked down the table and into the eyes of his wife, and she was smiling back at him. "To the lass I married, and I still can't believe how lucky I am. To my wife."

The toast was drunk, and Major Wheeler rose, greeted the newcomers and proposed the toast to the King and the Prince Regent. When it was done Anne van Daan caught the eye of Caroline Longford and rose to leave the men to their drinks. Manson got up. It had become his custom to escort Anne back to her rooms and he enjoyed it. This evening he had not reached her before Captain Longford stepped forward and between Anne and Manson, deliberately pushing him back.

"I'll escort the ladies back. Don't really want you near my wife, Manson, and if the Colonel saw how you look at his sometimes he'd feel the same."

It was said loud enough to turn heads. Manson felt himself flush. He stepped back with a slight bow. To his surprise, the Colonel's wife placed her hand very firmly on Captain Longford's arm and moved him to one side.

"Thank you, Captain Longford, it's kind of you, but I think my virtue is safe with Mr Manson and I enjoy his company. Why don't you escort your wife?"

She took Manson's arm and drew him towards the door. Outside she quickened her steps slightly to draw ahead of the Longfords. "I am sorry, Mr Manson, if he gives you grief about that, but I was not about to let him get away with it."

"It's all right, ma'am, I appreciated it. Worth the grief."

Anne looked up at him, laughing. "I'm so sorry you're going through this, Leo."

"It's not that bad. The colonel had a chat with me on the way here yesterday, and I feel better. Bit nervous about being in the field. And I'll miss talking to you, ma'am."

"Leo, you can't imagine I'm staying here the whole time, can you? Depending on the situation I shall be in the medical tent as close as I can be."

"And he lets you do that?" Manson said, startled. "Sorry, ma'am, that slipped out."

"It has slipped out of all the rest of his officers, Leo, don't worry about it." They had reached her door. "Go on, go back and enjoy yourself, and hurry up before he dumps Caroline and chases after you to give you a hard time on the way." She stepped forward, placed a hand on his shoulder and stood on tiptoe to kiss him lightly on the cheek. "Goodnight."

"Goodnight, ma'am." He turned to go, hoping the darkness had concealed his flush. He had seen her give the same light-hearted salute to Michael O'Reilly but she had not done it to him before, and he felt as if a Rubicon had somehow been crossed. He walked back towards the mess feeling happier than he had since Captain Longford had landed.

The following day Paul held a series of meetings with his officers and NCOs and outlined his instructions for training and drills and his views on discipline. When they were done he remained in his office with Johnny and Carl. Johnny went to the cupboard and took out a bottle and three glasses.

"Welcome back present," he said, opening it. "It's the best Madeira I've had in a long time. Present from a grateful local. Try it."

Paul sipped and nodded. "That is good. Anything I've missed?"

"Nothing you don't know. Wellington is watching Massena like a hawk, thinks he'll be on the move soon and he's hoping to give him a hard retreat. Our fever patients are mostly back on their feet, although poor Edmonds is in a bad way. We've done well, better than most regiments."

"Nan's isolation rules are pretty ruthless," Paul said with a grin. "She's banned me from going near Gerry Edmonds, says it would be inconvenient if I caught fever."

"I don't suppose she's likely to stick to that herself, is she?"

"No, she thinks she's immune to most fevers. And honestly I'm beginning to wonder if she has a point, it's extraordinary she's not killed herself the amount of time she spends on those wards. I try not to think about it. Rowena had it once, just after Vimeiro, and I honestly thought she was going to die."

"What are you going to do about the third?"

"I'm going to talk to Wellington, get him to agree a promotion for George Zouch, it's years overdue and he tells me he can pay for it. He can take over for now. When Gerry gets back I can either transfer George over to the 112th or if I've managed to get rid of Longford by then he can take over the 7th. What's your view of the new men, I saw you both doing the rounds last night?"

"Good on the whole. Kerr is a steady man and I like young Heron. Lloyd too – he's had a year with the cavalry as ensign, I believe."

"Yes. I don't think he could afford to keep up the lifestyle – a commission with us was cheaper. Although I'm told on the grapevine that the cost is going up which irritates me as it's likely to mean we get more idiots wanting to purchase in for prestige."

"Don't worry, Paul, they won't last," Johnny said soothingly.

"You probably said that about me when I first joined, Wheeler, and look where that got you."

Johnny laughed. "No, no, sir, you've got that wrong. Michael and I agreed early on that we thought you'd stay, it was us we weren't sure about..."

"Impudent bastard! What about Fenwick?"

"He seems old for a lieutenant."

"He is. Cousin to an Earl, he's a bit further up the social scale than we're used to, which keeps Longford off his back a bit, but they clearly loathe each other. He's twenty six and fairly broke although he's been saving for promotion. I want to see him in the field but if he's as good as I think he's going to be I'm going to find him a captaincy, hopefully without purchase. He's a cocky bastard but I like him." Paul sipped the wine and smiled. "I heard your discourse to Mr Manson last night, Carl, and I get the point. We do need more officers. We can manage during winter quarters but on campaign we're going to come unstuck. I'll talk to Wellington, and I'm going to put the word around quietly that I'm interested in transfers."

"You're planning on poaching good officers from other regiments."

"If I can get away with it. Specifically the light division."

"Robert Craufurd will eat your liver if he finds out what you're doing."

"Robert Craufurd is in England in bed with his wife. Shouldn't have gone if he didn't trust me to look after his division in his absence. It's not personal. I've also written to Nan's brother and he's replied with interesting news about the 115th North Yorkshire foot who are back in barracks. Not all the officers there were that fond of me but there were three young ensigns and one lieutenant who showed promise. All four are now lieutenants and they're all back in Thorndale under the newly promoted Major Walsh who was an arsehole I wouldn't touch with a bayonet. Benjamin Hendry can't afford promotion but he'll get it if he's out here with us. I've written to each of them casually mentioning that we're looking."

"Sir, you are a devious, thieving bastard and you are going to leave a stream of pissed off commanding officers in your wake if you pull this off," Johnny said.

"I hope so," Paul said modestly. "What did you make of the lads from the 112th?"

"Grey is good, a bit uncertain still but definitely the right material. Corrigan we know, does better in the field than in barracks but he won't idle about too much under your command he's worried about what you'd do to him. Mr Manson..." Carl paused and grinned. "Mr Manson is a very well brought up lad who is currently trying hard to make up for early mistakes by concealing what a thoroughly arrogant little bastard he actually is. He broken out yet?"

"Once or twice and I love it when he does. I'm impressed with how hard he's trying not to break out with bloody Longford. I'm not sure I'm going to do quite as well if that bastard doesn't back off, but hopefully we'll get him on a battlefield and he'll realise that the 110th is not the place for him after all."

Carl sipped his wine. "I'm surprised. You were very definite about Manson in your first couple of letters."

"Yes, I'm not often wrong, but I missed him completely. The stripes on Barker's back blinded me to some extent. Stupid thing to do, of course, but he'd been stuffed full of his father's antique notions on discipline from childhood, and he'd literally nobody to tell him what else to do. It was a horse guards shambles from start to finish, they shipped the 112th out here to get rid of them and to shut Wellington up about needing more troops and didn't give a shit how those two lads coped. The thing I missed, of course, was not Manson's mistaken ideas on how to deal with the situation, but the fact that at nineteen and with no experience he at least had the balls to try to deal with it. I'm hoping he shows a similar resilience with Longford."

"Be a shame if he transfers elsewhere and Longford stays. But he's being a right bastard, I caught him at it twice last night. He'll wear down that lad's confidence if we don't watch it."

"He might. I don't think so. I'm going out on a limb and saying that Leo Manson is equal to it. As long as he doesn't lose his temper, because he's got one, I'm telling you."

Wheeler refilled the glasses. "When are you going up to see Wellington?"

"I'll ride up now."

"At least you'll get more out of him than most of the army would. God knows why, but he talks to you."

Paul grinned. "I'm his lucky mascot," he said. "His career started to take off just at the time we met. Not quite sure why that's important to him, he's the least sentimental man I've ever met, but there's something in it." He stood up. "Just do your best to keep Longford off Manson's back as much as possible. If he pushes that boy to do something that gets him into trouble, I am going to wring his bloody neck!"

His officers followed him out and watched as he walked towards the stables. Michael O'Reilly came to join them. "Good to be back," he said with a grin. "It's been too quiet."

"Bet it was quieter here," Carl said with a laugh. His eye was caught by a figure crossing towards the officers block carrying an empty laundry basket. "Am I seeing things or is that the Simpson lass? I'd forgotten about her."

"I hadn't," Michael said with a laugh. "She's not Simpson, they never married. Trenlow."

Carl surveyed the girl with appreciative eyes. "Well she has blossomed!" he said. "Didn't realise how pretty she was. Found herself a man yet?"

"I'm working on it," Michael said with a grin and Wheeler shot him a look.

"I'm not sure that's what he meant, Mr O'Reilly," he said drily. "Leave the poor girl alone, with any luck she'll find a nice lad who will marry her and take care of her."

"And what makes you think I wouldn't take care of her, Major?"

"You'd be charming to her for a couple of months, Michael, and then you'd leave her high and dry for something new. And in the meantime you've sent a message to every one of the other officers and NCOs looking for a lass to warm their bed for a few weeks that she's available. Which is fine if that's what she wants, but I'm not sure it is. Anyway, I thought it was the aim of your life to talk Teresa Cortez into your bed. How's that going?"

Michael laughed, shaking his head. "Not bloody well. Teresa Cortez is giving nothing away to me, and believe me I've tried. As a matter of fact, I'm beginning to suspect there's somebody else, she's got that look recently. Wondered about Hammond, he's got an eye for a pretty girl."

"Well it's just as well for you, Michael, if you'd got that girl pregnant Nan would have gutted you, she's very attached to Teresa. Come on, let's get them out for training. If he comes out of the stables and we've not moved he'll start yelling. Although bizarrely I've quite missed being yelled at."

Chapter Nine

Lord Wellington received Paul in his headquarters building in the village of Pere Negro. He had taken over a big farmhouse at the edge of the village not far from the convent where Paul was billeted. There was plenty of space for the commander and several estate cottages for the rest of the headquarters staff. Wellington welcomed Paul with a warmth which told him that his efforts in Lisbon had been appreciated.

"How are you, Colonel?"

"I'm well, thank you, sir. Although don't ask me if I had a nice rest because I'll be rude."

Wellington laughed. "I've received more letters from the commissariat in the past few months than I have for years, Colonel. You've certainly woken them up."

"I had help with that, sir. I think they've taken a dislike to my wife. One of them told her she was a disgrace to her sex."

"Did he? Brave man, he should be in the field."

Paul laughed aloud. "It's good to be back. Good experience, I'll admit. But I've missed my regiment."

"Thank you, Paul. I feel more confident about my supplies thanks to you. For the first time I feel that there is actually a transport system in place which might work."

"I honestly wish I could take credit for that, sir, but I can't. Nan designed it from start to finish."

Wellington sighed. "If I had her at Headquarters, this war would be over faster I swear."

"If you had her at headquarters, sir, you would have other things on your mind and the war would take twice as long. Leave my wife alone!"

Wellington laughed aloud. "Yes, Colonel. But thank her for me, will you? And if ever I need to shake up the commissariat again I shall threaten to send you both back to them! How are the 112th?"

"Very well, sir. Coming on nicely."

"Really? I had feared your report would be less positive."

Paul laughed. "I'll just bet you did! Horse guards at their worst!" he said. "But we struck lucky. Two very junior lieutenants with literally no training or experience should never have been sent in charge of eight companies, it was a disgrace. And yet, I think they'll both make excellent officers. In fact one of them..."

Wellington regarded him with amusement. "Found a protégé, Paul?"

"Yes, sir. Not a particularly easy one, mind. But..."

"You have all my sympathy!" Wellington said unexpectedly. "Same thing happened to me once on a baking hot parade ground in India."

Paul paused and stared at him. Wellington laughed. "Have you forgotten that day, Colonel? You had just spent a week working double shifts in the hottest part of the day drilling and training two companies of sepoy infantry in order to get some of your men out of a flogging."

"Christ, no, but I'm surprised you remember it, sir."

"It was the first time I really remember you. Somebody – can't remember who – told me what was going on. It was a bit of a joke in the mess, they thought you were mad. I asked Johnstone and he told me a bit about you. I walked down that afternoon out of curiosity and I watched a boy of twenty-one showing off what he'd achieved with a company of sepoy infantry in a week."

Paul laughed. "I was an unconscionable show off," he admitted.

"The Indian old hands didn't like you. Complained that you spent time drinking with the enlisted men and failing to come to the mess like a gentleman. I was curious. Sending you out with that supply convoy the following day was a whim. You didn't even blink when I put you in command. Acted like it was your natural place."

Paul laughed. "Yes. I suppose that is how I feel about Lieutenant Manson. He's having a difficult time. Captain Longford has taken a dislike to him, and I can't be around all the time. But he's getting by. I want to get rid of Longford when I can, sir. I've some ideas about recruiting some new officers, I'm very short. But if you know of anybody who'll take Longford off my hands..."

"Nobody wants Longford, Paul, he's got a reputation. But I'll keep my eye out for something." Wellington paused. "In the meantime, I've a problem of my own to solve, and I'm going to recruit your help with it."

Paul eyed his chief. "Why is it that I'm suddenly concerned that your reminders of our long history had a purpose," he said.

"Because you're a suspicious minded young bastard, Colonel."

"No, sir, I've just known you for a long time! Better get it over with."

Wellington sighed. "All right Colonel. Massena is about to march out and I want to make it hard for him to escape."

"No arguments so far, sir."

"You know that General Craufurd is on leave back in England."

"Yes, sir."

"I was unhappy about letting him go. I understand that men who have wives and families..."

"Sir – you don't," Paul said quietly. "You and I are luckier than most. And I'm not going to explain why because you know."

Wellington stared at him for a moment and then gave a wry smile. "You mean that I don't really miss my wife, and yours won't leave you? I take the point, Colonel. Of the two of us I know who is to be envied. You'll know of the scandal back in London regarding the Duke of York?"

"I know what is said," Paul said. "His mistress admitted to selling military commissions at inflated prices and he resigned. Although my source tells me there is some doubt as to his involvement. I don't know him personally, sir, but I don't disagree with some of his ideas. To be honest I'm not sure his replacement as commander-in-chief is that much of an improvement."

"Sir David Dundas. Nor am I, Colonel. I'm curious about your source, does your father have military connections?"

Paul laughed. "Mainly in India, but he's cultivated people at Horse Guards to keep abreast. But my London gossip comes from a different source. I correspond fairly regularly with George Brummel."

Wellington stared at him in considerable astonishment. "Beau Brummel is a friend of yours?"

Paul smiled. "Not that close. But my father made attempts to introduce me into London society during my time at Oxford. With limited success, I'll admit, I was in a bad mood at the time. However I knew George slightly from Eton and we got on well. Spent some time in London together. Very different people, but we enjoyed a shared sense of the ridiculous and we've kept in touch. He is a marvellous source of London gossip."

"I imagine so," Wellington said, sounding amused. "Really, Paul, you never fail to surprise me. With the Duke gone, Dundas is making his own appointments to my army and he has sent me Major General Sir William Erskine, whom you will meet tomorrow at my reception. He is to take over the light division during General Craufurd's absence."

Paul sat very still, staring at his commander in chief. Wellington looked back at him very steadily. There was a long silence. Eventually, Wellington said:

"I know you are about to start swearing, Paul."

"I actually don't know any words rude enough to cover this," Paul said, taking a deep breath. "Was this your idea or Horse Guards?"

"What do you think, Paul?" Wellington sighed. "I have no choice but to accept him. He is politically very well connected, of the right rank and knows the right people."

"And according to popular gossip he is arrogant, inexperienced, blind as a bat and mad as a Bedlamite. Are you seriously proposing to allow him to command troops at all, let alone Robert Craufurd's light division?"

"I don't have a choice, Colonel."

"Why don't you send him out in command of my light company for a couple of days, sir? I can pretty much guarantee they will solve your problem for you."

"Colonel, murder is not a solution I can countenance I am afraid."

"What a shame."

Wellington shook his head. "I should know better than to confide in a relatively junior officer..."

"You should know better than to confide in me and expect me not to tell you what I think, sir."

His commander in chief smiled grimly. "Colonel, in a week or so we will be in the field, chasing Massena out of Portugal. I would like to cause as much damage as I can."

"And the light division would be perfect for that, sir, if you had the right commander."

"You're too young, Paul, and you don't have the right connections."

"Christ, I'm not suggesting you give them to me! Either Beckwith or Drummond are more than capable!"

"Paul, my hands are tied. He is here and I need to use him, at least until I can come up with a very good reason not to!"

"Well if you get Black Bob's division slaughtered under this imbecile, sir, I suggest you take leave of absence before he gets back, because he'll shoot you!" Paul said shortly. "What do you want me to do?"

"Excuse me?"

"Oh come on, don't tell me I'm here for a chat and a drink! I've spent four months working my arse off in Lisbon to get your bloody army supplied, I've come back ready to fight and you are about to give me a job that you think I am going to yell about! How long have I known you, sir? Cut line and tell me what it is!"

Wellington nodded. "You'll meet Erskine tomorrow. I want you and the 110th to operate under his personal command, in addition – but not as part of – the light division. You'll provide him with ADCs, try to give him some guidance...."

"You have got to be fucking kidding me, sir!"

"I knew you were going to start swearing, Colonel."

"You were absolutely right, sir! Is there something I've done recently to piss you off? Because if there is, I wish you'd just tell me what it is and I'll apologise! I have to be the worst person in the world for this job. Johnny Wheeler once told me I have the diplomatic skills of a five year old, and honestly, I think he was being generous!"

"Paul, listen to me for a moment. You will be in the thick of the fighting. I want you to act as liaison between General Erskine and the light division. And you'll also be in a position to report back to me. If things are going wrong, you are a man I trust to make difficult decisions without fear. God knows you've made up your own orders often enough over the years."

"Yes, in the heat of battle or when no other orders are available. I also fight very well under the command of a good general, by the way."

"I know you do, Paul, I commanded you at Assaye, Rolica, Vimeiro, Talavera and Bussaco. And you did exactly what you were asked to do on each occasion. Very well. But at Assaye you went in to help the 74th before I could get to you to give the order. And at the Coa you defied Robert Craufurd to double back and retake that knoll, saving the rest of his troops during the retreat. And that is why I want you within reach of Major General Erskine. Because you being there could save lives."

Paul stared at his commander. "Tell me this is a joke," he said, too angry to be polite. "You are giving Robert Craufurd's light division to a half blind lunatic with no experience of either war or command and you are expecting me to do what exactly?"

"Colonel, don't lose your temper with me!"

"Sir, I have already lost my temper with you, telling me not to is only going to piss me off more!"

"The light division needs a commander. I have to do something with him, his family are too influential for me to ignore. He's hopeless, you're right. So I'm putting him in charge of men who are going to be able to work round him. Beckwith and Drummond are good men, used to Craufurd. They'll know what to do if he makes a mistake. And if they don't..."

"Sir?"

"If they don't, you will," Wellington said quietly. "I'm putting the 110th under his direct command. You'll march with him, provide him with ADCs, make sure he's where he should be when he should be. And make sure that the light division knows what the hell is going on."

Paul stood up and went over to the window. "And what happens if that goes wrong?" he said quietly.

"It won't."

"It bloody well could and you know it. If I can't manage this, my lads end up dead, possibly taking half the fucking light division with them. And if I survive it, I'm neither senior enough nor well connected enough to survive what they'll do to me at Horse Guards. Either way you're in the clear. If I manage it, you'll get a slap on the back and political points. If I don't, you stand back and point and I'm going down!"

"You can do this, Colonel van Daan. You are probably the only man I would trust with it."

"You've got a very funny definition of the word trust, sir."

"I've not yet given you an order you've failed to obey, Colonel van Daan."

"No. And you haven't this time. I'll do my duty, sir. It's what I do."

"I know it is, Paul."

"Then you need to do something for me in return."

"Which is?"

"Before we set off, I want to borrow your man of business. I need to get my affairs in order. And I need you to give me your word that if he gets me killed, you'll make sure she's all right."

He had shaken his commander and he knew it. Wellington stood up. "Paul..."

"Your word, sir. I can get everything set up and ready for my lawyers at home. But the only thing my family knows about her is that I married the widow of a thief and a deserter, practically over my wife's grave. They're not supportive of us and they don't need to be. Sooner or later they'll meet her and get to know her and they'll think it's the best thing I ever did. But at the moment she's on shaky ground. So if I die, I need you to use every piece of influence that you have to make sure she gets what she's due."

"I will."

"You promise me."

"Colonel you have my word on it."

"And look after her. Nobody else can do it. I don't think any of them understands her yet the way you do, with the exception of Leo Manson and he's too young."

Wellington studied him for a long moment. Then he nodded. "I will. But it isn't going to be necessary. You'll be fine. You are better at this than you think you are, Paul, I wouldn't be doing this if I weren't sure of that."

"Well I appreciate your confidence, sir."

"I'll expect you and your officers at the reception tomorrow evening, Colonel."

"Yes, sir."

"Bring your wife."

Paul eyed his commander in chief. "Sir, when my wife hears about this one, you might be better off if I leave her at home," he said shortly. "But we'll be there. If you'll excuse me, I'll need to go and brief my officers about this. They'll need at least a day before they get over it enough to guarantee they'll be civil."

There was a grim resignation among the officers of the 110th arriving at Pere Negro on the following evening. Wellington's reception rooms were stiff with local dignitaries. Despite the relatively short distance involved, Wellington had insisted on sending his carriage for Anne. Paul was faintly amused at Captain Longford's surprise at being invited to share it with his wife.

"Does Lord Wellington usually do this?" he asked as he and Paul waited for the ladies to emerge.

"If he can. To be honest there's no need today it's so close Nan could have ridden even in evening dress but he likes to make the gesture." Paul glanced at Longford and grinned slightly. "He's got a thing about Nan," he explained. "Quite openly, it's a bit of an ongoing joke. Ah, here they are. My compliments, Longford, you've married a lass who doesn't take all night to get ready. That'll please Nan she's a punctual soul and it would drive her mad."

The two ladies emerged from the convent and Paul stepped forward, his eyes on his wife's face. She was wearing an evening gown in deep burgundy, his rubies showing off the graceful lines of her neck and shoulders. The shawl was a new gift, made from a black lace mantilla he had bought for her in Lisbon, and the sight of it draped over her shoulders brought back a completely inappropriate memory of her lying naked in their bed with it thrown casually about her. He suppressed it with an effort and went to take her hand, lifting it to his lips.

"Christ, lass, Lord Wellington is going to make no sense whatsoever tonight!" he said with a smile, and she laughed.

"Good. I hope he gibbers like a loon and makes a fool of himself, I am out of charity with him!"

Paul turned to Caroline Longford. She was dressed in pale blue crepe, her fair hair arranged enchantingly in curls framing her face and she looked very pretty. "You look beautiful, ma'am," he said with a smile and she flushed slightly and returned the smile. He handed both women in to the carriage and climbed in after them, observing with amusement that Longford could not take his eyes from Anne.

He was accustomed to losing sight of his wife quickly at these affairs. Wellington came forward to greet them and Paul introduced him to Longford and Caroline. He saw Wellington's eyes rest with interest on Captain Longford. He was well aware of Paul's long history of antagonism with the man although Paul knew that Longford was completely unaware of the fact. Wellington bowed over Caroline's hand and his eyes turned to Anne. They were smiling.

"Good to see you, ma'am. You are looking very lovely this evening. I have missed you."

Anne regarded him severely. "And you are not in my good books, sir."

"I rather expected not, ma'am. I am sorry, sometimes the exigencies of war do not make me any friends."

"That is all very well, sir, but if the exigencies of war cause me to lose my husband, I am borrowing Sergeant Carter's rifle and coming after you!" Anne informed him. Wellington gave a shout of laughter and kissed her hand again. Paul observed Longford's startled expression with considerable amusement.

"Don't worry, ma'am, Colonel van Daan is equal to the task I have given him." Wellington looked at Paul and smiled slightly. "I have a sheaf of transfer requests on my desk, Colonel van Daan. You may wish to come up tomorrow to go through them with me to see if there are any, which meet with your exacting standards. On this occasion I am going to allow you free rein with this, although looking at some of them, when General Craufurd gets back from leave he may well be the one borrowing your sergeant's rifle."

"Serves him right for going and leaving me in this mess!" Paul said caustically. He grinned. "Mind, if this means I get some good officers out of it I'm going to make the most of this while you're still feeling guilty. Is General Erskine here?"

"Yes. Come and be introduced, I have told him about you."

"I hope you've not given him Craufurd's assessment of me?"

"No, Paul, that would be unfair. Especially once Robert finds out what you've done to his division in his absence. Ma'am, will you come and meet the General?" Wellington's eyes were amused. "He is very near sighted, but I rather imagine the way you are looking tonight will cause him to focus rather better."

"It is to be hoped he has better control of his line of vision than you do, sir," Paul said grimly, and his chief laughed aloud.

"I will keep my eyes lifted to her face, Paul."

"You'd better, I'm still in a bad mood with you. Come on Nan, let's get this over with. Longford, Caroline, excuse us, would you? Go and join the others, they're just over there."

Carl greeted Longford pleasantly. "Ma'am, you're looking lovely this evening. Champagne, Longford? It's surprisingly good."

Captain Longford took a glass. "So that's the famous Wellington," he said. "Seems affable."

"You'll see him at his best when he's around Nan van Daan," Wheeler said with a grin. "She has a curious effect on him. He can be a grumpy bugger at other times. Sorry ma'am, my language needs work."

Caroline Longford laughed and accepted the glass of champagne Wheeler passed to her. "Thank you, Major. Please don't apologise. I would hate for you all to change your ways because I have arrived in barracks and I am already well aware that none of you do so for Nan."

Wheeler laughed. "We don't. Some of us did try at the beginning. I admit I was horrified at how casually Paul treated her at the start. We're well into our first year with her now and we treat her like one of the regiment. But we do need to remember to behave properly around other ladies or we'll all end up in disgrace."

She glanced around the group of officers. Longford had moved to speak to Kerr and Heron. "You won't," she said. "My father would have been very proud."

Wheeler smiled. "I hope so. It's run very differently under Paul. We're all aware of it but we've become very used to it by now, and it does work. I know Captain Longford is struggling to adjust, but..."

He was surprised when she shook her head gently. "Major, you and I both know that my husband is making no attempt to adjust. I am hoping some time in the field will help him to settle down."

He read with unexpected clarity, the unhappiness she tried hard to conceal. "He may well," he said gently. "Paul's perfectionism can drive men mad during time in barracks. When you're standing on a field watching French cavalry coming towards you and you see those men moving into square like an automaton, those early morning drills suddenly feel like a really good idea. I don't think it ever really hit me properly until I watched it just before Assaye on the day your father died. Do you mind me talking about it?"

"No. I only wish people would, I'm not a child."

"You're not. We'd all have been dead that day if it hadn't been for Paul. I was older and longer serving than him, but by then I was well aware that he'd something I lacked. It was hard even to resent it, it was so obvious. We lost your father in the first rush, Paul was on his feet over a rise reconnoitring the enemy. I was trying to call them into square but it happened so fast, we were all shocked. I remember him coming over that hill bellowing in a voice they could probably have heard back in Assaye, and suddenly the men started to move. Every morning sweating on that parade ground, and all those hours of musket drill with him yelling at them and they'd called him every name under the sun and I saw a hundred men just fall into place as if it were a drill ground at the sound of his voice. We survived that day purely because he was so annoyingly insistent that they had to be perfect." Wheeler drank and laughed. "Actually they were very slow back then, could do it in half the time now."

"I hope my husband comes to accept it," Caroline said with a little smile. "He does not really want to be here, but it proved too difficult to obtain a transfer without funds."

"Yes, I've never had the money to purchase promotions myself," Wheeler said ruefully.

"And yet you are a Major, sir. Hard work and ability, I suspect."

He laughed. "I want to say yes, ma'am, it makes me look good in your eyes! But I'm very aware, and I'm sure Captain Longford would agree, that being a close friend of Paul van Daan's doesn't hurt me. He has a genius for arguing a case at Horse Guards, he drives them mad." He offered her his arm. "Would you like to take a turn about the room with me and I'll introduce you to some of the other regimental officers. They're dying to meet you, Harry Smith and his cronies from the rifles over there haven't taken their eyes off you since you walked in. They're desperately short of pretty women to flirt with, so be warned, you'll be very popular."

Johnny remained beside her through the evening, aware of the fact that her husband did not go anywhere near her. Caroline appeared relaxed and seemed to enjoy herself. Late into the evening their host invited them out onto the terrace where long tables of food had been set out, and lanterns had been hung from the trees around the garden. There was a view out over the stream, with lights twinkling from the village beyond, and Johnny went to bring her a plate of food and at her invitation shared it with her, watching the scudding clouds across the darkness of the sky.

"Thank you for this evening, Major," she said suddenly, quietly. "I have genuinely enjoyed it and that has been largely due to you."

Johnny thought of several platitudes he could give in response and then discarded them. "I have too," he said, taking the plate from her and setting it down. "It's been a long time since I had the opportunity to monopolise a lovely woman at a party. Thank you, ma'am."

"My name is Caroline.".

"I'm not sure how your husband would feel about me using it, ma'am."

"I don't really care. And I don't think he does either. He doesn't want to be married to me and makes no secret of the fact."

"Then he's a bloody fool," Johnny said softly, and Caroline looked up, startled. He was aware that they were temporarily alone, the noisy headquarters party having moved back to the far end of the terrace. He could hear his commander's wife laughing, and the deeper tones of Lord Wellington, and he wondered where Paul was and if he knew that the General was paying his wife extravagant compliments in the starlight. There was a bank of laurel at the edge of the terrace, and acting on total impulse he stepped back and took her hand, drawing her into the shadows.

"Major..."

"Don't," he whispered, and bent to kiss her. He was half expecting the slap he so richly deserved. Instead her mouth parted under his and she leaned into him. He could feel the curves of her body fitting into his and he drew her closer and kissed her harder. He could feel her body shiver under his hands.

"Caroline..."

She reached up and he felt her hand caressing the back of his neck. Suddenly he realised that they were completely alone, the rest of the party having moved back inside, and he moved his hand from her waist to her breast and heard her make a small sound of pleasure.

"Sweetheart, I need to stop this," he breathed. "I am enjoying it far too much and you're another man's wife."

"I know." He heard her take a deep steadying breath. "I'm sorry, Johnny, I just...for a few hours there, I was very happy."

Johnny was suddenly angry for her. He swore quietly and pulled her closer again. "Just a few more minutes," he whispered, and she

An Irregular Regiment

reached up again to pull his head down to her. He kissed her again, savouring the feel of her in his arms.

"You are so lovely," he said, raising his head finally. "I really don't want to stop this, but we'd better before somebody comes."

"I don't want to stop it at all," Caroline said unexpectedly. "I'm sorry, Johnny. I know you can't, he's one of your officers. But I wish…do you know this is the first time since I realised I was pregnant with his child that I can remember feeling genuinely happy. Thank you for that. Please don't worry, I do understand. I just wish I'd met you first."

Johnny looked down at her and suddenly laughed. "You did," he said. "You won't remember, Caroline, you were still a child, probably around fourteen. It was just before we went to India that last time and your aunt had taken you to a concert. I was there with two or three other officers. Somebody introduced us to your aunt and you made your curtsey like a well brought up schoolgirl."

"Oh – I think I do remember now. I wouldn't have know it was you." Caroline laughed aloud. "How embarrassing. Did I have pimples and…?"

"You were beautiful," Johnny said softly. "I couldn't take my eyes off you. Very inappropriate given your youth and my straitened circumstances. As for him being one of my officers, I'm not so sure I give a damn about that actually, which is unlike me, I'm very strait-laced. I'm more worried about what happens to you if somebody comes out here and finds you like this with me." Gently he smoothed her gown back into place. "We'd better go inside. Kiss me again."

She did so with obvious pleasure, and then stepped back her eyes on his. Studying her, he said quietly:

"That's not the last time I'm going to do that with you. I'm just going to choose my moment a bit better next time. Come on, we'd better go inside."

He found his commanding officer talking to Carl. "Mrs Longford, are you ready to leave yet? I have been alarmingly civil to Major General Erskine, who is manifestly a lunatic, and have commiserated with Colonel Drummond and Colonel Beckwith on our shared misfortune and now I am taking my wife home before I give in to temptation and land a punch on Lord Wellington."

"Yes, he's on good form tonight," Johnny said with a grin. "I'm not sure he wasn't propositioning her on the terrace earlier."

"It wouldn't surprise me at all. When I escaped from Drummond and came looking for her he was feeding her cherries and telling her stories of his boyhood, while gazing with considerable enjoyment down the front of her dress. I think he's trying to provoke me to murder this week. I'm almost looking forward to marching, it'll get him away from her."

Caroline was laughing. "Colonel she would not encourage him!"

"You will excuse my language, ma'am, when I assure you that she bloody would, and often does! Between him and Craufurd, every headquarters party is a nightmare. Longford, are you ready? Seen my wife or has she eloped with the commander in chief?"

Anne appeared beside him. She was flushed and laughing and looked startlingly beautiful. "I have not," she said. "You do make a fuss, Paul, it's a good thing nobody takes you seriously."

"The only person here who thinks this is a joke is you, girl of my heart. The commander in chief is deadly serious about what he wants from you, and only the absolute knowledge that I would shoot him through the head stops him from making the attempt. Come on, I've been civil enough this evening. Let's get out of here."

He slipped an arm about her and drew her close, kissing her hard on the mouth. Anne gave a squawk of protest. "Colonel you cannot kiss me like that in the middle of a reception."

"I am asserting my rights as your husband as publicly as possible. Don't worry, lass, they're all used to me by now, I can't shock them any more. Ah there you are, sir. Very pleasant evening. I am taking my wife home, while I still can. Let me know when you're going off to chase Massena, won't you?"

"My sources tell me it will be very soon, Paul, so keep them at the ready. You did very well with General Erskine, he is pleased with you."

"I should think he is, it's the most pleasant I've been in years."

Wellington laughed. "I am impressed. Don't forget to come up to look at those lists tomorrow. Mrs Longford, good to have met you." His blue eyes moved to Anne and he was smiling. "Ma'am – a delightful evening. You are as charming as ever."

He lifted her hand to his lips and looked at Paul. Paul was laughing. "Put her down, sir, I'm taking her home. Good night."

In the carriage he gave a sigh. "Thank God that's over. Longford, I've been discussing you with Wellington and Erskine. I'm going to assign you and Pat Corrigan to Erskine's staff, he doesn't have one to speak of and I'd rather he had one or two men I know around him. George Zouch can take over the seventh for a while, it'll be good practice for him."

Longford looked startled. "Thank you, sir."

Paul regarded him in some amusement. "You're so obvious, Vincent. You're wondering why I should do you a good turn. Well I'm not, I'm giving you a job that would drive me completely up the wall. But you might quite enjoy it, we'll see. If you can keep on his good side and prevent him from driving me to murder, it might even lead to a promotion, and a staff post, which would suit both of us."

"Yes, sir."

"Mrs Longford, did you enjoy the evening? You were a wild success, the 95th have fallen in love to a man, you'll need to watch her, Longford, you can't trust a rifleman." He glanced at his wife mischievously and she shook her head.

"If you even mention Lord Wellington again this evening, Paul, you are sleeping in Carl's room!"

"I am mute, love of my life. Although I'm looking forward to seeing what he has for me tomorrow, he's feeling excessively guilty which could be very useful. Thank God we're here, I find one of those parties more tiring than a month on campaign. Good night, Longford. Ma'am."

The following few weeks were spent working hard with Paul's battalions, integrating the new men into the 110th and getting the British and Portuguese battalions used to working together. Paul was delighted with the progress Johnny and Carl had made with the Portuguese troops. He stood watching them one afternoon when he had organised an impromptu parade to give the men the opportunity to show off their new skills.

"They're looking bloody good, Johnny." Paul glanced at his friend. "Well done. I hope you're as pleased as you ought to be."

"Revoltingly smug," Wheeler said with a grin. "We've genuinely enjoyed working with them, they're good lads and I like the officers." He glanced over at the officers block. Anne was seated in the shade in a folding chair and beside her was Keren Trenlow, her dark curly head bent over a book. "What's going on there?"

"Reading lessons," Paul said. "They started down in Lisbon. The girl never learned but she must have expressed an interest and Nan has been teaching her."

Johnny called an order to Sergeant Carter to stand the men down and then fell into step beside Paul, Carl and Michael as they walked back to their billets. Anne looked up and smiled.

"All done? I'll be up to change in a few minutes, we'll just finish here."

"How's it going, Keren?" Carl asked and the girl looked up.

"Very well, sir. I'm enjoying it, it's not as difficult as I thought it would be." She closed the book. "Shall I call Teresa for you, ma'am? I'm sure she's around."

"Don't worry, Keren. Can you bring up some hot water for us? And perhaps you can do my hair for me."

"I will, ma'am. May I…"

"Borrow it," Anne said with a smile. "Practice as much as you can. You're doing amazingly well."

"Thank you," Keren said, getting up. "I'll be up as soon as the water is hot."

Anne disappeared into the block, sketching a wave at the men.

"I need a wash myself," Carl said. "Anybody seen Ned Browning about, I'll get him…"

"I'll bring it," Keren said. Carl looked at her and she smiled. "No extra effort, sir."

"Thank you, lass." Carl watched her move away. "How is she doing, Paul?"

"Very well. To be honest, I thought she'd quickly take up with one of the lads. I'm sure she had a few offers when we were in Lisbon." He shot a glance at Michael who laughed.

"I've not given up yet."

"You need to bloody leave her alone, Michael. My wife's got very fond of her, if you upset her…"

"I'm not going to upset her, sir. And may I say it's rich coming from you!"

Paul laughed. "I keep telling you all, I'm a reformed man," he said. "But you're right, I can't lecture you about this with a straight face. All the same, I am going to be severely pissed off if you get that lass pregnant and Nan has to find something else to do with her. She's a hard worker and she's easy to have around. I…"

"And being that easy on the eye doesn't hurt," Carl said mischievously. "I've bloody seen you looking, I'm surprised Nan doesn't slap you."

"Nan doesn't care who I look at, lad, as long as I'm not stupid enough to do anything about it. Which I wouldn't. And I'm only human, she's very pretty. I don't blame you, Michael, but I'd much rather she took up with one of the men and found herself a husband."

"With your wife teaching her to read and write and Teresa teaching her Spanish, she might find herself a bit over-educated for most of our lads," Carl said with a laugh. "I'm going to change."

In his room he had removed his coat and sat down to take off his boots when a tap on the door heralded Keren with a heavy jug of water. Carl went to take it from her. "Tell me you didn't carry two of these up!"

She laughed. "I'm stronger than I look, sir."

"You must be! Thanks, Keren."

"You're welcome, sir." She glanced around the room and noticing his coat thrown across the bed, went to pick it up. "Do you want me to get the stains out of this?"

"I'm not sure it can be done," Carl said, sitting down again. Keren put the coat down and came forward, kneeling before him.

"I'll see what I can do with it. Unless you'd rather one of the other women…"

"No. If you don't mind, you can take the laundry and mending as well. Maggie Bennett usually does mine, but I know she's got more than enough to do." Carl sighed with relief as she eased off his boots. "Thank you. But you don't need to be waiting on me."

"I don't mind, sir. Mrs van Daan doesn't need me that much. She's got Teresa and she's very independent." Keren laughed. "At home I used to help up at the big house sometimes, when they had house parties and needed extra maids. Some of the ladies there didn't seem able to brush their own hair. Mrs van Daan can get herself completely ready without help apart from someone to button her gown at the back. She can even do her own hair if she needs to."

"Yes, she's always been that way. She didn't even bring a maid when she first came out married to Mr Carlyon. I can remember Rowena nagging her about it. She used to send her maid in to help Nan until she found Teresa. Is that what you did - worked as a maid?"

"Sometimes. In the season I helped in the fish sheds - when the catch came in. I hated that - the smell. And up at the mines too, in the sorting sheds. Da is a miner."

"And your young man?"

"He was too, but he couldn't settle to it. Couldn't settle to anything. When the recruiters came through he joined up. I cried for days but then he asked me to go with him. Some of the men had been telling him it was possible for a woman to sneak on board the transport."

Carl nodded, watching as she moved around the room with quick efficiency. "It was a mad thing to do," he said quietly and she looked around at him.

"I know. Knew it very quickly, but it was too late to go back. But I was alright until Jem died…"

He sensed her sadness and got up. "Look Keren, it's all right. Here, I mean. Nan is really happy with you. No need to rush into anything else and certainly no reason to go back to that bastard Simpson."

She shivered. "I wouldn't. Not now. But thank you, sir. You're very good."

She looked up at him and smiled and then moved away, scooping up laundry. "I'll get this back to you as soon as I can," she said, and was gone. Carl went to pour water into the basin and realised he was smiling. Something about the Cornish girl amused him. He wondered what she made of Michael's determined attempts to persuade her into his bed and realised in some surprise that he hoped she would hold out. He suspected that she was worth rather more.

Chapter Ten

Marshal Massena, having managed to maintain his starving army in scorched countryside considerably longer than Lord Wellington had thought possible, ordered his retreat to begin in early March.

Wellington had been anxious through the winter that Masséna might be reinforced by Soult's 5th corps and had stationed a reserve force under Beresford along the south bank of the Tagus including units at Almeirim and Salvaterra de Magos. Communication issues had prevented Soult from pushing through to reinforce Massena. He was aware that Wellington was prepared and had read reports of the strength of the British defences.

Despite Wellington's efforts to starve the French army into retreating, the troops under Masséna had displayed surprising fortitude through the winter months. A large number died from disease and illness but the lack of provisions only really began to take effect in the early months of 1811, and Paul was trying not to think about how the French had survived those months and what must have happened to those Portuguese who had not elected to flee with the British behind the lines of Torres Vedras.

There had been limited action through the winter, although the 110th had been called on several times while Paul was in Lisbon to repulse French incursions, caused more by starvation and desperation than any serious attempt at invasion. In January there had been a temporary panic when Portuguese militia had been defeated by part of the French 9th corps, and Wellington had recalled Trant, Wilson and Miller to reinforce the defences. The French had retreated and the British troops were dispersed to their original positions.

In February Marshal Foy arrived bearing orders issued by Napoleon instructing Masséna to hold his position until reinforcements had pushed through from Spain. French supplies were almost exhausted, and when nothing materialised after another two weeks, Masséna called a meeting with his lieutenants, during which a plan of action was drawn up. Knowing that no further offensive action could be attempted whilst food was in such short

An Irregular Regiment

supply he proposed to retire back to the Mondego, where they could replenish and await reinforcements.

Preparations began over the last few days of February as baggage was dispatched to the rear and caissons were destroyed to free up horses. On March 3rd, Ney was ordered to march for Thomar where he, Drouet and Marchand would provide cover for the retreat. Torres Novas was evacuated, leaving a reduced force at Santarem, Punhete and the Rio Major. The troops under Reynier and Junot remained in their original positions to convince Wellington that no retreat had begun yet, buying the French forces valuable time. Wellington was resolved to launch an attack only after reinforcements had arrived in Lisbon, but a delay in their arrival caused him to think again.

On 5th and 6th March, the final French troops pulled out of Santarem and the Rio Major and Paul received notification that General Erskine would be marching out with the light division and the 110th the following day. Like Wellington, Paul had been hoping to receive reinforcements in the shape of his new officers, and five men had recently transferred from the various regiments of the light division. In addition he had received and accepted transfer requests from four officers of the 115th Yorkshire, but they had not arrived by the time the summons came.

He dined with his officers and his wife the night before the march, seating himself beside her as he seldom did, watching her through the candlelight with painful awareness of their impending separation. She smiled at him finally and reached out to take his hand. "Are you all right, Paul?"

"I was wondering the same about you," he said quietly. "Honestly, I'm surprised you didn't make more fuss about not being able to come with us."

"It's all right, Colonel, I understand," his wife said. "You don't have enough information about where you're going yet, and you'll need to move well ahead of the commissariat. I shall stay here, be a good wife and bully the commissariat into getting your supplies to you."

He had not expected her to be so understanding and he lifted her hand to his lips. "Thank you, girl of my heart. Believe me, the minute you can join me, you will." He stood up and took her hand. "I've to be up early," he said quietly. "Come to bed."

His expression quickened her pulse. She rose, nodding, and caught Leo Manson's eye across the table, shook her head slightly and he smiled and nodded. Paul said goodnight to his officers, and she was aware of more than one of them smiling slightly behind their hands.

He gave her no time to undress herself, picking her up as soon as he had locked their door and carrying her through into the bedroom. Setting her down he reached for the fastenings of her gown and she stood still, amused at the impatience of his fingers on the small buttons.

"You're in a hurry, Colonel."

"I hate these bloody buttons," he said with a soft laugh, sliding the gown off her shoulders into a crumpled heap on the floor. "Makes me wait longer than I want to."

"You're a greedy man sometimes Paul van Daan."

"I really am. Give me a minute to undress and I'll show you just how greedy I'm feeling."

She laughed and went to the bed, slipping out of her chemise and sitting to remove shoes and stockings. She had barely finished before he joined her, easing her back onto the bed, his mouth moving over her body with exquisite gentleness until she was sighing with pleasure.

"I was imagining this round about the loyal toast," he whispered, and she laughed.

"You're a bloody liar, Colonel, you were thinking about this as they brought the first course in."

He gave a choke of laughter and lifted himself above her. "I actually was. Possibly earlier. Have to make the most of you, lass, I'll be dreaming about you for a week or two."

"Oh...Paul..."

She gasped as he moved into her and he laughed and kissed her again. "Mind, I'm rather intending you'll be counting the days yourself," he whispered, and she drew him closer, arching her body into his.

"I'll be counting the hours, love," she said softly, and he smiled down into her eyes and began to move.

They lay finally, entwined in the darkness, listening to the rest of the officers making their way back to their quarters. She felt his quiver of soft laughter. "Noisy bastards."

"Aren't they? Are they all going to be hung over tomorrow?"

"Nice march in the fresh air will sort that out. Leo Manson's a tactful little bugger, isn't he? Did you tell him his services as escort weren't needed tonight?"

"Not really, he catches on fairly quickly."

"Yes. Mind you, I've a suspicion the entire mess knew what my plans for the evening were."

"The way you were looking at me over pre-dinner drinks, Paul, I imagine so," Anne said, laughing, and he joined in.

"I don't care. Not at all ashamed of how I feel about you, lass, and half of them would swap places with me if they could." He kissed her gently. "I suspect half the army would. I am so lucky, Nan."

"So am I," she whispered, and suddenly he laughed.

"I'm also revoltingly smug. I can remember looking at Rowena at times and thinking how well I'd done for myself. Used to look at other lassies and think they weren't as pretty as she was. Or as good to be around." The amused blue eyes scanned her through the darkness. "Then I walked into a snowbound shepherd's hut in Yorkshire and a girl in a blue cloak turned and pushed back her hood and looked at me. I think my heart stopped beating for a while, and when it started again it wasn't mine any more."

She reached up and caressed his face in the darkness. "They all think they know you, Colonel, but they don't know what a completely hopeless romantic you actually are, do they?"

"No, lass, I keep that one quiet, it doesn't go with my public face at all," he said, laughing.

He kissed her and they lay close, listening to the sound of voices outside. "Who the bloody hell is that?" Paul said irritably.

"It sounds like Captain Longford," Anne said, listening.

"What the hell is he doing giving a speech at this hour of the night? He's...oh bloody hell, he's giving Leo Manson a dressing down about something isn't he?" Paul moved away from her and got up. He went to the window and looked around the curtain. The courtyard was dark but there was just enough light to see the dark shapes of the two men. Manson was standing to attention. Longford stood before him. Paul pushed open the window very quietly and Longford's voice became clearer.

"It is not the place of an arrogant little bastard like you to correct your betters, Mr Manson. If it were down to me I'd have you running around this parade ground for the rest of the night, but I'm aware that you're an officer and that would not be appropriate. Your men are a disgrace and your attitude stinks, and I...."

Anne had been silently counting in her head. She had reached eight.

"Captain Longford!" Paul bellowed, and his wife buried her face in the pillow to stifle her laughter. "If it is your opinion that I wish to be kept awake for the rest of the night by your whining, allow me to correct you! I have absolutely no idea what it is that Mr Manson has done to offend you and I rather imagine he has even less idea than I have, given the rambling incoherency of your discourse, but given that we are going after Massena tomorrow it would be more helpful if you would both go to bed and let those of us who intend to be fit to fight get some bloody sleep! If you are not in your quarters by the time I count to ten making literally no sound whatsoever I am going to come down there and kick your arse all the way down to the river where I will throw you in for an early bath! Save your bloody posturing for Major General Erskine in the morning, I am sure he will appreciate it more than I do! Now move, sir!"

Longford disappeared inside the convent door without speaking. Manson had not moved. "Mr Manson, come up please, I want a word."

The boy saluted and moved towards the door. Paul closed the window and reached for a shirt. "Do you mind for ten minutes, Nan? I'm sorry."

"No, love, of course I don't. Although I'd prefer it if you'd remove my shawl off the sitting room floor first, it looks as though I undressed in a hurry."

He was pulling on plain dark trousers, slipping his feet into shoes. "Wouldn't want to give that impression, would we?" He went through and scooped up the black lace. Laughing he threw it to her and she draped it around her bare shoulders provocatively. There was a tap on the door. Paul came to her and bent over her. "Be right there, Mr Manson," he called, and slid his hand under the lace shawl to her breast. She gasped and bit back the sound she wanted to make.

"You bastard," she whispered, and he laughed softly and moved away from her, closing the door.

He opened the door and Manson saluted. He looked tired and depressed. Paul opened the door further. "Come in."

"Sir, it's late and we got you out of your bed. I'm sorry."

"Come in. If that had happened an hour earlier when I was otherwise occupied he'd have got the contents of a chamber pot between the eyes for disturbing me." Paul closed the door behind him and went to pour two brandies. "You all right?"

"Yes, sir."

"What brought that on?"

"I was talking to Captain Withers about the retreat, sir. I disagreed with him about what he thought Massena would do. I didn't mean to be rude, didn't think I was and Captain Withers seemed fine with me, but Captain Longford..."

"He used it as an excuse. Again." Paul passed his junior the glass and Manson drank appreciatively. "I'm hoping that his new duties as official arse licker to General Erskine will keep him off your back a bit, Mr Manson."

"I hope so, sir. Thank you."

"You're welcome, Leo. Nervous?"

"A bit."

"Well I'm not going to tell you not to be, because everybody is. Including me, and I've done this a few times. But I've a lot of faith in you, I think you'll do well."

"Thank you, sir."

The bedroom door opened and Paul turned to see his wife emerging. She had dressed in her blue velvet morning gown. Paul was fairly sure she had not bothered to put anything else on, and the garment clung to her reminding him of how she had felt in his arms a short time ago. He glanced at his lieutenant and masked a grin at the boy's determined effort not to stare. He was doing very well, better than some of Paul's more experienced officers often did. Her hair was loose about her shoulders and she looked rumpled and content as if she were still warm from his embrace.

"It's too late to ride two miles back to the farm," she said with a smile at the boy. "Come on, you can use Captain Edmonds' room, the bed is made up although I probably should have aired it. But I doubt you'll care tonight. I'll show you where it is."

"Thank you, ma'am," Manson said gratefully. Anne glanced at Paul and he nodded. She led Manson along to the room and he paused on the threshold to light his candle from hers.

"Good night, Leo. Sleep well."

"Good night, ma'am."

Anne returned to Paul, locking the door behind her. "If you don't find a way to deal with him, Paul, I'm going to shoot him," she said quietly.

"I know. Perhaps Erskine will get him killed."

Anne slid into bed with him. "Don't even joke about that, love."

"It's all right, Nan, I'm too good at this to let Erskine get me killed. Thanks for that, by the way, I'd forgotten Gerry's room was free. Not sure he'll sleep much, mind, he looked very down."

She discarded the robe and slid into his arms and he laughed softly. "I'm not sure I'm going to be sleeping that much, either. I just think I'll be enjoying it more than Manson. Mind, I'm not the only one who is going to be looking knackered in the morning. While I was hanging out that window yelling at Captain Manson it did not escape my notice that the sergeant of my light company was emerging from the stable block with his arm wrapped very tightly around a lassie, and I'm not sure they were inspecting the horses in there."

"Really?" she said, laughing. "And was it...?"

"Yes, girl of my heart, it was indeed Teresa. She's taken her time about it, I thought Michael O'Reilly would be the one to storm that particular citadel, but it looks very much as though he has been cut out by his sergeant which will piss him off when he finds out." He laughed and moved above her. "I'm sure Michael will find consolation somewhere else. Now where was I when bloody Longford interrupted me?"

"I'm not sure where you were, Colonel, but I think we both know where you wanted to be," Anne said, laughing, and drew him down to her again.

He was already washed and dressed and outside the mess, a mug of coffee in his hand, when the messenger rode in the following morning. Dawn had barely begun to touch the darkened sky but he could hear the sounds of his men moving about, preparing breakfast ready for their march. As the young ensign rode in through the gateway Paul was joined by Johnny Wheeler. He glanced at his commander and grinned.

"You look tired. Enjoyed your little speech to Longford, mind. He interrupt your sleep or something else? You sounded pretty pissed off."

"I was, for a number of reasons. I'm about to ride out leaving my wife behind for an unspecified period of time, I've better things to do than listen to him bullying the junior officers in the dark."

"You'd think Longford would feel the same way given the lass he's married to. She's wasted on him."

Paul shot his deputy a surprised glance. "She is. Lovely woman. She'll probably be glad of the break from him, he's barely civil to her."

The ensign was dismounting, approaching Paul with a letter. He saluted. Paul responded, taking the note. "Morning, Ensign. Name?"

"Ensign Morrison, sir, first battalion 52^{nd,} third company. Attached to General Erskine's staff."

Paul smiled, opening the letter. "How's it going, Ensign?"

"Not sure yet, sir."

Paul grinned. "Very diplomatic, I might need your advice on that this week, lad, diplomacy is not my forte." He scanned the note and took a deep breath, looking up as Wheeler and Swanson approached.

"Change in orders?" Carl asked.

Paul passed him the note. "General Erskine's compliments. He will be ready to march at around noon."

"Noon?" Wheeler looked around him. "Well we're up a little early then."

"We are. I rather imagine Drummond, Beckwith and Marshal bloody Ney are up a little early as well. The difference between us and the French is that they will be moving out shortly and we will not. However, I shall remain calm, this is Wellington's problem, he can deal with it." He glanced at the young Ensign who was regarding him nervously and smiled. "The good news is we've time for a proper breakfast before we march."

He looked up to see Sergeant Carter approaching. "Orders, sir?"

"We're having a relaxing morning, Sergeant. Stand them down, would you, and go and tell the mess orderlies we've time for hot food. It seems General Erskine is in no hurry and doesn't want to see our faces before noon."

Carter grinned. "Looking at the expression on your face right now, sir, I should think he wouldn't want to see it much before midnight, but he doesn't know that yet, poor bastard. I'll let them know, they can get some proper food into them. What time we setting off then?"

"We'll do a full inspection at eleven, should give us plenty of time." Paul glanced at Morrison. "You can join us for breakfast, Mr Morrison, and I'll introduce you to Captains Longford and Corrigan who are going to be joining you on the General's staff. They can ride back with you ahead of us."

"Yes, sir."

"Assuming Captain Longford is awake. He had a late night."

"He did, sir," Carter said with a grin. "Heard you having a bit of a chat with him about it."

Paul glanced at his sergeant. "I know you bloody did, sergeant," he said quietly. "And you didn't hear me from your nice warm bunk in barracks either, did you?"

Carter looked at him, startled. Paul met his eyes in some amusement. After a moment Carter relaxed. "No, sir. Notice you weren't sleeping either."

"I was trying hard not to, Carter, although it wasn't easy with that racket on the parade ground."

"You have my sympathy, sir. Cut my evening short as well." Carter saluted and moved off to relay the new orders and Johnny glanced at Paul.

"What was that about?" he asked.

Paul glanced around to ensure he would not be overheard. "While I was explaining my views to Captain Longford out of my window last night I spotted my light company sergeant on his way out of the stable block when he should very definitely have been asleep in his bed, and he was not alone."

"Really? That's not like Carter the day before we march. In fact it's not like him to be sneaking a whore into barracks in the first place. Should Carl have a word?"

"No, it's fine. He didn't sneak anybody in and it wasn't a whore, Johnny. He's taken up with Teresa Cortez."

Johnny's eyes lit up with amusement. "Has he by God! Nan know?"

"She's got her suspicions. I think she approves in principal. When Michael O'Reilly was trying his best to get that girl into his bed a year or two ago he got an earful from my lady – who was not officially my lady at the time - that he won't forget in a hurry, but she's said nothing to Danny. I was just testing the waters there to see what his reaction was, but he didn't miss a beat. I'm not sure he cares who knows which is probably a good sign. Come on, let's go into the mess. If bloody Longford isn't already there I'm going to kick his door to wake him up after last night."

"Seen Manson this morning?" Wheeler said.

"Yes, he was up at dawn to ride over to the farm and make sure Grey and the men are ready to march. Looks tired, I'm not sure he slept much."

"No. I'm really hoping your plan keeps Longford off his back."

"So am I. I'm running out of ideas, short of shooting the bastard and that one keeps coming back to me." Paul nodded. "Looks like he's up, mind, or at least his wife is. Good morning, ma'am. I'm sorry you've been roused from your bed so early on false pretences; we're not marching until noon. Will you join us for breakfast or eat in your rooms?"

"Oh. I could join you…"

"Please do." Paul raised his voice. "Jenson, will you go and tell my wife about the new orders and ask if she'll join us for breakfast since we've time."

"Yes, sir. She awake then? Thought she might be sleeping in this morning."

Paul grinned. "If I come over there, Freddie, I can move a lot faster than you and I'll hit you over the bloody head with that wooden leg! And it's nothing to what she'll do if she hears you."

"Just on my way, sir."

"Johnny, will you take Mrs Longford in for me. I want a quick word with Mr Manson, I can see him riding in."

He moved away and Wheeler took Caroline's hand and smiled at her. "Come and have breakfast with me, ma'am. It's a treat I wasn't expecting before I rode out so I'm going to make the most of it."

"Yes, you'll all feel better for it."

Johnny met her eyes. "I wasn't talking about the food, Caroline, as you know very well. Did you sleep well, you look tired?"

"I'm fine. My husband was not in a good mood, he had words with Colonel van Daan…"

"Caroline, your husband is an imbecile who bullies the men and the junior officers. But if he's taking it out on you as well you need to tell me because I promise you…"

"No, Johnny, he doesn't. He's bad tempered but…"

"Look at me!"

She looked up startled into the steady grey eyes and Johnny lifted her hand to his lips. "We've not known each other very long, love, so I can't tell if you're lying to me or not. I don't know how much you know yet about Nan and her first husband but she spent two years concealing from us the fact that he was beating her on a regular basis and that ended with him almost shooting her. Men who beat their wives don't stop. Things don't get better. And it does not happen in this regiment. It particularly doesn't happen to a woman I'm starting to care about. So if he ever lays a finger on you, even just once, you are to come straight to me, you understand me? Ever! I saw what he did to her at the end and I am not having that happen to you!"

He saw a sparkle of tears in the blue eyes. "He hasn't, Johnny, I promise you. But if he ever does, I will tell you. Thank you. Since I married him I've felt so alone. I don't feel that way any more."

"Good. Because you're not. Come and eat, love."

Paul moved forward as Manson and Grey rode in at the head of their eight companies. Manson looked around puzzled and Paul came forward.

"Punctual as ever, Mr Manson. A wasted effort this morning, I'm afraid, we've been delayed until noon. Mr Grey, tell your lads to go and join the light company and get some hot food into them, we may as well make the most of the extra time. And then into the mess, George is serving breakfast shortly.

"Yes, sir." Grey dismounted and moved over, shouting orders to the NCOs. Manson swung down from his horse, and handed the reins to Private Browning.

"Thanks, Ned."

"You all right this morning? You were up with the dawn."

"Yes, sir, we're both mad aren't we?"

Paul laughed. "Bet I had a better night than you did, lad."

"Don't show off, sir, it's unbecoming in a senior officer."

The remark was so unexpected that Paul began to laugh and could not stop. "You cheeky bastard!" he said. "Get your arse into the mess to eat and hope I don't tell my wife about that one. Morning Michael. Take Mr Manson away before I punch him."

"I will, sir, we've a use for him this week." Michael glanced across to where Keren Trenlow was crossing the yard with a pile of clean shirts. "Are those mine, lass?"

"Yes, Lieutenant."

"Put them on my bed, would you, and take the money from my purse, it's in the drawer."

"Thank you, sir."

Carl Swanson joined them. "Morning, Keren. A bit early."

"Yes, sir. I've put your laundry away and put two clean shirts in your pack. And the tear in your black pantaloons is mended, but they're getting so thin they're going to fall apart soon."

"If the uniform orders would ever arrive, I'd have some new ones," Carl said laughing. "Going to have to do what the men do and start robbing dead Frenchman soon. Thanks, Keren. You can take the money for mine out of Lieutenant O'Reilly's stash, he owes me three shillings from cards last week."

"I do. Forgotten that. Shouldn't play with an officer living on his pay, he never forgets the debt!"

Paul was laughing, shaking his head. "You two have been owing each other money since week two in Melton!" he said. "How you've kept track over the years..."

"Just waiting for him to get himself killed and I'll be in profit," Michael said cheerfully. "Which reminds me, how is it that she puts your laundry away for you and packs your bloody kit and I have to do my own? You pay her extra for that?"

"No, Michael, she just likes me better," Carl said with a grin, moving towards the mess. "I don't grope her every time she goes past me."

"That was intended to make her like me more."

"Well it's not working, is it?" Carl said, laughing. "Morning Nan. Trying to give Michael some advice on his technique with women, he's failing badly."

"Mrs van Daan knows there is only one woman for me in the world!" Michael said, placing his hand on his heart. Anne studied him with apparent interest.

"That's as may be, Michael, but if I see you put your hands on my maid without her express invitation one more time, you are going to lose them which will make it much harder for you to hold a sword. She's very young and very unsure and she thinks she has to be nice to the officers, but I intend to make it very clear to her that does not include warming their beds for them when they're too lazy or too clutch-fisted to go to the brothel. Are we very clear?"

"Admirably so, ma'am. My apologies."

"Accepted." Anne nodded and walked into the mess and Michael glanced at Carl who was laughing so hard there were tears in his eyes.

"You're failing worse than I thought, O'Reilly."

"Bastard!" the Irishman said, laughing. "Come and eat."

Marching north with the light division after Massena, Paul was quickly aware of his chief's frustration at being unable to guess the next movement of the French. He was determined not to allow his supplies to become a problem, and his own scorched earth policy combined with the depredations of the French during the winter meant that he needed to remain close to his supply train or risk his troops becoming very hungry.

Embittered by their long and difficult winter the French troops took their revenge on the towns and villages through which they were obliged to retreat. The population, already starving, was subject to a level of brutality, which sickened Paul. The French soldiers went on an orgy of rape, torture and murder and their officers seemed unwilling to intervene, and possibly on occasion actively encouraged the excesses of their troops. Bodies of civilians often littered the streets of the towns and villages through which they passed, and in one village just south of the former French headquarters at Torres Novas, a sound alerted Paul and he went across to the burned out ruins of the church and found a huddle of ragged creatures peering out of him in mute terror.

"Oh Christ," he whispered, and sat down, summoning the Portuguese Anne had been teaching him. "Are there others hidden here or is it just you?"

"Only us, Senor." The woman was hard to place, probably no more than thirty but so thin and emaciated that she looked like an old woman. She had three children with her who could have been any age between twelve and six, like small walking skeletons. Paul called Michael over.

"Michael, we need to feed these people. Just a little for now. When the supply wagons come up they can have more and we'll get them back to the lines to be taken care of."

"I'll get some food together, sir, most of us are carrying a bit. Who's the lassie?"

Paul turned and studied the frightened face peering at him through the burned out walls. "It's all right, come through, you'll be safe."

"She won't!" the woman spat. "French whore. They took her and she went with all of them to feed herself. No wonder she looks good."

"I tried to give you food!" the girl said. She was only in slightly better condition than the older woman and there was a bruise on her face and finger marks on her arm. "They didn't give me a choice!"

Paul went to meet her. "Hush, lass, I know. Come on, she'll calm down. We'll find food for you all and then we'll send the hospital wagon back with you, it can come back up."

On March 8th Wellington arrived in Torres Novas and he watched while the French retreat was beset by a number of small skirmishes. It was clear that Massena was in full retreat, but the confusing criss crossing of various sections of his army were cleverly designed to confuse the British of his full intentions, and made it hard for the harassed general to know where to concentrate his forces.

"I don't think he wants to retreat all the way back to Spain," Wellington said, leaning over a folding table covered with maps. "He'll try to get to the Mondego valley. It's still fairly untouched, he'll be able to find enough food there to wait for reinforcements. So we need to stop him, gentlemen."

He glanced around the tent at the commanders of his various divisions. Paul was standing at the back, his arms folded and his face expressionless. Ostensibly he was there as aide to Sir William

Erskine, although his presence had been privately requested by Wellington.

"The Mondego river is the only thing stopping him then," Cole said. "We've only got the Portuguese down there."

"They won't stand," Wellington said quietly. "We've destroyed the bridges, but if they're hard pressed they'll run or they'll be slaughtered. The French are desperate and the Portuguese militia doesn't have the training, the experience or the fire power to hold them off."

"Best tell them to retire, then," Paul said quietly. "Not much point in letting them get slaughtered."

His commander smiled slightly. "I already have, Colonel,' he said. "If they're pressed. They still have to find a way across the river, they'll need to hold one of the bridges long enough to make a repair and I'm not sure they can, with us on their heels."

"Well we hope not, although the way they're bobbing about it's hard to know exactly which heels we'll be snapping at," Paul said. "He's got me confused already."

"Which is something of an admission for you, Colonel," Wellington said. "We'll have to split our forces and hope we get it right. General Erskine, I'm sending the light division along with Pack's Portuguese Brigade up after Ney, you'll march tomorrow."

"At dawn, sir?" Paul said innocently, and Colonel Pack gave a choke of laughter, which he hastily turned into a cough. Wellington glared at him and then turned his arctic gaze onto Paul.

"If you think you can manage that, Colonel."

"I'll do my best, sir, although my lads do like a lie in," Paul said. Erskine had not spoken throughout the briefing and appeared to have fallen into a daydream, which was probably just as well, Paul thought. He was unlikely to have appreciated the remarks of his so-called aide, but Paul, who had needed to manage several difficult skirmishes over the past three days while keeping Erskine from doing anything especially rash, was not in a conciliatory mood.

He walked to the horses beside Sir Denis Pack with whom he was on excellent terms. Pack clapped him on the shoulder.

"How are you holding up?" he said. "Thought Erskine had dozed off in there. You're doing a grand job, was talking to Drummond the other day and he's singing your praises. I think if it was left to him he'd recommend you be put in command rather than Erskine."

"Well somebody might need to take over if I lose my temper and shoot him, Denis, but I promised my wife I wouldn't, so I'm trying," Paul said with a grin.

"Women! Always making unreasonable demands!"

"She doesn't want me cashiered apparently. Although it's almost worth it."

Pack chuckled. "Shouldn't worry about that, Paul. When Black Bob Craufurd gets back here and finds himself short five of his best junior officers, you won't survive to be cashiered."

Paul grinned. "You heard about that?"

"I did. Was that your payment for taking on Erskine?"

"In part, I applied some strategic blackmail." Paul looked around, exasperated. "Where the hell has he wandered off to now?"

"He just rode out with Captain Longford, sir," Paul's orderly said, bringing up his horse. "The Captain sent his compliments, said the General had urgent things to do and couldn't wait around for you."

"Good. With any luck they'll get intercepted by Marshal Ney on the road back to camp and that'll get rid of Erskine and Longford. Good to see you, Denis, I'm glad we've got your lads with us tomorrow. The light division and the 110th will be on the road at dawn, by the way, even if General Erskine isn't! I'm not bloody waiting for him again."

"See you tomorrow, Paul. I'm assuming your lass isn't with you?"

"No, she's back in Pere Negro fretting. This is too uncertain, couldn't risk her. She'll be up when she can."

Pack laughed. "How you went from the worst womaniser to the most devoted husband in the army I'll never know, but it suits you, lad. See you in the morning."

Over successive days, Wellington's army pursued the French, following the smoke on the horizon, which marked the passage of the angry and starving Frenchmen. They passed burned out villages and wrecked churches, convents and monasteries, and the tortured bodies of local villagers who had tried to resist the French use of their houses, their food supplies and their women haunted Paul's dreams at night. Ney's rearguard consisted of two divisions but Junot's corps was not far ahead and Paul was very conscious that if pushed too hard the French could easily turn back with 35,000 men, considerably more than the British whose divisions were widely scattered trying to cover all possible eventualities as Massena continued to baffle Wellington.

Only the Light Division and Pack's Portuguese Brigade were available to follow Ney, moving fast and carrying little. By agreement with both Drummond and Beckwith, Paul encouraged Erskine to push the men hard, keeping as close as possible to the French without pressing them so hard that they felt the need to turn and fight. He was unwillingly impressed by Ney's skilful tactics. He was fairly sure that the Marshal was deliberately keeping the English busy to give Massena time to find a way to cross the Mondego.

It took until 11 March for the 3rd and 4th Divisions to catch up. Ney had taken up a position at the town of Pombal, with Junot only five miles further north. When the British appeared in strength Ney sent one of his divisions to the rear, keeping Mermot in position on the hill above the town, with one battalion in the castle of Pombal.

Seeing the isolated battalion, Wellington decided to attempt to cut it off. A battalion of Caçadores and two companies from the 95th rifles were ordered to attack across the bridge at Pombal, with the Light Division in support, while Picton was sent off to the left to outflank the French position.

Elder's small force managed to fight its way across the bridge, and up to the castle. When Ney realised that the battalion in the castle was in danger of being cut off, he led four battalions from the 6th Léger and the 69th Ligne down from the heights, sweeping Elder's men back out of the town. He then blockaded the main street and set fire to a number of houses, before retiring back up the hill with his entire force.

With Drummond and Beckwith in support, Paul led his men grimly through the streets of Pombal. Privately he thought it a wasted effort. The French fires and blockades made it almost impossible to progress and hand to hand fighting through the narrow ancient streets was frustrating at best and dangerous as night approached.

"Might as well pull back, sir," he said to Erskine, during a pause in the fighting. "Most of the French force has already gone, we're losing men and there's no point if we can't stop them. The third division has just arrived, we should pull out and wait for daylight, catch them then."

"I don't agree," Captain Longford said loudly. "Can't pull back now, we'll look as if we're admitting defeat. We're cutting through them, it's worth carrying on."

"I agree with Longford, Colonel," Erskine said. "Don't know what bloody Drummond is doing over there I've hardly seen them. Longford, get over there and tell them to press on. Get that blockade cleared!"

"Yes, sir." Longford shot a glance at Paul and Paul looked back at him steadily. As Erskine moved away to speak to another officer, Longford wheeled his mount to take the message to Colonel Drummond.

"Captain Longford," Paul said quietly.

"Sir?" Longford's tone was insolent.

"You get my men killed just so that you can ingratiate yourself with General Erskine, and I'll bury you in the same grave as them, so watch yourself. And be polite to Colonel Drummond because if I hear you've not been, I'll kick you off that horse."

Without awaiting a reply, he turned away and moved back into the fray. The heat from the burning houses was intense, and he was aware that there were very few French skirmishers left. Briefly he considered pulling his men out against Erskine's orders, but he decided against it. They were in little danger now although they were wasting their time. Eventually Wellington would send the order to pull back.

Under cover of darkness the French fell back to Redinha, a picturesque village on the banks of the river Ancos. At first glance to Paul the French position looked vulnerable with Mermet's division on a plateau to the south and Marchand's to the north, with the narrow bridge over the Ancos linking the two. Wellington was very aware of how close he was to the main French forces and waited patiently for the arrival of the 4th division and the news that the 1st and 6th were close by before beginning his attack at around two in the afternoon.

The 3rd division was sent to attack the French left and Erskine was ordered to take the light division to the right. The attack lasted less than twenty minutes before Ney ordered Mermet to retreat back across the river. The light division poured after them, and the French suffered heavy casualties on the bridge, but managed to get the bulk of their forces across. Paul ordered his skirmishers forward and they pursued the enemy carefully until they were in danger of being cut off. He pulled them back with no casualties and awaited Wellington who was approaching with his staff.

"Nicely judged Colonel. General Erskine, start getting your men over, slow and steady, no unnecessary risks, please. Clear those bodies off the bridge first."

Paul motioned to Carter. "Sergeant, get the first company clearing the bridge, light company and the first and second of the 112th in support. I don't think they'll double back, they're forming new lines beyond the village."

"I agree," Wellington said. He had his telescope to his eye. "Get us over, Colonel, fast as you can."

"He is not in command of the light division, sir!" Erskine said suddenly. "I am in command!"

"Indeed you are, General," Wellington said, his tone patient. "Is there somebody else you would prefer to clear the bridge? Really it is of no moment, as long as it is done."

Erskine did not reply, merely stomping off. Paul glanced at his commander. "I'd like to point out, sir, that for once it wasn't me who was tactless there."

"You're doing very well, Paul. We're all impressed."

"I hope it doesn't go on for too long. Sooner or later I'm going to crack." Paul nodded to the distant French. "The minute we get over there, they're going to retreat again, you know that, don't you, sir?"

"I do. He's doing a good job of holding me up, that's for sure. But my scouts tell me that Massena is still not across that river and we're getting closer. I don't think he's going to make it, Paul, and the only other way for him to go is back to Spain. Which is exactly where I want him."

"What the hell has Massena been doing all this time, dandling his toes in the water and drinking champagne? I could have got my lads across in half the time! And you bloody did at Oporto!"

"I have no idea, I'm simply glad of it," his chief said. "How is your young protégé getting on? Seen much action?"

"Yes, sir. He's a born skirmisher, he's fast, he thinks on his feet and his men will follow him. If he can manage to stay alive, he's going to be a name you'll want to remember."

"Excellent. Don't get him killed, will you, Paul?"

"Try not to, sir. I'm getting very attached to him."

"Yes, that can happen. It causes one to make all kinds of allowances which one would never make for somebody else."

Paul did not look around. "It doesn't stop you for using me to shovel shit when it's needed, though, sir, does it?"

"No. But then I know you'll always do it. And you'll do it better then most."

"Thank you, sir. Right, that's it. Distract Erskine, will you, I want my light company over first and he'll countermand my order if he hears it. We'll get them and Drummond's rifles out there, they'll do some damage while we get the others over and then we can outflank him and make him run away again."

Wellington laughed aloud. "Paul, have you actually taken command of Robert's light division? He is going to be very cross with you."

"He'd be a damned sight more cross if I let Erskine get them all killed, sir. I thought this was what you wanted me to do, even if you didn't say so."

Wellington was still laughing. "Following orders, Colonel, I am going to distract the General who is supposed to be commanding this assault."

"Don't let Longford get involved, either, he's a pain in the arse."

"Yes, Colonel." Wellington gave an ironic salute and rode off.

Paul watched him go with a slight smile then turned to give the order to Captain Swanson. The past weeks had felt endless to him, reining in his temper and trying to work around Erskine under very difficult circumstances. He missed having Anne with him to talk to at the end of the day. His officers were being incredibly supportive, but he was ruefully aware that it was his job to display no doubts and no fears. While he presented his regiment with his usual calm authority they would not waver, no matter how little faith they had in Erskine's erratic leadership. The officers and men of the 110th trusted implicitly that he would not blindly follow a stupid order which would get them unnecessarily slaughtered and he wondered how many of them understood that it could cost him his career.

He could say it to Anne. For the first time in his life he had somebody beside him to whom he could say literally anything. His first wife had provided him with love and stability and practical comforts but her affectionate domesticity was no substitute for his second wife's formidable intelligence and understanding. He could talk to her about his self doubts and uncertainties in complete confidence and he was missing her desperately. He needed to maintain his public face of cheerful calm in the face of Erskine's potentially lethal incompetence and he was doing it alone.

To his considerable surprise the person he found most useful was Lieutenant Leo Manson. The boy seemed to have assumed an unofficial role as Paul's ADC during the march. He was there to provide a listening ear when Paul felt like talking, and although his youth made him naturally diffident about putting forward his own opinions, when encouraged to do so, he showed an astonishingly mature grasp of the situation. Paul found him a very restful companion. He was naturally quiet beside Paul's boisterousness but he was beginning to come out of his shell and Paul enjoyed both his dry wit and his razor sharp intelligence. He had the sense that Manson's upbringing had stifled any tendency towards independent thought and now that he was being given the opportunity to spread his wings he was beginning to show his true colours. With Corrigan absent at General Erskine's side, the 112th was being run by Johnny Wheeler with Manson, Grey and four new young Captains from the light division. Manson was younger than any of them and had less experience but Paul watched him take the lead with considerable amusement. He wondered if the boy realised yet how much potential he had.

As Paul had predicted, Ney retreated once his flanks were in real danger, this time pulling back to the village of Condeixa. Once again Wellington's men moved up to outflank the French, encouraged by the news that Massena had still not found a way across the river. He had run out of time. In a series of increasingly angry communications with his subordinates, Massena abandoned any hope of maintaining a presence in Portugal and began the long retreat to the Spanish border.

On 13 March the French army turned east, and began the march back to Spain. Ney was left behind at Condeixa, with orders to delay the British for as long as possible. His task was harder now because his line of retreat was to his left, and could be quite easily cut by any British outflanking move. On 13 March Wellington sent the 3rd Division around the French left, and Ney was forced to abandon Condeixa and retreat five miles east to Casal Novo another small village of cobbled streets and exhausted and starving people.

Chapter Eleven

Paul awoke chilled and damp on the morning of the 14th. They were travelling light, well ahead of the commissariat and sleeping on open ground. It was foggy and cold and around him his men were stirring with no temptation to sleep late although dawn was a long way off. The sound of a horse approaching brought him to his feet.

"Colonel van Daan."

"Over here." Paul stood up and moved over in the direction of the voice, and recognised the lively grey ridden by Captain Grant, one of Wellington's aides. "Morning, Roddy, get any sleep?"

"Not much, sir. Yourself?"

"Surprisingly yes, although I'm as stiff as bedamned, feel like I'm eighty instead of thirty. Orders?"

"Any orders will be for me, sir!"

Paul turned at the approach of General Erskine. "Good morning, sir."

"Morning, General." Grant saluted. "These orders are for Colonel van Daan, sir. Lord Wellington would like to see him up at his lines."

"What about?" Erskine said huffily.

"I'm afraid I don't know, sir."

"I'll be back as soon as I can, sir," Paul said pleasantly. "Won't see much action first thing, by the look of things. Until this lifts we can't even see if they're still there or not."

"I doubt they will be. We've got them on the run now. We'll be marching out after them, I imagine."

"Very possibly, I can't see Ney making a major stand, but we'll be able to see more once this lifts, it normally does by mid morning." Paul glanced across to where Jenson was leading out his horse. "Morning, Freddie, he all ready?"

"Yes, sir. You want me to come up with you?"

Paul shook his head. "No, stay and get something to eat. I'll be back soon. Let Major Wheeler know where I've gone, will you?"

"Yes, sir."

Paul swung himself up onto Rufus' back and set off beside Grant. "How is he?"

"Grumpy this morning. We managed to get his tent up last night and there's hot food, but of course he doesn't give a damn about that."

"No but I do, and if he's not eaten it, his breakfast is in my sights."

Grant laughed. "You do like to wind him up, sir."

"Like a clockwork toy. I feel it's my responsibility with General Craufurd away. When's he getting back?"

"Don't know, sir. Lord Wellington has written to him saying that since he abandoned his command he might not get it back when he returns."

"Bollocks, he wouldn't dare give it permanently to anybody else, they'd mutiny," Paul said with a laugh.

"Only if you put the idea in their heads, sir. Going to get your light company to show them how it's done?"

"My lot have never actually mutinied, Roddy."

"No, sir. But there's always that feeling that they just might. Here we are."

Paul dismounted and handed Rufus to a groom. He approached the private on guard by Wellington's tent with a smile.

"Morning, Sam."

"Morning, sir. Bloody cold." The man ducked his head into the tent. "Colonel van Daan is here to see you, sir."

"Send him in, Gates."

Paul went into the tent. His chief was sitting behind his folding table, reading a letter. An untouched plate of food sat to his left, and he was drinking from a steaming mug. As Paul approached and saluted, Wellington looked up and over the top of his letter.

"Don't touch it!" he said. "Yours is over there. Sit down."

Paul lowered his tall frame into a camp chair and picked up the plate and mug. "Thank you, sir, you have possibly just saved my life."

Wellington gave a small smile. "I promised your wife I would," he said. "Besides, it isn't fair on your men if you miss a meal. I wanted you to see this. It came in from my scouts late last night."

He passed the letter to Paul who read it quickly. "Jesus," he said, half laughing. "Are you telling me we nearly picked up Massena and didn't know it was him?"

Wellington pulled a face. "Can't blame the Germans, how could they have expected Massena to be so far from his main force? Apparently he's furious, is blaming Ney and has even suggested that Ney tried to get him captured deliberately."

"Massena's losing his mind. Ney has saved his arse over and over this week. It's his own bloody fault he couldn't manage to get over that river. Is he starting to panic?"

"I think so. We're not going to risk a big battle, Paul, however much London would like me to. I'll take anything I can get out of this, but the main thing is to kick him out of Portugal. After that we can concentrate on Spain." Wellington studied him. "You've done very well this month. Better, to be honest, than I'd expected. Can you stay with him until Robert gets back? Only another few weeks, I'm hoping."

"I thought you told General Craufurd you were giving his command to somebody else, sir?"

Wellington pulled an expressive face. "I have told General Craufurd a number of different things over the last week. Writing rude letters to him helps to vent my spleen somewhat."

"Sir, he needed a break. He's not been well, and you need to remember that while most of your officers were sitting in Viseu or Pere Negro with their feet up planning cricket matches and organising amateur theatricals, Robert Craufurd has been out on the border skirmishing with the French pretty much all the time."

"So have you, Paul. When did you last see your older children?"

Paul smiled slightly. "Two years ago. Same as you, sir. I'm luckier than Craufurd, Nan is here with me. But you should stop writing rude letters to Craufurd, he's surprisingly sensitive, they'll upset him. You need to vent, do it with me instead, I've the hide of an elephant. As for Erskine, I'll do my best. It is hard work, mind, but Drummond and Beckwith are being incredibly supportive which helps. I am worried I'm making too many decisions. I'm junior to both of them. But often I'm the one on the spot when he drifts away or does something mad." Paul finished his meal and sipped the hot coffee appreciatively. "Was that all you wanted, sir? Because I ought to get back. I don't like leaving him for too long."

"There was one other thing. When Craufurd gets back, I'm going to increase the size of his division. He's up to the job and we need more light infantry." Wellington hesitated. "I'm going to add a third brigade to the light division, and you'll command it, Colonel. You've trained your entire regiment to be able to operate the same way, I'm going to ask horse guards to officially designate the 110th as light infantry. I'll detach the guards, put them over with the third, and I'll probably give you some more Portuguese and a couple of companies of rifles."

Paul felt his heart flip. "Sir – I'm not going to say no here, but you know perfectly well I'm ridiculously young to be commanding a brigade."

"You can work with Craufurd and you're more than up to the task, Paul. If Robert approves of you – and he does – I've nothing more to wish for. We'll talk more once he's back." Wellington gave a slight smile. "After all, it should be a sinecure after taking command of the entire light division without letting General Erskine know you're doing it!"

"You're not wrong there. Thank you, sir. I'm assuming this is not for general knowledge yet."

"No, let's wait until Craufurd is back and then we'll work out the details. Heard from your wife, by the way?"

Paul shook his head. Wellington laughed and picked up a folded letter from the desk. "Then enjoy," he said.

Paul took it, recognising his wife's flowing hand, and smiled. "You sure this isn't for you, sir?"

"Oh I had one too. It was very pleasant but I think there were hidden threats in it regarding your safety. I believe she is missing you."

"I'm missing her. Keep waking up in the night wondering where she is."

"Waiting for your return, I suspect. Go and read it, Colonel."

"Yes, sir."

Outside the tent he realised with wry amusement at his own childishness, that he could not wait. The air was still cold and damp but the early light of dawn would be sufficient for him to read. Wellington's camp was on the edge of a ruined farm and he found a place on a crumbling stone wall and sat down, opening the letter. She had the knack of filling the space without the need for crossed writing. Even the sight of her familiar hand warmed him in the cold of the morning.

"We are a camp of doleful women," she had written. "I have forced a confession from Teresa, since her gloomy countenance needed some explanation, and she has admitted that she is pining for your light company sergeant far more than she had expected to. I hope he is missing her too, I shall be cross if he is not.

"More surprising is Caroline, since I would not have thought that she cared two pins for her worthless husband, but she asks me for news as frequently as Teresa. I feel sorrier for her since it is clear that Longford cares nothing for her and I am frankly amazed that she should be missing him so much, and worrying about him so greatly, since she is worth so much more than him.

"As for me, I am missing you as much as I would have expected which is a great deal. I know that you are busy and active and have no time to sit and pine, and I know that makes no difference whatsoever, since you are quite capable of pining while on the move. I love you, and since it is hopeless to tell you to take care of yourself, I will tell you to take care of your regiment, since that is something you will take seriously. Give them all my love. Tell Carl that Keren has expressed her anxiety by cleaning his room from top to bottom and mending garments, which probably did not need it. Tell Michael to behave himself and look after you, since you will not. Tell Leo I miss talking to him.

"Hurry up and chase Massena out of Portugal, love of my life, and come back to me. I'm cold at night and I need you."

He stood up, tucking the letter inside his coat. Absurdly he felt tears pricking behind his eyes. He wondered of all the things she had not told him, all the minor irritations and bothers of daily life or the bigger tragedies of death and illness. Some of his fellow officers received letters full of domestic dramas and it weighed on them heavily at times when they needed their wits about them. She had told him nothing to worry him. She had made him laugh and she had managed to convey in warm, witty prose, the strength of her love. He walked back up towards his horse and mounted, smiling his thanks to the groom, walking Rufus at a relaxed pace back towards the village and the lines of his regiment. He no longer felt cold or depressed.

Into the joy of his silence, gun fire intruded with shocking abruptness. Rufus reared his head abruptly, and Paul reined in, trying to assess where the sounds of battle were coming from. There could be no doubt, they were up ahead where the 110th and the light division should be silent and watchful, waiting for the fog to lift. The glow of Anne's letter was blown apart, and he set spurs to his horse and began to gallop forward into the thick, cloying mist.

He arrived at Erskine's command post into a babble of argument and shouting. Around him he saw a collection of officers, Colonel Drummond and Major Wheeler among them, frantically trying to argue with Erskine. Behind him stood Captain Longford, silent and tight lipped.

Paul slid from Rufus, tossing the reins to Jenson who was waiting to take him, white faced and worried. "Thank God you're back, sir."

"What the hell is going on?" Paul bellowed, and the men fell silent, turning to look at him. Paul looked instinctively to Johnny and then diplomatically, shifted his gaze to Colonel Drummond.

"George, what's happening?"

"Christ, Paul, I'm sorry. We've been trying to reason with the General. He's sent out troops into the fog. He's assumed that it's just a line of pickets they're dealing with but I think it's more...."

"Of course it's bloody well more, that's serious gunfire up there. Who is out there?"

The silence told him what he wanted to know and he whirled towards Wheeler. "Johnny...?"

"Three companies of the 52nd, all eight companies of the 112th and our light company."

"I did not order the 110th light company into the field!" Erskine shouted. He seemed beside himself. "Your officer disobeyed a direct order and advanced! I shall have him court martialled, sir, and..."

"110th, to me!" Paul roared, and his voice had cut through the babble of sound around him, silencing them all. Through the blanketing fog he heard the shouts of his officers and NCOs, the call of his buglers and the footsteps of his regiment running into position. They moved so fast he knew they must have been standing there, at arms, waiting for the order. He looked at Wheeler and then back at Erskine who seemed to have lost the power of speech.

"Why the 112th?" he said. "It doesn't make sense, they're inexperienced troops..."

"General Erskine thought it would be a minor action and would help to season them, sir," Captain Corrigan said. He glanced across at Longford and his glance was murderous. "He had advice on that. Permission to join you?"

Paul nodded. Erskine blustered:

"Captain, you are a member of my staff..."

"He's a member of the 112th, sir, and he wants to help his men." Paul glanced at Drummond.

"Paul, I'll have my lads ready in fifteen minutes and I'll ride up and speak to Beckwith. We're with you."

"George, I've no idea what we'll find up there."

"Well best find out together, Colonel."

Paul nodded. He glanced across at Jenson. "Freddie, will you take Rufus and get up to Lord Wellington, tell him what's going on."

"I will, sir."

"This is my light division, sir!" Erskine roared and Paul turned on him.

"Well pick up a sword and come and defend it then, sir!" he said, and turned away, bellowing orders to his officers and NCOs.

His men were advancing cautiously as the fog suddenly began to lift. Paul sent up a silent prayer of thanks and then paused, his lines hovering behind him, waiting to see what visibility brought. Their advance was taking them down the hillside and across a narrow ravine then up a steep road on the opposite side. As the fog lifted Paul stared up the hill and his stomach gave a lurch in sheer horror. The hillside was covered with the dark masses of blue-clad French soldiers and in the midst was a solid red dot up on the ridge; the red coats of the 52nd, the 112th and the 110th light company in the middle of Marshal Ney's division.

"Oh Jesus Christ, it's Ney's whole force up there. They're being slaughtered." Paul was aware that his voice came out as a croak. He turned and looked over the nine companies of his regiment. Beyond them, although he had not asked, were his Portuguese battalions, ready and watchful. Paul took a deep steadying breath.

"110th advance. Hit them as hard as you can. When they turn, form square and keep firing. The rest of the light division are on the way and Wellington will be close behind, we only have to stand for a while. We're outnumbered here, lads, but that's never worried us before!"

They moved over the rough ground, fast and lethal, stopping behind low walls and small hillocks to fire round after round into the enemy. It was hard to miss, there were so many of them. When his companies felt threatened, Paul called them into square. Around him men fell and he deliberately did not allow himself to know how many and from which companies. Gradually, painfully, they made their way up the hill onto the road.

He was fighting with sword, leaving the shooting to men who could. Getting closer to the beleaguered troops he saw that they had formed three squares. One was clearly the 52nd, another was a small square consisting of his light company and the third was formed by the inexperienced men of the 112th.

"Sir."

Paul glanced behind him, taking the opportunity to catch his breath. "Zouch?"

"Beckwith and Drummond's men just engaged, sir. Sent up a message to say Lord Wellington is bringing up the 3rd division to hit them on the left. Just need to hold on."

"Thanks George." Paul felt a surge of relief. His eyes swept the field, assessing the situation. "Johnny!" he yelled. "Help is on the way, the third is taking the left! Pull them up onto the right, concentrate fire and push them over, we'll outflank them."

It was easier now with the French taking heavy fire from the rest of the light division. Fighting mainly in skirmish formation, the 110th pushed their way up the hill and Paul was conscious of the pressure of numbers easing as more and more of the light division fought their way up to join his men. It was exhausting fighting their way uphill, and the men were tired after two weeks of constantly marching and fighting every day, sleeping in the open and carrying their heavy packs. There was little sign of their exhaustion in their movements. Operating in pairs they moved through the French lines, picking off Ney's men with ruthless efficiency.

He knew with the sixth sense of experience when the French began to retreat. Pausing, he reached for his canteen and took several gulps of water. A man ran up beside him and he glanced around.

"Busy day, Kerr. Your lads all right?"

"Doing well, sir," the borderer said. "I'm pissed off, mind, they didn't tell me it was this much bloody hard work when I signed up."

Paul gave a choke of laughter and passed his canteen to the man. "They're pulling back, the third is outflanking them on the left. One more push and we'll reach our squares."

"Yes sir. Don't know how bad it is, but they're still standing." The other man studied him curiously. "You in trouble, sir? I'd heard Wellington doesn't like his officers showing too much initiative."

"He'll be all right. I doubt Erskine will be sending me a birthday gift, but I wouldn't want it. Hookey's used to me. On this occasion, I think it's why I'm here. Come on, get them up."

They reached the 52nd just as the rest of Drummond's brigade caught up with them. The French were in full retreat as the 3rd

Division began to move around the French left. Marchand pulled back towards Mermet's division, two miles to the east, and the two French divisions began to form up on a new line.

"Colonel van Daan."

Paul paused at the sound of his commander's voice. "Sir."

"I'm taking Beckwith and Drummond's men over personally. General Erskine is resting."

"Yes, sir. I expect he needs it after today. Permission to go to my men, sir? I'd like to see what's left of my light company. Be good to know."

"Get yourself over there, Paul. The good news is that the commissariat wagons have just caught up, there's plenty of food and some medical staff." Wellington's eyes studied him. "You all right? You're bleeding."

Paul glanced down, aware of pain in some surprise. His left arm ached and was soaked in blood. He examined it briefly. It hurt but the wound was not deep and he could still use the arm. "Not serious, sir."

"Well get it looked at, you told me that at Assaye and you turned out half crippled for the rest of the year. When you've sorted out the wounded get yourselves back to the lines."

"We can join you, sir."

"You don't need to, Picton is sweeping them up. Stay away from Erskine, I'll make sure he keeps out of your way for a day or so. That was a very impressive charge, Colonel van Daan. Look after the rest of my new brigade, General Craufurd will shoot me if I get them killed before he's even had a chance to lead them into battle."

"Just at the moment, sir, I would pay a sizeable chunk of my fortune to see that grumpy bastard riding over the horizon."

"So would I, Paul. But you've done a fine job of causing mayhem in his place, he'll be proud of you. And I think I see one face you'll be glad of approaching. Do I understand he went in against orders?"

Paul turned. Carl Swanson was limping towards him. His face was black with powder and he looked hot and exhausted. There was blood on his coat, staining his left side but he looked very mobile. Paul smiled slightly. "No, sir, I gave Captain Swanson his orders."

"From my command tent, sir?"

"That's right, Lord Wellington. My responsibility."

His chief laughed. "See to them, Colonel. Well done."

He rode off and Paul bent to clean his bloodied sword on the damp grass and sheathed it then went to meet Carl.

"I am so bloody glad to see you," he said simply. "Well done. How bad is it?"

"Not good, but it would have been a damned sight worse if you'd not come in when you did. Where's Erskine?"

"Hiding behind a tree if he's taken Wellington's advice seriously. Is Michael all right? How many, Carl?"

"Still finding out. Michael's fine, gone over to help the 112th. A fair few of my lads wounded, but so far only one dead that I know of, young Smithson."

"Jesus, he's only been with us since Christmas."

"I know. And he went down defending his sergeant, who is wounded."

Paul shot him a sharp glance. "Bad?"

"He's taken a bayonet through the shoulder and he's really pissed off! But the lads from the 112th took a pounding before we got to them. I'm just going up there."

Paul felt sick. He made his way up the hill. The 52nd had broken square and were limping around checking their dead and wounded, assisted by others of the regiment who had reached them by now. Paul lifted a hand in acknowledgment to one of their Captains who sat bleeding steadily into the grass from a severe looking leg wound.

"You all right, Ben?"

"No, sir, but thanks for coming in so hard. Saved our arses. Fucking Erskine! He needs shooting!"

"I'm working out how to do it without being seen."

"The rifles have renamed him Ass-Skin."

"Sounds fairly charitable to me." Paul passed on and jogged up to the 112th As he approached he could see men of his light company helping their shocked and bleeding comrades to sit or lie down. He glanced at Carl. "Where are the officers?"

"I don't know." Carl was moving faster. It was customary for the officer commanding to run to report immediately. Paul began to run up to the remains of the square. He stopped when he got close enough.

"Oh Jesus Christ."

He made his way over to the exhausted men of the 112th, who were beginning to break ranks, seeming finally to have realised that they were no longer under attack. One or two of them ran to their fallen comrades to see if any still lived. Johnny Wheeler was directing some of his men to search the surrounding area for wounded. Carl was kneeling on the ground beside a fallen man. Paul joined him. Sergeant Williams lay on his back. The sword must have taken him across the throat and almost decapitated him.

"How many?" Paul asked. His throat was dry and his voice came out hoarsely. He reached for his canteen, but Carl was quicker and passed him his.

"I've counted twenty of ours dead, more wounded, but I've not made it into the square yet."

Paul turned and walked over to the remains of the square as men helped their injured companions to sit or lie on the ground. Every face was shocked and exhausted. Young Private Terry was holding the colours, his knuckles white on the pole. He appeared uninjured but there were tears streaming down his face, and Paul looked down and saw that Will Grey lay on the ground beside him. There were so many stab wounds and slashes on his body that it was impossible to say which had killed him. Private Burns was kneeling beside him, crying openly. Paul placed a hand on his shoulder feeling very sick.

"Burns, where is Mr Manson?"

"Here, sir." The voice was so quiet Paul could barely hear it, but he ran to where Manson sat a few feet away, surrounded by five dead French infantrymen. His sword lay by his side, stained red. He was soaked in blood and there was a gash on his cheek.

"Good to see you, sir," Manson said. "Are the light company all right?"

"Christ, yes!" Paul said. He was looking around him at the scale of the slaughter. "I can't believe you held them, Leo."

"Grey's dead," Manson said. "And all the NCOs. I'm sorry, sir, I couldn't…"

"Mr Manson, don't waste your breath talking nonsense to me. You held them, lad, I am bloody proud of you."

O'Reilly appeared beside them. "I've sent some of our men down to the camp for stretchers," he said quietly. "We'll lay out the dead here. Good to see you, sir, I was getting a bit worried back there."

"Glad you're all right, Michael. How's Carter?"

"He's in pain but he's still talking which is a good sign. Bayonet wound, some bastard Frenchman got him on the ground and stabbed him several times in the arm and shoulder. He'd have been dead if young Smithson hadn't rushed in, he's cut up about him."

"Any other dead?"

"Not of ours, sir, we were lucky. These lads took the brunt of it, no question." Michael was looking down at Manson's white, exhausted face. The boy had closed his eyes. "I thought they'd break, no experience of something like this. They held better than the 52nd. Poor Grey. I really liked him, he was shaping up to be a good officer."

Paul nodded. "How many?"

"Trying to count up now, think there's around a hundred down, probably forty dead. Most of them are ours from the 112th, some from the 52nd. Christ, this was so unnecessary."

"French?"

"Light losses. Bastards had us outnumbered. We should never have been up here in that fog."

Paul nodded and knelt down by Manson again. "Leo?"

The boy opened his eyes. "Sir?"

"You'll be all right. I'm going to get you back to the wagons and we'll get you back to Nan, I'd rather she treated you."

Manson nodded, exhaustedly. Paul beckoned to Private Terry. "Come over here, lad. Leave the flag. You've saved it. Come and sit by Mr Manson while I see what else needs to be done. Keep talking to him – he may not reply but he'll know that you're there and that's good." Paul put a hand on Manson's uninjured shoulder. "I'm going to find out what medical staff we've got and where they've set up. I'll be back very soon."

Busy with his dead and wounded, Paul took no further part in the action during the rest of the day. Under Wellington's personal direction, the British carried out a more skilful outflanking manoeuvre over to the east and the French were forced to retreat again. The same happened again later in the day at Chão de Lamas. After being turned out of this position Ney retreated six miles to the Eça River and joined up with the rear of the 8th Corps with no further fighting that day.

Paul saw nothing of Erskine. Both Drummond and Beckwith came down to find him during the evening. With supplies having arrived, Paul had set up a full camp without waiting for orders from Wellington, and set his men to providing hot food. His light company, expert scavengers, had been through the French dead and wounded at speed although there had been little food to steal, they had done surprisingly well for money, and had looted blankets for their wounded. There was one hospital wagon with a young surgeon and two orderlies, and Paul had commandeered him ruthlessly to dress his men's wounds.

Sending his men out to scout in the gathering dusk he had discovered two poorly guarded baggage wagons pulled by emaciated mules. His men had despatched the French sentries and brought the wagons back to camp. They had proved to contain what appeared to be the officers baggage, and Paul had given permission for his men to go through the packs under Captain Swanson's supervision, taking anything they might find useful. His interest was not in the baggage but the transport and he sent Hammond and five men of the light company to bully fodder for the mules out of the commissariat.

The losses had been considerable although not as great as he had feared. Of the eight companies of the 112th, comprising around six hundred men they had lost fifty one plus Private Smithson of the light company. There were no deaths from the rest of the 110th although a number of men were wounded. They were bloody and exhausted and angry to a man, and having settled them in camp for the night, Paul took himself up to Wellington's tent.

He found Thomas Picton with the General. Wellington waved him in. "Find a chair, Colonel, and have a drink. Picton and I are discussing plans for tomorrow."

"Sir." Paul seated himself and accepted a cup from Wellington's orderly. "Thank you, Sean. How's that shoulder?"

"Feeling better, sir. Almost fit to fight again. Yourself?" The Irishman nodded at Paul's bandaged arm.

"It's sore but fine. Not all my lads were so lucky."

"No, sir."

"How many did you lose, Colonel?" Picton said.

"Fifty two, all but one from the 112th. All their NCOs and young Will Grey, one of the two officers who came out with them. I think the 52nd lost around twenty plus wounded. I'm holding burials at first light."

"I'm damned sorry, Paul."

"So am I, sir. We've managed to acquire a couple of wagons, I'd like permission to send our wounded plus those from the 52nd back to the lines."

Wellington nodded. "Of course. Will you escort them?"

"No, sir, this isn't serious. And I am not leaving my men to be butchered by that fucking lunatic again. Until you get rid of him or I shoot him, I am going to be glued to his side for the duration of this campaign, and you need to trust me when I say that he is not going to enjoy it."

Picton gave a short laugh. "Hate to say it, but I wouldn't want to be in Erskine's shoes. You'll need to send an escort back with them. French are all over the bloody place, I think we've got Ney pinned down now but can't speak for stragglers."

"No. With your permission, sir, I'm sending Carl Swanson back, he's got a bayonet wound in his side that would have killed him if it had been six inches to the right. I'll send an escort from the 112th, they'll want to see Mr Manson safe."

"How is he, Paul?" Wellington said quietly.

"He'll be all right, sir. I want him back at the lines, he'll be better in Nan's hands. And I want her to take care of Danny Carter as well. Manson is very quiet, he's upset about Grey and the rest of his men. He's very young for such a big loss under his command."

Wellington smiled slightly. "I rather imagine you remember how that feels, Colonel."

"Yes, I do. Which is why I want him around Nan, they've become very close and she'll be a big help. We've space for the wounded from the 52nd as well."

"Are you sure you don't want to go with them, Paul?"

"No, sir, I'm fine here." Paul shot Picton a look. "Wouldn't want anybody to think I can't do my duty because I want to see my wife."

"Christ, Colonel, nobody thinks that!" Picton said shortly. "I spoke out of turn after Bussaco. Shouldn't have done." His lips twitched slightly. "Met your wife at some reception a few months back, first time I've spoken to her properly."

"Did you, sir? Hope she was civil."

"She was charming. On Bob Craufurd's arm, he looked bloody pleased about it as well."

Paul smiled. "He's very fond of her, she makes him laugh."

"That's quite an achievement, he's a bad tempered bastard. She's a lovely woman, clever as well. You're a lucky man."

"Thank you, sir, I know it. I'd love to see Nan, but I've a job to do here. She understands that."

"She's one of the few officers' wives who actually seems to," Wellington said. "There are times when I'd choose to send all of them home, but I'd keep yours here, Paul. She's understanding and she's very useful."

Paul grinned in spite of himself. "She is, sir. Although at a guess, I'd say that the way she looks doesn't hurt much either." He stood up. "I'd like to send the wagons off early tomorrow. Once they've gone I will track down General Erskine and attempt to mend some bridges although it's going to kill me to do it. One thing that I haven't mentioned is the role played in this by Captain Longford, whom I am fairly certain gave advice to send the 112th into action.

Just at the moment I'll leave him alone, but when we get time to breathe, I am warning you that I'm going after him. It might be worth your while to come up with an idea of how to get rid of him for me, because if I can't come up with anything better my light company are going to bloody shoot him and bury the body, they've a great regard for Leo Manson to say nothing of Sergeant Carter. If you'll excuse me, I need to go and write to Lieutenant Grey's family."

Wellington nodded. "I'm damned sorry, Paul, I know you liked him."

"I did. He was a very promising young officer and I have to go and lie to his mother and tell her he died a gallant and meaningful death. That's going to stay with me for a while. Good night sir. General Picton."

Chapter Twelve

The days crawled past for Anne. Since her marriage to Paul they had not been separated for more than the occasional night and she was ruefully aware that she had not realised how badly she would miss him. It did not help that she knew he was in danger. She had always hated, in the days before she had married him, to watch him ride out to fight. It had not been her right then to kiss him goodbye although she had done so on many occasions. She had thought in her ignorance that it had been easier for Rowena who had at least the comfort of knowing that if he survived he was coming back to her arms. Lying awake in their shared bed, missing the sense of him by her side, she realised it was no comfort at all.

There was plenty to do. Four days after the 110th left, Captain Gerald Edmonds slipped quietly away in his sleep. Arranging for burial and writing to his family in England, Anne wondered if she should have told Paul in her letter and decided against it. He would learn soon enough and there was no point in upsetting him when he needed his wits about him. Anne's other fever patients were doing well and ready for discharge and she took the opportunity while the wards were empty to scour the church which she was using as a hospital from top to bottom with the assistance of Teresa, Keren and Caroline Longford. With no sick or wounded to tend, she wondered if she should send Dr Daniels, the young regimental surgeon, on to find Paul where he might be of more use.

Anne was vaguely troubled about Caroline. Teresa's distracted misery was understandable. Her relationship with Sergeant Carter was very new and she was clearly frantic about his safety, which knowing Carter's propensity for being in the thick of any fighting Anne thought was very reasonable. Caroline's husband was unlikely to be heavily engaged, and Anne had seen no signs before of marital devotion. But the young woman was obviously very anxious and Anne gave her what comfort she could, curbing her own fears so as not to worry Caroline.

The absence of news, although understandable, was frustrating, and when Anne heard the sounds of arrivals late one morning she ran down from her sitting room hoping for a message from the front. She was disappointed. Instead she found four officers, dismounting in the courtyard. All four of them were dressed in very new looking uniforms of the 110th. Two pack mules were laden with their baggage, and they handed their horses to Gibson in the yard, looking around them with interest. Anne smiled slightly and came forward.

"Gentlemen, I'm guessing you're just up from Lisbon?"

The oldest of the four turned. She recognised him immediately and could see that he recognised her; his eyes widened in surprise. He came forward, surveying her with considerable interest. She was dressed informally in one of the loose morning gowns she generally wore around camp, her long hair loose down her back, caught back at the sides with two combs.

"Yes, ma'am. Newly transferred to the 110th, just out from England."

"Welcome to Portugal, Lieutenant."

"I think we've met, ma'am, although I didn't expect to see you here," the man said. "It's Mrs Carlyon, isn't it? The last time I saw you was in Yorkshire and you were very newly married. Did Carlyon transfer in to the 110th?"

She was conscious of the very open stares of all four men. When she had married Lieutenant Carlyon she had been seventeen, desperately unhappy and only too well aware that her new husband had boasted around the officer's mess that his hasty wedding to the Howard heiress had been brought about by the fact that he had already enjoyed her favours and that her angry father had insisted on a speedy marriage in case she was pregnant. She had attended several parties in the company of her new husband and had been very conscious of the broad appreciation the officers had displayed of her beauty. They had sniggered very openly behind their hands about her and it had added to the misery of her early weeks of marriage. There was something of the same manner about Lieutenant Hendry now. His eyes moved over her body, taking in her loose hair and informal dress with an obvious appreciation, which was wholly inappropriate with a married woman.

"You're as lovely as ever," he said, bowing over the hand she had offered him. "Something of a treat finding you here."

Anne smiled. She was conscious that Gibson, who would normally have followed the grooms back to the stables to help with the horses, had remained where he was. Now he moved forward, stepping deliberately close to Anne. The men of the 110th were very protective of Anne. It had begun even before she had married Paul, when she had been left alone after Talavera and had travelled back to Lisbon under their protection. Clearly Gibson had picked up on a perceived lack of respect in Hendry's tone.

"Do you want me to stay, ma'am?" he asked, his eyes on Hendry.

"Don't be impertinent!" Hendry said, glancing at him. "You can get our bags unloaded and do something useful."

Gibson regarded him without replying or saluting. It was a study in silent insolence and Anne could not help laughing aloud.

"It's all right, Charlie. These gentlemen have just transferred in from the 115th Yorkshire, just down the road from where I grew up. They remember me from my first marriage and it's confused them a bit, but they'll be fine."

"First marriage, ma'am?" Lieutenant Franklin came forward. His manner was more civil. "Did something happen to Lieutenant Carlyon?"

"Yes, he was killed." Anne did not propose to give details, they would presumably hear the gossip at some time. "I married for the second time around seven months ago. He was a widower too, his wife died in childbirth. I should have introduced myself formally straight away, Lieutenant. Anne van Daan, wife to the colonel of the 110th. I think you'll remember him from Thorndale." She rested gentle eyes onto Hendry's startled face. "He will be pleased to see you lot, he's short of officers just now."

Franklin had gone scarlet. "Ma'am, sorry, didn't realise."

"How could you?" Anne said with a laugh. "I don't look much like the colonel's lady, do I?"

"Sorry, ma'am," Hendry said stiffly. "Didn't realise you'd married Colonel van Daan."

Anne smiled slightly. "Gibson, can you unload the bags and take them up. Captain Breakspear has allocated quarters in the seminary, they should be all ready. Get Keren and Teresa to help you unpack." She looked at the four men. "Come through into the mess and have a drink and I'll fill you in on what is happening. Paul is currently with Wellington chasing Massena out of Portugal and I suspect he'd like you to join him as soon as you can."

They followed her through into the mess. Anne was amusedly conscious of their discomfort both at her casual appropriation of her husband's duties and her complete unconcern about being found en dishabille by four relatively strange men.

Sergeant Kelly emerged. "New officers, ma'am?"

"Yes, George, just arrived. These are Lieutenants Hendry, Franklin, Ray and Ryan formerly of the 115th Yorkshire foot. They were stationed at the Thorndale barracks years ago when the Colonel was seconded there to sort out a few problems. I think he was there for six or seven months so they had plenty of time to get used to him."

Kelly brought wine and biscuits. He was laughing. "Doesn't usually take that long, ma'am. Wonder how General Erskine is doing?"

"I'd give a lot to know. Sit down, gentlemen. This is Sergeant George Kelly who runs our mess. He's not up at the lines because there's not enough food going up to make it worth taking a cook, and he'd end up punching the commissariat when they messed up the ration orders. I hope food is getting through, mind, or Paul will be like a bear with a sore head. Have some wine."

Lieutenant Ryan accepted. He seemed unable to take his eyes from her face. "I can't believe you're here, married to the Colonel," he said, shaking his head. "I mean..."

He broke off abruptly, and Anne laughed. "It's all right, Lieutenant. Best get the air cleared so that you can forget about me and concentrate on your duties, because you know the Colonel well enough to know that's what he'll expect. There was a scandal surrounding my marriage to Lieutenant Carlyon, and I am well aware that he fanned the flames to his own advantage, because he wanted to marry me for my father's money. So you'll have heard all sorts of stories from him at the time which will have caused you to treat me with less respect than you might have done."

All four faces were scarlet. Franklin glanced up, appalled at the mess sergeant. Hearing the conversation he had put down his tray and was standing listening, his arms folded across his chest, his expression forbidding.

"Ma'am, I didn't mean..."

"I know you didn't, Lieutenant, it's been a shock finding me here instead of decorating the quartermasters department on the arm of Robert Carlyon. In addition to whatever Robert told you about me, I'm also aware there was gossip in some quarters about my friendship with Major van Daan. I expect Robert fanned that as well, it's just the kind of thing he would have done to make my life difficult. What I want to say to you is that it was three years ago and I'm a lot older and wiser now. I don't give a damn about you lot sniggering in the mess over my so-called loss of virtue with my late husband. You were young and stupid then too and I don't suppose it ever occurred to you how much you were upsetting a very vulnerable young girl."

"Ma'am..." Lieutenant Ray looked appalled. "I swear we'd no idea..."

"Of course you didn't. The thing that you need to know is that my husband has no idea either. If he had the least notion you'd behaved that way towards me, not one of you would be here, no matter how much he needed new officers. He asked for you because he thought he saw potential in all four of you back then. It's your job to prove him right. You'll find the 110th runs very differently to any other regiment you've been near. He thinks you can fit in and he's not often wrong. As for me, we start again from here. You'll see a lot of me, I spend most of my time with the regiment. I help the quartermasters and I work in the hospital. I'm on good terms with all the officers and I hope that will include all of you. I'm also on good terms with the men as you might have gathered by Gibson's attitude."

Hendry was looking slightly sick. "I'm sorry," he said quietly. "This is the strangest conversation I think I've ever had with a woman, but I swear I'd never really thought about how much we must have upset you back then. I've two sisters of my own and I'd hate to think of anybody behaving that way towards them." He glanced across at Lieutenant Franklin with a slight smile. "We all laughed at Franklin back then, he kept on saying that what Carlyon was talking about in the mess wasn't right when he was marrying you, but I suppose we just didn't think."

Anne smiled at Franklin. "Thank you. I wish I'd known I'd a champion at the time, it would have helped. But it's over now and we were all very young." She looked at them. "I am unconventional which tends to upset some people. There is gossip and you'll hear it. My recommendation is don't repeat it around the mess here. Or in front of the enlisted men. They're very protective of me and of Paul and somebody will punch you if you say the wrong thing."

"We wouldn't, ma'am. And we're grateful you've been so frank. It can't have been easy for you. When did Carlyon die?"

"About a month before I married Paul, which gives you a very big clue as to what you'll hear from the headquarters gossips at some point. They're not right, but it hardly matters. I'm his wife and I hope we'll be friends."

She rose. "I'll leave you to your wine. Gibson will come and let you know when your rooms are ready, you'll have a room each, we're lucky, we've got plenty of space here. One of the eccentricities of the 110th is that I dine in the mess as does Captain Longford's wife, you'll meet her later. I generally leave early so that you can all drink and swear as much as you like. Caro and I have been dining in solitary splendour for weeks so I hope you'll all join us today, and I'll send a message to headquarters, if they can find it the way Lord Wellington is hopping about, to see what Paul wants to do about you lot."

She dressed carefully for dinner that evening. Since the regiment left she had not bothered to do so, and Caroline had followed her lead, often dining in her day dress. Despite missing Paul, it had been fun spending time alone with Caroline Longford. Since Rowena's death almost a year ago Anne had not had a female friend of her own station. She found Caroline a pleasant and easy companion in the same way Rowena had been, but she was sharper than Rowena with more of an edge to her wit, and she was well educated, having earned her living as a governess before her marriage. They had sat late some evenings, talking and laughing. Anne had shared, in a very limited way, some of the problems of her own first marriage. It was hard for Caroline to do the same, given that her husband still lived, but she had admitted to Anne how difficult she had found it losing the child, which had been the acknowledged reason for her wedding.

Anne was amused at the effort the four new officers had made to look presentable. She introduced them to Caroline and to Dr Oliver Daniels, the regimental surgeon and as Kelly supervised the first course and the wine she asked them a little about their background. None of them were married. All had purchased their commissions, and both Hendry and Franklin hoped to purchase up to Captain when a vacancy became available. Anne did not elaborate about Paul's chronic shortage of officers. He would make his own decisions about promotions. Ryan was an Irishman from Cork and had an older brother in the service, currently in Cadiz. All four of them were carefully respectful, apparently trying to make up for any sense of over familiarity from earlier.

They were coming to the end of the second course. The wine had caused all four men to relax, and Hendry even went so far as to flirt a little. Anne responded with cautious amusement. He would learn quickly how the relationship with Paul's officers worked, but until he had the opportunity to do so she did not want to put him in a difficult position should he misunderstand her free and easy manners. Experience was teaching her to be more careful around men she did not really know.

"What is that?" Caroline said suddenly, and Anne looked up, listening.

"Somebody arriving. A messenger, perhaps?" Anne stood up. "I'll go and see."

"I'll come with you, ma'am," Franklin said, getting to his feet. Anne nodded. She was halfway to the door when it opened and Anne stared in horror at the bloodstained figure before her.

"Carl! Jesus Christ, what happened? Is he all right?"

"He's fine, Nan, no need to panic. But we had a bit of an unfortunate time a couple of days ago and I've come back with two wagons of wounded."

Dr Daniels was on his feet. "We need to get them into the hospital. I'll go over and get set up, ma'am."

"I'll get changed and get my medical bag. Have you an escort, Carl?"

"Yes, we brought back the first and second companies of the 112th. Most of the wounded are from there, we've a few from the light company and some from the 52nd." Carl seemed to notice the other men for the first time. "You must be the lads from Yorkshire. Welcome. Captain Swanson, light company. "I'm sorry about this."

"Don't be." Hendry stood up. "Ma'am can we help?"

Anne looked around. "You can if you don't mind getting dirty, I'll need help to move them into the hospital, it's set up in the church. It's completely empty at the moment which is a first for me."

"What about Gerry Edmonds?" Carl said. Anne met his eyes and shook her head.

"I'm sorry, Carl."

"Oh Christ, so am I. I liked Gerry although we argued a lot. Does Paul know?"

"No, I didn't mention it in my letter. Thought it wouldn't help."

He smiled. "You're a good lass, Nan. You manage this well. But I've bad news for you too. We lost Will Grey."

"No." Her eyes scanned his face. "What about Leo, Carl?"

"He's with us, Nan. Not too serious, but he needs treatment. And he's upset about Grey. And Danny Carter isn't so clever either, couple of fairly deep bayonet wounds. Paul wouldn't let the surgeons pull them about too much, we got the wounds dressed and brought them back to you."

"I have trained that man well! Gentlemen, I'm sorry..."

"Don't be. Going to run up and change and then I'll be back to help." Hendry saluted and moved past Carl and the other three followed. Carl watched them go.

"That looks promising."

"Doesn't it? I knew them slightly in Yorkshire but they've grown up well, he'll be pleased. Let me go and change. Caroline, forgive me."

"I'll do the same," Caroline said. "Are...are the other officers all right, Captain?"

"Captain Longford is fine, ma'am he wasn't engaged."

"No. What about your officers."

"All well. Paul has a scratch on his arm..."

"I'm translating that!" Anne put in.

"Yes. It's a big scratch. But it's fine. All the others are all right."

Caroline seemed to relax. "I'm glad." She looked across at Sergeant Kelly. "Should we get food for the escort, Sergeant?"

"A good thought, ma'am. I've some bread made for the morning but I'll put it in now and we've the beef stew which I can heat up. Don't worry about it, I'll see to them."

With the help of the escort and the new officers, the two wagonloads of wounded men were carried into the hospital. Anne had set up two trestles in the surgery area, one for her to work and one for Dr Daniels. As Sergeant Carter was lifted gently onto the boards she felt slightly sick at the amount of blood soaking his clothing. The long face was white with pain and his shirt was a mess where he appeared to have been sick in the wagon.

"Danny?"

He opened his eyes. "Ma'am. Glad they brought me back here. Didn't like the look of that field surgeon."

"So am I. Lie still for me, let me have a look."

She peeled back the shirt and glanced across at her orderly. "Gibson, can you lift him for me, I want to get this shirt off and wash him thoroughly. Bloody field surgeons, they're quick enough to amputate a leg but they can't be bothered to wash a wound!"

Carter laughed weakly. "Don't, it hurts to laugh. Just hearing you start swearing makes me feel better. Ma'am..."

"She's on her way, Sergeant," Anne said quietly. "Just sent her for some rum."

As she began to bathe the bayonet wounds Teresa came into the room. She came forward quickly, slid her hand under Carter's head and lifted him to help him drink. He did so, his eyes on her face.

"I'm all right, lass," he said quietly.

"You are not all right!" Teresa said angrily. "You have holes in you! And now I am going to have to worry about you all the time!"

"Sorry about that," Carter said mildly. He winced as Anne probed and picked out pieces of cloth from one of the wounds. "You're as pernickety as the Colonel, ma'am, he looks just like that when our rifle drill is four minutes slower than he thinks it should be."

"And did those endless hours of drill help at all this week, Sergeant?" Anne said.

"We'd be dead without them," Carter said. "You heard about Mr Grey?"

"Yes."

"All their bloody NCOs, every single one of them. Manson is cut up about it, trying to work out if he could have done something different. Shit! Sorry ma'am, that hurts."

"It would do, it's very deep. I'm going to have to put a couple of stitches in this one, Danny. Was there anything different he could have done?"

"No. He was bloody amazing although he's too upset to realise it yet. How old is he – twenty? He'd pulled them into square by the time we got up there, did better than the 52nd they need some extra drill practice and no mistake, they were bloody hopeless in the fog, kept tripping over their own feet. Thank God it was too wet and too foggy for artillery or we'd all be dead. They were going for the 112th, it was the biggest square, they thought they could break through, they'd cavalry. Got through once, he went and stood in the breach and fought them off while Grey closed it off. That's when they cut Grey down and then they were all over him and Manson. I honestly thought them both dead. Captain Swanson put us into skirmish formation to keep them busy while the 112th got their square closed. They went for the NCOs deliberately; thought the square would break if there were no officers but I could hear his voice, steady as a rock, directing the men lying on the ground. I'd serve under him and you know how fussy I am, ma'am." He laughed suddenly. "All that bloody drilling in the dark down in Lisbon, not surprising the fog didn't stop him. He's a ballsy little bastard."

Anne finished her stitches and reached for a dressing. Teresa had brought a cloth and was bathing Carter's face, which was black with powder and mud. Anne finished off and glanced at the orderly. "Can you get him to a bed, Gibson. You can find somebody to give you a hand with the stretcher."

"I'll do it, ma'am." Lieutenant Ray came forward from the door. "Where do we find a stretcher?"

"Gibson will show you. Thank you, Mr Ray."

"You been taking up with new officers, ma'am?" Carter said, amused. "The Colonel won't like that."

"He'll like this lot, Carter, they leave their dinner to come and haul the enlisted men into the hospital. Although if I get any more lip from you I'm telling him to drop you."

Carter laughed. "Yes, ma'am."

Anne glanced at her maid. "Go with him, Teresa, get him settled. And get somebody to bring Mr Manson through, would you?"

She found Manson barely conscious which made it easier to clean and stitch his wounds. They were not life threatening although she suspected loss of blood was making him weak. He had little to say and Anne did not ask him questions. There would be time enough to talk.

Carl Swanson waited patiently on a bench just inside the church while the men were treated. His own wounds were painful but not serious and he could wait. Leaning back against the cool stone wall he closed his eyes feeling the exhaustion of the past few days wash over him.

"Here."

He felt a hand on his and opened his eyes. Keren Trenlow was sitting beside him holding out a cup. He took it with a smile and sipped. The brandy warmed him.

"Thanks, lass."

"Why don't you come up to your room? I've taken up some hot water and I can look at that and call Mrs van Daan if it needs treating. You'd be more comfortable in your own bed."

Her young face was concerned and Carl wondered how ill he looked. Suddenly the idea of a wash and a clean bed was very appealing. He set the cup down on the bench. "You're a life saver," he said with a grin. "Hold on a minute, it's hard to get up…"

"Let me." She held out her hand and he let her pull him to his feet. She led him outside and back down to the convent, up through the hall and into his room. The lamps were lit and a jug and bowl of water were on the table along with a wine bottle and some bread, cheese and sausage. Carl looked round at Keren. She was closing the door.

"Lass, thank you. Look, I'll manage."

"No you won't. Let me."

He yielded without argument and she stripped off his coat and shirt and seated him on the wooden chair. Carl sat silently under her ministrations and when he was clean she examined the bayonet wounds in his side.

"I'm going to dress it for you. I expect Mrs van Daan will want to have a look at it tomorrow but it's not urgent, I think sleep is more important. And food."

She dressed the wound competently and poured wine for him, then brought him a clean shirt and the loose trousers he wore about camp. While he changed, she went to his pack and began to unload it, tossing the clothing into a pile for laundry. "I'll do these for you tomorrow," she said. "What's this?"

Carl turned, dressed, and laughed aloud. "I took your advice about trousers, Keren. We ran across two wagons of officers baggage and I took a leaf out of the light company's book and looted to my heart's content. They're a good fit. There's a couple of shirts and some new boots as well. Feel quite well off."

Keren was laughing. "I'll get them washed. Eat."

"Come and join me, I'll never eat all this."

She hesitated then came forward and shyly sat down. He poured the wine into two cups and touched his to hers with a tired smile. "To survival," he said. "Keren, thank you for this. I can't tell you how good it feels to be clean and fed."

"You're welcome, sir."

Carl studied her as they ate. Since her return from Lisbon, Keren had been attracting a good deal of attention from both the officers and men of the 110th. He remembered thinking in those first days after Anne had taken her under her wing that she was a pretty child but he had not really paid that much attention to her. When she had arrived back at the lines she had offered to take on his laundry and mending and he appreciated the amount of effort she put in. He did not employ an orderly or a valet, being unwilling to pay somebody from his slender means to do something he could manage perfectly well for himself. Jenson and Browning both helped out when needed but he was aware that he was beginning to enjoy Keren Trenlow's constant presence as she cleaned his quarters and managed his kit with considerable efficiency.

Several of the other officers, especially Michael O'Reilly had begun to speculate about their chances of persuading the girl into their beds. It would not be an unsuitable arrangement, Carl supposed. Since she had left Simpson she had shown no signs of looking for another man in the regiment and he was not sure that he blamed her, but she was pretty and very sweet and sooner or later presumably somebody would persuade her either into a marriage or a liaison.

She looked up and smiled at him. "I'm going to go. You should get some rest, you look exhausted, sir. I'm glad you're safe, I've been praying for you."

Carl watched her as she rose and began to clear and felt suddenly a jolt of desire at the sight of her trim form moving about the room. Firmly he suppressed it. She was too young and too vulnerable and he hoped she would find some nice young NCO who would marry her. Getting up he stretched gingerly and winced. She came forward quickly.

"Into bed. Now. You're in pain. Come on, stop pretending that doesn't hurt."

He let her chase him into bed and lay watching her as she bundled up the filthy laundry in a shirt. "Thank you, Keren."

"Go to sleep. I'll speak to Mrs van Daan and I'll be back to see if you need anything."

She moved to the door with the bundle. On impulse Carl said:

"Would you be doing this for Mr O'Reilly if he were here, Keren?"

She met his eyes steadily. "No, sir," she said. "But if Mr O'Reilly were here, we both know he'd be trying to persuade me to get into bed with him, so it's a little different."

Despite his good resolutions Carl laughed. "Please don't think I'm not tempted," he said. "I honestly don't think I could, though. And besides, you're worth more than that. But I am grateful."

She smiled. "Sleep," she said, and left.

Working steadily into the night Anne was aware of how exhausted she was, unusually so for her. She supposed it was due to sleeping poorly for several weeks, missing Paul. She sat through the night with Manson, leaving him sometimes to return to the ward, checking on the men. Teresa sat beside Carter, holding his hand. Sometimes they were talking softly, at other times he appeared to be sleeping. Anne watched them, touched by their obvious attachment. She had been watching this relationship develop and it had taken a long time. Since before she had married Paul the men of the 110th had become used to Teresa helping with their wounded and sick and Anne knew that a number of them had made approaches to the Spanish girl. Teresa had resisted all temptation.

Anne wondered how many of them knew why. Teresa had been a young novice in a convent not far from Salamanca when the French invaded and took over the nunnery, killing the older nuns and raping the younger ones. When they marched on she had been left starving and desperate and had turned to prostitution, attaching herself to the Portuguese army on it's retreat towards Lisbon. By the time Anne met her she was working at an army hospital and her experiences seemed to have put her off any relationship with a man for good.

Sergeant Carter had exhibited more patience than Anne would have thought possible in his careful courtship of her maid, and Anne had watched their friendship developing over more than a year, amused and impressed at his determination. She was not sure at what point Teresa had capitulated but it was very clear that they had moved well beyond friendship and Anne was pleased. Teresa had been her support and lifeline during the time she had been married to Robert Carlyon and had been the only person who knew that Robert beat her. Their relationship had moved well beyond that of mistress and maid and Anne would have been sorry to see Teresa embarking on an affair with a man who wanted nothing more than a bedmate. She did not think that of Carter and watching them together now Anne was happy although she wondered for how long she was going to be able to rely on Teresa's services as her maid. A good thing that Keren Trenlow seemed to have settled so well.

Anne had sent Browning over to the farmhouse and had Manson's possessions brought up to Captain Edmond's old room and she settled him there. He slept heavily but awoke in the early hours to find her sitting beside him. Anne stood up and moved towards him, placing her hand on his forehead.

"How are you, Leo?"

"Sore." His young face was grey and drawn with pain. "But better than some. Did you stitch me up?"

"I did, and I'll thank you not to give me so much needlework next time." Anne reached into her bag and drew out a small flask. "Here. Compliments of Mr O'Reilly, apparently, he gave it to Carl for you. He said to tell you that it's what was left of your grog ration as he's drunk the rest."

She held the flask to Manson's lips and he drank, then lay back with a sigh. "That is not army grog," he said.

"No. I rather suspect that is part of Michael's stash of best French brandy. But it may help a little with the pain and help you sleep."

He seemed more relaxed already. "I'll be all right, ma'am – on my feet in a week or so. But I keep thinking about Will Grey."

"We all do. Did you see…?"

He nodded. "I was already down by then. They'd broken one side of the square and we were desperately trying to push them back enough to close it up again. I knew that once they were in, it was all over. They cut me down and were all over me, and then Will and two of the men stepped in and I just watched the three of them die, right in front of me. There was one tirailleur standing over Will just stabbing him over and over. He must have known he was already dead."

He closed his eyes and she could see tears wetting his cheeks. Reaching out she wiped them away with her hands and he smiled wearily.

"Danny Carter told me what happened, Leo," Anne said quietly. "He said that you carried on directing the men while lying on the ground. You held the square when all the other NCOs and officers were dead."

"My men held the square. I just shouted a lot."

Anne squeezed his hand. "That's your job, Leo. Thank God it wasn't worse. I'm guessing the Colonel is furious."

"Yes, ma'am. But he's being very good. I think he's cross with Captain Longford. It was his idea to send us out into the fog and General Erskine listens to him."

"Something really needs to be done about that man!" Anne looked around. "I've moved your things down, you can have this room. You can't be up in the farmhouse on your own."

"Is Captain Edmonds…?"

"He didn't make it, Leo. The fever had weakened him too much."

"I'm sorry. I didn't know him well but I liked him. So many deaths."

Anne leaned forward and kissed the young face. He was only a year or so younger than she was, but she felt many years older tonight. "I'll check on you again later. Have another swig or two of Michael's brandy, since I can't believe he gave it to you, and sleep."

"I will. Thank you, ma'am."

Anne got up and moved to the entrance to the door. Unexpectedly she felt a wave of nausea and caught the wall to steady herself. It did not help. The room swirled around her, spinning faster and faster, and then she felt herself falling forwards, heard a startled yell from Manson, and knew nothing more.

She awoke to see Oliver Daniels looking down at her with concerned eyes. "Nan – welcome back. Here, drink this."

Anne took a sip from the flask he offered. "What happened?" she asked.

"You fainted."

"Rubbish!" Anne said indignantly. "I have never fainted in my life!"

"Well then this will be a first. No, lie still for a moment, you're as white as a sheet. I don't know how long you've been lying there, Manson says he'd been yelling for about five minutes."

"Leo?"

"Yes, he saw you fall. Got himself up and to the door to shout for help."

Anne shoved Daniels' hands away and pulled herself into a sitting position. "If he's pulled those stitches, I'm going to…"

"Nan, he is fine. I've checked. When you sew up a wound it has a tendency to stay sewn up! Sit still, for God's sake, I can see you're still dizzy. Browning has gone to get Caroline and we'll get you to your bed."

"I'm here," Caroline's voice said, and Daniels stood up and stepped to one side as the other woman knelt beside Anne. "What happened, Nan?"

"Apparently, I fainted," Anne said. "It's a new skill, I didn't know I knew how."

"Let's get you up and to your bed. Let me lift you..."

"No, Oliver, I can walk. I'll be fine, just very tired. Probably worrying too much."

"You need to rest. Take her back to her room, Mrs Longford and get her settled."

Anne slept heavily through the night, and woke early with her stomach churning. She made it out of the room and down to the latrine before she was sick, and then went weakly back to bed. She slept again and awoke close to noon to find rain pattering against the windows and Keren Trenlow bringing her tea.

"Thank you, Keren."

"How are you feeling, ma'am?"

"Much better. Hungry. Is that bread I can smell?"

"Yes, ma'am, George baked another batch this morning. I'll get you some with some cheese."

"How are the wounded, have you been down?"

"All doing well, ma'am. Captain Swanson ate his breakfast and then he ate most of mine which I think is a good sign..."

Anne laughed. "Keren, did you stay with him all night?"

The girl blushed. "Some of it, ma'am. It's not what you're thinking. He just...I like him, ma'am. He's always polite, always respectful. He makes me laugh. I told him you'd been teaching me to read and when he couldn't sleep he asked me to read to him. Said it helped with the pain. I promise you, there's nothing wrong in it..."

"Keren, I know. Thank you for looking after him. I neglected him yesterday but I'll have a proper look at that wound later although I trust your judgement. You're turning into a very good nurse." Anne finished her tea and eased herself out of bed. "I must look a fright. Hand me my brush and comb would you? I don't know what's the matter with me, I never sleep like this. And my back is aching. Perhaps I've strained something cleaning that hospital last week, we did go a bit mad." Anne pulled on her wine coloured robe and sat brushing her long hair. "I'll be fine. Just need a bit more rest."

Over the next week, Anne forced herself to rest more. It was not as difficult as she had expected. There were no more fainting fits but she found herself more tired than she could ever remember. She watched anxiously for signs of fever or other illness, but apart from a feeling of nausea which seemed to come and go she had no symptoms apart from the exhaustion. Both Keren and Caroline fussed over her and she allowed them to do so. The wounded men were beginning to improve. Carl Swanson seemed itching to get out of bed and Anne gave Keren credit for keeping him still and quiet while he needed time to rest and heal. She was amusedly aware that her young protégé had developed a tendre for Captain Swanson, which was touching in its innocence. For all Keren Trenlow's experience of men, she still seemed very young and naive. Anne was continuing to help her with reading and writing and she had proved a quick and able pupil. Putting her head around Carl's door late at night to check that he was well she was amused to find Keren practicing by reading aloud to him.

"It's good of you," she said, alone with him the following day, checking his wound. "That's healing well. She's so keen to learn..."

"I'm not being kind, Nan. It genuinely helps, I don't sleep well with this. She's very restful for such a young lass. Reminds me a bit of Rowena. I like her and it's good of her to sit with me, she doesn't have to."

"No." Anne smiled slightly and took herself back to her room to rest. She slept for an hour most afternoons at present and awoke to find Keren bringing her tea and a noise from outside.

"What is that, Keren? I wonder if it's the uniform supplies finally. I wrote them the rudest letter I could manage so I suspect they'll be here soon."

Keren had gone to the window. She laughed. "Not supply wagons, ma'am."

Anne turned her eyes wide. "Not..."

The girl nodded, smiling. Anne ran to the window and looked down. There was a swirl of colour in the yard as the troops marched in. She could hear the voice of Michael O'Reilly dismissing the men to their billets. In the centre a tall figure was swinging down from a big roan gelding, looking around him. Anne knew what he was seeking. She got up and ran to the door.

"Ma'am, you cannot go down without shoes on!" Keren said, catching her arm.

"It wouldn't be the first time," Anne said, obediently pushing her feet into black slippers. She ran lightly down the stairs and out into a light drizzle.

"Paul."

He swung around, took three steps to reach her and pulled her into his arms, his mouth coming down hard on hers. She kissed him, her senses full of him, her body pressed close to him. She felt his hand buried in her hair, holding her even closer as if he could not let her go.

"Bonny lass, I've missed you," he whispered.

She stepped back finally and surveyed him. "You're hurt. The arm I knew about, Carl told me. What have you done to your head?"

"It's not serious, bled a lot. Flying debris from gunfire. We'd another skirmish the day after I sent the wounded back. And another the day after that. I'm hard put to remember the last time I spent a day without fighting the French, it's worse than last year up on the border with the light division and that's saying something! I'm completely shattered and really hungry, the commissariat finally caught up with us but the Portuguese one never arrived so we shared our rations with them. How are our wounded?"

"All mending. Carter is doing very well but he can't get up because Teresa is holding him down. Carl has had a lot of pain but he's mending well now. Leo is the worst, but he's doing surprisingly well and itching to be out of bed, he's as bad as you are! Your new officers arrived."

"Have they? Good, we'll need them. How is Gerry?"

She met his eyes. "Paul, I'm sorry."

"Oh God no!"

"I didn't tell you. Thought it couldn't do any good."

"No, that was the right thing to do, lass. I'll miss him, though; he's been with me for a long time. I'll need to write to his family."

"I already have, but they'd probably appreciate a letter from you."

"Thank you, love." Paul surveyed the yard, which was beginning to empty. "I'm looking forward to a bath, a meal, a drink and a very long time in bed with you. Are you all right, you look tired?"

She slipped her arm about him as they walked to the stairs. "I've not slept well," she confessed. "Missing you, I think. Is Captain Longford back? I didn't see him."

"No, he's elected to stay with Erskine. We'll rejoin them in a few days. It looks as though we've a break while Massena squabbles with his generals and decides which way to go, and I think Wellington felt I might be better away from Erskine for a few days so he suggested we come back here, get our wounds tended and get fed properly. He'll send a message if he needs us fast, he knows how quickly we can move. This is my reward for not killing Erskine so far." Paul glanced across. "Looks as though Johnny is explaining to Caroline. Jenson, if you're about to start messing about with hot water, desist and get some rest, you look half dead."

"I've got the orderlies heating water, sir," Keren Trenlow said coming forward. "Mrs Bennett has taken her tub up to your room. Won't take long."

"Keren, thank you." Paul smiled gratefully. "Christ, it's good to be back. Should be quiet around here for a while, Wellington has stood down all the Portuguese militia."

"He's confident."

"He can be. Massena may not know it yet but he's not coming back to Portugal. I think Ney has more of a grip. Wellington's spies tell him the two are at loggerheads and that Massena is likely to dismiss Ney. Which will suit us very well, he's a clever bastard and I've seen more than I need to of him this month."

He sat down tiredly in the chair and Anne knelt to pull off his riding boots. "Let me look at that arm," she said.

He smiled and eased himself out of his dusty coat. "I think everything I own needs laundering three times over. Including me. I'm sorry, lass, I'm truly foul."

"Paul, you're the best sight I've ever seen." Anne poured water into the basin from the jug and brought it to the low wooden table beside him. She set it down and went for clean cloths and dressings and brought the brandy and a cup. She poured and handed it to him and he drank and gave a sigh of satisfaction.

"That's good. You want one?"

"No, I'm a bit off brandy and wine at the moment. Seems to make me feel a bit sick."

He winced slightly as she began to clean the wound, and then sat quietly watching her face as she worked. He felt almost as though he had forgotten how beautiful she was and it was hard to take his eyes from the delicate perfection of her face. She reached up to bathe the cut on his head and he caught her to him suddenly, kissing her hard, his hand slipping into the front of her robe. She leaned in towards him and unexpectedly he felt her flinch. He drew back, studying her.

"You all right?"

"Yes, love. I am tired, don't know why." There was a tap on the door and Anne went to admit a procession of women and orderlies bearing jugs and buckets of hot water. "I've had a bit of sickness, perhaps I ate something that didn't agree with me."

He caught her hand and drew her back, studying her with sudden anxiety. "That's not like you. Any fever?"

She shook her head. "No, nothing. Honestly, Paul, I'm fine."

Keren poured the last of the water into the tub. "She fainted last week, sir."

"She did what?" Paul said, horrified. "Nan, I have never known you to faint, I'm worried."

"But I feel fine now. It's all right, Brownlow, just leave the towels on the bed." Anne watched the procession leave the room and bolted the door firmly. "Into that tub and stop fussing around me, Paul van Daan!"

"Bully." He was laughing, stripping off his clothes. "I wonder if it's big enough for two."

"I don't think so, but I'm happy to help you."

He sat relaxed in the steaming water as she knelt beside him, soaping him and washing the weeks of grime and powder from his hair and body. The heat soaked into him, relaxing tired muscles and he felt drowsy and content under her hands. He was aware of a change in her movements even without opening his eyes and he grinned, reached for her hand and moved it.

"A little lower, I think," he said softly. "God that feels good."

"You're getting me soaked," she said laughing and he opened his eyes and surveyed her.

"Best take it off then lass," he whispered, and reached to draw the robe over her head. "Do you know, this tub is bigger than you'd think. Come here."

She knelt before him, letting him soap her body, his mouth on hers, and the feeling of him touching her after the past month of longing for him was heaven. When he was ready he picked her up and carried her to the bed, dried them both gently and then settled her back and moved over her with exquisite gentleness. She was melting, her bones feeling liquid in her body, every part of her tingling with sensation and he was slow and tender when she had expected impatient passion, reducing her to silent tears of happiness as she lay in his arms afterwards feeling warm and safe and loved.

"That was literally one of the best experiences of my entire life," he said softly. "I can't believe how much I missed you, lass."

"Me too, Paul. I've felt as though part of me was missing. How long do you have? Can you stay a few days?"

"I can, girl of my heart, and when I go I'm intending to take you with me. We're marching up towards Sabugal with full camp which means tents, supply wagons, a hospital and my wife lying in my arms every night which is what I really need!"

"Oh Paul, thank God. I really didn't want you to go without me again so soon."

"But you weren't going to say so, were you?" He kissed her very gently. "Thank you for this month, bonny lass."

"Heavens, I've done nothing."

"Yes you have. You've given me what I needed. You've stayed where I asked you to be and tended my wounded and written me a letter that I swear I'll carry with me until it falls apart to remind my why I love you so much. I know how hard it's been for you, and to be honest I didn't know how you'd be. You're the bravest lass in the world, it's not easy for you to stay and wait, but I know now you can do it. I never have to worry that you'll go haring off and worry the life out of me, and that is so important."

"Is that what you thought I'd do?" she asked.

"I didn't know. It's hard for some of us to obey an order. God knows I've struggled with that myself this past month. But I know you can at need." He laughed. "I cried when I got that letter, it made me feel so bloody good."

She reached up to kiss him. "I love you, Paul."

"I love you too, lass." He shifted away and reached down to his coat, which lay on the floor. Pushing himself up onto one elbow he passed her a small cloth drawstring bag. "Sorry it's not wrapped, I was short on tissue paper."

Anne sat up, opening the bag. She tipped the contents out onto her hand and gasped as the late afternoon light caught the sparkle. She held the necklace between her hands and let it spill through her fingers.

"Paul are these...?"

"Yes, they're real. I'm fairly good at diamonds, my father has traded in the Indian market for many years; it's partly how he made his first fortune. He'll go wild when he sees these, mind, they're rather spectacular. I bought them from a Portuguese officer. He claims they were his mother's and that might be true or they might have been looted. Not many in this army are going to give him a decent price for them, he was overjoyed and it was still a steal, so we're both happy. Here let me."

He fastened the necklace and reached for her hand mirror. She studied her reflection then put the mirror down and moved back into his arms.

"You have a lot of money, don't you?" she said quietly.

"Yes." He looked at her and laughed. "Didn't you realise?"

"No. I mean I always knew your family was wealthy, but I think it has only just dawned on me..."

"Don't let it bother you, Nan, its not very important. Except that it makes it easy for me to buy you something beautiful every now and again, which I enjoy doing."

She looked up at him. "Thank you, Paul, although I'm not sure what that was for."

"For making me the happiest man in Portugal. And probably Spain as well." Suddenly he moved, bent his head to her breast and teased her with his tongue and she gave a shiver. He laughed.

"Girl of my heart, you are ridiculously sensitive just now, are you aware of that?"

"Yes, although I'd not realised until now because you've not been here."

"I only mention it because I'm curious. For a lass who's been feeling sick and had no appetite you're looking remarkably bonny." He moved his mouth lower and kissed her abdomen and then down to her tummy and she giggled.

"You're tickling me."

"I'd like to do a lot more than that with you, darling girl, but we'll have to wait until later, I can smell dinner and I am starving." He was still kissing her tummy, nuzzling her.

"You look as though you're trying to eat me," Anne said with amusement and he looked up, his blue eyes alight with laughter.

"Well there's slightly more of you to nibble on just now, Nan, but you clearly have absolutely no idea, do you? When did you last bleed? I'm working it out as before Christmas when we were still in Lisbon, you were as grumpy as hell for a few days. Anything while I've been away?"

She froze, staring at him, her mind in a whirl. "No," she whispered. "But you know how irregular I am, Paul. It's not unheard of for me to miss a month."

"No. But that's not a month, it's almost four. You're permanently tired, you've been sick, your appetite is all over the place and you've just fainted for the first time in your life. Your breasts are so sensitive you're wincing every time I touch them and I am absolutely certain, girl of my heart – and I've spent a lot of time enjoying your very lovely body so I am the man to know – that you are slightly more rounded here than you were a month ago. Come here – lass, don't cry, I thought you'd be happy!"

"I am," she sobbed, moving into his arms. "But Paul, I was so sure I couldn't!"

"I have never known why, there was always an even chance it could have been Robert. There has never, on the other hand, been the slightest doubt that I could. I can't believe you didn't realise."

"I feel so stupid! But all I've thought about this past month has been you."

He held her, stroking the shining hair until the storm passed. When she was settled in his arms he said:

"This is probably the time I should give you a long list of all the things you shouldn't do while you're carrying my child, bonny lass."

"I wouldn't if I were you," she said and he laughed.

"I'm not going to. You've been incredibly well with this, nothing like my poor Rowena. We'll just take it one day at a time. But now that you know you're not sickening for something, I need you to promise me you'll eat better."

"I will. Actually, I'm starving just now. Do you want to tell people?"

"They'll work it out fairly soon. Personally I want to shout it from the rooftops. It's up to you."

"We'll tell them, I think. I need to get dressed. I'm surprised they've left us alone this long."

Her husband began to laugh. "I'm not," he said. "They're probably hoping I'll forget to come down at all. I have been in the worst mood this month. By the end of it I'm not sure there was a single one of my officers who hasn't thought about shooting me. I'm lying here wondering if they've locked the mess door to keep me out."

Anne was laughing. "You'd never know it looking at you now," she said. "Get dressed and get yourself down there, you need to go and greet your new officers. Just let me put a dressing on that arm, I want to keep it clean. Can you send Keren or Teresa in for me to do my hair?"

He nodded, moving across to his clothes chest. "The joy of clean clothing. Keren seems to have settled in very well."

"Yes, she's been a big help."

"That's good, you'll need a bit more help than usual in a few months."

"If she can spare the time from coddling the Captain of your light company," Anne said, reaching for her robe.

He turned to look at her, his face alight with laughter. "Does she do so?"

"She does. I'm not sure what he thinks about it, but she definitely has a tendre for him."

"Knowing Carl he might not have realised, he's always had a tendency to underestimate himself. She looking for a protector, do you think?"

"Not at all. I've a suspicion she's had plenty of offers. I know Michael has tried fairly hard, but she's remained determinedly unattached. I think she genuinely likes Carl."

"Well she's got good taste then, but he's unlikely to make the most of his opportunities. He has all the scruples I always lacked."

Anne got up and reached for her robe then moved to collect the dressing she had laid out. She dressed and bandaged the angry wound then helped him into his mess coat and smoothed his still damp hair, laughing.

"You can't get the smile off your face, can you?" she said.

"No. I've had the worst month. Losing so many men, and I was worried I was going to lose Leo. I've got so much to tell you, Nan. But all I can think about right now is that we're going to have a child."

"We've plenty of time. Go on, get yourself down there and cheer up your officers."

He walked into the mess to find most of his officers assembled, drinking. Looking around he smiled slightly, thinking how different they looked from the tired, filthy men who had ridden in a few hours ago. Suddenly he grinned and went forward. "I wasn't expecting to see you up and around. Does Nan know?"

"No, it'll be a nice surprise for her." Carl was seated in an armchair. "It's much better and I'm bored with being in bed. Although it's had its consolations."

"Carl you cannot have been fit enough...."

"Only you would think of that, Paul. Thanks Johnny."

Wheeler put the wine glass on the side table and passed another to Paul, studying him. He laughed. "You look like my commanding officer, but you definitely don't sound like him. There's a thing on your face that looks suspiciously like a smile and you've not sworn at me once in five minutes. What's happened?"

"We all know what's happened," Michael O'Reilly said joining them. "Had a good afternoon, have you, sir?"

Paul was laughing. "Do I need to apologise to you all individually or will a group one do?" he said.

"Make it part of your speech later, some of your new juniors are trying to work out how to get back to their old regiments," Wheeler said with a grin.

"I know, I've been ghastly. A combination of Erskine, too much fighting, not enough food..."

"And missing your lassie. I hope you're bringing her with you next week, the difference she makes to you is shocking," O'Reilly said. "If she's not going, neither am I."

"She'll be there. Although at some point I'm going to have to look at alternative transport for her. I'm not sure at what point she won't be able to ride, but..."

They stared at him, open-mouthed. Then Carl got up and clapped him on the shoulder. "Christ, no wonder you're grinning from ear to ear! She just tell you?"

"Yes. Not sure even Erskine could piss me off now."

"Congratulations, Paul. How is she?"

"She seems amazingly well to me. Far better than poor Rowena was at this stage. She'll be down shortly. I'm just going to say good afternoon to the new lads."

"Go ahead. They'll be pleased to see you, they've not been round you for the past month."

Paul laughed and moved away and Carl sat down again cautiously. "It's not going to be easy to wipe that smile off his face at the moment," he said, amused. "I'm trying to imagine Nan as a mother and at the moment my imagination is stumped."

"She surprises me so often I don't even try to guess any more," Wheeler said, looking across the room. "Caroline, welcome. Come and join us. It is very good to be back, even for a short time, in a civilised place."

Caroline Longford gave him her hand and he raised it to his lips. "I'm so glad you're all back safely," she said. "I was so sad to hear about Mr Grey."

"Thinking about your father?" Wheeler said softly and she nodded.

"It is hard not to. By the time I received the news he had been dead some months, it is a long way to India. I'm guessing Mr Grey was not married. He was so young."

"Yes. Paul has written to his parents. A sorry waste." Wheeler studied her. Under cover of the general conversation, he said quietly:

"Caroline, what are you going to do next week when we march out? Nan is coming with us. Has he written to you?"

She shook her head. "Not a word. I thought he would come back with the rest of you..."

"Were you worried?"

"Not about him, Johnny. Although I've been horribly anxious about you."

He took her hand. "I'll talk to Nan and Paul but I think you'll have to come with us."

"I'm not equipped for camp life, Major. I don't have a tent..."

"We can provide everything you'll need, ma'am. Nan will help. Unless he has another plan for you, but you certainly can't stay here on your own."

She nodded. Johnny realised he was still holding her hand. It felt frighteningly natural to do so. He squeezed it slightly. "Caroline, at some point we need to have a conversation. We rather left things up in the air before I left."

"I know. But Johnny, you're under no obligation to me," Caroline said quietly. "A few moments on the terrace...I know it's easy to get carried away."

"Is that what happened for you, lass?"

She laughed and looked up at him. The expression in her eyes made his pulse quicken. "No," she said. "But I thought it might have been for you."

"You don't know me that well yet, Caro. They'll be up late tonight, but if you're still awake come down and meet me by the well. It's a fine night, we can walk down to the river."

She nodded. "I'll be awake," she said. "Nan is here, I must join her."

"We both will," he said, drawing her hand through his arm. "It's good to be back, Caroline. And it is really, really good to see you."

Her smiled warmed him. "You too, Johnny."

Anne came into the room and Paul turned to watch her approach, conscious that the eyes of most of the men in the room had turned towards her. She was wearing soft muslin shot through with gold and the elegantly wrought diamonds were about her neck, drawing attention to the line of her breasts. She had arranged her hair differently, the influence, he suspected of Keren Trenlow, and he approved the shining braids threaded through with gold ribbons, dressed low on her neck. Beside him he heard Lieutenant Ryan catch his breath. Smiling slightly he went forward and took her hand, lifting it to his lips.

"I'm aware of the urge to say something unsuitably poetic but it would shock my officers," he said quietly. "I love your hair."

"Thank you, it's Keren's idea." She smiled beyond him at the four officers from the 115th and then looked past them and frowned. "And what is Captain Swanson doing down here?"

Carl got up and came forward. "Hoping for a good dinner. Don't shout at me, Nan, I'm fine. Congratulations."

You had better be, Captain. Since Leo isn't here you can take me in to dinner and then I can keep an eye on you. I see Johnny is taking care of Caroline."

Carl nodded. "It looks like it," he said. "Paul, what are we going to do about her when we march?"

"I think we need to take her with us, Carl. Teresa will stay here with the wounded and a few orderlies since I'm not sure we're going to prise her away from Danny Carter but we can't in conscience leave Longford's wife unprotected here, no matter how uninterested he seems in her welfare. We'll take her with us and Nan can keep an eye on her, they get on well. I hope she'll be all right with that."

Carl was watching Caroline Longford, laughing up at Major Wheeler. "I'm sure she'll be fine with it," he said quietly.

Chapter Thirteen

It was after midnight when Major Johnny Wheeler left his room and walked down through the silence of the courtyard towards the well. He was aware of a feeling of guilt weighing down on him. During the past month he had thought of Caroline Longford daily, the memory of her in his arms warming him through the coldest nights. But it felt wrong somehow to actively plan to meet her with her husband still out in the field.

She was waiting for him in the shadow of the trees, a slender figure wrapped in a dark cloak, anonymous until he reached her and she looked up into his face and smiled.

"I'm glad you're back safely, Major Wheeler."

He smiled and shook his head. "It is very good to see you, lass. I'm still not sure I should be doing this, but I've spent the past month wanting to."

She stepped forward and he drew her into his arms, his mouth finding hers and the world spinning and steadying as he felt the passion of her response.

"Christ, lass, I'm guessing I wasn't the only one," he said finally, lifting his head. "But we should have a conversation..."

Caroline shook her head firmly. "No we shouldn't, Major, or you'll talk yourself out of this. And I've spent the past month deciding that I want to do it."

Her determination amused Johnny. He studied the pretty face, framed with fair curls and thought that she was rather lovelier than he had remembered. During his weeks in the field he had convinced himself that for her, the moments in his arms on the terrace had been a temporary madness which she would want to put behind her. Something about her demeanour told him he had been very wrong. Like him she had clearly spent time remembering the moment and she had obviously made up her mind that it meant more to her than a kiss in the moonlight. Looking down into her eyes he felt a little rush of happiness that she had spent time thinking of him at all.

"Are you sure, Caro?"

"Yes. Aren't you, Johnny?"

"Very sure. I'm just trying to be chivalrous here, but I'm not sure you want me to be."

"I don't."

"Come on, then, lass. The sisters kept a feed store down here, it's dry and warm and very private and that's probably all I need just now."

She had gained confidence in his absence, and he allowed her to take the lead. Thoughts of her absent husband faded in the warmth of her body and the soft sounds she made as he made love to her with careful tenderness in the dark shadows of the wooden store.

They lay together afterwards, her fair head pillowed on his shoulder and he listened to her quiet breathing. "Caroline..."

She shifted to kiss him. "Don't talk too much, Johnny. I just want to lie here and think about how lovely that felt."

He was silent, looking at her, wondering. Suddenly, as if she was reading his thoughts, she said:

"He is quick and silent and not particularly gentle. And it is horribly awkward. I know nothing of such things but I rather imagine it is how a man would take a prostitute. I used to cry at first, but now I have learned just to put up with it in silence."

Johnny felt rage flooding through him. He did not speak, unable to form the right words. She twisted her head to look up at him. "That was what you were wondering, wasn't it?"

"Yes," Johnny said. "I was thinking it was none of my damned business what you do with your husband but I've just changed my mind. You're a very lovely woman, Caroline. I don't understand how you came to married to a man like him. Tell me if I'm stepping out of place here, darling girl, but I am not doing this because I was looking for a quick tumble. I care."

She smiled slightly. "I know you do, Johnny. You're not a man to take a risk like this for something that doesn't matter."

"I doubt I'd be well thought of if this came out, Caroline, but we both know you're taking the bigger risk, especially given the bastard you're married to. Why the hell did you get involved with him?"

She sighed. "I was stupid, Johnny. My aunt died, I'd very little money. The house had to be sold and I found a post as a schoolmistress. Not much money but I could live in, I didn't have many expenses. There was some prize money owing to my father. I'd tried to contact Horse Guards, was getting nowhere. I remembered that Colonel van Daan – he was only a captain then of course – had said that I could call on him if I needed help. I thought perhaps if a serving officer wrote to them..."

"I see. And we weren't there."

"No. But Captain Longford was very kind and very helpful. He did manage to obtain the money. I was very grateful. He asked if he could see me again and we met a few times. It was very decorous, until one night. He took me skating, the lake was frozen, it was close to Christmas. I used to go with my father sometimes as a child. There were booths set up selling mulled wine and hot pasties and lanterns around the lake and a bonfire. It was romantic and it was fun and I had several drinks which made me reckless."

"I think I can guess the next part, Caroline." He was surprised at how clear and how painful the images were.

"Probably. He took me into the trees and we made love. I don't remember much about it. It was quick and awkward and afterwards I felt very ashamed."

"And you were pregnant," he said quietly.

She nodded. "I did not tell him. Afterwards he made no attempt to contact me again. I was not sure what to do. I had a little money, thought perhaps I could go away somewhere quietly to have the child although I was not sure how I would support myself after that. I was friendly with the wife of my father's man of business and I confided in her. She was very angry with Vincent, thought he had taken advantage of me. She went to Colonel Johnstone. I have often wondered if he would have been so determined to see me married had it not been for my father. Captain Longford was furious, but he could not refuse to do so."

"No, I imagine not. And you lost the baby."

"I was devastated. And relieved. I know that sounds horrible. And then we were both trapped. He was so angry. He told me he did not want me and would not come near me again. But he changed his mind. I was convenient and cheaper than a brothel."

"Oh Caroline..." He drew her closer. "I have always disliked that man but just at the moment I'd like to kill him."

Caroline snuggled into him. "I know. But Johnny, although I hate it, I do wonder if he is so much worse than a lot of other men. How many couples marry for love, honestly. I know very well that Nan didn't the first time around and she had it much worse than I did, he beat her. Vincent isn't really interested in me other than the use of my body from time to time. But he isn't horrible to me either."

"Your description of your sex life suggests otherwise, love." Johnny kissed the top of her head very gently. "I know you're probably right. We don't know what happens in other people's marriages and I can't imagine marrying a woman I barely knew for money or any other reason. But I do know that if I had, I'd try to make her happy."

"I know you would, Johnny. You're that kind of man. I'm not excusing Vincent. He's just a very angry man and having to marry me has probably made it worse." Caroline tilted her head back to look at him through the darkness. "Johnny, I am tied. I know that. But having this with you has made me so happy. I wish you had been there when I wrote to ask about the prize money."

"I wish I'd been the one to take you skating in the moonlight, Caroline." He studied her and laughed suddenly. "I can't guarantee I wouldn't have done what he did, you're too lovely to resist. But I promise you you'd have enjoyed it more, and I'd have wanted to see you again."

They walked back up to the edge of the courtyard and he kissed her and watched her go, his heart already aching.

"Tomorrow?" she asked, turning.

"Yes. I hate to say this, but I'm going to make the most of this, lass."

"When do we march out?"

"About a week. Caroline..."

"Johnny, no. No point in talking about what might have been or what can't be. Just let me enjoy this while I can."

Johnny studied the clear purity of her face in the moonlight. He was conscious of a feeling he had not known for many years, since he said a painful goodbye to the girl he could not afford to marry. Thrown together with Caroline Longford he had thought only of easing her discomfort at being ignored by her husband in the new surroundings of the 110th. It had moved very quickly so far beyond that and it was pointless now to pretend otherwise. "Caro, I'll do whatever you want me to do. Literally. You need to let me know if this gets difficult for you, but until you do I'll be with you as often and as much as I can."

Caroline reached up and kissed him very tenderly. She was smiling. "I thought you were very staid and respectable, Major Wheeler, you've surprised me."

"I am, love. Which ought to give you a clue as to how I feel about you to make me ignore all that."

He watched her go and stood for a while in the cold air thinking about her. It occurred to him with rueful amusement that he was potentially putting his commanding officer in a very difficult position. If Captain Longford were to realise that his pretty, neglected wife was finding consolation in the arms of his senior officer he would have every right to complain to his colonel. Despite himself the picture amused Johnny. When Lieutenant Robert Carlyon had first arrived in Lisbon with his beautiful young wife, Johnny had been censorious of her informality and flirtatious manner and deeply concerned at the burgeoning friendship with Major Paul van Daan whose reputation with women was well known throughout the army, and he had not hesitated to make it clear to his friend what he thought. He tried to imagine the expression on Paul's face at being confronted by an outraged Longford complaining that his conventional second in command was conducting a passionate and highly unsuitable affair with his wife. He was still laughing at the image as he went to bed. Paul would not know whether to yell or laugh.

The 110th and 112th marched north towards Sabugal four days later. Carl Swanson was well enough by then to march with them. Paul was aware that both Lieutenant Manson and Sergeant Carter were frustrated at being left behind but he accepted his wife's judgement and left them with his other wounded in the care of her orderlies and Teresa.

Anne rode beside Paul. She felt a huge sense of relief and of belonging, being out with the regiment again and she could sense the pleasure it gave him to have her there with him. They rode at a steady pace keeping close to the baggage wagons and camped each night in relative comfort. Anne was aware of a new watchfulness in her husband and she was faintly amused. Her sickness and tiredness seemed to have vanished and she felt astonishingly well although she was aware now of the slight swelling of her belly. She suspected that several of Paul's friends had questioned his decision to bring his pregnant wife up towards the battlefield and she was fiercely proud of his determination not to allow her condition to change the nature of their relationship.

They reached Wellington's lines after six days, and found the camp sprawling over several miles. Paul gave instructions to his men about making camp and then rode up towards his commander's tents with Anne.

As he lifted her down from the saddle, Lord Wellington emerged from his tent. "Colonel. Welcome back. All well at the lines?"

"I think you've got them too busy up here, sir."

"We have. You'll not have much rest, Paul. Massena's army is lying along the Coa. We're expecting to engage within the next day or so."

"That's all right, sir, had a nice break. Where's General Erskine?"

"Camped up past Drummond's brigade, you should go and pay your respects. Take your wife, he'll forget all about his bad temper with you."

Paul laughed. "Why do you think I brought her up here?" He glanced at Anne and she laughed and nodded. "Although we might be a little restricted in a few months, sir. Not sure she'll be spending so many hours on her feet."

Wellington paused, staring. Then he broke into a smile. "Congratulations, both of you. You look very well, ma'am."

"I am, sir. Hoping to see the back of Massena soon."

"We'll be sure of it, ma'am." Wellington took her hand and kissed it. "It is good to see you, I've missed you."

Anne lay in Paul's arms that night, feeling the warmth of him against her. "Will it be today?"

"I think so, love."

"Adam tells me they've set up in a deserted winery on the edge of Sabugal. Oliver is already there and I'm going to ride over in the morning."

"Take an escort, the lines are all over the place. And don't overtire yourself."

"I won't." She reached up and kissed him. "I love you, Colonel."

"I love you too, lass."

Paul had spent some time with Wellington and the commanders assessing the French positions. The French 9th Corps was to the north, forming the extreme right flank in the vicinity of the fortress of Almeida. The 6th Corps was in the centre while the 2nd Corps was at Sabugal on the extreme left flank. The 8th Corps was considerably to the rear. After some thought, Wellington had chosen to turn the French left by launching the Light Division, around the back of Reynier's 2nd Corps who were posted on some heights behind the town. This attack was to be supported by a frontal assault using Wellington's four other available divisions.

Marching out into a misty morning Paul was conscious of Anne watching him leave. Her horse was ready to take her down to the hospital and at the top of the rise he paused and watched her mount and ride out. She did not know that he was watching her and he stood immobile, seeing the slight figure on Bella, flanked by her orderlies, riding down to the hospital. He knew a familiar urge to call out to her and order her back to the tent and if possible back to the lines where she would be safe. He restrained himself with an effort and turned his horse. His other officers were around him, mounting up. Johnny Wheeler moved to join him.

"Worried?"

"Yes," Paul admitted. "It's hard not to be, Johnny. I lost Rowena to childbirth and I tried so bloody hard never to put her in danger. With Nan that's going to be impossible, she won't stand for me hovering over her like a hen with one chick. I want to tell her to rest and put her feet up and let Keren wait on her but I know she isn't going to do that. And how can I give her orders given the risks I take?"

Johnny laughed. "Paul, are you aware that most men see it as their right to give their wives orders just because they can?"

"That's not how Nan and I work, Johnny."

"I know it isn't. And I like that. I think you have the best marriage I've ever seen."

Paul shot him a startled glance then laughed. "Jesus, Johnny, you've changed your tune."

"It took some getting used to. And I will admit that when you married her, I was not convinced that you'd be any different than you were with Rowena. I'd known you since you were twenty one."

"I was a bastard to Rowena. Makes me cringe even to think about it. But that changed. I just hope she knew how much she came to mean to me."

"She did, Paul. And she'd be happy for you and Nan."

Paul smiled. "That, I know. She pretty much gave me my orders about Nan on her deathbed and by then I'd learned to listen to her. Jesus, what is Carl doing this morning? I swear to God he has days when he needs a nursemaid to get him ready!" He raised his voice. "You ready, Carl?"

"Almost." Carl ducked back into his tent and looked around.

"Are you looking for this, sir?"

He turned and found Keren Trenlow holding out his water bottle. He took it with a grin. "I'm having one of those mornings, he'll be yelling in a minute. Thank you, Keren. I'm not sure how you came to be acting as my orderly but I have to say you're prettier than Browning, and I think you're more efficient."

She blushed slightly and Carl admonished himself silently. "I'm sorry, that was uncalled for, I'm beginning to sound like Mr O'Reilly..."

Unexpectedly the girl's eyes flashed. "You're not, sir. You don't grope me every time I go past, and when you pay me for doing your laundry or mending you don't drop the money down the front of my dress!"

Carl paused at the tent flap. "He does what?"

"I'm sorry, I shouldn't have said that. You need to go. But you're nothing like him."

Carl walked back into the tent. "How long has this been going on?"

From outside there was a bellow. "In your own time, Captain Swanson."

Carl walked to the entrance and looked up at Paul. "I'll be five minutes, get them going, I'll catch up." He looked at O'Reilly. "Lead them down, Mr O'Reilly, I'll be with you shortly," he said, and saw Paul's eyes narrow in puzzlement at the chill in his voice. He nodded and Carl walked back into the tent.

"Sir, you need to go, this isn't important."

"It's important to me. For how long has he been treating you like this?"

"Since we came back from Lisbon. He wouldn't hurt me, sir, I know that. It's just that it gives some of the others ideas. One of the other girls told me there's a book open among some of the junior officers as to who I'll go to bed with first."

Carl was conscious of a spurt of pure fury. "I wonder why I've not been invited to join that particular bet?" he said. "Lass, I'm so sorry, they should know better and O'Reilly is being an arsehole. I'm guessing he made you an offer and you told him no?"

"Several times."

"When I get the chance I'll make sure he hears it loud and clear. He's been picking at me about it for a while but I thought he was just joking, it didn't occur to me that he was annoying you." Carl reached out and tucked a loose strand of hair back behind her ear. "I'll deal with him," he said quietly.

"Thank you," Keren said softly, and he felt, as he so often did, a rush of longing to take her into his arms. He controlled it with an effort and smiled slightly, moving past her.

"Take care," she said suddenly and he paused, looking down at her. She looked back steadily with clear brown eyes. "Come back safely. I couldn't bear it if you didn't."

Something about her expression broke the dam of his self control. He stepped towards her and scooped her to him with one arm. He kissed her hard, feeling her lips parting under his, feeling her body pressed against him. She clung to him, kissing him without restraint and Carl felt his resolve melting away.

"Oh Jesus, lass, I wasn't going to do this," he whispered, and she reached up to caress his face.

"I know you weren't, Captain," she said softly. "I was beginning to think you were the only officer in the 110th who really wasn't interested. And that was a shame because you're the only one I wanted."

Carl felt a rush of pleasure. He laughed and kissed her again. "Of course I'm interested, I'd have to be bloody mad not to be. Keren, I have to go but I'll be back. But lass, you need to think about this. They'll make just as many assumptions with me as they would with Michael."

"I know. The difference is that with you it would be worth it."

Despite himself Carl smiled. "I do like a lass who knows what she wants, Keren. But you're too young and I shouldn't be doing this."

"We can talk about my age when you get back, Captain. Best get going, he'll be yelling again in a minute."

He nodded and ducked out of the tent. He swung himself into the saddle and his friend shot him a questioning glance. Carl shook his head. "Tell you later."

Paul nodded and turned his horse.

"Ready to go, Major?"

"Yes, sir. But we've got company." Johnny nodded and Paul stared through the mist, puzzled. A small group of men were marching in, two horses at their head. Coming out through the mist he was astonished to recognise Lieutenant Manson leading one of the horses and Sergeant Danny Carter leading the other. On their backs were two of the wounded from the 112th and Paul realised in growing bewilderment that the rest of the wounded from the 112th and his light company were marching in neat lines behind.

"Mr Manson!" Paul bellowed, dismounting and moving forward. "Would you mind explaining to me what the devil you mean by..."

"Sir, not really his choice!" Carter cut in forcibly and Paul stopped. Manson's face was white and set. Paul looked up at the man seated on his horse and saw blood staining the front of his coat. Carter was leading Manson's spare horse and the man astride it had his arm in a sling and looked fit to pass out.

"Carl!" Paul yelled. "Ride down after Nan and get her back up here! Jenson! Make sure there are tents set up for these men, I don't want them in the hospital if I can help it!"

He reached up and carefully lifted one of the men down. "Johnny, bring the other lad, put them in our tent for the time being. Carter, any of the others this bad?"

"No, sir, but a few of them are definitely not fit to fight."

"None of you are supposed to be fighting, that's why you were left back at the lines." Paul lowered the man down onto his mattress. "Easy, lad, you're here now. What's his name, Leo?"

"Christie, sir. Took a ball to the chest. He shouldn't be out of bed."

"Paul, what the hell happened?" Anne erupted into the tent and dropped to her knees beside Christie as Johnny came forward with the other man and set him down alongside. Paul rose and stepped back. He turned to Carter and Manson. Both looked tired and pale.

"What happened?" he said quietly.

"We had a visit from the provost marshals, sir. Came with quite a force. Searching for malingerers on the orders of General Erskine."

"Erskine?" Paul said, incredulously. "He can't remember his own name, let alone how many troops are wounded and where they're billeted!"

"No, sir, that thought occurred to me," Manson said tightly. "Ordered every man from the 110th and 112th out of the hospital and lined them up. They'd a surgeon with them, didn't know him, ginger haired and going bald."

Paul and Johnny looked at each other. "Craddock," Johnny said.

"He pronounced every man fit for duty and told us if we didn't march up to join our regiments we'd be arrested as deserters."

"What about the 52nd?" Carl asked.

"Didn't go near them."

Anne stood up and looked over at Keren who had appeared in the doorway. "Is that my bag, Keren? Thank you. Will you bring some hot water…where's Teresa?"

Paul had only just realised that she was not present. He looked at Carter's white, set face. "Danny?"

Nobody spoke for a moment and Anne moved forward. Her expression was one of dawning anger. "Sergeant Carter, where is my maid?"

"In prison, ma'am."

"What?"

Paul put his arm gently about his wife. She looked as though she was about to explode. He studied his young lieutenant. "What happened, Leo?"

"I argued with them. A fair bit. Some of the guards took matters into their own hands, started hauling the lads out of bed. Christie's wound opened up again." Manson glanced at Carter. "Sir, Teresa lost her temper a bit at that point. She went for the man. They've arrested her for assaulting him."

Paul looked at Carter. "Tell me you're joking," he said quietly.

"I'm not joking," Carter said. "They said she was a camp follower, subject to army discipline, refused to accept that she was Mrs van Daan's maid or my fiancee. She'll come up before the next board and I imagine they'll order a flogging, sir."

Paul could feel his wife almost quivering with anger. "They called my maid a camp follower? Before I'm finished with them they are going to wish they'd not done that! Jenson, go and get Bella."

"Ma'am, Teresa is back at the lines. You can't ride back there. And besides, it won't do any good. One of the reasons they gave for doing this was that none of us had been certified sick by a proper medical officer. According to Craddock we'd been treated by an unqualified and untrained female who has no standing in the army and was a disgrace to her sex."

"Which is actually untrue because Oliver Daniels was with me. But I'm not riding back to the lines, Danny," Anne said with ominous calm. She looked at Paul and he nodded.

"Go. Take Jenson. And Keren. Not Caroline in case you happen to run into Captain Longford, I don't want her to hear what you're likely to say to him. Get Norris or Daniels down here if you can."

Anne shook her head. "I don't think so, Paul, I want Mr McGrigor."

"The surgeon-general? Yes that ought to do it. Be careful, girl of my heart, remember you've two of you to worry about now."

"I will. I have. And we're both furious. I know you have to go, Paul." Anne reached up to kiss him. "I love you and don't worry, I'll take care of them."

"I know you will, lass, thank God you're here. Tell Wellington that if he doesn't send a message back to the lines about Teresa right now I am coming after him with a bloody sword!"

When she had gone Paul turned back to Manson and Carter. Carter looked somewhat relieved. "Think he'll do it?"

"With Nan in that mood? He'd better or she'll take a bayonet to him. This is bloody Longford's doing of course, but the provost marshals will have taken to it with gusto, they loathe me with a passion and they don't often get a sniff near my regiment. When I get hold of Major Courtney I'm going to throw him through a bloody window, unpleasant little shit! And I don't even want to think about what Nan is going to say to Cradock the next time she runs into him. In the meantime we need to get these lads settled. Caroline can help with that. I wish I could stay to help but I can't."

"No, sir. Permission to march with you, sir?"

"Mr Manson, you're wounded."

"I'm fine, sir. Been marching for six days, no problems. I can fight."

"So can I, sir," Carter said.

Paul studied them. "Neither of you look all that good, but I can't tell if that's because you're still sick or if it's because you're so pissed off."

"Both, sir, but I'll be better in the field than sitting around here fuming."

"All right. Unload your kit, Mr Manson, and join your men."

"Sir."

As he walked away, Paul glanced at his sergeant. "Something tells me I might need to intervene on Mr Manson's behalf with the provost marshal," he said quietly.

"I think you might, sir."

"What did he do?"

"Could have been worse, sir."

"You mean he didn't shoot anybody."

Carter laughed. "Exactly. He was bloody rude. He's got a mouth on him, that lad, when he gets going it's hard to stop him. At the end of it Courtney told his lads to arrest him along with Teresa. Mr Manson pulled a pistol on him and told him that he'd been ordered to march with his men and he was bloody well going to do it to make sure they got here in one piece. They didn't argue much but they'll remember it. It was pretty obvious early on that Christie and Andrews weren't going to make it on foot, so Mr Manson suggested they use the horses and we'd lead them."

"So he came here on foot."

"Pretty much, sir."

"Is he fit to fight, sergeant?"

"I'd say so, sir. He's a tough little bugger."

"He is. All right, let's get going. I'm happy to leave this up to Nan, she'll see the others settled."

"I'm guessing Captain Longford put them up to this, sir?"

"I'd guess so. He hates Mr Manson for some reason. I'll find out when this is over. Come on, Sergeant. Good to have you back despite the circumstances." Paul paused suddenly, aware that in his anxiety about his wounded men and his sheer fury at what had happened, he had missed something. "Sergeant?"

"Yes, sir."

"Did I just hear you refer to Miss Cortez as your fiancee?"

"Yes, sir."

Paul regarded him owlishly. "Did I know about this?"

"I'd say you do now, sir."

"Does Nan?"

"Not officially, sir, it's fairly recent. But I doubt it's much of a surprise to her. You all right with it, sir? I should probably ask Captain Swanson officially, but…"

"I'm delighted, Danny. I'd quite like to kiss the bride but she's not bloody here, being locked up for doing her job. I am going to fucking kill somebody for this, I'm just trying to decide who gets it first! Come on."

Paul's men were positioned on the river bank with General Erskine and Colonel Beckwith's first brigade. The fog was so thick it was impossible to see the enemy and sounds were muffled and hard to locate in the silent whiteness of the morning. Paul waited, shifting impatiently. He could hear no signs of the approach of Drummond with the second brigade.

He could hear orders going out and the sound of bugles and drums and he rode forward. Captain Corrigan was seated on his horse watching General Erskine talking to Beckwith.

"What's going on, Pat?"

Corrigan turned furious dark eyes towards him and Paul felt a sinking sensation in the pit of his stomach. "He is a bloody lunatic, Paul. He's ordered Beckwith to cross and engage the enemy."

"Oh not again! In this fog? He must be mad, nobody will try to do anything in this. Wellington won't march his other divisions in support until he can see where he's marching them. If he's managed to escape from my enraged wife yet, which is by no means certain. Didn't he learn anything from the last fiasco?"

"Apparently not."

Paul rode over towards Beckwith. Erskine had moved away and Paul noticed that he was in conversation with Captain Longford. He glanced back at Manson and saw that the younger man was watching them as well. His golden eyes were stormy but he made no attempt to move and he seemed to have himself under control. Paul looked back at Beckwith who pulled a wry face.

"We're going in. I'm not happy about it but orders are orders. General Erskine is going off with the cavalry to reconnoitre crossing places and he's left orders that Drummond is not to follow me in when he gets here without specific orders."

"How can he give orders if he's buggering off with the cavalry?"

"God knows, Paul, but will you make sure Drummond knows what's going on when he finally gets here? I'm worried we'll get no support, Wellington will never march in this, he's got more sense."

"Sydney, you could refuse to march."

Beckwith shook his head. "I can't, Paul. Whatever I think of him, he's in command."

Paul bit back his instinctive response. "I know. I'll keep an eye on things. If I'm worried I'll come in and make sure Drummond does as well. Go carefully."

"We will." The colonel eyed his junior in some amusement. "Are you aware that in the mess they have started to refer to you as Wellington's mastiff, Paul? He has you lined up for every job nobody else wants to do. Don't you get tired of it?"

"At times, yes. But on the plus side I lead an interesting life. Although I'm sick of Erskine. Would you excuse me, sir, I need to have a word with Captain Longford. Good luck. I've got your back."

"I know you have, Colonel." Beckwith saluted and turned to join his men and Paul rode over to Longford. He saluted Erskine.

"Sir."

"I'm taking the cavalry to look at possible crossing places, Colonel van Daan. Captain Longford has my orders."

"I'm sure he does, sir. Take care, won't you, this fog is very deceptive."

"I will. Hold until I get back or send further orders." Erskine saluted and rode off. Paul looked at Longford.

"Captain Longford. I understand you suggested that the provost marshals pay a visit to my wounded."

"General Erskine's orders, sir."

"On your advice I have no doubt. Sadly most of them have arrived here in no condition to fight. My wife is taking care of them after having a chat with Lord Wellington on their behalf."

"Surgeon's decision, sir, not mine."

"And who told you, I wonder, that Cradock was practically the only surgeon in the army by now who objects to my wife's work?"

"He's not the only officer to object to it, sir. A fair number of them think that she shouldn't be doing this."

"Fortunately for the health of my regiment, Lord Wellington disagrees, Captain. When this is over we'll have a chat about this, I can promise you. In the meantime I'd suggest you do nothing to remind me of your existence."

He turned his horse but Longford's voice arrested him.

"Colonel van Daan."

Paul turned back. "What?"

"It isn't just the surgeons, sir. She shouldn't be out here. She shouldn't be doing this. She is the most beautiful woman I have ever seen and she should be back in Lisbon or London living in luxury, mixing with royalty, not the scum of your regiment. You claim to care about her but you let her spend time with criminals and vagabonds and I don't care how much it pisses you off to hear it, you should take care of a woman like that properly, or one day she's going to find a man who will!"

Paul studied him. "Longford, that speech made you appear almost human," he said. "I'm aware of your admiration of my wife, but your problem is all you see of her is a lovely face and a charming smile. There's a lot more to her than that. She's here because she wants to be."

"Well you shouldn't let her, it's your job to take care of her."

Paul felt the remains of his temper slipping away from him. "And what about your wife, Longford? Do you even know where she is? Don't be a bloody hypocrite, you've no idea how to treat a woman and you certainly don't deserve one like Caroline! Don't think I'm unaware of your views on my wife, I've seen the way you bloody look at her. You'd better keep on the right side of Erskine and get yourself onto his staff permanently because after what you did this month you have no place in my regiment, and I certainly don't want you anywhere near my wife! Now piss off and stay out of my way!"

In almost complete silence the officers and men of the 110th and 112th stood listening to the sounds of Beckwith's brigade engaging the enemy. The mist remained like a damp blanket over the river and surrounding hills and there was no sound other than the distant call of bugle and drum and the firing of muskets. Paul wondered dismally how effective firepower would be in this weather. They waited, ears pricked for the sound of Drummond's brigade approaching or for some messenger with orders, but nothing arrived and nothing changed. Twenty minutes crawled past, then half an hour, then another fifteen minutes. Paul felt like shaking his pocket watch although he knew it was working perfectly well. Time seemed to have slowed down.

"This doesn't feel right," he murmured. "Bloody Erskine, where the hell is he? Has he got lost in the fog? And where is Drummond, he should have been here by now."

"Drummond is on his way up, sir, just had a runner from the Portuguese, they can hear him approaching. He won't have hurried this morning, probably assumes we're all sitting here waiting for the fog to lift. He can't have any idea Beckwith is engaged."

Paul stood, his telescope in his hand. It was not worth attempting to use it; the mist and rain were still too thick. Even the sharp cracks of musketry were muffled by the weather.

"It doesn't feel right," he said again, glancing at the small group of officers huddled around him. "Where the bloody hell is he? We need to get the second in."

"Orders were very clear, sir. Drummond is not to go in support."

"Not even sure how far back Drummond is," Johnny said. "They shouldn't have gone in so soon, not everybody was in place."

"Perhaps the weather will lift," Carl said, glancing up at the grey sky. "Can't see a bloody thing."

"Well that's no handicap to fucking Erskine, he's as blind as a bat anyway!" Paul said.

"General Erskine to you, Colonel," Longford said.

Paul turned and looked at him and Manson remembered suddenly how it had felt when he first arrived to have those deep blue eyes regarding him with mild contempt.

"You open your mouth again Longford, I am going to kick you into the river." He turned back, and Manson watched, seeing how intently he was listening.

"What do you think, Paul?" Wheeler said quietly.

Paul shook his head. "My gut is telling me to go in."

"Your gut doesn't like inactivity, Paul."

Paul glanced at him and smiled. "No, I'm trying to balance that against my fear that Beckwith and his men are getting slaughtered out there. And our bloody commander has pissed off with the cavalry and couldn't be found even if he was likely to be of any use. Which he isn't. I need to make this decision now and send back to Drummond."

"Can you get a message to Wellington?"

"Too far. For it to matter a damn I need to go now."

Carl's eyes were on his face. "This is what you've been dreading, isn't it?" he asked quietly. "Since he first got you babysitting Erskine."

"Yes. Bad enough last time, but it was so bloody obvious a rescue was needed, and Wellington was close at hand. This is on me. And I know damned well that's why he put us here. I go in, and I could get every one of us killed. And if I survive it, my head is just the right size and shape for the Horse Guards block. They'll slaughter me, I've given them so much bloody grief over the years they'll be selling tickets. And if I don't go, we could lose the first brigade of the light division, I'll never forgive myself, and questions will be asked at Horse Guards about why I didn't go in and send for Drummond."

"Paul, everybody knows Wellington doesn't like his officers taking the initiative. You can't be blamed for that."

"And he knows it's what I bloody do, Johnny. Why else did he put me here?"

He looked out again at the blank mist. The sounds of battle reached them faintly on the air. "Get the rest of the officers over here. And I want Carter, Hammond and Stewart."

"Yes, sir."

They came at a run and he summoned Jenson with his horse, mounting and holding Rufus steady so that he could look down over them.

"We're going in," he said. "Not much time here. I'm sorry if I've got this badly wrong and get you all killed, but I can't sit here and know that Beckwith and his men are out there getting slaughtered. We're going in line, light company ahead as skirmishers. It's your job to get in as close as you can, take out their skirmish line and then get back and tell me what the hell is going on." He looked across at Manson. "Mr Manson, I need to take in the line companies. I want Carl to lead in the Portuguese. Will you go in with Michael and the light company?"

"Yes, sir."

"On our way in, you obey my orders to the letter. All of you. Once we're up there and can see what we're doing, I'll let you loose, but nobody is to take the initiative here until I say so." Paul glanced across. "Mr Heron, I want you to get back to find Colonel Drummond and tell him what the hell is going on here, let him know my decision. He's a bloody good officer, I think he'll make the right choice. After that you get on up to find Wellington and tell him as well. You may have a way to go, I don't think he was in place when Erskine sent Beckwith in. Clear?"

"Yes, sir."

"Get going. Freddie, take Rufus and go with him. I want two of you in case of accident."

"Yes, sir."

"Captain Longford, I want you to go in search of General Erskine. If you find him, give him my compliments and tell him I've advanced and that I expect Colonel Drummond to do the same shortly."

"Against his orders."

"He'll work that bit out himself, Captain, if he can remember what his orders were. If he forgets, I'm sure you'll remind him." Paul nodded. "That's it. Buglers and drummers at the ready. I want Beckwith to know we're coming, and we'll need their signals in this fog. On my word."

They moved away at a run and Manson went forward to join Michael O'Reilly. The Irishman grinned at him. "Welcome to the light company, laddie. You all right to fight, you're as white as a sheet?"

"I'm fine, sir." Manson was frowning. "Why is he so insistent on us obeying orders? He doesn't normally say that."

Michael glanced across at him with a quick smile. "Well spotted," he said. "No he doesn't. He wants it to be very clear that we all have absolutely no say in this. No democracy here. He didn't ask for Johnny or Carl's opinion back there although he normally does before he makes a decision."

Manson studied him through the mist. "Because if it goes wrong it's his responsibility. Nobody else can be scapegoated."

"That's right."

"Wellington's a bastard," Sergeant Carter said beside him. "He lets them go yapping at the Colonel's heels he's going to get more than he bargained for."

"You threatening the General, Sergeant?" O'Reilly said, lifting his arm to call his men forward.

"I wasn't talking about me, sir. It'll be the end of kissing her hand and whispering sweet nothings at the headquarters ball. I don't know if he realises it, but she'll carve his liver out and send it to Horse Guards in a box if he does anything that hurts her man."

"Christ, yes," Michael said, looking amused. "Hope this goes well for his sake."

They marched into eerie silence. Paul had drawn his sword. Across the lines his drummers beat a steady marching rhythm, which made it easier for his men to keep in touch. They made their way steadily up the hill. He watched his light company moving ahead. Their line was uneven, each pair of men covering each other, running up and past each other then dropping into firing position.

He had watched them so many times on the training field, had run with them and yelled at them and called them names, and he felt his stomach clench knowing that the decision he had just taken might get many of them killed.

"Enemy sighted, sir. Mist's lifting." Carter's voice floated back to him.

It was true. Gradually the mist almost seemed to be rolling back up the slope where Paul's men were advancing. Ahead between the skirmishers he could see a solid block of blue coats and he gave the signal to halt and peered up assessing the situation.

"What's happening, Sergeant."

"I'm going up to see. Stay there."

The voice was Manson's and Paul saw his tall wiry figure running nimbly up a rise to the right, keeping low and moving fast. He wanted to laugh, to make a comment about how quickly Manson had forgotten his orders about not taking the initiative, but he bit it back and watched. Manson reached the top and dropped flat, pulling out his telescope and the 110th waited, silent. It seemed very clear that the French had no idea they were there.

After a few minutes Manson rose and skidded back down the rise and ran back to Paul. "Sir."

"Just awaiting my orders, Mr Manson," Paul said gently and the boy flushed. Paul grinned. "Get on with it, Leo," he said.

"They're pinned down over by the trees. There's some stone walls there, taking cover behind them. Quite a few down, sir, looks like the 43rd has taken the brunt."

"Firepower?"

"Well they won't have been firing much in the rain but it's over now, so it's about to start up again. And it looks like they've got two guns over to the right. Outnumbered sir, like you thought."

As he finished speaking there was the crack of musket fire, and then bigger, the crash of field guns. Paul swore and looked around at the expectant faces of his officers.

"Michael, get the light company out as skirmishers, drive those bastards back, they don't even know you're here. Johnny, take the 110th and hit them hard on their left. I think Beckwith came over too far north, he should have come up behind but he's hit their flank - not surprising in this fog. Go and kick their arses for them. Carl, take the Portuguese and come up further round. Pat, take the 112th and go with him. Sergeant Carter. Twenty men of the light company, your best shots, with me and Mr Manson. We're going up on that rise to shut up those guns and frighten the shit out of the musketry. Move!"

They were running, the thudding of their feet louder now that the mist had cleared. He heard, running fast through the long grass, the twenty men of his light company and he glanced around, smiling inwardly at how easy it was to guess which of them had been selected for this. To himself, he admitted that as commander he should probably not be putting himself at risk with them, but the rise would be a good vantage point for the field as a whole. He looked at Manson. The boy was moving freely despite his recent injuries, the golden eyes intent and steady.

Up on the rise he directed his men into position and surveyed the field. Grimly he watched his main force move into action. With the rain lifted their muskets were workable, and he sensed the shock of the French as the 110th hit them with a solid wall of fire, taking the pressure immediately off Beckwith's beleaguered troops. He heard a few ragged cheers float across from the men of the 43rd, pinned down behind the stone walls as they realised that help had come.

Happy that his troops were in place and doing their jobs he turned his attention to the two French guns. It would be difficult at this point to reach them and disable them, there were too many French troops in the way and he did not have the men to cut his way through. But his rifles were accurate and had a long range and the gunners and men surrounding them were easily within reach. He was aware that once they began to direct fire onto the guns they were going to become a target for an infantry charge to stop them, but the men with him were the best he had and he hoped they could hold out until Drummond reached them. It should not be more than twenty minutes or so.

The gunners ran for cover as the light company fire hit them, and he watched as the remains of Beckwith's men, no longer under such fierce pressure, began to emerge and reform. He saw the Colonel on horseback, blood streaming from what looked like a nasty head wound, wheeling around to see where the covering fire was coming from. He recognised Paul and lifted a hand, a grin spreading across his face. Paul acknowledged with a salute.

It was a long twenty minutes. As more of the French began to realise what was happening, a column formed up and Paul called his men into line and sent a rolling volley of rifle fire into the approaching troops. Even so there was a limit to what could be done with so few men. He was looking around him, assessing the best line of retreat when the column was hit by a hail of fire and Paul saw Michael O'Reilly leading his skirmishers in to the left with such effect that the French crumbled and began to retreat in some disorder back up the slope.

He turned. "Mr Manson."

"Yes, sir." Manson called the men over and they recommenced firing on the guns and the French musketry again. The remains of Beckwith's men had rallied now and were moving forward, fighting in close hand to hand combat up the slope. They were joined halfway by the 110th and Paul watched with approval as his men advanced in good order, pushing the French back.

"Sir, we've got trouble," Carter called, and Paul turned and swore softly. The 4th Leger had rallied back up on the slope and was advancing steadily on the left and two squadrons of cavalry seemed to be coming in from the right.

Even with the arrival of the 110th and 112th, the Allies were hopelessly outnumbered. Paul saw them waver and halt, and then heard the bugles sounding the retreat. Once more the 43rd were forced back to the shelter of the stone walls, followed in good order by his own men. Paul directed his skirmishers to give covering fire and could see Michael organising the rest of the light company to do the same.

"Sir," Manson called. "The 2nd brigade is coming up. On the right."

Paul felt relief flood through him. He turned to look and saw Drummond's men advancing steadily. Already the French were turning to face the new attack, but numbers would be more even now. He glanced across at Manson.

"Mr Manson, I'm going down to join the regiment, I want to get them up on that crest and push the French off. Can you keep those guns off us?"

"We can, sir."

Paul glanced at his sergeant, who grinned. "If he says we can, sir, we can. Mind, if this goes wrong and it comes to a close fight, I'm getting behind him, I've seen him with a sword."

Paul laughed. "Good plan, Sergeant."

"How you getting over there, sir?" Hammond enquired.

"I'm going to run really fast, Hammond, and if any French bastard gets in my way I'm going to kill him. Simple plan really. Could do with some covering fire, mind."

"Yes, sir. Don't get killed. Why you can't be like a normal officer and use a horse beats me."

"I lead infantry, Hammond. What do I need with a bloody horse? I'm off. If it goes wrong and you're too hard pressed, pull back to those trees and you can cut up round and join the others."

He hefted the sword in his hand, swinging it twice to loosen his arm and nodded at Manson. "You've got command, Mr Manson."

"Sir. Don't trip up."

The monumental calm of his young lieutenant impressed Paul. He studied him for a moment feeling a sudden certainty that this boy, out of all the dozens of young officers who had served under him, was destined to reach the heights if he did not get himself killed. He laughed, shook his head and turned to look at the line he must follow.

Taking a deep breath he began to run. He was unchecked racing down the small hill and across the boggy ground at the bottom, his boots splashing through the mud. As he turned up towards the stone walls behind which the Allies were sheltering there was a sudden crack alarmingly close to his ear and the muskets were onto him. He kept low and weaved from side to side. The crack of his rifles could be heard, and the musket fire died down. Movement to his right caught his eye and he swung around, realising that two cavalrymen had noticed him and broken away from the main charge.

Paul spun around swinging his sword into the dragoon's thigh. The man screamed, dropping forward over the saddle clutching the leg as blood spurted high. Paul turned again and as the second cavalryman slashed down at him he dropped to the ground and rolled away. The dragoon pulled up sharply and wheeled his horse and Paul ran towards him, stabbing upwards before the Frenchman had recovered from the shock of a man on foot pursuing him. The dragoon fell from the saddle and Paul continued his run, aware of pain from his upper arm where the first dragoon had caught him with the sabre. The wall was in sight. Paul slid to a halt beside it, took a flying leap, skidded down the slope in a hail of musket fire and landed laughing and breathless at the feet of Carl Swanson.

"All well, Captain Swanson?" he asked cheerfully.

"You are a bloody idiot!" Carl said furiously. "Have you any idea what Nan would have done to me if she'd found out I'd let you do something as stupid as that? Haven't you noticed that it is the job of the regimental colonel to sit on a damned horse and look important, not go haring off around the field with a sodding target painted on him?"

"And haven't I been telling you all for years that he's not fit to be in command?" Michael O'Reilly said. "It's Wellington's fault, he should never have promoted him. You all right, sir? You're bleeding."

"Not much. Drummond is here and we can get out there and push those bastards back up to the crest. And then off it. Carl, get them lined up! Where's that bloody bugler, do I need to do everything myself?"

"Be good if you included the rest of us occasionally, sir!" Carl said scathingly.

"You're very confident Wellington is on his way, Paul," Michael said.

"If Drummond got the message, so will Wellington. The fog has lifted, he'll be here in minutes."

"And Erskine?"

"Erskine can piss off, I'm bored with him. Form line, Major Wheeler!"

"Yes, sir. Permission to speak, sir."

"As if there was any way I could stop you, Major Wheeler."

"You are a frigging lunatic who will get yourself killed one of these days. And if you've left Manson up on that rise, you are going to get him killed too, he is twenty, recovering from a wound and has less than six months of experience!"

"And after today he'll have an awful lot more, Johnny. It's how we learned. Get them ready."

It was a short and bitter struggle. They fought, initially with firepower and then with bayonet and sword and the light division regained the crest as the French fell back in confusion. Colonel Beckwith was still on horseback, riding to the front with the skirmishers, his face and shoulders soaked in blood, calling out to his men. He waved cheerfully at Paul as the 110th came up.

"Colonel. Knew I could rely on you, sir. And Drummond. Wait until Craufurd hears about this!"

"He'll say I was too rash, sir. I'm taking men over to take that howitzer out of action."

"Appreciate it, Van Daan."

Paul turned and summoned Carl with a wave. "Captain, we'll take the rest of the light company over. Keep them low, we can hit them from the side."

Carl nodded and turned, shouting orders. Paul looked back across to the rise. The twenty men of the light company had formed two ranks and were firing steadily down onto the advancing French. None of the enemy had yet made it onto the slopes and although he could not hear over the noise of battle, he could see Manson standing, sword drawn, calmly calling the shots. He watched for a moment and felt again, the absolute certainty about the boy.

"Ready, Paul."

"Let's go. Keep low, fire at will."

They moved forward in line, repulsing any attempt of the French to stop them. By now Drummond was making inroads onto the field and the French were falling back fast. The gun was in sight and Paul yelled, and his men moved forward, swarming over the gunners, their guards falling back quickly, running from the lethal rifle shots and bayonet charge of the light company.

Pausing to catch his breath, Paul looked back. The Allied line was now formed behind one of the stone walls. A squadron of Dragoons had surmounted the hill, in a desperate charge and were firing over it with their pistols, when a rolling volley slammed into them and Paul saw them fall, only two remaining to gallop back. A second and stronger column of French infantry was pushing up the face of the hill towards the howitzer and he yelled commands and his infantry turned and fired. The first rank fell almost to a man and the second stepped forward but more hesitantly. The 110th fired again and some of the French wavered and began to retreat, the deadly volleys pushing them back.

Paul paused, looking over the field. The French had broken, were beginning to run. "Jesus, that was close. Reynier cannot have known what the hell was going on or he'd have sent in his whole force."

"Not so good, Paul. Merle might be on the run, but Foy's brigade is on his way up."

"We'll hold them. Wellington is on his way."

He took a deep breath and looked across at Carl. "You all right?"

His friend nodded, grinned at him. "Fine. Christ in heaven, Paul, Johnny is right. You're a bloody lunatic, if Nan could see what you do out here she would go mad! Is Manson all right over there?"

"Manson is keeping them occupied which is his job. Come on, let's go and have a chat with the 17th and the 70th ligne. The 52nd are taking a hammering over there."

He turned to shout orders, and the 110th moved back into the fray against the charging French squadrons, crashing into their flank as they attacked the 52nd. Vaguely he was aware, swinging his sword and cutting down men as he advanced, that the weather was clearing further. It gave a new level of visibility across the field and he could see movement coming from the west. His heart lifted further.

"Wellington," he said briefly, and O'Reilly followed his gaze and grinned.

"Might be time for Reynier to rethink."

"I would."

The two French squadrons charged again upon the flank of the 52nd and a British squadron of the 16th Light Dragoons followed them into the fight. As the weather cleared even more it was clear that Reynier had seen the British divisions advancing from the west. The 5th Division were crossing the bridge at Sabugal and Picton's 3rd Division were advancing fast on the flanks of the 17th and 70th. Fighting on the crest, watching the French fall back, Paul could hear orders shouted through the French lines.

"They're retreating," he called. "Careful in pursuit. Rain's coming down again and we won't be able to use much firepower. Get them off the field and then back off, lads!"

He watched as his men pushed the French into a cautious run and then into full flight. They were too well trained to pursue beyond his orders and gradually they fell back. He stood, suddenly completely exhausted, and realised that his sword was still stained with blood. Crouching he wiped it clean on the grass and listened to the sound of the French retreat.

"Colonel van Daan."

Startled he looked up and saw his commander looking down on him from his horse. "Sir. Glad to see you."

"I had your message. It was extremely succinct."

"Seems to have worked, sir."

"Any idea of losses?"

"No idea, sir. I think we've done all right, but Beckwith's brigade might have suffered. Once they're pushed back we'll see about the wounded."

"The nearest hospital?"

"Just over the Sabugal bridge, sir. They've set up in a deserted winery. My wife is there."

"Yes, I saw your wife earlier."

"I'll just bet you did."

"Are your wounded all right, Paul? I am sorry, I'll be having words with Major Courtney. Disgraceful behaviour."

"I think they'll be all right, sir, although I'm worried about Nan's maid."

"Don't be, I've sent a message telling them to release her and provide an escort up to the lines here. Give them something to do. McGrigor is furious with Cradock, he thinks he let personal spite affect his medical judgement."

"I think he's right, sir. I accept that Nan is not a surgeon, but Dr Daniels was with her when she made those decisions and besides, Cradock should have taken one look at some of those men and known they weren't fit to march or fight. Lieutenant Manson gave up his horses and walked here with the men to make sure they survived the journey."

Wellington nodded. "I've just spoken to General Erskine, Paul."

"Yes, sir."

"He'll be moved to another command. General Craufurd is on his way back. I think perhaps somebody else should take their turn at taking care of Sir William."

"I'm glad to hear it, sir."

Wellington gave a small smile. "Well done, Colonel."

"Thank you, sir. Did I do what I was supposed to do? Because your orders weren't all that clear."

"You did, Colonel. It's a shame we weren't able to do more. I had hoped..."

"Your plan was a good one, sir, but General Erskine made a mess of it, I'm afraid to say. A wasted opportunity. May I ask a favour of you?"

"What is it, Colonel?"

"I don't want Captain Longford back. He seems happy with General Erskine and if Erskine will take him I think it would suit both of them. Longford bullies the men and my junior officers and it's bad for morale."

"If the General wants him he can stay on as Erskine's ADC although formally he'll still be on your payroll."

"I'll happily pay to keep him away, sir. Permission to go and see how many men I lost in this almighty fuck up?"

Wellington saluted. "Permission granted, Colonel. Carry on."

Chapter Fourteen

With his plans for remaining in Portugal in tatters, Massena marched north to the fortress town of Ciudad Rodrigo, and Wellington's army went back to camp to bury their dead, treat their wounded and rest after the weeks of exhausting pursuit. With his men making their way back to camp Paul removed himself over to the disused winery at the edge of the pretty little town where he knew he would find his wife at work. Lord Wellington had moved his staff into the castle as guests of the Portuguese governor and had invited Paul to join him and his commanders for dinner but Paul had declined the invitation.

He stood watching Anne, unseen, as she dealt unflinchingly with an atrocious wound on a rifleman's leg. The man bore her probing stoically, distracting himself, Paul was amused to note, by gazing at Anne's face as she bent over him. She straightened finally and put her hand to her lower back.

"There, that should do it, Corporal. Hold on a minute and I'll get someone to help you over to the ward. Don't try to put any weight on that."

"I'll take him," Paul said quietly, coming forward, and she looked up her face lighting up.

"Paul. I thought you were never coming. You all right?"

"I am. Glad that's over. Where am I taking him?"

"I'll show you." Anne glanced at her orderly. "Gibson, I've finished here now, will you pack up my instruments, please?"

"Yes, ma'am."

"And Gibson – wash them! If I find blood on one of them I'm coming after you with a bone saw!"

"Yes, ma'am."

Paul hoisted the Corporal who appeared shocked at being carried by a ranking colonel and Anne led him through to the wards. "I miss Teresa," she said. "I don't have to keep telling her what to do, she just knows!"

"She'll be back soon."

"I hope so, Danny is so worried. Put him over here, Paul."

"You ready to go?" he asked when he had carefully settled the man on a mattress. Anne nodded.

"Yes. I'm getting tired now and my back is aching."

"Good girl. Come on then, let's get up to camp, I'm hungry."

"Is Leo all right?"

"He's fine." Paul put his arm about her and drew her outside. "I've sent him back with Carter and Hammond, they'll make sure he rests a bit. But honestly although I'm pissed off he was dragged out when he shouldn't have been, he proved his worth out there today."

She glanced up at him. "You all right, Colonel?"

He nodded. "Glad of a break myself. I have been invited to dinner with Wellington and the other generals up at the castle. Celebrating a valuable victory, which would have been a lot more useful if we could have taken out as many of them as we should have. But still, we've done what we intended. Spain next. Can't wait for that mess."

"And what excuse did you give to Lord Wellington?" Anne enquired as he lifted her up onto her horse.

"I didn't. I just looked at him and he laughed and told me to go back and get drunk with my men. I'm not sitting down at a table with Erskine tonight and Hookey knows better then to try and make me. He'll digest his dinner better if he's not worrying about me blowing up."

They arrived back at camp to find the officers and men of the 110th wearily unloading weapons and kit into their tents. Anne went into the tent to change and Paul checked on his officers. He found Carl Swanson talking to Sergeant Kelly beside one of the cooking fires.

"All right, Carl? How's your side?"

"Sore, but it's fine. I've just been in to see Manson. He's exhausted, but I think he would have been anyway with what he's done today." He eyed his commander. "Something of a baptism of fire."

"Yes. Johnny thinks I was wrong."

"If he'd died up there, Paul, you'd have found it hard to forgive yourself. But I suppose you needed to put him to the test, didn't you?"

Paul glanced sharply at him then laughed. "You know me so well, Carl. He passed."

"I know. And I'm glad. I'm not sure I could do what you do."

"You could if you had to. Michael, you all right?"

The Irishman approached. "I am. Looking forward to supper and a drink. Or three. Glad that's over, I think we'll get a break for a week or two now."

"I imagine so. Give the wounded a chance to heal without being dragged out of their beds. I'm hoping I get a chance to have a chat with Courtney. You look shattered, Carl. Go and get changed and come and have a drink, we've all earned it. I think I see Keren taking hot water into your tent."

"I will," Carl said. He glanced over at Michael. "I'm glad you survived, Michael, we've been friends for a long time now. But just for the record, if you don't back off Keren Trenlow and stop treating her like a lass for sale in the Lisbon stews, I'm going to kick your arse so hard you'll be wishing you were back out there with the 70th ligne trying to gut you. She's not a prostitute and she's told you no. You've got the urge, get down to the brothel or find some pretty local lass who's willing and not too expensive, but leave that girl alone! And you might want to let the rest of the arseholes who are betting on your chances know that if I find out who they are, they are going to be on early drill for the rest of their miserable lives in this army!"

Both Paul and Michael regarded him in considerable astonishment. Carl nodded pleasantly and walked back to his tent. Paul turned his gaze to Michael.

"Have you by any chance been behaving like an arse, Michael?"

"No more than usual, sir, but it appears the lassie is well protected. Has he got an interest there himself, do you know?"

"I've no idea, if he had he would be unlikely to tell me. Carl's well past the age where he'd make a bet on a girl in a tavern, Michael. What the hell is this about a bet anyway?"

"Oh it's just a joke among some of the officers, sir, nothing serious. She's a pretty lass, it's not surprising some of them are interested."

"Well if she's spoken to Carl about it, I'm guessing she's not finding this particular joke very funny. I'd take his advice if I were you. If you're annoying her and my wife finds out, you'll get a lot worse from her than you would from Carl, and you bloody know it. Go and get changed."

As Carl entered his tent he found Keren pouring hot water into the enamel basin. She had set out soap and shaving kit on the folding table. Hearing him she turned and smiled, then went to the chest to get out a clean shirt and the loose coat he wore around camp. Carl went to his bed and sat down with a sigh of relief.

Keren put down the towel and came forward. "Let me," she said, kneeling down. Carl opened his mouth to protest and then closed it, realising with wry amusement that he was so stiff that he was not sure if he could bend far enough to pull off the boots. She removed them and set them aside and he got up.

"Thanks, Keren."

He went to the basin and took off his coat, wincing. She took it from him and went to hang it up. "It's soaked. I'll get it cleaned up when it's dry."

Carl eased his shirt away from his body. He was soaked through and completely filthy, but he was aware that some of the stains were red. Carefully he peeled the cloth from his side, wincing, and then he felt her hands on him, helping him.

"Let me look."

She drew the shirt over his head and reached for the sponge carefully cleaning his chest and side to examine the wound. "It's not too bad, opened up a little but I don't think you'll need to see Mrs van Daan."

"Thank you." Carl realised with grim amusement that he was no longer conscious of the pain of his wound or of any of his other aches and pains. Her nearness was distracting him. He took a deep breath and reached for the sponge, but she held onto it.

"Let me help you. You're filthy, how on earth do you get so dirty out there?"

He splashed water over his face and hair, reaching for the soap, laughing. "Powder, mud and blood mostly, a battlefield is never a clean place, we all come back looking like this."

She reached for the jug and poured more water over his head to rinse off the soap and he reached for the towel at the same moment she did, his hand closing over hers. He held on and she looked up at him quickly, an expression in the melting brown eyes which made him catch his breath.

"Sir…"

"Don't move," he said softly, wiping the towel over him, still holding her hand. Dropping it he moved closer and bent to kiss her, his hands sliding up her arms to her shoulders. She returned his kiss without restraint or hesitation and he wondered when he had made the decision to do this. It had been coming for a while.

"Would you believe me if I told you that I thought about this halfway through that bloody battle?" he said against her hair. "Surprised I didn't get myself killed out there imagining just how you'd look with no clothes on."

She gave a breathy laugh. "You didn't…"

"I bloody did. But since I managed to survive it, I've a feeling I should find out just in case I start imagining things again."

He moved his hands to the laces at the bodice of her simple gown and she stood looking up at him, her eyes steady on his, dark with desire. Carl slid the gown back and moved his lips to her bare shoulders as he dealt with her chemise. She wore nothing else, having no money for complex underclothes and he picked her up and carried her to the bed, laying her back gently and standing up to remove the rest of his clothing.

He was surprised and touched at how shy she was. He supposed that her previous lovers had been a lad of seventeen and a drunkard with no care for her pleasure, and she was still very young. It was the reason he had not acted before on the attraction between them, but Michael O'Reilly's determined pursuit had made him realise that he was being naïve. Sooner or later somebody was going to wear down her defences and take her to bed, and he had accepted in those moments before riding to battle, that he could not bear the thought of seeing her with anybody other than him.

He concentrated on being gentle and patient, reining in his desire and focusing on her, and her wide-eyed astonishment at her own pleasure was well worth the effort. When they were done he shifted his weight from her and leaned over to kiss her.

"Now that was definitely worth coming back for," he said softly.

"You were so gentle," she said, almost wonderingly and it told him more than he cared to know about her previous experience of men. He kissed her again, feather light.

"You all right, lass? I didn't hurt you?"

"No. Not at all. I didn't…I've never really felt that way before."

He was startled to see tears in the brown eyes. "What's wrong, Keren?"

"Nothing. I…it's silly."

"No it's not, not if it makes you cry in my bed. Come here."

He pulled her gently against him and lay holding her. After a while she stirred.

"I should go, sir, they'll be wanting…"

"What did you call me?"

She looked startled. "Sir…"

He brushed her lips with his. "Carl. Say it."

She was smiling, shaking her head. "What if I forget and say it out there?"

"I'm expecting you to."

She studied him. "You're a gentleman. I'm a miner's daughter. A camp follower…"

"Keren, stop it!" Carl reached up and smoothed her tumbled curls very gently. "Is that what this is about? Because if you think I'm about to offer you money for what we just did you're going to be awfully disappointed."

She met his eyes steadily. "Since I separated from Simpson and started working for Mrs van Daan a fair few of the officers have offered me money to do what we just did," she said.

"Please don't tell me which ones, it will piss me off. I've spoken to Michael. He annoys you again you can either hit him or come to me and I'll do it for you. You do not have to put up with that."

She reached up suddenly and kissed him and he felt himself wanting her again. He pulled her close, pressing her slender body against him and smiled against her mouth.

"You do realise if we don't go outside soon one of them is going to come in here looking for me and get something of a surprise."

"Do you care?" she asked.

"Not at all," Carl said, and bent to kiss her again, hard.

It was beginning to get dark finally when he slid from the bed. She reached for her clothes and he watched her as he dressed, feeling a huge sense of content. When she was ready she moved to pick up his dirty shirt and he laughed and went to put his arms about her.

"Leave it until morning. Come and have supper with me."

She looked up uncertainly. "Sir...Carl, they're going to guess."

"Do you care?"

Keren reached up and caressed his face with a tenderness which touched him unexpectedly. "No. But you probably ought to. I don't expect anything from you, you know that don't you?"

Carl felt a tug of emotion which he knew he had not felt for a girl for many years. He gave a slight smile.

"Well I've a few expectations of you, lass, but we'll work that out as we go along. Listen, Keren, I don't know what this is to you, but for me it's not just an hour's pleasure with a pretty girl. I've spent a lot of time with you, and being with you makes me feel good. Just now that's enough for me."

She reached up and kissed him for a long time. Lifting his head he laughed softly. "What was that for, sweetheart?"

The brown eyes were steady on him. "Every one of them has been making me feel like a prostitute for the past few months, without laying a finger on me," she said. "You make me feel like a lady even when I'm in bed with you. Thank you, Carl."

Carl kissed her again. "I'm more and more coming to the conclusion that somebody needs a punch. Come and eat," he said.

He took her hand firmly and drew her outside, standing for a moment looking up and down the lines. The light company were camped just along from his tent and he walked down to where Cooper and Dawson were tending a cooking fire.

"Evening, sir. You look a bit cleaner. Your wound all right?"

"It's fine, Cooper. What the hell happened to your ear?"

Cooper touched the bandage. "Shrapnel, sir. Took a chunk off. Mrs van Daan tells me it won't affect my good looks, though."

"She's got a funny sense of humour," Dawson said with a grin. "Drink, sir?"

Carl took the bottle and drank. "Thanks, Dawson. Everyone accounted for?"

"Yes, sir. Not a bad day for us, no deaths, a few wounded. The second didn't do so well. Eight dead and Mr Aldous not looking so good."

"I know, poor bastards. I saw them hit, musket fire. All went down in the same volley. Best shooting the French have done in this campaign, they were unlucky. But Nan got the shot out of him, and he'll do better in her care than most of the surgeons. He might be lucky."

"Sir, is it true the Colonel's wife is in the family way?" Cooper asked.

"It is, Cooper."

"Bloody hell! How the hell is he going to get her to calm down and put her feet up?"

"I have no idea, Coops, and I don't suppose he has either," Carl said with a laugh. "That smells good and I'm starving. Come on Keren, come and get supper."

He moved back up to join his friends and found Carter distributing drinks. Camp chairs and upturned crates had been set out around the square and Carl sat down with a sigh of relief and looked across at Manson. "Better?" he asked.

"Much." Manson raised his wine cup with a smile. "Somehow the knowledge that Massena is currently marching on an empty stomach, without most of his officers' baggage and in the opposite direction to me has cheered me up considerably. Ma'am, do you need a chair?"

He made as if to rise but Caroline Longford shook her head and took a seat beside Major Wheeler on an upturned box. Carter brought her a drink and she smiled her thanks. Keren had gone to help Corporal Hammond who was handing out bowls and spoons and there was a rising babble of conversation as the officers of the 110th and 112th talked over the day. When she had done she took a bowl for herself and looked around and Carl smiled at her.

"Come and sit, there's space here."

It grew dark and Paul got up to add wood to the fire. Through the darkness he was aware of a horseman walking up and he remained on his feet.

"Captain Longford. I thought you'd be celebrating with General Erskine."

Longford dismounted and looked around for somebody to take his horse in some irritation. Nobody moved. After a moment, Paul grinned. "Browning, would you?" he asked quietly. "Are you joining us for a drink, Vincent?"

Longford's eyes moved over the group and rested on Carter and Hammond who were stretched out on their blankets at Anne's feet, drinking wine. "I prefer an officer's mess to be for officers," he drawled.

"Yes, I'm picky about who I drink with myself, but I'll make an exception this evening," Paul said, and there was a ripple of laughter. Paul shook his head. "Vincent, we're all alive which is a blessing after today. Why don't you just sit down, have a drink, and pretend to be part of the regiment for once. You might even find you enjoy it."

"I came to speak to my wife," Longford said shortly. Paul glanced across at Caroline who rose, setting down her cup. She looked flushed in the firelight and his heart ached for her as she came forward to join her husband. He watched as they moved away into the darkness, and Paul glanced briefly at Wheeler and looked away.

An Irregular Regiment

She was gone for some time, and when she returned she was alone. Without speaking, Wheeler got up and went to meet her and they moved quietly to the shadow of the tents.

"Johnny – my husband wants me to join him. General Erskine wishes him to remain as his aide, and Colonel van Daan has agreed. He will send an escort down for me tomorrow."

"Oh Christ," Johnny said softly. "Caro..."

"Johnny – no. We both knew this was likely to happen. I am glad we've had what we have, but I am married and I am tied."

"I'm not sure that I care."

"I care. For both of us. It will be all right." She reached up and kissed him very gently. "I will write often to Nan, so you'll have news of me."

He nodded. "Can you come back..."

"In a little while. I am going to pack, but I'll join you all for a last drink. Go back now."

He watched her walk down to her tent and then turned.

"Not sure I'm that keen on you whispering in the darkness with my wife, Major," Longford drawled, and Johnny turned back to find him coming through the tents.

"Not sure I care, Longford."

"I find it hard to believe that a model of rectitude like you is doing anything he shouldn't be, Wheeler, but perhaps I got you wrong! Not that it matters much now. Whatever she's been doing, she'll be doing it with me now. Looking forward to it, I must say. She's a taking little thing. Looks very nice with her clothes off in the lamplight, and if you've been teaching her a few new tricks in bed, I'm only too happy to benefit from that."

Wheeler felt rage flood through him. "You piece of shit," he said quietly. "She's your wife, Longford, treat her with respect or I'll...."

"You'll never know anything about how I'm treating her, Major. I could be doing whatever the hell I like to her. Think about that when you're marching into Spain, being a hero. I wonder if she'll think of you when I'm..."

He broke off with a sharp intake of breath, and there was an ominous click in the darkness. "Vincent, I thought you'd gone," Paul said pleasantly. He was holding a pistol to the side of Longford's neck. "No, don't move, I'm a little jumpy tonight. I'm glad you came back, I've been wanting a chat with you about Leo Manson and the rest of my wounded men. I'm assuming it was you who gave Courtney and his bloodhounds the idea that my regimental hospital was a hotbed of skivers and malingerers?"

"What if it was? I wasn't there, had no control over what they found!"

"You're right there, Vincent, and I'll deal with Courtney and Cradock presently. For now, let us be clear on one point. I can't stop you taking your wife with you. But how you treat her is very much my business. You might be seconded to Erskine but you're still one of my officers, and she is my wife's friend. Nan will expect to get very regular letters from her, and if she gives just one hint that you are being anything other than respectful and gentle with her, I will come after you with half a dozen men from my light company, and we are going to quietly put a bullet in your head and bury the body. And you need to believe me when I tell you it will never be found. Are we perfectly clear about that?"

"Yes," Longford said.

"Good. Now piss off! I'll escort Caroline up myself when she's ready and not before, and I'll make very sure that General Erskine understands her position – and mine. And you will stay away from Mr Manson, while you're about it. I do not know what your problem with him is, but he is out of your reach now. Turn around, walk away and don't come back. Good evening."

He stood watching as Longford retreated. Johnny did not speak. Eventually Paul said quietly:

"I'll talk to Nan. She and Caroline can work out a code phrase for Caroline to alert her if she's in trouble. He won't stop her writing, he's too much of a coward, and he knows I'd go up there after him if we don't hear, but he might read the letters first."

"Yes. He's the type." Johnny turned and looked at Paul and there was a glimmer of amusement through the pain. "Did you actually just point a pistol at General Erskine's latest ADC, Colonel?"

"I did. Quite enjoyed it. Not enough people in life have pointed guns at Vincent, he needs more of that in my opinion." Paul uncocked the pistol and slid it back into his coat pocket. "Given what he's done, he's lucky I didn't pull the trigger. Johnny, I'm sorry. I don't even need to look at your face to know how you're feeling."

"You're probably the only man here who actually does. I don't know how you stood it for two years."

Paul remembered the sheer misery of watching Anne with her first husband. "Neither do I." He turned to look at Johnny. "Go to her. You've got one night. I'll make sure you're not disturbed."

"Paul..."

"Johnny, in a few weeks time I'm going to be given command of the third brigade of the light division, and you are going to be promoted to lieutenant colonel as my second in command. And you cannot be sleeping with the wife of one of your officers."

"I'm sorry, Paul."

"Or if you are, I can't know about it. But I will do whatever I can to keep her safe, I swear it."

Johnny gave a soft laugh. "How did you know? Did you see us?"

"Christ, Johnny, you are talking to the world expert on falling in love with a married woman. It was so bloody obvious. To me, at least. And I suspect Carl is aware although he's not said anything, he's too tactful."

Johnny glanced across at him. "Commander of a brigade. What are you now, thirty?"

"Two months off."

"Christ, Paul. And are you serious...?"

"Yes. I've already spoken to Wellington. You're beyond the point now where purchase is an issue, Johnny."

"I am. It feels strange. Do you remember all those years ago on that first voyage to India, you told me to stick close to you if I wanted promotion?"

"I do. I'm surprised you didn't throw me overboard. I was such an arrogant little bastard back then."

"You haven't changed a bit, Paul. It's just that now you're in charge so it doesn't matter so much. Thank you."

"For what?"

"Oh – Christ, for everything. For giving me a career when I might not have had one. For fighting every step of the way for each one of my promotions, which I know you have. For teaching me how to be better at my job."

"I'd have said that was rather the other way round."

"No. I might have helped for the first year or so, but you didn't need me after that."

"Yes I bloody did, Johnny. And had it occurred to you that if I'd not been there it might have been you Wellesley noticed back in India?"

"It wouldn't have mattered if it had been. I might well have made Captain, but I wouldn't have done what you did." Wheeler smiled. "I'd never have rallied the men during that skirmish just before Assaye – not as quickly as you did. I'd have waited for orders at Assaye. When you showed up last month and Erskine had sent the lads out into that fog, I was still standing there arguing with him. You just turned up yelling and we went in. And earlier today, you basically took command of the light division without any authorisation whatsoever."

"All that is probably true. But there are just as many times when I'd have done something rash, or opened my mouth at the wrong time, or got half my company slaughtered and the person standing beside me telling me to calm down and not be an arsehole was you. You might well not be where you are if it hadn't been for me. But I'm damned sure I wouldn't be where I am if not for you." Paul smiled slightly. "I'm going back to drink with the enlisted men. Go and see your lass, Johnny, and make very sure she knows you'll be there for her if she needs you, because married to that bastard the day might come when she does. I've not said anything to the others yet about promotions. Let's get our dead buried and recover for a day or two."

"What next?"

"Wellington wants them out of Almeida, but something tells me Massena will fight for that one, it's his last foothold in Portugal."

"Yes. I wonder where he'll send Erskine next."

"A long way from Black Bob Craufurd and me if he's got any sense. She'll be all right, Johnny. Women are a lot tougher than you think, look at our lasses. Nan endured two years with Carlyon. Teresa survived the French army. Keren Trenlow was half beaten to death by that bastard Simpson and look at her now."

"I've never felt this way," Johnny said quietly. "Is it always this hard?"

"Christ knows. Ask Danny Carter who is sitting over there drinking, wondering if his lass has been strapped to a whipping post down in Pere Negro and given thirty of the best for assaulting a provost marshal."

"And you're about to take your pregnant wife north into Spain. Aren't you?"

"If she wants to go, Johnny."

"She will."

"Probably. Go on, get out of here. Good night."

He watched Johnny go and then moved back to the fire. His wife was leaning forward to hold out her cup to be refilled. Leo Manson had given up his chair to Keren Trenlow and was sitting cross legged on the floor in front of Anne. As she leaned forward she placed a hand on Manson's shoulder to steady herself, and he looked up and said something which made her laugh. Paul stood watching them for a moment. Then Anne seemed to sense his presence and looked up, smiling.

"Come and sit down. Is Caroline coming back?"

"No, she's gone to pack and she's going to bed. We'll talk later."

She nodded and he wondered if she knew. Her hand was still resting on Manson's shoulder and he grinned, thinking how much it would have annoyed Longford.

"Tired, girl of my heart?"

She sat back. "Yes. But in a good way. Worried about Teresa. Lord Wellington promised that he'd make sure she was brought back in one piece but that rather depends on how quickly his letter reached Pere Negro. Do you really think they'd flog her?"

"Courtney is a toad, and unfortunately he'll push for it because she's attached to the 110th and he hates me. But it depends on who is on the disciplinary board, if there is a friend of mine on it she should be fine." Paul leaned over and kissed her. "I'm sorry, lass, some of this is down to me. I don't always make friends."

Anne glanced around her. "You've made a few," she said quietly.

He sat beside her holding her hand listening to the talk and the laughter. Tomorrow they would rise and go and bury their dead, and he wondered how it must seem to an outsider seeing them like this when the bodies lay close by awaiting burial. The men up and down the lines had lost friends and comrades, and they were in everybody's thoughts tonight, but it seemed more fitting to remember them like this than in solemn silence with flowers and incense.

Further down the lines there was the plaintive sound of Private Flanagan's fiddle, no riotous dance tune tonight but a love song, the notes cutting through the noise and the laughter until men fell silent listening. He saw Carl reach out and touch Keren Trenlow's arm. "Sing for us, lass," he said, and she nodded and stood, her hands folded demurely at her waist and sang. She had an unusual voice, powerful but low for a woman with a husky tone that gave depth to the story of love and loss. Paul wondered how Carl had known she could sing.

He glanced across at his wife and saw the sparkle of tears in her eyes. Anne seldom cried and when she did she tended to do it silently and without fuss. He shifted his chair closer and drew her near and she put her head onto his shoulder and sat listening until the song ended.

It was quiet for a while and Keren sat down on the ground, close to Carl's legs. Paul watched curiously. He was very aware that the girl had developed a tendre for his friend but for the first time he wondered how Carl felt about it. Carl was not Michael O'Reilly. He was very scrupulous in his dealings with women and Paul thought it unlikely that he would put the girl in a difficult position in the regiment, although watching them tonight as she looked up, laughing at something he had said, Paul felt that it was rather a pity. She was growing into her new role surprisingly quickly and he suspected that already she would not settle well into a relationship with one of his men.

Leo Manson turned, lifting the wine bottle and Paul held out his cup with a smile and let him pour. "All right?" he asked quietly, and the boy nodded. He was sitting awkwardly forward, and Anne seemed to notice and put her hand on his shoulder again, easing him back to rest against the edge of her chair. He looked up at her and smiled.

"Jesus, we're all terribly serious all of a sudden," Michael O'Reilly said with a laugh in his tone. "This is usually the job of the Major but he's buggered off to bed early, the idle bastard, he must be getting old. Gentlemen – and ladies – will you raise your cups for a moment if you've not drunk it all, and let's have a toast. To Colonel van Daan and his lovely lady, and to the poor wee bairn they'll be raising in this madness."

The toast was drunk, laughingly. Paul lifted his cup in response, smiling. "Well you've toasted my wife, Michael, so let's have another. To the 110th and the 112th, to Lord Wellington – and to Spain."

They drank, and then the talk began again and the laughter resumed. Anne was there, still resting against him, his child barely noticed yet growing inside her. His regiment was around him, depleted and bloody in places but still whole, still complete. Erskine was being moved on and he had survived the experience with both his life and his reputation intact. Paul sat back and allowed the comradeship and the sense of belonging to wash over him. He felt her stir beside him and he turned his head to kiss her forehead. He sat still and quiet in the darkness and the warmth of the fire, thinking about how fortunate he and Anne were in each other and let himself feel, just for this short time, nothing but happiness.

Author's Note - may contain spoilers

This is the second book in the Peninsular War saga and it was more of a challenge than I expected although I thoroughly enjoyed it.

The story of the lines of Torres Vedras is worthy of a book of it's own. It was the most extraordinary military achievement and the fact that it was managed without the French realising it was happening is astonishing. The lines were never actually finished to the extent that Wellington and Fletcher intended, because they were not needed. Despite several more years of advance and retreat, Wellington was never pushed back onto the lines again. I visited the lines earlier this year when I was writing this book and the sheer scale of the project is breathtaking. For anybody interested, there are a couple of blog posts from my trip on my website at the following links:

http://www.lynnbryant.co.uk/320-2/

http://www.lynnbryant.co.uk/the-lines-of-torres-vedras-day-two/

One of the challenges of following the story of Paul and Anne van Daan during the years of the Peninsular War is knowing how much to cover in each book. The first book was longer and covered a much greater time period, from 1802 when Paul first joins the regiment all the way through to just before the battle of Bussaco in 1809. This book covers a much shorter period, less than a year. I was astonished while researching the books just how quickly things tended to move during Wellington's war. There really wasn't much down time.

These books are the story of a regiment, but not just the men of the regiment. There were always women who accompanied their men, wives and girlfriends, some officially part of the army and others local women who had taken up with one of the men. They played a valuable part in the day to day life of the army, doing laundry and mending, cooking and acting as nurses. Many of them were incredibly brave, putting themselves in danger to find their wounded menfolk. They lived in often appalling conditions and were seen as a nuisance by Wellington and many of the other officers, and there was very little provision for them or their children, many of whom died from sickness, cold or malnutrition on the long marches. I researched their story to make mine as believable as possible, but some of what I learned would seem like sensationalist fiction if I included it.

This is a novel, not a history. It is also a love story. But it is also a tribute to the men and women of the army and the extraordinary courage they have often displayed in terrible circumstances. What I've learned through researching these books is that regardless of my views on any particular conflict, and accepting that there have always been times when the army has got it wrong, I have a completely different level of respect for the armed services and what they do.

By the Same Author

An Unconventional Officer (Book 1 of the Peninsular War Saga)

It is 1802, and two new officers arrive at the Leicestershire barracks of the 110th infantry just in time to go to India. Sergeant Michael O'Reilly and Lieutenant Johnny Wheeler have seen officers come and go and are ready to be unimpressed. Neither of them have come across an officer like Lieutenant Paul van Daan.

Arrogant, ambitious and talented, Paul van Daan is a man who inspires loyalty, admiration and hatred in equal measure. His unconventional approach to army life is about to change the 110th into a regiment like no other.

The novel follows Paul's progress through the ranks of the 110th from the bloody field of Assaye into Portugal and Spain as Sir Arthur Wellesley takes command of the Anglo-Portuguese forces against Napoleon. There are many women in Paul's life but only two who touch his heart.

Rowena Summers, a shy young governess who brings him peace, stability and lasting affection.

Anne Carlyon, the wife of a fellow officer who changes everything Paul has ever believed about women.

As Europe explodes into war, an unforgettable love story unfolds which spans the continent and the years of the Peninsular War and changes the lives of everyone it touches.

An Uncommon Campaign (Book 3 of the Peninsular War Saga)

It is April, 1811 and Lord Wellington has led his army to the Spanish border where the French occupy their last stronghold in Portugal at Almeida. As the two armies face each other in the village of Fuentes de Onoro, Colonel Paul van Daan finds himself in command of a brigade and is trying to manage resentment at his early promotion. His young wife is carrying her first child and showing no signs of allowing her delicate situation to get in the way of her normal activities much to the disapproval of the rest of the army.

With General Craufurd not back from leave and Lord Wellington's army looking uncomfortably stretched, Paul is concerned that for once his commander in chief has made the wrong decision which might endanger not only the light division but the whole Allied army. And if that is not enough, Paul encounters a French colonel during battle who seems to have taken their rivalry personally with potentially lethal consequences for his brigade.

A Redoubtable Citadel (Book 4 of the Peninsular War Saga)

In the freezing January of 1812, Lord Wellington pushes his army on to the fortress town of Ciudad Rodrigo and a bloody siege with tragic consequences. In the aftermath of the battle Colonel Paul van Daan and his wife Anne take a brief trip to Lisbon to allow Paul's family to take their young son back to England. With his career flourishing and his marriage happy, Paul has never felt so secure. But his world is shattered when his young wife is taken prisoner by a French colonel with a personal grudge against Paul. As Wellington's army begins the siege of Badajoz, the other great Spanish border fortress, his scouts and agents conduct a frantic search for the colonel's wife. Meanwhile Anne van Daan is in the worst danger of her life and needs to call on all her considerable resources to survive, with no idea if help is on the way.

A Respectable Woman (Book 1 in the Alverstone Series)

Philippa Maclay is the daughter of a missionary who is left alone to make her way in the restricted society of mid nineteenth century London. Taking a post at a charity school in the East End she is torn between her love for her work and the girls in her care and her relationship with Major Kit Clevedon, a man to whom she can never be more than a diversion.

Kit Clevedon knows that he should stay away from the young school teacher he first met in the African bush but his attraction to the girl who lives in a different world to him is rapidly turning into something a lot more.

A Marcher Lord (Book 1 in the Borderers Saga)

The Anglo Scottish border in 1547 is a land at war. Jane Marchant, recently orphaned, arrives from France to live with her English aunt and uncle and finds an unhappy household. A rash decision to act as messenger for an injured English courier takes her across the war torn border and into the hands of William Scott, Lord of Crawleigh, a baron loyal to the Scottish crown.

As the war rages between the two nations, Jane finds unexpected peace at Crawleigh castle and realises that loyalties are never that simple in these border lands. But with secrets of her own to hide, can she reconcile her duty to her country with her feelings for the Scottish Lord who has become her protector and her friend?

For Lord Crawleigh, the English girl is a distraction and a temptation. But how can he trust her when she will not even tell him her name?

A Regrettable Reputation (Book 1 in the Light Division Romances)

In 1816 war is over, Napoleon in exile and Regency England is at peace.

Mr Nicholas Witham, land agent at the Yorkshire estate of Lord Ashberry has found a haven of quiet, far from the bloodshed of war and the horror of Waterloo. With poachers and lost sheep his most pressing concerns, Nicholas is not seeking anything more exciting than the occasional trip to York and a game of cards with friends.

The tranquillity of Ashberry is about to be disrupted by the arrival of Miss Camilla Dorne, a young woman of doubtful reputation, sent away from London by her guardian to avoid the consequences of a disastrous and very public love affair with a disreputable officer which has broken her heart.

The last thing Camilla wants is to be thrown into the company of another army officer, past or present. But she discovers that a lost reputation can bring unexpected freedom and possibly a second chance at happiness.

With the shadow of war firmly behind him, Nicholas is ready to move on, but poverty and rising prices bring rumblings of discontent and rumours of Luddite activity in the industrial towns, and as violence erupts, the land agent of Ashberry finds himself swept up in a new conflict where the enemy is hard to identify. Faced with a stark choice between love and duty, Nicholas is beginning to realise that he may not have left the regiment behind at all…

The Reluctant Debutante (Book 2 in the Light Division Romances)

Cordelia Summers is the only daughter of a wealthy City merchant. Strong willed and clever, she has a horror of being married for her money and resists her father's attempts to push her into society in the hope of making a good marriage.

Giles Fenwick, Earl of Rockcliffe is a scarred, cynical Waterloo veteran who unexpectedly inherited the title and has no interest in making the society marriage that the polite world expects of him.

An inauspicious first meeting in a common inn leads to a surprising friendship between the Earl and the merchant's daughter. Neither are looking for romance or marriage, but thrown together during the London Season, both Giles and Cordelia begin to realise that not all marriages are created equal…

Printed in Great Britain
by Amazon